I0635717

The
AMBER
NECKLACE

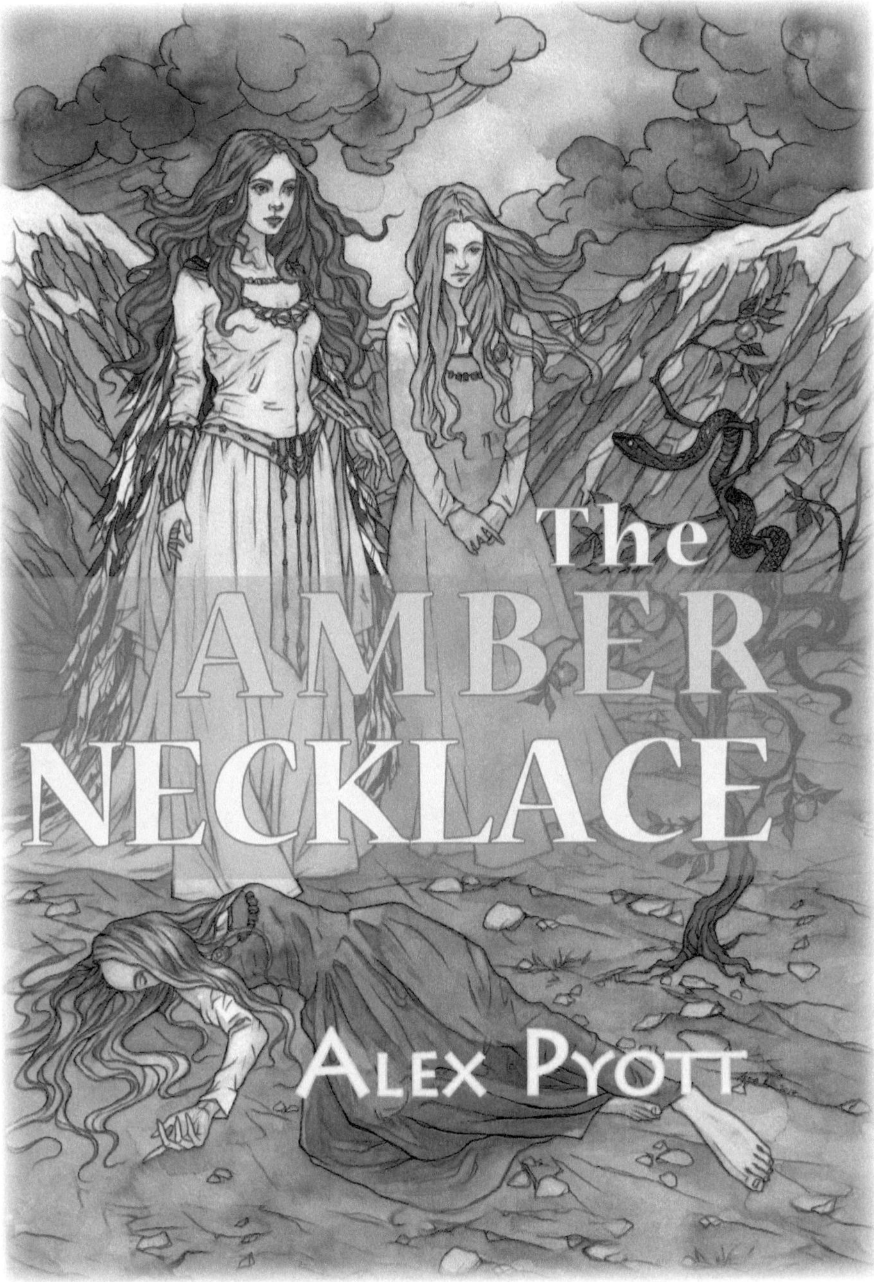

The
AMBER
NECKLACE

ALEX PYOTT

Bink Books
Bedazzled Ink Publishing Company • Fairfield, California

© 2019 Alex Pyott

All rights reserved. No part of this publication may be reproduced or trans-
mitted in any means, electronic or mechanical, without permission in writing
from the publisher. Except for historical characters, all characters are fic-
tional. Any similarity to actual persons, living or dead is strictly coincidental
and not intentional.

978-1-949290-02-8 paperback

Cover and Interior Art
by
Līga Kļaviņa

Cover Design
by

Bink Books
a division of
Bedazzled Ink Publishing Company
Fairfield, California
http://www.bedazzledink.com

Prologue
The Raven's Suffrage

"WATER IS THE lifeblood of humankind . . . and snakes and frogs and worms and bugs and corpses and maggots and—Ugh!" Ylva screamed. Her sealskin boot had just squelched down into a stinking sludge puddle of peat. "May a goat eat Odin's balls!" To add to her torment, the heavily laden clouds that raced across the sky began to shed their burden.

"This journey is beyond reason!" She wrenched her foot free with a plop that was followed by the stench from decaying reeds.

No one had asked her to come along; her clan shunned her. They believed her a witch. She wished she was one. It would be easier to be a witch than what she truly was. "Best not to think about it," Ylva whispered to herself.

In the days prior, most of the village had made their way to the island for the ritual, while the old and crippled stayed at home, caring for the infants. The sea crossing, in the stomach-turning swell, had almost undone her. It wasn't the motion of the waves but the dread of what waited in its depths. *Only simpletons don't fear the sea.* But that was the company she kept. Simpletons, who, when daylight winks to night, would drown a girl in a bog on a small treeless island, ages away from halls with roofs, in hope that the gods would ensure their harvests.

"Are we there?" Ylva yelled to a group that had stopped just ahead of her. No one answered, and she kept going, pushing her way between the miserable, tired, and mud-covered villagers in their sodden woollen jerkins and apron-skirts. The clan was poor and traded little, such that the men had only knives to measure their bravado, and only a few of the women wore fancy beads or brooches that had been handed down from mother to daughter.

Ylva squeezed to the front and snuck up to stand next to Gudmund. He was a tall broad-shouldered man with blond hair and an unremarkable beard. As the chieftain, he was also unremarkable in his deeds, lacking any reputation. This was likely the reason he had commanded all to come and perform the ritual.

The gathered clan waited. They were surrounded by tall reeds and stood in front of a peat-filled pool, which promised certain death. Ylva guessed why the elder had picked this place. The sun would rise behind a central tor, and its rays would be split by a crack in the rock. *This place must see the sun first. In the middle of a stinking, foul, death-laden bog of a goat's hairy—*

"Move, Ylva, you are in the way again," Gudmund said, before elbowing her aside. Ylva waited a moment and then went back to stand beside him. She was slender, tall, and almost the same height as Gudmund. He could easily knock her away, but she knew he wouldn't; like all the others in the clan, he, too, feared she might have powers.

A pink-lined bank of cloud was slipping to the west, keeping the sun at bay, while behind them, waves of a grey sea crashed rhythmically against the shore.

Ylva gathered her hair, twisting it into a braid and tucking it into the shoulder strap of her woollen hangerock.

A girl was brought forward, still a child. Her hair was brown and loose about her shoulders, and although she was being brave, her hands trembled at her sides.

Ylva poked Gudmund's arm. "It's raining. Can't this wait? You won't see the sun anyway."

"No, it must be done."

"What about somewhere else? Over there perhaps?" Ylva pointed deeper into the marsh. "The gods would see that as more courageous."

"No more from you," he growled at her.

This won't do. Ylva made a noise with her tongue, and then cleared her throat to distract the others from her secret call. The elder was wailing words and then more words to gods who Ylva knew weren't listening.

A large raven circled and landed on a dead branch sticking out of the reeds. A few people gasped.

Ylva poked Gudmund again. "Bad omen," she said, and pointed at the bird. "The Norns are disappointed." She knew more than she told of the Norns; the weavers of fate who controlled the destinies of mortals and gods. And it was safe to say the Norns didn't give a whelp's ass what Gudmund and his elder were doing at this moment. But Ylva did. "You must select a different offering," she suggested.

Gudmund nodded, gazing at the bird, which tilted its head and stared back.

The chieftain turned to the people of his village. "Bring your girls forth. We must select someone else. And be quick! There's not much time."

This wasn't what she had in mind, but the brains of men often turned as a wheel in a single track. The villagers began to shuffle around; unwed girls were pushed back, to hide behind their parents, while the foolish ones or the ones not paying attention ended up at the front. During the commotion, Ylva clicked her tongue, and the bird in response clacked its beak.

"How do we choose?" Gudmund asked the elder whose idea it had been for the ritual. The woman turned to him, hesitating. Her hair had not yet turned grey and was still chestnut-blond. Ylva needed this to be so, not for now but for a happening in a hundred years. The rest of her didn't matter.

"They need to walk past the bird. When the raven flies away it will mean it's the right offering," Ylva interjected.

The elder raised a hand to reprimand Ylva for speaking, but she mustn't have thought of anything else. "Yes, that is correct. But be quiet!" She wacked Ylva hard on the back of her head. "You walk past first."

As Ylva did, the elder stomped her foot, attempting to startle the raven. The bird opened its wings and Ylva gave the tiniest shake her head. "Don't you dare," she mouthed. The raven closed its wings and shifted from one foot to the other.

The elder frowned, turned, and shoved the nearest child towards the raven.

One by one, unmarried girls were paraded past. The raven's head tipped in their direction and then at Ylva. Each time, Ylva gave the faintest shake of her head, until all the girls had gone by without being chosen.

"Foolish idea, Ylva, the raven is still there. And the time is now!" the elder cursed.

"We are not done," Ylva informed her. "You are unwed."

Gudmund nodded. "That is so."

"I am widowed and too old," the elder hissed at Ylva.

"Let the ears and eyes of the Norn decide. You're the only one left."

The daylight dimmed. Gudmund's muscles tensed, and his fingers curled into white-knuckled fists. "Walk past!" he ordered before shoving the elder.

"Very well," she muttered, slipping past the bird with catlike steps.

Ylva clicked her tongue.

The raven spread its wings and clumsily flapped off its perch, almost crashing in the bog before flying towards the hill. As it rose, the clouds parted and the sun came into view. There was a simultaneous intake of breath as the villagers fell to their knees. The sun was being concealed by a great disc slipping over its surface and blocking its light. Ylva knew it was the moon, but the others understood nothing. They wouldn't appreciate that nowhere else in the universe did the masses, proportions, and distances make the celestial event possible. And for that to exist, with life to witness, was far from a random coincidence.

Gudmund didn't hesitate. He picked up the elder by her waist and threw her into the boggy pit.

She didn't die well, cursing Ylva, screaming, trying to drag herself out, but the more frantic her flailing, the deeper she sank until all that was left was an outstretched hand. Then that, too, disappeared under the wretched muck with a plop from a bubble of air. Ylva stilled and reflected on events to come. *She will do. Close enough to the goddess's child . . . And, in a hundred years, the differences won't be noticeable. The monk will heed her message.*

She moved to stand beside Gudmund and shaded her eyes. Through the gaps between her fingers, she watched as the sun was consumed. "You now need someone younger and wiser to council you," she told Gudmund. Her eyes were still locked onto the spectacle unique in all of the heavens.

Gudmund crossed his arms, causing his muscles to tighten against the brass rings about his biceps. "You mean you."

"There is no one else."

He sighed before muttering, "As you desire, witch. So be it."

When the mightiest of all things was quelled, leaving behind just a garnet red ring of flame, Ylva turned away. "So begins a thousand years of sorrow." She wiped her face using the crook of her elbow. "With the blood of life, there are tears; not even the sun and moon can change that."

The Purple Clematis

August 2013, London

TODAY, AS WITH all the days before, Jade would go through the motions and appear normal. There wasn't an alternative. Disorder or not, life goes on. She swiped the alarm on her phone and dug herself out of the small gap between the bed and wall, where she slept. She showered and dressed with each step debated. Finally, issuing one instruction at a time, she turned the lock and opened the door.

London in the morning had a disorder all its own. Jade hurried with her head down, following her usual route from her flat in Holborn to Fleet Street. The tube would have been quicker but she couldn't travel on it anymore. So she carved a path through the heterogeneous crowd as it swarmed in all directions.

She was on time. But time was relative. To everyone else she was late. She deposited her bag on her desk and prioritized the coffee machine as her first port of call.

"Meeting," Max, the deputy editor, told her as he whizzed past.

Without accelerating to catch up, Jade followed, heading towards the chief editor's office. Once there, as an act of self-preservation, she zoned out. Minutes passed, with yelling and swearing, and then her name was mentioned.

Brian Connell, the editor, had asked her a question.

"Sorry?" Jade said.

"Are you good with the assignment, Platt?" he barked.

"Absolutely."

"We're done, then." Brian waved everyone out.

Sally forth to the altar of caffeine! Jade's neurons commanded. Sally wasn't there, but every Tom, Dick, and Harry were. She waited, hoping, to all things mighty, that the pot wouldn't run out before she could get a cup, or worse, have less than a cup left, forcing her to make a new pot.

Max nudged her shoulder. "How are you today?"

"Fine, thanks," she said, offering her most propitious stock response.

"I take it you didn't hear what Brian assigned you."

"No, I wasn't listening. What did I agree to?"

"An exclusive story on the Prince of Cornwall's supposed new girlfriend."

"Really?" Jade rubbed her temples. "Jesus, you should've said something. I'd switched off."

"I hadn't noticed," he joked.

"You know I don't do royal gossip."

Max grinned. "You're committed now."

It was Jade's turn at the coffeepot and she used all her volumetric prowess to judge how much she could take to avoid having to make a new brew. "Who cares about royals anymore?" she muttered while feeling guilty for having shoved the pot back with only half a cup left. "Shit . . . Who is this girlfriend?"

"Jade, read the papers sometimes. At least the one you work for!" Max laughed.

"Why would I read that rag?" she muttered under her breath. She was in a rut and she knew it. But she liked her rut; it was deep and safe. *Maybe not a rut. More like a trench.* She began to pace in a small circle.

Max touched her on the shoulder. "Hey, it's a simple story. Don't worry about it. And it's Freya Rykkel. She is a model from Norway. They were seen together yesterday." He sipped his coffee before muttering, "This tastes worse than usual." He dabbed his mouth with the back of his hand. "Actually, I'd be surprised if she's the prince's new fling. Not much is known about her. But I understand she's at this year's London Fashion Week. There's a main press event at six this afternoon, so it should be a doddle. Fashion questions, then the prince."

"God. Is this what I've become, a bloody tabloid reporter?"

"It's better you do it to keep Brian honest. And it could lead to something more interesting."

She sighed. "Alright, alright. Where is the fashion show this year? The Strand?"

"That's right. Somerset House."

Max patted her on the shoulder again and with a note of compassion in his voice he added, "You'll be fine." He had been watching out for her since she had returned from Syria. She hadn't been the same since then.

Half an hour later, Jade debated asking the taxi to stop so she could bail on the whole thing. She'd have to make up some excuse, but it wouldn't be the first time. *Everything is so hard now.* She pulled out her phone to find out more about Miss Rykkel. There were very few details except that Freya Rykkel was a very elusive twenty-six year old from north-western Norway. A picture showed Miss Rykkel leaving The Ivy restaurant in the West End. Next to her was His Highness, the Prince of Cornwall, third in line to the throne, while behind them were security personnel directing them towards a waiting car. Jade pursed her lips when she noticed the reporter for the story was a junior hack who had been brown-nosing the editor. *Why has Brian given this to me? Is this all he thinks I can do now? Just quit.*

Jade was about to phone Brian when the cab pulled up to the curb. She jammed her phone back into her jacket. *Do it and get it over with.*

She crossed The Strand and entered through eighteenth-century stone arches into the courtyard of Somerset House. The area was covered with a great marquee, and a large electronic display announced, "London Fashion Week."

Inside, the marquee was packed with mingling groups of reporters, designers, agents, models, and celebrities. She navigated through the flow of people, stopped, and retrieved her gum from inside her coat pocket. Chewing helped to reduce her constant anxiety but only by a small amount.

In the opposite corner was a woman who she thought might be Miss Rykkel. Jade manoeuvred around a group of fashion designers and their human mannequins, only to discover that the woman had disappeared.

"Was that Freya Rykkel?" she asked a man standing close by.

He looked at Jade with curiosity. In fact, he scrutinized her from top to bottom: her wrinkled jacket, faded jeans, waxed-canvas camera case, and finally, back to notice her press pass. "Miss Rykkel has left. She doesn't talk to reporters."

Jade suddenly felt very self-conscious. "Damn." She ran her hand down her face; her anxiety was making her weary. She looked around to see a woman ducking through a side flap of the marquee. She took a few steps in that direction when a hand gripped her elbow.

"Leave her be," the-handsome-and-I-know-it model said.

"I'm just looking to do a quick interview."

"Don't pester her or everyone here will kick your ass."

Great, she has a horde of size zero assassins. One I can handle, maybe even a dozen, but not the complete spring collection. Why am I doing this?

Jade pulled free of his grip and dove into the crowd in pursuit of her quarry. An unzipped flap of the marquee fell still, offering a clue. She slipped through to find herself outside in the unused part of the courtyard. Just a few steps ahead, a woman in an elegant white dress stepped furtively across the cobbled ground before stopping to remove crystalline shoes. The feathery fabric of the model's skirt made it appear as if a swan had just died in the courtyard.

Jade slowed her pace, continuing until she stood before the pile of plumage. "Freya Rykkel?" Her question came across rather clamorous, and she grimaced as the words echoed against the neoclassical facades.

"Yes?" Freya rose and straightened; a pair of high-heel shoes dangling in her hand.

"Um" was as much as Jade could muster as their eyes connected. Freya's piercing blue irises had an intense ring of green at their edges, while her face was strong and commanding. Chestnut-blond hair fell in fashioned disarray along her slender neck, around which hung a delicate amber pendant on a silver chain. She wore a voluptuous ankle skirt of layered down feathers, which ascended into a bodice embellished with purple threads, depicting a clematis. The evening sunset completed the image, providing a canvas for the haute couture fashion.

Jade coughed, trying to clear the gum suck in her throat. Panicking, she swallowed it down.

"Are you okay?" Miss Rykkel asked, moving closer.

"You took my breath away," Jade stammered. She paused to gather herself and felt her cheeks warm. "Sorry, that just slipped out."

Miss Rykkel smiled. "Please, call me Freya," she said with a slight accent.

Jade ran her fingers through her hair. The once-pixie-style trim was now unruly, and her fringe had to be parted to keep it out of her eyes. *Stunning, front-page fashion-magazine perfection; Photoshop not required.*

"It's rude to stare," Freya reprimanded.

Jade blinked. "God, sorry. Kind of a photographer's trait . . ." Embarrassed, she whispered, "I'm such an idiot."

Freya scrunched up her eyes. "Are you sure you are okay? You are talking to yourself."

Jade mustered a smiled as she tried to remember why she was here.

"You know, I think there is something wrong with you. Are you simple?" Freya asked.

Jade cleared her throat. "I don't think so. Well, I wasn't earlier."

"Do you remember who you are?" Freya was speaking as if to a small child, with mischief in her eyes.

I should just quit. But Max, he would think I'm pathetic. "I . . . Sorry, what?"

Freya gave a puzzled laugh.

Jade gathered herself. "Let me start again."

"It might be better to plough forward."

"Sure, um . . . I'm Jade Platt, a photojournalist from the *United Herald*." Jade shifted from one foot to the other; her nerves were now controlling her body, and she was uncertain if she'd blown her chance to get an interview, although she was not sure it mattered anyway. *I'll quit when I get back.*

There was an awkward pause as Miss Rykkel appraised her. "I am trying to escape," Freya blurted, before spinning around and heading towards a pair doors with a sign that read "Event Dressing Rooms."

Jade stared after her, stunned.

"Come on," Freya called back, the soles of her bare feet appearing fleetingly under the raised hem.

Jade managed to catch up and followed her through the doors.

Freya touched her forearm. "If you can wait for me here. I will just be a minute." She disappeared up a sweeping staircase.

She is like Cinderella. Glass slippers and all. But seriously, why am I doing this? Minutes passed, and Jade wanted to leave. She questioned again why she'd been given the assignment. But she knew exactly why. Since being wounded in Syria, her days as a conflict-zone reporter were over. The doctors had advised her not to do anything stressful. But now, all Brian thought she could do was chase down gossip for a paper that once wrote news stories rather than fiction. *Screw this. Just go.*

Someone tapped her on the shoulder, and she turned to see Freya dressed in a vintage brown leather jacket, a white button-up blouse, and dark blue, ripped jeans.

Glancing down, Jade took stock of her own attire. *A tramp's terrier would be better—*

"You are lost again?" Freya asked with a quick smile.

"Jesus, sorry, I'm just . . . Never mind."

"I can't never mind something I was never told."

"Sorry?"

Freya leaned in close. "You say sorry a lot, and your cheeks are red."

What? God she's beautiful. "Sorr—Um, nervous, I guess."

"You're not much of a reporter if you get nervous."

"I'm better with ugly people." Jade cringed as soon as the words left her mouth.

Freya gave a compressed smile, causing her dimples to show. "You are so odd. Cute, but very odd."

Cute? Jade's mouth opened slightly as she tried to think of a response.

"You came for an interview, right?" Freya asked.

"Yes."

"Good, I have my questions ready for you, Jade."

"Your questions?"

"Yes, so let's get a coffee." Freya took Jade's arm and led her along a corridor. "Secret way out," she whispered while putting on a pair of sunglasses.

They left Somerset House by an emergency exit. A group of photographers had their backs to them, and they snuck past and crossed The Strand before turning left into a narrow lane.

"Miss Rykkel, so, just to confirm, you're okay with doing an interview for the *United Herald*, which would touch on your relationship with the Prince of Cornwall?" Jade asked, her brain cells finally firing, but really, she couldn't believe she was going through with this for the paper.

"Call me Freya. And to answer your question, no. But it will be good to have something more accurate in the news than what I saw this morning. So let's get it done. As long as I can trust you to report what you are told?"

"Of course," Jade said quickly. "And thank you." Some of her tension eased. She would treat this as an editorial.

After a few more confusing turns, they finally arrived at a small, neglected coffee shop.

"I like this place. It's old and unspoiled. I've come here a few times this week. Sneaking out to hide here," Freya said.

Unsurprisingly, the café smelled of old newspapers and ground coffee beans. There were six white marble tables, surrounded by worn Thonet chairs. On the walls were posters from 1960s Hollywood films and old black-and-white pictures of stars. Jade stopped to look around the room.

"Do you do that to everything?" Freya asked.

"Do what?"

"Study everything."

"I don't know. I guess I do. An old habit, I suppose."

"It's okay. You must be a detail person." Freya smiled. "Have you been here before?"

"No. It looks interesting." Jade glanced at one of the pictures. It was a signed photograph of Audrey Hepburn. "I wonder if these are originals."

"I suspect so. This place is old." Freya leaned into Jade to examine the picture as well. "You know, you look like her."

"Who?"

"Audrey Hepburn, when she was in *Breakfast at Tiffany's*. It's one of my favourite films."

Once they were seated at a small table by the window, Freya squinted at Jade and wrinkles formed on the bridge of her nose. "You are also like someone I knew many years ago. You're not her, are you?"

"I don't think so. We've not met before. I would've remembered," Jade said seriously.

"Maybe you have amnesia?"

Jade smiled. "I don't think so."

"Hmm. I don't know. I—"

A portly man interrupted her. "Good afternoon, *Kjønnshar*. I'll be with you shortly."

Jade glanced at Freya in puzzlement over the name.

"*Kjønnshar* means pubic hair in Norwegian, but he is not saying it right," Freya explained.

Jade released a sudden laugh. "What? You told him your name was pubic hair?"

"Sure, why not. He doesn't know. It's better than most names I tell people."

A moment later, the man returned. Jade assumed he must be the owner. "What can I get for you today?" he asked.

"A coffee, please and one for my friend, Enkel," Freya answered. "And something, some pastries. I don't mind which." When the man left, she turned to Jade. "*Enkel* means simple. So I ordered for you. I don't want to overstretch you."

Jade rolled her eyes. "Thanks a bunch."

There was an awkward pause, and Jade glanced down to see Freya's necklace against her pale skin. "Beautiful," she said.

"You mean my boobs or my necklace?"

Jade put her hand on her forehead. "God, not your boobs, I mean—"

"You don't like my boobs?"

"Freya!" Jade stammered. "I was looking at your necklace."

"What's wrong with my boobs?"

"Nothing, they are—" Jade was hugely relieved when the man placed two coffees and a selection of patisseries.

"Thank you," Freya said. "Do my boobs look okay to you?"

"Um, Yes, *Kjønnshar*, they are fine," the man stammered and beat a hasty retreat when they both burst out laughing.

"You're incorrigible," Jade said.

"Yes, of course." Freya smiled and took a sip of her coffee. Jade did the same, uncertain when she should start the interview. Freya surprised her by touching her hand. "Did you mean it when you said I took your breath away?"

Jade hesitated. "Well, yes. I'm sorry I said that out loud. I suspect it happens to a lot of people when they meet you for the first time."

"I don't know. No one has said that before." Freya bit her lip while she studied Jade. She then picked up a chocolate croissant and waved it in front of Jade's mouth in small circles. "Eat it, you are way too skinny."

Jade tried to bite it but instead collided with it, sending small fragments of flaky pastry over the table and causing a smear of chocolate across her cheek.

"Oh my God!" Freya said. "You're so messy. Were you born on a farm?"

"No!" Jade laughed.

"Then why is so much of what you eat on your face?" Freya picked up a red paper napkin and wiped the chocolate from Jade's cheek. "There. You look almost presentable."

"Gee, thanks."

"You're welcome." Freya paused, her features tightening. "I'm sorry. I was being a bit childish. A trait I'm stuck with."

"It's okay." It was odd behaviour, but endearing and nothing to be sorry about.

There was a rapping sound against a misted windowpane and a face came into view. Freya smiled in recognition and waved the person in.

A woman in her mid-forties entered the café. She struggled to close an umbrella while still talking on her phone. She was dressed in an expensive tailored suit with immaculate white stockings and blue mid-heel shoes.

"Yes, I found her. She is in a coffee shop . . . Yes . . . okay, bye." She turned to Freya, who stood, causing Jade to do the same. The woman embraced Freya and kissed each cheek. "There you are! Everyone is expecting you back at the post-event party. I was getting so much grief I thought I better come and find you."

Freya smiled. "I'm sure that's not really why you're here." She opened her hand towards Jade. "This is Jade. She's a photographer."

Jade didn't think of herself as a photographer but rather a reporter. She was about to correct Freya when the woman kissed her cheeks. Jade never really got the kissing-cheeks thing, and she had to save herself from the embarrassment of instinctively being intimate.

"Hi, I'm Karen Felds. I try to keep Freya out of trouble. But I fail most days."

"It would be pretty boring if you were good at your job." Freya laughed. "You found me now. But I'm not going back without a fight."

"You know I'd win." Karen ordered a tea and finally deposited herself on a seat at their table. "So, seriously, are you coming back?"

"No, Jade needs me for the rest of the evening." Freya said this so matter-of-fact that Jade did an obvious double take.

"Really?" Karen responded with sarcasm.

"One moment." Freya rotated on her seat to face Jade. "Are you free?"

"Sure," Jade said without hesitation. Part of her thought it would be great to get the assignment done and over, while another part wanted to spend more time with Freya. Her world was a very different place.

"See, Karen. Busy, busy."

Karen's tea arrived, and after a sip, she started an animated conversation with Freya, which ended in a graceless concession. "I'm too tired to debate this with you. So okay, I will hold the fort again. But please, next time tell me where you are going. It's such a pain to track you down. I wish you'd get a phone."

"What, and feel guilty about ignoring your calls?"

They sat around the table in silence. After a moment, Jade tried to defuse the tension as though the fault was hers. "You are a model at the show?"

Freya turned to Jade. "No."

"Oh. I thought you were."

"Well, a young designer from Oslo asked me to wear her creation. I don't normally do it, but I wanted to help."

"I see. So you're not a model?"

"No. Karen makes me go to these things." Freya shifted in her chair and glared at Karen.

"I don't." Karen clanked down her teacup.

Freya continued to stare. "You do."

A couple of seconds thawed before Karen spoke again. "I better get back. Remember, you need to be ready to leave for New York by ten. I don't want to be searching all over London for you."

"Do not worry. I'm never late."

"Freya, you are always frigging late." Karen stood and collected her clutch purse and umbrella.

"Which airport do I need to be at?" Freya asked.

Karen struggled with her umbrella again. "No. We are to meet in the hotel lobby, as I was telling you this morning and this afternoon."

Jade stood and went to help Karen. She took the umbrella from her and freed it but not opening it fully.

Karen paused. "Which paper do you work for and what is your full name?"

"Jade Platt, I work for the *United Herald*."

Karen grimaced. "All interviews should be cleared by me. I don't approve this one."

"It's fine, Karen," Freya snapped. "I will make sure she sets the record straight."

Karen sighed. "No, the press always twist things."

"She won't do that," Freya insisted.

Karen glanced from one to the other. "Alright, but I want to see the editorial before it is released. Let me give you my number." As she rattled it off, Jade listened but didn't enter it into her phone. "Please add it to your contacts."

"It's okay, I've got it."

"I'd be happier if you'd put it in your phone." Karen's angry words were hidden in honey.

Jade entered the number without asking for it to be repeated.

"Ring me so I have yours."

Jade did, and when Karen's phone rang, Freya chimed in, "Get that, Karen, it's from someone important."

"Very funny. I should remind you I deal with all of your calls."

Freya stood and kissed Karen's cheek. "I know. And thank you."

Karen picked up her umbrella. "Okay . . . Be good," she said before darting out into the rain.

Freya turned and stared at Jade. Her sapphire-blue eyes had darkened. "You must not judge by just observing an instant. You reporters are all the same," she said in slow, measured tones.

Jade's confidence instantly drained away. *She's been playing me.*

"I don't think you reporters understand the impact when rumours are spread to make money. A lot of the work Karen is doing tonight is to clarify they are not true. I am not involved with the prince." She paused. "Actually, *rumours* is the wrong word. *Lies*, I think is better. It was your paper that made up all those lies yesterday."

Jade hadn't yet read the published story on Freya. She yanked out her phone and pulled up her paper's website while Freya lambasted her. As she read the headline, sickness rose in her gut. It was slanderous. Beyond that, insulting. *Hell. I shouldn't have allowed this.*

"Are you listening?" Freya snapped. "Are you responsible for the story this morning?"

A dark pressure closed around her.

"If you knew anything about me at all you would know it is a ridiculous assumption, as I'm not attracted to men, never mind English royals. Saying I am model is one thing but—"

Jade wavered. She tried to control the building shame that was consuming her. But since the event, a simple sense of guilt caused her anxiety to overflow. There was no way for her to break the cycle. The terror from the past jumped to the front of her mind without any rational thoughts hindering its progression. She gripped her forehead as the sinking feeling changed to a free fall and desperately tried to force her hand into her pocket to find her pack of gum. She felt faint as the pressure increased. *Why is this happening . . . now?* Freya's rebuttal had triggered it. She crossed her arms and bent forward. Guilt, horror, and fear all screamed at her that she was in mortal danger. An image of tar-blacken smoke and flame appeared in vivid colour in her mind. The tingling, that told her that her breathing was defunct, spread across her face and hands.

Freya placed an arm around Jade's shoulder.

"*Hei, hei,*" Freya said softly. "Are you okay?" Her voice was filled with concern.

Jade blinked, untangled her arms, and managed to pull out her packet of gum with shaking hands. "I need to go . . ." She attempted to stand, but Freya wouldn't let her.

"You are panicking. You need to breathe slower."

Counting to four and holding her inhales and exhales, Jade attempted to calm herself.

Freya took Jade's hand and squeezed. "Just relax. I'm here. We have plenty of time."

After a few minutes, Jade drank some of her coffee. Her hands still trembled.

"I didn't think my English was that bad," Freya tried to joke.

"No, it's okay. It's not you," Jade muttered.

"It was me," Freya said. "I am so sorry."

Jade shook her head and clasped the coffee cup in two hands. "No, it's not your fault. You are right to be angry."

Freya rubbed Jade's back in slow circles. "No interviews today. I need to take you home."

She hadn't been touched by anyone in years, and it was like being released from an eternal tomb. A long breath reverberated as it left her trembling body.

"I have you." Freya signalled the café owner. He was standing a few feet away, twisting a tea towel in his thick fingers. "Can I have the bill? I need to take her home."

The Magpie

THE RAIN HAD eased, and the air smelled of London as Freya held Jade, leading her through the narrow passage to the main road. The way their footsteps echoed on the wet pavement made Freya uneasy.

There was an unnatural stillness as they passed a small square crammed with bushes and dominated by a mature beech tree. A magpie hopped near the bottom of a wrought-iron gate.

Freya stopped when she saw the bird and instinctively leaned close to Jade. She was taken aback; it had been a long time since any message had been given to her. *What the hell, what are you saying to me?*

"Is something wrong?" Jade asked.

"Shh, I'm trying to listen."

The magpie goose-stepped back and forth, as if it were on parade. It squawked and shook rain out of its feathers.

Freya yelled at the magpie in Norwegian, "Shut up, fat pompous bird! How can I trust what you say?" The bird turned, snapped its beak at her, and flew off into the beech tree. Freya pulled on Jade's arm and soon they were standing on The Strand, where Freya hailed a taxi.

"I take it you don't like magpies?" Jade asked.

"No. They often lie."

At the curb, Freya helped Jade into the waiting cab.

"Hey, don't be sick on my seats," the driver told Jade as she climbed in.

"That will depend on the quality of your driving," Freya snapped back.

"Funny," the cab driver said as he pulled out into the sodium-lit street.

After about fifteen minutes, they arrived at a narrow, five-storey Georgian terrace, close to the British Museum. Jade took her keys out of her satchel but dropped them as she got out of the cab. Freya fished them out of a stream of dark water running along the curb. She rose and kept hold of them.

"You don't have to come up, I'm fine," Jade said.

Freya gave her a look of cold determination and took her arm. There was no way she was going to let Jade out of her sight with the night being what it was. "Lead the way."

Jade's flat was on the top floor, and Freya opened the door for her. Inside, high Victorian ceilings gave a sense of space in the studio kitchen and lounge. Sash windows at the far end of the room overlooked a wooded park, only barely visible in the night.

Jade carefully placed her satchel on an old oak desk. Freya noticed how sterile the apartment was. There was little in the way of family memorabilia and the place appeared as a tidy office rather than a home.

"Are you feeling better now?" Freya asked.

"Yes. Can I get you a coffee?"

Freya was nervous and trying to hide it. She was worried about leaving Jade, if she wasn't well, and disturbed by what the magpie had told her. "If you don't mind me staying, I will sort out dinner. I'm hungry. We can eat together. Okay?"

"Sure. That would be nice." Jade walked to the coffee table, picked up the remote, then put it down again. She turned and looked unsure where to go.

Freya took her arm. "Why don't you take a bath and relax? I will sort out dinner."

Jade nodded before disappearing into her bedroom.

Freya went into the kitchen area and searched through each of the cupboards, looking for food.

"I don't think I have much." Jade had her nightclothes under her arm. "We might need to get a takeaway," she said before heading into the bathroom.

Yes, Jade is right, the cupboards are bare. Freya found nothing but pasta. The fridge held more interest, but only for a minute. She yelled back to Jade, "You should be embarrassed." She paused. "Unless you are a part-time biologist. I'm sure salsa is not supposed to be brown with black spots. How do I order something?"

Jade didn't answer, so Freya went to the bathroom door. "You okay in there?"

A mumbled yes was just audible.

"I will go find food," she said, grabbing the door keys.

As she headed down the stairwell towards the ground floor, Freya saw a light underneath the door of the apartment below Jade's. She stopped to knock.

"WAKE UP, SLEEPY." The words were melodic, and Jade stirred.

Coming to, Jade rubbed her face. Embarrassed, she positioned her arm over her breasts. "Guess I dozed off."

Freya was kneeling beside the tub. "Sorry, I forgot how private you English are. Your bath was overflowing, so I turned off the tap. I didn't want you to drown in your sleep."

"Thanks."

"Food will be here in a minute. Will you be long?"

"No, I just need to wash my hair."

Freya picked up the shampoo bottle from the sink behind her. "Lean forward to keep your modesty."

Jade hunched forward as Freya scooped up water from the bath to wet Jade's hair. "This won't take long. Your hair is rather short." The sensation soothed a tension she had endured for so long without knowing it was there.

Five fingertips, each one discernible, glided along her scalp, massaging in the jasmine-scented shampoo. "You have been in the battles," Freya said sympathetically.

She's seen my scars. Jade let out a long breath and just nodded when Freya asked if she was okay.

Freya finished washing out the shampoo and there was a knock at the door. She gave a meaningful smile. "That will be dinner. Don't be long."

How can she look at me and smile? Jade bowed her head, her eyes shut and jaw clenched, while tears welled up. *Why is she being so kind to me?*

When she was dried and dressed in a pair of light grey jogging bottoms and a worn black T-shirt, Jade entered her living room. She was surprised to see her coffee table covered with a selection of deli food. She took in a spread of olives, stuffed red peppers, cheeses, samosas, satays with dips, a large loaf of bread, and a wooden chopping board containing a selection of charcuterie. A bottle of white wine marked the boundary of the banquet.

"Where did you get this from?" Jade asked in amazement.

"Sit down, before your mouth hits the floor." Freya laughed and handed a glass of wine to Jade, who had positioned herself at the end of the sofa. "I am not sure the wine is good."

Jade was aware that Freya was speaking quickly. "I don't understand, where did you get this?"

"Your neighbour, Sara, provided it."

"Sara, just below me? Why would she do that?" Jade scrunched up her forehead.

Freya sliced off a piece of bread and cheese and handed it to her. "I asked."

But Jade didn't take in the answer. So many things were now confusing; it was like a different world, a dream.

Freya put the bread and cheese back on the table and took Jade's hand. "Sorry. I didn't mean to rush you. I want you to eat because of how thin you are."

"Where's the food from?"

"Well, I was not sure what to do and I have no money," Freya said, even quicker than before. "So I knocked on your neighbour's door, explained the situation and that you were not well. I suppose in my conversation, I made her feel guilty that she had not been a good neighbour, so she brought up food." She paused for breath. "Does that answer your question?"

The room was silent except for the sound of muffled traffic driving on wet roads.

"Your apartment is very nice. You're lucky to have it."

"Not really," Jade muttered.

Freya looked at her quizzically.

She didn't want to explain and probably shouldn't have said anything. She was seventeen when she had started at Oxford, and that summer when she came back to London, her mother had disappeared. As a young adult, she'd just accepted her mother's behaviour. But looking back, she knew her mother must have been mentally ill. She wasn't certain she missed her. A memory drifted by of a woman with wild black hair with white streaks and old, grey eyes. Her mother had always refused to have her picture taken, and that mind's eye image was all she had. The police never found her, so when she finished at Oxford, she sold their home and bought the apartment.

She turned to Freya. "Why are you here?" she asked, and then wished she could take it back.

But Freya seemed unfazed. "If I answer this will you eat something?"

Jade nodded.

"It would have been hard for me not to come here and help you. It is the way I am. Why would I not?"

"But you don't know me," Jade responded.

Freya laughed, causing Jade to smile. "You are silly. What do you mean I don't know you? I know your name. I know where you live. I know who you work for. I know you have a good memory. That you are a photographer. You are kind and not selfish." She reached out. "Hold still." She picked a lose hair from Jade's eyelashes. "I also know that you need some caring. What type of person would I be if I didn't care about other people?" She took a sip of her wine for the first time. "And—well, that is enough for now." She picked up the bread and cheese and handed it to Jade. "You agreed. Please eat this."

Jade took a bite and Freya put both arms around her and hugged her, almost tipping over the wine glass that was squashed between them. "Good, good." She released Jade and snaffled a samosa, stuffing it in her mouth in one swoop.

Jade felt her cheeks burn. *She is starving. She's been waiting all this time for me to eat!*

Freya piled Parma ham onto a roughly sliced piece of bread. "Not seen someone eat before?" she said with her mouth full. She swallowed. "I will stay here. I could make up a reason, but I want to make sure you are okay."

God, what does she think about me, that I'm so broken?

"I would be worried for you. We can sit and talk. There is a lot of food." Freya carried on talking about how nice the food was, how kind Sara had been, how she was not looking forward to going to New York, how it must be great to be so close to the British Museum, and that she would spend every day looking around it if she lived here, all said in apparent random order, without hesitation.

Jade silenced her by touching her forearm. "Please stay."

Freya smiled. "Okay. But you need a lock on your *kjøleskap*. I don't want the salsa killing me in the night."

Jade laughed. "What's a *kjøleskap*?"

"Your fridge. I want no part of your unnatural biological experiments."

She watched Freya as she bent to place items on a plate for her. Her hair had fallen forward, still in waves from the afternoon's fashion show. Freya glanced at her through the strands, then pushed them around her ear and handed Jade the plate.

Jade forced herself to eat, while wishing Freya hadn't seen her in the bath. But Freya was right. She had lost twenty pounds in the last year and her doctor was warning her that she needed to improve her diet. She just didn't feel like eating; it seemed *irrelevant*.

Remembering that Freya said her favourite film was *Breakfast at Tiffany's*, Jade put it on the TV, and sure enough, Freya was glued to it. She didn't even notice Jade clearing up.

She looks tired. "I will get you something to sleep in."

Freya unstuck herself from the film and turned her attention to Jade. Her expression was that of a schoolchild caught not paying attention in class. "Pardon?"

Jade laughed. "I was thinking you look tired and I should get you something to wear. You can sleep on the sofa."

Freya flicked her attention back towards the TV while Jade spoke. "Let me pause it."

Even after it was paused, Freya still glanced at the TV, as if not trusting it to stay put.

Jade grinned. "You are really enjoying the film."

"I've never seen it. It's amazing."

"I thought you said it was your favourite?"

"It is."

"Wait, how can it be your favourite if you have never seen it?"

Freya's eyes widened in surprise. "Oh, I mean—I mean I haven't seen it like this before."

Jade blinked twice, still puzzled, and just laughed and got up to find a set of nightclothes for Freya.

When Freya was changed and the sofa had been made into a makeshift bed, she asked, "Will you watch the rest of the film with me?"

Jade hesitated.

"Please," Freya pleaded.

"Sure." Jade sat down next to her and pointed the remote at the TV.

"Wait," Freya said, picked up a pillow, and put it behind Jade. "Let's get comfortable." She leaned into her, pulled the blanket over them, and nestled against Jade's chest. "Ready," she whispered.

Jade un-paused the film and felt awkward at first, but with Freya's warmth next to her she was able to relax. She didn't really know this woman, but for whatever reason, she felt she could trust her.

Freya was again absorbed in the classic film and sought out Jade's hand, which she took and held against her chest. Jade felt the smooth stone of the amber necklace against the back of her fingers. A soft tingling warmed her stomach as she dozed off.

A gasp from Freya woke Jade up. On the screen, Paul had just told Holly he loved her. Holly had gotten up and started to walk out of the reading room. The camera panned by a blonde sitting at a desk and watching their encounter.

"What's wrong?" Jade asked.

"Nothing, go back to sleep."

Lesser of Two Evils

July 2012, Aleppo, Syria

THE SUN HAD just risen, and birds sang in what remained of a Byzantine courtyard.

Even here, they sing, Jade thought as she put on her ceramic bullet-resistant jacket.

A member of the Tawhid Brigade called to her, "Are you ready?"

"Yes," Jade said and looked for James. He was a few yards away checking his camcorder and batteries.

"James, come on!" she called out to him. "Nizar, where are we going today?"

"We will visit a market here in Aleppo. You can talk with the people who are still here trying to survive."

Jade had found it hard to believe that anyone remained in Aleppo, which was once the financial capital of Syria. But now all that was left were ruins upon ruins of bombed-out buildings marked with bullet holes. The ancient city had been turned into an apocalyptic battleground with multiple factions attempting to gain control. She had been there a week, embedded with the Tawhid Brigade rebels and it was still hard to take in the total devastation in every direction.

"What's the route going to be like?" Jade asked. Sporadic rifle fire answered her, echoing between the empty, rubble-filled streets.

Nizar tapped Jade's vest. "You should take that off. It's better you appear as a boy today."

If Nizar was advising this, it meant the journey to the market was risky. Jade knew that appearing as a Syrian teenage boy would offer more protection than calling attention to the fact she was a journalist. She had used this persona before and took advantage of her hazel hair, small breasts, and dark tanned skin. Being identified as a Western woman in a war-torn country would serve her up as a possible hostage to one of many militant groups. She shuddered, remembering her colleagues who had died in the most brutal ways at the hands of extremists. She slowly removed her vest and pulled out a dirty tan camo jacket from a backpack.

A dented, green Toyota pickup truck pulled up with three rebels sitting in its bed. Each held battered Kalashnikov rifles. Nizar put his foot on the top of the rear tyre and stepped into the back. He told Jade and James to get into the cab. Even before Jade closed the passenger door, the pickup sped away.

It was late July and Jade expected the temperature to rise to a sweltering forty degrees Celsius. The Toyota raced towards a market just north of Bustan al-Qasr. Its location was on the border of a contested area between rebel and regime forces. Jade had her DSLR out and was taking pictures as they drove along. James was filming from inside the cab through a missing rear window.

Two rifle shots sounded. The rebels in the open bed of the pickup all ducked with their weapons pointed towards the possible source of the gunfire. Nazir reached in through the rear window, slapped the driver hard on the shoulder, and pointed violently forward. The driver accelerated, creating a cloud of chalky dust, which trailed the vehicle. They arrived at the market with no more incidents and Nazir told Jade it was safe.

Jade had learnt long ago not to just take advice when it came to her own safety. She scanned the market, which was an odd mix of stalls, coffee vendors, and collapsed buildings. She took her time and checked the skyline for possible sniper vantage points. She also used her telephoto lens to inspect a slender minaret which stood close to the market. Most of the time she wished she would see something and know there was a threat. This was better than being unsure. In truth, she knew no area was safe. Snipers in the Bustan al-Qasr market, just half a mile south, were shooting people at a rate of ten a day and this included children.

James pointed. "Come on, Jade, that trader is okay to talk to us."

Jade nodded and walked over to a man who was selling a small selection of vegetables. He was leaning against his stall and beside him was a young girl. She was perched next to a sack of carrots and looked no older than twelve. She didn't wear a niqab, but a lime-green shirt and jeans. She swung her legs slowly and watched the events around her. What was different about the girl was that she had dark skin, chestnut-blond hair, and blue eyes with a green rim around the irises.

Jade considered how rare such genetic traits were in the eastern Mediterranean. She remembered reading about blond blue-eyed farmers, ancestors of Europeans, who lived near the dead city of Serjilla in the north-west part of Syria.

Jade smiled at the girl as James asked the man how the conflict had affected life here. The girl smiled back with one corner of her mouth. Beside her was a wooden drawer, which must have been part of a side table at one point. It contained a magpie's collection of trinkets and beads. Words written on a flat stone next to the drawer suggested they were for individual sale.

"Hi, my name is Jade. What is yours?" she asked in Arabic.

"Aaina," the girl answered. "Are you a boy or girl?"

Jade laughed. "Girl." She reached into her satchel and took out a package of chewing gum, which she gave to Aaina.

"Thank you."

"You are most welcome. Your name is pretty. Do you know it means mirror?"

Aaina shook her head.

Jade turned to the merchant.

"Wait. You are Jade!" Aaina's eyes were impossibly large as she glanced between Jade and her box of trinkets.

"Yes." Jade gave an amused smile, watching the child frantically shifting through the items in her container.

Aaina pulled out a wide ring of metal and inspected it, rotating it close to her nose before handing it to Jade. "This is for you."

Jade took the ring. It was grey with tarnish and would fit on a finger if she tried, but it was not a continuous ring. The metal had been bent into that shape at some point in the past. "How much is it?"

"Oh no, it's never for sale. It's for you."

"Well, thank you." Jade was about to put it in her camera case when Aaina grabbed her sleeve.

"No, keep it very safe."

"Sorry. Is here in my pocket okay?" Jade pointed to a button-up breast pocket on her shirt.

Aaina looked dubious but then nodded. "I guess so." She shifted her attention to the packet of gum.

Jade turned and introduced herself to the merchant. She asked if it was okay to take a few pictures of him and his daughter. The man threw his hands up in a gesture of "Why do I care?" Jade took out her camera. She had a great angle with a line running from Aaina to her father and then down the street, with a pair of ruined apartment blocks in the background. As she took a few pictures, an aircraft entered the camera's frame. She kept the trigger down and captured a dozen images. There was no sound from the approaching plane but its altitude was lowering. Jade suddenly acknowledged what it was.

"MiG! MiG!" Jade screamed and spun to find James. She reached for the girl who was just a few feet away. "Run!" she shrieked and managed to catch Aaina's wrist. But Aaina's arm was also being yanked by her father, who was heading across the street in the opposite direction.

"No!" Jade said desperately. "There! The barriers!" She had earlier noticed a pair of concrete street barriers pushed to one side along the pavement and only ten strides behind her. She lost her grip on Aaina for a split second, but it was enough to cause her to fall, her forward momentum sending her to the ground. At the same moment the Toyota she had arrived in skidded to a stop in front of her. The two men in the back were continually firing at the MiG with their rifles, while a third was aiming an anti-aircraft weapon in its direction.

The Toyota cut off the escape path for Aaina and her father fleeing to the other side of the road.

The MiG opened fire. Its ballistics streamed towards their target and tore through the thin metal of the pickup and the rebels within it. Aaina's father went down. He had been directly in the line of the straying bullets.

Jade was on her feet again but could no longer see the girl or James, and out of instinct darted towards the barriers. In the brief moment it took her to get to them, her world changed.

From the corner of her eye, she saw a projectile falling from the MiG's undercarriage. She had located Aaina, who was hunched up against the wheel of the Toyota, and James, who was not moving and lying in a growing pool of blood. The bomb hit, no more than fifty yards away with the sound of cracking lightning. The explosion carried her as she dove over the barriers.

A cloud of thick grey smoke spread around her as buildings collapsed on the opposite side of the street. She caught a glimpse of the MiG's engine as it turned and disappeared from view. She started to crawl back towards the barriers she had been thrown beyond and noticed she was leaving a trail of red handprints on the pavement.

Her adrenaline was fading, and delayed pain hit her. She could see that her left side was drenched in blood, a large hole torn through her shirt. The street was deadly silent, then panicked voices rose in all directions. Those voices were quickly overpowered by gunfire, which came from all directions.

She dragged herself to the barrier's edge. Her hand pressed tightly against the hole through which her lung was attempting to breathe. She glanced over the barrier to see the Toyota now on its side. Its engine compartment and front tyres were burning.

The impossible became true. Aaina was there, huddled in a corner of the upturned vehicle. Her knees against her chest with her arms crossed around them. Her green shirt was stained with blood from a cut on her head. She looked back and forth with eyes full of fear.

A zing passed Jade's ear and cracked behind her as a sniper's bullet narrowly missed her head. "Shit!" She felt a hand pull her down below the barrier.

It was Nizar. "Stay down!"

Jade could barely breathe and the pain was overwhelming. Her eyes rolled up as she tried to ride out the agony.

"Stay still," Nizar ordered. Out of his rucksack, he pulled a roll of duct tape and wrapped it tightly round and round her chest without removing her shirt. "The regime is launching an assault here. I must leave you." He rummaged through her satchel, found her press identification, and stuck it to her chest. "The regime will find you. I must go."

"A girl . . . beside the pickup near the rear . . . It's on fire!" Jade managed through waves of pain.

Nizar glanced towards the pickup but only the top portion was visible from below the barricade. His expression was grim as he gripped Jade's shoulder. "To Allah we belong and to Him is our return." He crawled along the barrier and then stood. He ran towards the girl but took no more than a few strides before a sniper fired. He fell to the ground, not moving.

"No!" Jade screamed. Pain followed the words. She hunched forward against the barrier. She couldn't move. The agony was too great. She thought to call out to Aaina and tell her to flee, but she was afraid. *Would that sniper just kill her as she ran?*

Jade's camera was still around her neck. The body was badly damaged, but a quick test showed it still worked. She lifted it up above the barricade and pointed it in the direction she hoped was the back of the pickup truck. She clicked the trigger and let the camera take a number of pictures. Two more sniper rounds sounded over her head as she lowered the camera. She examined its cracked screen and scrolled through the images. Most of them had missed their target, but two contained Aaina. She was still there, small and fragile sheltering against the bed of the upturned truck.

One of the burning tyres popped and sent up a plume of smoke. *There is no choice!* Jade started to sob and yelled out with the little strength she had left, "Aaina! Run! You must run!" Her voice trembled. "Allah is with you! Run, Aaina!"

Jade was uncertain but she thought she heard the thud of a footstep on flexing metal. She lifted her camera again and pushed the trigger. She tried desperately to point it the right way without being able to see its direction;

the pain in her chest caused her hand to shake. The camera rapidly took its shots but on the fourth click the petrol tank of the Toyota exploded and sent a flash of flame in all directions. Fragments from the blast pinged off the building behind Jade. A spinning lump of metal just missed her head. Her camera lay beside her and she could no longer lift it. She popped open the side panel and removed the SD memory card. With trembling, unfeeling fingers she undid the button of her breast pocket and tucked it in. She tried to stay conscious, listening to the crackle of flames and increasing gunfire, then all went black.

A SHROUD OF cool orange and grey replaced the darkness. She was panting in short shallow breaths, but not screaming. There was something moist and warm on the back of her neck. *Am I hurt again? Is it blood?*

She tried to move her hand, to touch the back of her head, but it was wedged under her. She opened her eyes but only saw a blurry criss-cross pattern. There was something against her back. She managed to turn and found herself looking into a pair of blue eyes, partly concealed by dark blond hair.

In the background, a DVD repeated its menu sequence for *Breakfast at Tiffany's*. She let out a long, slow breath. She was safe.

In a whisper, Freya complained, first in Norwegian and then in English, "What are you doing?" Her nose was almost touching Jade's.

"I'm just going to give you some space."

Freya blinked; her hair was catching on her eyelashes. Jade climbed over Freya, stood, and switched off the TV.

She was about to turn and head into the bedroom, when Freya took hold of her wrist. "Stay here," she whispered.

"It's okay. You need space to sleep."

"No . . . You don't understand," Freya said almost too softly for Jade to hear and pulled her towards the sofa. "I don't want to be by myself."

She knelt in front of the sofa. "What's wrong?" she whispered.

Freya took a long breath and let it out. "I—I'm tired. Please stay here."

Jade stroked Freya's forehead and brushed her hair away. "Shift up so I can get in."

With Freya's arm around her, she listened to her breathing and wondered what was unsettling Freya so much. She didn't know her at all and it was impossible to say. But Jade had seen her eyes. She had seen that same fear before in another pair of blue eyes.

With Freya snoring softly behind her, Jade stayed awake until dawn, when the glow of the city's lights was replaced with the blues and whites of the rising sun.

She gently slipped out of Freya's embrace and headed over to her desk. She flicked on her laptop and opened a small metal tin that once held a geometry set. She had used it in school and kept it all these years. Now it contained SD memory cards from her camera, as well as other mementoes given to her on her travels. She tipped it out onto the desk. She spread the contents around with her fingers, moved aside a broad, grey ring of tarnished silver, and examined the labels on the SD cards until she saw one that read, "Aleppo, Syria, July/12." The sight of it caused all her confidence to drain away. Panic set in and her hands trembled. Her face tingled with pins and needles.

I can't do this . . . You can't live in fear forever.

She held the open tin just below the edge of the desk and quickly brushed all the items back into it before replacing the lid.

A desperate need came over her and she moved quickly back to the sofa. She lifted Freya's arm, climbed back in, and pushed up against her. Freya made a soft murmur, but nothing more. Jade's anxiety faded and after a moment, she fell asleep with Freya's arm around her.

A Second Chance

JADE'S MOBILE BUZZED on the coffee table. *Why is sleeping so exhausting?* She picked it up to see Karen's name below the time, which read 10:43 AM. Jade immediately swung her legs out and sat to attention on the sofa.

In the background, the shower was on, and she could smell a pot of coffee brewing.

"Jade Platt," she answered and tried not to show her nervousness. She suspected Karen was not the type of person to hold back.

"Hello, Jade, this is Karen Felds." The words were formal and business-like. Jade took in a breath and prepared herself. She wasn't sure what Karen would make of Freya staying the night.

"Is Freya with you?" Karen asked in a neutral tone.

"Yes, she is in the shower. Do you want me to get her?"

"No, she doesn't do phones," Karen continued. "I'll come over and collect her."

The call ended abruptly after Jade gave her the address. She was pretty sure Karen didn't like her. She knew this shouldn't matter, but it bothered her. Her head ached and she was desperate for a coffee to cut through the fatigue that she always felt, no matter how long she slept.

She stood, and her phone rang again.

"Hey, Jade," Max said in his reassuring mid-Atlantic accent. He had worked with her for a long time, and after Syria he supported her. He even sometimes credited his stories to her to cover up her reduced contributions to the paper. When Jade complained that he didn't need to, he just responded that she would do the same for him.

"Are you coming in today?" Max said without sarcasm.

"Ah . . . was I needed?"

"I guess you also missed that part of the meeting yesterday," Max said and Jade knew he was teasing her about her absences. "Brian was asking for an update on Miss Rykkel."

"One second . . ." Jade walked to the end of the room and pushed open the sash window. She stepped out onto the fire escape and sat on the windowsill in the sunshine. "Okay, go ahead, Max."

"I told Brian you were still working on Miss Rykkel." Max must have realised what he had said. "That came out wrong."

Over her shoulder, Jade saw that Freya was out of the shower. She tried to concentrate on the call. Max had started into a long string of complaints about Brian. She held the phone away from her ear and waited for him to stop. *He's right, but who bloody cares.*

"Sorry, I've been going on a bit," Max said.

"It's okay—"

Freya placed a slow kiss on Jade's cheek and handed her a full coffee cup.

"Morning," Freya said. She was still damp from the shower and wrapped in a too-small bath towel, which exposed sensuous thighs. Jade took the coffee as her stomach leapt into her mouth. All she could do was stare. "You should have joined me."

"Sorry?"

"Never mind." Freya smiled.

Oh . . . the shower.

"If that's Karen, tell her I left an hour ago." Freya backed away from the window but then flicked her towel open and closed quickly. She doubled over, laughed, and darted back into the bathroom with her bottom exposed.

Jade's whole body tingled. "Oh my God . . ." she muttered.

"Are you there?" a distant voice asked.

"Sorry, Max," she said, flustered.

He laughed. "So my statement about Miss Rykkel was not completely incorrect."

"Geez, Max. No. She just slept here. I wasn't feeling well and she—"

"It's okay. I believe you." She could tell he was amused. "Did you find out about her and the prince?"

She composed herself. "Max, that's all made up. She is upset about it."

"I know," Max said dryly.

"You know?" Jade paused. "What—Why was I assigned to the story if you knew it was bogus?"

"I'm not sure you want to hear this."

"Just spit it out." She was annoyed now.

"All right. Brian wanted you to cover it, okay? He didn't trust me to do it the way he wanted. Look, Jade, Brian is an asshole. And I am hoping to persuade the board to get rid of him."

"I know that."

"Look, let me explain," Max said. "Brian was all over that picture of Miss Rykkel. He wanted to use it as an exclusive story. But of course, like a professional, I did my research."

Jade shifted on the windowsill and then took a sip of her coffee as she listened.

"I then handed all the information to Brian. I explained there was no relationship between them. Later I found out he'd asked one of the juniors to make up that gutter-press nonsense. When I asked him why, he just told me to *f*-off, that he was the editor and he knew how to sell papers."

"God. You know, I hate this stuff." Jade sighed. "Why was I assigned to it?"

"That's the bit I didn't want to tell you."

Jade paused, then realised why. "You don't need to. He thinks I'll just do what he wants without complaining, and take pictures he can use with any old crap he makes up."

"I'm afraid that's about it."

"Well, there's no story here. So he can go to hell."

"I think he's just done that. And with two royals involved, there will be big consequences." Max paused.

Jade sipped some coffee, thought a moment, and almost spit it out. "Wait! You said *two* . . . not *a* royal . . . but two." Her chest tightened.

"Yes?"

Jade glanced behind her and saw that Freya was now dressed and finger-combing her hair.

She lowered her voice. "Are you telling me—So you're saying that Freya happens to be a bloody Norwegian princess or something."

"Possibly."

Jade glanced at Freya, who smiled back. Putting on a brave face, Jade waved awkwardly and turned away.

"Hell, Max," she whispered, "Why didn't you tell me? I've a goddamn princess getting me dinner . . . Shit, wait . . . Washing my hair. I've seen her ass for Christ's sake."

"Whoa! Too much detail." Max laughed loudly. "Calm down. There is some connection to the royals in Norway, but it's a bit confusing. My researcher had to do a lot of digging and some of it not through normal channels. So right now I don't know exactly. Maybe you should ask her?"

"God no. I can't ask things like that, especially if it's meant to be a secret. She already distrusts the press." Jade stood. Freya had started to walk towards her. "Anyway, she's off to New York in a minute."

"Why not go with her?"

She didn't reply. Freya was too close and would've overheard. There was a knock on the door. "I have to go!" she said in a panic and hung up.

Jade stepped back through the window and faced Freya. "That'll be Karen. She phoned while you were in the shower to say she was coming over."

Freya took Jade's hand. "Before she comes in, thank you for letting me stay and letting me sleep here."

"Of course, Miss Rykkel." Jade winced. *God, foot-in-mouth disease.*

Karen called from behind the door.

"Sorry, that was a weird thing to say. I guess I'm a bit flustered," Jade said.

Freya gave Jade a reassuring smile and squeezed her hand.

The knocking became louder.

"I better get that." Jade trotted to the door with her fingers entwined with Freya until their arms were extended and their hands came apart.

Jade opened the door and Karen strode in.

"You're late," Freya said, as she applied lipstick.

Karen looked like she was about to explode, but Freya put an arm around her.

"Thanks for collecting me. And before you get angry, Jade wasn't feeling well, so I stayed the night, and I slept well." Her voice rose on the last word.

Karen took a moment to inspect them. "You do look rested. But we need to hurry. I have your bags from the hotel. Are you ready to go?"

Freya hesitated, clenching her hands together, and then releasing them quickly. "All right," she said and looked at Jade. "I guess I better say goodbye." She leaned over and kissed Jade's lips.

Jade wavered, sorting through a stack of facts and emotions. *She is royalty. She's incredible. She kissed me. I need to get into the office and get Brian off Freya's back . . . Karen's here and I'm still in my stupid PJs.*

Freya paused as if waiting for something, then turned and left with Karen.

Jade just stood there, wondering what had just happened.

FREYA'S HEART FELT tight in her chest as she clopped down the last few steps onto the pavement. She sighed. *The timing of this trip is so awful. I hope Jade is all right. It can't be her. Can it? I don't know.*

By the curb, a silver Audi Saloon waited, and once she was inside, the driver asked Freya, "Heathrow, correct? Which terminal?"

Freya sat with her hands clasped. "Wait!"

"Why?" Karen said. "We don't have much time to get our flight."

"I don't want to go."

Karen rolled her eyes. "You need to. We already discussed this."

"No, I don't need to. It's you who needs me to," Freya snapped back. "I don't want to go. I've had enough of doctors asking questions, poking me, and testing all manner of things. I don't want to do it anymore." She took in deep breaths that were more like gasps.

"You know this, but I will say it again. This is different. It's a specialist unit; they will try to sequence the genome in some of your cells and compare it to an old sample to find out what might be the cause. These doctors aren't like the others you have seen."

"No. It's time to call it a day." Freya took hold of the door latch. "I'm going to spend time with Jade."

"Jade—God, not another lost puppy. Freya, she'll be fine."

She glared at Karen, who stiffened in the seat. She pulled the latch and shoved violently. It hit the end of its hinge and bounced back. She pushed it again and stepped out onto the pavement. The driver glanced back but said nothing.

"You were a lost puppy once! Do I have to remind you?" she said over her shoulder. She slammed the door closed and walked back in to Jade's building.

JADE STOOD AGAINST the wall near her front door for countless minutes as she ran through the events of the last twenty-four hours. *I'm such an idiot!* She banged her head against the wall—thud, *useless!* thud, *loser!* thud, *stupid fool!* She stopped reprimanding herself and was surprised that the banging continued. She frowned at the door then opened it and stared at Freya.

"You . . . you came back," Jade stammered.

"Yes, of course." Freya looked Jade up and down. "Are you having a pyjama day?"

Jade stared at her. "Pyjama day?"

"Yes, you're still in your pyjamas. So I was wondering if you plan to just lounge around all day. I'm not judging, by the way; it saves on washing I suppose. But if you get dressed you can take me somewhere."

"I'd—I thought you'd gone to New York."

"Let's go out. Get dressed and I'll explain once you are ready. Okay?"

Jade slowly nodded.

"But can you send Karen a message on your phone? She will be upset with me."

"Sure." Jade felt happy. She couldn't believe that Freya had come back. She thought she would never be given a second chance.

Vikings!

THICK BLACK CLOUDS ploughed across the London sky as Jade and Freya walked along Bloomsbury Place. The avenue was close to Jade's apartment and ran in front of the British Museum.

"It might be busy," Jade said. The pavement was lined with centuries-old London plane trees whose leaves had started to turn brown as autumn approached. "Have you been here before?"

Freya nodded. "Yes, many times. But there is an exhibition I want to show you."

They continued in silence until they arrived at the iron gates that marked the entrance to the colossal museum. The forecourt was full of tourists. Jade hated crowds but not the people themselves; to her it was affirming to see so many different nationalities coming to visit historical works of art.

It's better than destroying them. Her mind drifted to the antiquities of Aleppo bombed into dust. She remembered an old mosque she had once visited. Its painted frescos pocked with bullet holes, and the looted rooms where rays of sunlight reflected on dust, then slouched in a corner, a decaying body and its stench. She closed her eyes and shook away the last image.

Freya yanked on her coat from the other side of the open gate. Rain drops splattered the ground and the horde of tourists quickly took shelter where they could.

"You were disappearing on me." Freya pulled Jade in so that she was up against the gate's bars. She smiled. "I think something has come between us." She laughed. "You have put up your barriers again." She shrugged. "Maybe that last joke doesn't work."

People weaved around Jade, while others opened their umbrellas in a panic, as if the rain would melt them.

"It seems we have reached an impasse," Freya whispered, while half smiling and with a cheek against an iron rail. "Are you going to tell me what you were thinking about?"

Jade blinked. "Nothing. I was distracted, that's all."

Jade gazed at Freya's eyes, hidden behind her lashes. Freya didn't use much makeup, but her lashes were impossibly long. The depth of the blue behind them was incredible. She lifted her hand up between the rails and brushed away a strand of Freya's blond hair with her fingertips.

Jade blinked and dropped her hand. "I'm—"

Freya stopped her with a kiss. Jade's stomach felt like a thousand butterflies had just been set free. She could feel Freya's smile in that kiss. It was full of joy.

The rain was heavier and the crowd had thinned out. A group of Italian teenage boys were taking photos of them with their phones.

"We are getting our picture taken." Jade looked towards the boys.

"Does it bother you?" Freya whispered.

"No. I was just concerned for you."

Freya glanced at the boys. She then frowned. "You could be right." She took Jade's hand. "Let's go in."

Jade couldn't move as Freya was still on the other side of the gate and held her hand between the bars.

"Come on," Freya said.

Jade laughed. "I can't. You need to let go."

Freya tightened her grip. "I want to hold your hand from here to the museum. You must find a way."

Jade kept smiling, but she was confused. "You're serious?"

"Yes."

"Freya, it's pouring."

There were now only a few people by the gate. Most had taken shelter under the colonnade of the museum. A security officer watched them, amused but not about to interfere.

"I'm not moving without your hand," Freya said.

Jade swallowed; there was something about her tone which told her this was not just a game. She couldn't see any obvious gaps in the bars.

"I don't see how it's possible."

Freya leaned against the railing.

Jade twisted her hand gently, but Freya was not going to let go. The rain had dampened Freya's hair and raindrops had darkened her leather jacket.

Jade put her other hand between the bars. "Take my hand."

"I can't. I'm already holding it."

"Use your right one."

Freya did as she was asked. Now both of her hands were held between the bars.

"Now let go of the left."

Freya did and they moved along the gate one pace. Jade repeated this twice and never lost contact. Once free, but still holding hands, they ran for cover towards the south entrance.

Freya stopped at the enormous neoclassical pillars and pushed Jade against a column and kissed her. Jade's arms wrapped around Freya in a long, slow kiss, which left her breathless.

"You see . . ." Freya panted. "Things, which . . . might seem impossible . . ." Her eyes were big and her face flushed. "Always have a way."

"You're amazing," was as much as Jade could get out.

God, that was a lame thing to say. She winced and wanted to slap herself. *What am I doing here?* She started to pull away but Freya stopped her.

"What is wrong? What are you thinking?" Freya asked.

Jade swallowed. "That I'm clumsy and I don't understand you most of the time."

"Not understanding is a perquisite to most things worth knowing." Freya tucked her hair around both her ears. "And you are not clumsy, you're just a *kanin* . . . a rabbit. You just think too much, and then you're not sure what to do. There's too much fear in your brain." Freya half smiled. "I got lipstick on you." She rubbed it off with her thumb. "You know you don't need to think about everything. Something's you just feel." She entwined her fingers with Jade's.

"I'm afraid to do that," Jade whispered to herself.

"I'll remind you. It's not serious." Freya brushed rain out of Jade's hair. "Come, I want to show you something in the exhibit. But first, I'm hungry."

Freya seemed to know her way around and made a beeline for the Great Court. This was the area of the museum's library, created a decade ago, and it housed the new reading room. Freya pointed up and Jade saw a domed lattice of glass, which spanned two acres of space.

"I always think it's impressive," Freya said.

"Yes," Jade agreed before being yanked to a cafeteria area at the rear.

As they waited in the queue to be served, Jade crossed her arms, aware of how many people glanced at them. Freya seemed unfazed by the attention. When the cashier told them the total, Freya turned to her and muttered, "Sorry."

Jade paid, and they looked for an empty table.

"You can have our table," a woman said to Jade. She got up, as did her partner.

"You're not done. It's okay, we'll wait," Jade said.

"It's fine," the woman said. "We're in a hurry anyway."

Freya smiled back and touched the woman's arm as she picked up her coat. "This is very kind. Thank you."

The woman nodded. "You're welcome."

Jade sat down. "Do you get this reaction everywhere?"

"What do you mean?"

"People staring and others giving up their seat for you."

Freya shrugged. "It happens a bit. People are kind. But I suspect they recognised me from the newspaper."

"I don't think so. They, like me, think you are beautiful."

Freya poured the tea and gave it to Jade. "So, you think I'm beautiful?"

"Yes, I'm sure everyone does."

Freya placed a sandwich in front of Jade. "You know, you say things in the oddest ways."

Jade felt her cheeks warm. *Jesus, I'm an ass.* A hand touched hers and she glanced up. Freya was leaning forward, her face a few inches away from her.

"Listen, I think what you say is sweet and unguarded," Freya said in a voice that made all the other sounds fade away. "Have confidence. Who wants to be magnolia?" She leaned back. "Look at that amazing sandwich you have. Wow, I bet it really tastes fucking awesome," she said loudly with a strong accent.

People at nearby tables turned to look, and two kids laughed.

Jade smiled. "I guess you want me to eat it."

Freya nodded and Jade took a bite.

"Magnolia?" Jade backtracked.

"Yes, magnolia. It's a colour."

"But why magnolia?"

"It's a bland colour everyone uses to paint the inside of their houses."

"Oh. Yes, it's good not to be magnolia." Jade laughed. "So, what colour am I?"

"Well, not black, if that's what you thought I would say. Anyway, black is not a colour. I think you are more like a rainbow behind a cobwebbed pane." Freya focused a serious smile at Jade. "Eat the sandwich that I specially acquired for you."

Jade picked it up. "I paid for it."

"True, but sometimes, someone with a ladder needs to clean the windows. Or get someone to eat a sandwich."

Jade stared at her in mid-chew and then finished her bite. "You're very random."

Freya laughed, leaned in, and gave her a quick kiss. "And you're very cute," she whispered.

Jade felt self-conscious and clocked that people were watching them. She wanted to get on firmer ground, so she changed the subject. "So why didn't you go to New York?"

"I wanted to spend time with you." Freya took a sip of her tea.

"But really, why?"

"I wanted to spend time with you."

"Oh. But you're a—" This was not the right time to bring up her royal status. "I don't understand."

"Did I say it wrong? I just thought we could spend some time together." Freya was fiddling with her necklace. "I should have asked."

"It's fine. I'm just surprised."

"It is okay?"

Jade smiled and felt warmth in her chest. "Yes, of course."

"Good, I've a lot to talk to you about. Eat up. I want to show you the exhibition."

"What's it about?"

"Vikings!" Freya hit her fist on the table, knocking over an empty teacup. Jade slowly put down the crust of her sandwich. The people next to them had turned to stare.

Freya's face reddened and she got up. "Come on. I'm embarrassing myself now."

JADE, WITH FREYA at her side, entered a specially provisioned area entitled "Exhibition: Ancient and Postclassical Mythical Deities."

The expanse opened into a dimly lit, large room filled with display cases containing items that were highlighted by spotlights. The exhibit was busy, and after Jade examined a few of the relics on display, she lost track of Freya.

She frowned and scanned the gallery, and then she spotted her, gracefully meandering around the artefacts related to Old Norse folklore. Freya stopped and looked into a square glass cabinet at waist height. She turned and beckoned Jade to come over.

Inside the case was a single figurine no more than an inch high. Freya knelt at the same level as it and tugged Jade down.

"Look," Freya said.

Jade raised her eyebrows in surprise but not at the display. Freya tapped the case with a finger that was shorter than normal.

"This is twelve hundred years old," Freya said. "You see the hair and garment is that of a woman. She has no beard."

Jade gazed at Freya.

"Jade, pay attention!"

Jade blinked. "I am."

"She is not a farmer or field worker or even a slave. She carries a sword in her right hand and in her left a shield. It's known that women Vikings fought alongside men, but this is not a female warrior. She's a Valkyrie. Only a few have ever been found as artefacts."

Freya put an arm around Jade's waist. "The Valkyrie chose who died and who lived in the field of battle. They chose from the dead who go to the afterlife in the field Fólkvangr or go to Odin's great hall, Valhalla. Do you know this?"

"A bit, yes," Jade said.

"There is a hole, see? Through the hair. This was worn on a cord as a necklace by a *læknir*."

"A *læknir*?"

"A healer. The figurine is of a Valkyrie representing peace and mercy."

Jade understood, as she was familiar with classic mythology from her Oxford studies. "I like it. It says a lot for something so small."

"I love it as well." Freya stood, pulling Jade up with her. She looked right and left before hunching over the cabinet. "It's why I want you to steal it for me," she said in a low voice. Her tone was dark and demanding.

"What?" Jade said, shocked.

"Not so loud," Freya whispered. "Do it now. While no one is looking—"

"Freya, I'm not stealing it."

Freya burst out laughing. "That's good. It would be hard for me to visit you in prison." She tamped down her amusement. "I'm sorry, that was a bad trick. You don't need to steal it. It's already mine."

"Yours?"

"A family heirloom. I lent it to the organizers of the exhibit."

Jade started to relax. "Impressive."

"Come on, one more thing to see."

Jade followed her to another display case.

Freya tapped the glass again.

"What happened to your finger?" Jade asked.

Freya held up her finger, examining it. "Oh I forgot about this. You get used to things. It was cut off with a knife, long ago." She turned back to the exhibit. In the display case was a small tablet, the size and thickness of an atlas.

"*Burney Relief (Queen of the Night) 18ᵗʰ–19ᵗʰ century BCE*," Jade read.

"You don't need to read that." Freya poked Jade's shoulder. "It's wrong anyway."

Jade laughed. "Okay, tell me about it."

Freya locked arms with her. "I'm going to. Well, it's about four thousand years old; it's supposedly the queen of the night. But these things get confused. And it has been changed." She paused and rubbed her nose. "You see, the winged female figure in the centre? Well, she holds two rods and rings, symbols of eternity and divinity. No one knows why there are two. She has the feet of a hawk." She pointed. "And she stands on two cats. Beside are two ridiculously large owls." She faced Jade. "You see that the wings. They are the same as I showed you on the figurine?"

"I guess." Jade rubbed her temple. "This is a Valkyrie as well?" She decided it was better to humour Freya than try to get an explanation for what this was all about.

Freya laughed. "No. Valkyries aren't real."

"I know that. This is mythology. It's all superstitions with truths mixed in," Jade said.

"How many truths? And, how much myth?"

"Mostly myth."

"Really," Freya muttered while biting her lip. "You sure?" She wandered away from the cabinet.

Jade took the opportunity to read the full description:

> Queen of the Night, 18ᵗʰ–19ᵗʰ century BCE, Mesopotamian terracotta relief originally painted. The exact identity of the deity is under debate, but it is believed be Lilitu (or Lilith), Inanna, or Ereshkigal, the Queen of the Underworld.

She skipped forward:

> The name Lilith comes from the Hebrew term meaning "night creature". Lilith appears in Jewish religion as the first wife of Adam, expelled for disobedience, or in Christian religion as the serpent that persuaded Eve to eat the forbidden fruit. For some, Lilith was the liberator imparting knowledge and this has been misrepresented to ensure obedience. Although there is much conjecture involved with these assertions.

"What time did Karen say she would come to get me?" Freya asked, stepping up next to her.

Earlier in the day, at Freya's request, Jade had sent a message to agree on a time. Jade looked at her phone. "Three. But it's three now."

"We have ten minutes. Karen knows I'm always late, so she allows extra time."

"Freya," Jade tried again. "Why'd you want to show me these things?"

Freya blinked at her. "You're smart, and I need your help to work something out. I guess we haven't time now to talk about it more."

They glanced at each other in awkward silence, then they both spoke at once.

"You go ahead," Jade said.

"Okay . . . I'm kind of worried, that I might have come on a bit strong to you today." Freya twisted the pendant on her necklace.

"It's fine—"

"Let me explain. Well, I will probably embarrass myself." Freya took a deep breath. "I've a lot going on and not much time. I really want to spend more time with you. It's a silly thing to say, but I think—Um, I want to help you get on your feet, and to be honest I need your help as well. But really, there is a lot hidden in that head of yours and I want—I think you need someone to share it with. I'm hoping you would like to spend more time with me. I make sense?"

"Who wouldn't want to spend more time with you? I'd love to."

Freya dropped her necklace. "Good, Good." She took Jade's hand. "Let me know if I'm being overly affectionate. Not everyone appreciates it."

"I find that hard to believe," Jade said. "You said you needed my help?"

"We better find Karen. Come on." Freya took Jade's hand and led her out of the gallery.

OUTSIDE THE GATES, Karen leant against the Audi as she talked to a police officer. She could see Freya and Jade walking down the steps. She sighed to herself when she saw them embrace briefly.

"I'll be going now," Karen told the officer when he handed back her ID.

"Do you need assistance from Special Protection Branch?" he asked.

"No, Freya is pretty low profile."

The officer nodded towards the other side of the street. "It doesn't look that way."

Karen turned to see half a dozen reporters with heavy photography equipment, taking pictures of Freya.

Jade had spotted them as well and was crossing the street towards the paparazzi, leaving Freya to meet Karen.

"Let's go!" Karen ordered, opening the car door.

Freya was twisting her necklace as they climbed into the car.

As the Audi pulled away, Karen caught a glimpse of Jade arguing with the group of photographers.

Kari's Courage

EIR SAT ON a large log next to a smouldering fire as long shadows of the fjord's mountains drew across the land and sea. The temperature had dropped and she was cold. Everyone else was in the great hall keeping warm, but she refused to go in. Her eyes stung from the smoke of the fire, but she didn't move. The smoke deterred the swarms of midges, which came out at this time, and she didn't want to be up all night scratching bites. A cold gust cut through her woollen dress, causing her to shiver. She thought about going into the hall to join her father, but she was furious with him.

No, they can burn in Helheim! Her father had denied her yet again. She had been taught by her mother all her life and expected to take on her mother's duties, looking after the sick and injured of the village as a *læknir*. But her father just said, "No, you are not ready," and told her she must take a husband. She didn't want to, and the thought of it made her shudder.

Eir sighed; she knew it was not his doing. He was just a shell since her mother had died last year. It was Ragnvi who had influenced his decision. Ragnvi snaked her way around him, hoping to gain status and become a chieftain's wife. Eir knew that despite her efforts, it wouldn't be long before she had a new mother.

She took a section of her long blond hair and weaved three strands into a tight braid. It was not right to have her hair bound, being unwed. *Why should I do as I'm told!* Without a ribbon to tie the end, she let it fall and unwind. She leant her chin on her hands and put her elbows on her knees, enclosed in her thoughts as the smoke of the fire subsumed her. She wanted the gods to tell her what to do. *Perhaps Frigg will speak to me or the Norns will give me a sign.*

She was about to cry, for the injustice of it, for the death of her mother, for the loss of her father's spirit and the sly Ragnvi, who was taking away her life. "I'm not going to cry," she said and gritted her teeth. Her mind tried to revisit an image of her mother's face. She could no longer see it clearly, but her feelings formed a picture and she started to weep. The effort of her tears kept her warm until she could no longer endure the repeating cycle.

Eir looked up to see the night sky bright with stars. She'd been there a while. The fire was now diminished and gave off little heat. She stared at the embers as their intensity rippled in the wind.

A heavy sheepskin was thrown around her, causing her to jump. Kari pushed up next to her and held the fleece in place with a thin arm across Eir's shoulder.

"Are you still angry?" Kari asked.

Eir said nothing.

"You will freeze if you stay out here much longer. Eir, come inside, please."

"A *karl* is giving me orders now! I don't care if Hel takes me to Nifelheim," Eir snapped and looked at Kari.

Kari then thumped her palm hard on her forehead. "Stop being a *haensa griss*!"

Eir stared in disbelief. She knew that Kari didn't like being teased that she was just a *karl* from a farming family, and before that, a *thrall*, while Eir was the daughter of a chieftain, the ruling class, and a *jarl*. But they joked about it all the time.

Kari hit her again, but missed Eir's shoulder and punched her chest. "You heard me, *haensa griss*."

"Hey! Stop punching me."

Kari tried to thump her again, but Eir caught her hand and twisted it. Eir was stronger than Kari and easily turned her wrist and bent it back.

"Ow, ow . . ." Kari winced. "That hurts. Stop!"

Eir bent Kari's wrist back harder, now playful. "Then don't hit me."

"Ouch! Stop, stop, please stop!"

"No more name calling," Eir said, and released Kari's hand.

Kari rubbed her wrist and looked wounded.

"You know you're calling me a chicken piglet. That doesn't even make sense." Eir laughed.

Kari glanced at Eir mischievously. "You *are* a *haensa griss*!" She laughed.

"Why are you calling me that?" Eir asked. "You could have made up something better."

Kari gazed into Eir's with her unusual brown eyes. "Because you are being a coward, sitting out here in the cold, waiting for your Norns to offer a golden fate. Well, they won't, so stop being a piglet and feeling sorry for yourself. Don't let things just happen to you. You're a *jarl*."

Eir allowed her head to fall on Kari's shoulder and enjoyed the peaceful quiet for a few moments. "Let's go inside, it's cold."

They walked wrapped in the fleece until they pushed through the thick drapes of hide that covered the entrance to the great longhouse. In the centre of the vast space, Rangvald crept around the tall flames of the hearth. He raised and lowered his voice in a dramatic fashion as he told a tale of battles from far across the sea.

A number of the women and men watched Eir enter. She could never get used to the attention she drew. In their eyes, she read lust, envy, hatred, and sometimes all three.

She asked her father once, why do they look at me so? His response didn't help. "You were born with gifts from the goddess Frigg," he would say. He had been telling her that since she was a child. It meant that she was pretty.

"That's what you always say." Eir had rolled her eyes.

"And one day you will know why."

She never understood what that meant and assumed it had been the ale talking.

After they entered, Kari started walking to the corner where she must sit.

Eir caught her hand and whispered, "I'm not a *haensa griss*."

Eir expected Kari to say, "You are," but instead she said in a serious tone, "No. So don't be one." Kari pulled away and disappeared into the darkened shadows of the hall, with the fleece bundled in her arms.

Eir manoeuvred to the head of the room where her father was sleeping in an embrace. He lay against Ragnvi as her fingers brushed along his bearded cheek. Even in the dim light of the hearth fire, Eir could see Ragnvi watching her. Her hawk-like eyes followed every step. The courage Kari had given her wavered, but she clung on to it and moved to take up a spot a few paces behind her father. She sat and rested against one of the large timbers, which ran up to support the ceiling.

Many in the hall were still awake and listened intensely to Rangvald. Although they had heard the tale many times, they still watched Rangvald's movements as he acted out the words. Eir smiled to herself. Everything was pretty much as she expected it to be. Her life might change for the worse, but it was comforting to know that some things would always be the same.

She tried to spot Kari but couldn't. Kari's darker skin and eyes made her stand out in a crowd, but not in the smoky shadows of the hall. Eir was a year younger, and they had always been friends, even though it was frowned upon. Eir couldn't imagine how this would change when she had to take a husband.

She'd thought that if she became the tribe's healer, she would be able to have Kari help her. But Ragnvi had taken that away. Her anger bubbled up again. She wanted to get up and yell at Ragnvi as loud as she could, *Get out, get out, leave my father alone!* The thought of doing it made her feel a little better. Kari had told her she needed to act and not just hope the Norns would weave her a new path. But what did Kari know of those spinners of fate? Kari came to the village as a Christian slave, and although she had tried to adopt their ways, Eir knew she still clung to her single God. Eir closed her eyes and tried to think of what to do.

IT WAS AFTERNOON when Eir made her way to a hut on the edge of the land her tribe farmed. Beyond this, the meadows changed to steep, rocky scrub and climbed towards the mountain peaks. A friend of her mother's, Gjertrud, had come to her, secretly avoiding Ragnvi's attention and had asked Eir to come see to her son. He had been sick for a day and was getting worse. Eir was puzzled why he was in such a remote building normally only used to tend to the caribou herd. Gjertrud told her the elders feared his sickness and would no longer allow her to keep him in the village.

They followed a faint path in the lush grass, which ran along the edge of a low cliff. Below, she heard the waves of the sea crashing against the shoreline, followed by the rattle of rolling pebbles. Eir tried to make conversation with Gjertrud, but she was not in a mood to speak. The wind had picked up and Eir's hair blew around her face. She stopped and opened the sealskin bag that hung across her chest. She pulled out a short bind of leather and struggled to tie her hair in the wind. Gjertrud took the tie from her and looped it to fix a ponytail.

"Thank you," Eir said.

Gjertrud nodded. Worry lined her face. "It will be dark soon," she muttered.

They arrived, and Eir squinted to see inside the small log building. She kept the door open to let in what light she could. In the corner, on a pile of old straw, a small boy lay.

"How old is he?" Eir asked and pulled away the skins that covered him.

"Four."

Eir felt his forehead. He was wet with fever and cold to touch. She leaned over and put her head against his chest. After a few moments she could just make out a faint heartbeat.

Gjertrud stood close by, trembling with her fingers against her lips. "Is he—?"

"He is alive." Eir examined his chest and arms. There was no sign of pox. She looked inside his mouth and saw that his tongue was dry and white as chalk. "Has he been throwing up his food?"

"Yes, and worse."

"Did he eat anything unusual before this?"

"No. I thought maybe he had an upset tummy, but then he became quiet and hasn't moved."

Eir continued to examine the child. "I see no bites," she said softly. "Did he go anywhere or do anything out of the ordinary?"

"No. He was with his father in the morning, mending nets. He wasn't like this until last night."

"Is Halvard also sick?" Eir remembered the boy's father and that he was a kind man.

"I don't know. He went away on the boat before sunrise to catch the tide."

Eir considered the child. She had seen this condition twice before when she'd been learning her skills. Both those times it had been a viper's bite, but there was no bite on the boy.

"Try to think. What did they eat or drink before this?"

"Barley and milk, bread, then herring, with carrots and mushrooms."

"Did you eat all of these as well?"

"Mostly yes, but I don't like carrots or mushrooms, so—"

"Wait, you didn't eat the mushrooms?"

"No."

"Where did the mushrooms come from?" Eir asked.

"I don't know, Halvard brought them in. He said he had traded a carved walrus tusk for them."

"Do you know who he got them from?"

"No, he didn't say."

Eir paused, gathering herself before standing.

"He's been poisoned by the mushrooms," she asserted confidently. "We must take him back to the great hall. We need milk thistles, boiled goat's milk, and dandelion root. My mother's stores will have some of those, but we must keep an eye out on the way."

"The elders won't let me take him back."

"Who won't? Which elders?"

"All of them. Well, Ragnvi told them the illness would spread and he must be taken away. The others agreed."

The mention of Ragnvi's name made Eir's blood boil. She bent down, scooped the child up, and held him against her shoulder.

"She is wrong. We are taking him to the hall." She turned and carried the child from the stable.

The wind had picked up and was bitterly cold as it blew in from the northern sea. The child she carried still felt warm against her, but she didn't think they would make it in time to do any good. She stopped and handed the boy to his mother to carry with a grim expression. Gjertrud took her son and held him tightly to her chest.

By the time they arrived at her father's longhouse, Eir had been able to gather a few thistles and dandelion roots in the dark. The place was empty as she expected; her father had gone with the fishing boats that morning and they had not returned yet.

Eir lit a whale oil lamp from a reed that she had used to capture a flame from the central hearth. She gestured for the boy to be placed on a small cot made of willow and began preparing the medicine. When it was ready, she slowly fed it to him with her finger. She hoped that it was going down his throat. She cleaned up, turned to the cot, and discovered that Gjertrud hunched over him, praying; a cross at the end of a necklace held between her hands. She hadn't known Gjertrud was a Christian. The only other person she knew who wore a cross was Kari.

She closed her eyes for a moment. Sharp nails dug into her shoulder and spun her around.

"Fool! Why have you brought him here?" Ragnvi seethed. "You condemn us all!"

Ragnvi's Rage

EIR FACED RAGNVI, the witch who was destroying her life.

Ragnvi glared at Eir with hatred. "You have brought death here! Servant of Pesta!"

Eir shuddered at Pesta's name—the creature of death that brought disease. "He was poisoned; he doesn't carry a plague." She turned to console the boy's mother, who was kneeling beside him.

Ragnvi was quiet for a moment and then took small, nervous steps backwards. She stopped and pointed a finger at Eir. "You have brought him back and now others will die. Helvíti will welcome you, plague carrier." She disappeared into the shadows of the longhouse.

In the morning, Eir didn't eat but instead went to the spot where the longboats were normally beached. She scanned the horizon; they still had not returned. This was often the case—it depended on the weather, the catch, or if they were chasing a pod of whales. A whale was a prized catch and the whole clan would celebrate, but this could take many days and sometimes a few lives. She was hoping to get news of Halvard, the father of the boy who had also eaten the mushrooms. He had left with the boats the previous day. Eir was confident the boy was poisoned and wanted to see how his father had fared. If he was alive, she would ask him whom he had traded his ivory scrimshaw with, in exchange for the mushrooms. Eir knew that Ragnvi would be doing her own poisoning; telling the elders she had brought the boy back and now others would die.

Eir couldn't see any sign of the boats' sails and the cold wind bit deep into her. She pushed herself off the smooth stone on which she was perched and walked back up to the great hall.

"How are you today, *fagr minn*?" Kari said. She popped her head out from behind a goat she was milking.

Eir smiled and climbed over the split logs of the pen. She perched on the edge of Kari's low stool and shoved her sideways to make room.

"Hey, this is not big enough for both of us." Kari laughed.

"That was a nice thing to call me, but I'm not beautiful," Eir said.

Kari shot her an incredulous look. "Your goddess Frigg would be jealous of you."

Eir felt herself blush, looked away, and sat in thought for a moment.

"Sometimes I wish I was a *thrall*," Eir said in a wistful tone. "I could stay here and look after the animals."

"No, you don't. It's very boring. Do you want to milk Erica?"

Eir watched Kari milk the old goat. "No."

"I didn't think you did." She laughed.

"Well, maybe I would, if I didn't have to be anywhere near Ragnvi."

"She's an old goat. And you're a *brusi*." Kari bumped Eir off the stool.

"I'm not a he-goat." Eir managed to get a foot down before completely falling over on her side.

On the wind, she heard someone calling her name. She scanned the field but couldn't see who was calling, so she leapt out of the pen and ran up the hill towards the shouts. When she was closer she could see it was Ylva, one of the elders, and called back, "What's wrong?"

Ylva waited until Eir was closer. "Two of the children are ill. The same as Halvard's son."

"No, that can't be—"

"Come." Ylva turned and marched away.

Eir hurried to follow her. Ylva looked to be forty, and for as long as Eir remembered, she had been forty every year. She was slim, tall, and her dark hair was streaked with grey. She had special status, as no one else in the clan was older. She spoke to few and many avoided her. Her acrid remarks and ill humour kept people at bay. Some even feared she was a witch, but Eir's father respected her and often sought her council.

Ylva led Eir to the great hall, where the ill children had been placed. They were wrapped up and close to the always-burning hearth. It was midday but the hall was dark as it had no windows; it was only possible to see by the flames of the fire, which cast orange light and created flickering shadows. Eir inspected the children, who were no more than six years old.

"They're the same. They've been poisoned. But I'm not sure how," Eir said.

Ylva signalled the mothers of the sick children to come forward.

When they women did not speak, Eir understood she was supposed to talk to them. She looked at them nervously. "What did they eat this morning?"

"They ate with the other children. Porridge," one woman said, while stroking her daughter's feverish, damp forehead.

"How many children?" Ylva asked.

"Many," Ingrid said. "It's easier to feed the little ones at the same time."

"I know," Ylva snapped. "What was in the porridge?"

"I don't know." She bowed her head with tears in her eyes.

Eir waved to Ylva, indicating she wanted to speak. She lifted Ingrid's chin. "Do you know who made it? I need to know if it's the cause of the sickness."

Ingrid shook her head and looked to the other mother.

"It was brought by a *thrall*. I think her name is Dotir," the woman said.

Eir gasped, put her hand over her mouth, and whispered to Ylva, "That's my *thrall*. She makes meals for my family . . . I didn't eat this morning and my father is fishing. She must have given our breakfast to the children."

"We need to find her. And you must prepare for others," Ylva said.

Eir nodded. "First I will tend to these with the remedy I made last night."

When Eir finished, she went to stand with Ylva outside the hall. Her thoughts were on what she needed to do to make more medicine. Out of habit, she looked out to sea. She closed her eyes and exhaled in relief. A strong breeze was blowing offshore and she saw the square sails of a vessel tacking against the wind. It had rounded the cliffs that marked the entry of the harbour and soon would be beached on the pebbles.

But why only one? Where is the other? Rán, please bring all home safely. She had always thanked Rán, wife to the god of the sea, and so far it had always brought her father home.

She turned and walked a few steps.

"There she is. She brought death to us." Ragnvi screeched. She pointed an accusing finger at Eir. Behind Ragnvi were the women of the village and a few of the older men who hadn't gone to sea. Three were carrying sick children, all looked tearful and afraid.

"You don't know that, Ragnvi. This is something else," Ylva said.

"She brought the plague-ridden boy here last night, when I told all to keep him away. Now our children are sick and will die!" Ragnvi's face was red and spittle flung out between the words.

Eir had never seen such rage before. She took a step back. "I didn't. Halvard's son was poisoned."

Kari ran out from behind the crowd and stood with Eir, her small delicate face hardened and she looked ready to fight. "This is not Eir's doing. Leave her be."

"Be quiet, elf," Ragnvi commanded and turned to the group. "Eir is cursing us and wants our children dead. She brings Pesta to us." She pointed at Eir. "Look at her. No one appears so perfect without dark *seiðr*."

The crowd rumbled their agreement.

"Kill her, my child is dying!" a young mother yelled.

Another mother picked up a fist-sized stone and threw it at Eir.

"Eir!" Kari yelled and stepped in front of the path of the stone.

The stone hit Kari in the centre of her forehead and she slumped down onto the muddy ground.

"Kari!" Eir knelt and put an ear to Kari's chest. Nothing of Kari moved.

The crowd was now subdued. A few people backed away from Ragnvi and the woman who had thrown the stone.

Eir looked at Ragnvi in anguish. Then she saw it. Hanging around her neck on a cord of leather was an ivory figure of a whale. The one Halvard had traded for the poisonous mushrooms. "It was you . . . the scrimshaw." Eir pointed at the necklace.

Ragnvi touched the scrimshaw and ran towards Eir. Ylva grabbed her arm, but Ragnvi twisted free. She collided with Eir, knocking her to the ground and then hit Eir's face in a fury. "Shut up! Shut up, witch!"

The stone that felled Kari was within arm's reach. Ragnvi flung out her hand, picked up the stone, and sat on Eir's chest.

Eir waited for the blow and closed her eyes the moment before impact.

WARMTH BRUSHED ALONG her cheek. She tried to get up but couldn't. She tried to see but her eyes wouldn't open and her breath wouldn't fill her lungs. She listened for her heart but no sound came. It happened again: the soft warmth across her face and her neck. She wanted to speak. Her own distant scream engulfed her. That sensation again, over her eye and down her nose. *Help me*, she thought. *Please.*

Of course, child, a voice came to her. *Your eye should open now.*

Eir tried to open her eyes, but only one honoured her command. She looked into a twilight of dark grey. Cumulus clouds raced across the sky, while pure white lightning danced between them and struck the ground without a sound. A woman knelt at her side with a cloak of black and white feathers, a head of wavy red hair, lips of red, and a walrus-tusk-white gown threaded with green. Behind, off in the distance, a black stallion stood still, dressed in silver armour with wings folded at its sides. The stallion snorted and stomped its hooves, its head shaking impatiently.

Help me, please. Eir tried to speak.

Your body is dead, child, the woman said.

I must get back, I must stop Ragnvi, I must save Kari, I must—

Shh, child.

Eir could feel fingers stroking her hair.

No! I must save my father from that evil, I must protect the children, I—Oh Kari . . . Her thoughts wept tearless sorrow. *Take me back, læknir!*

I am no healer, the woman snapped. *I am Frigg, the Assented, daughter of Njord.* Frigg moved her head back in surprise. *I know you . . .*

Eir frowned at her. *You know me?*

The goddess Frigg shook her head, her lips narrowed, and face reddened. *Hush, Eir! This is not what I agreed. This is not what I wanted for you. The Norns had promised, now they cheat us both!*

Frigg jerked up, spread out her black-and-white-feathered cloak, and drew it around her. She paced to the stallion with her head down.

Don't leave me! Eir screamed.

Frigg turned back to Eir, and her demeanour had changed. Tears rolled down her cheeks and her shoulders hung low. She knelt beside Eir again. *This was not to be, my child. I will undo this. You won't be bound here.*

Frigg moved a hand across the length of Eir's body and released Eir's soul. Eir stood beside Frigg and looked down on herself.

Frigg collected Eir's body in her arms. "Come, my cherished. It's time for these games to end."

Bound

"WHEN CAN I go back?" Eir asked. She was in a glade set between the peaks of snow-covered mountains. The sky was moody and majestic clouds from time to time shielded the sun.

"It's not that simple to leave Asgard," Frigg said.

"Yes, my lady," Eir said, remembering her manners.

Eir took a few steps in the direction they were heading.

Frigg gave a sad smile. "Wait a moment." Her red hair fluttered in a gust of wind. "This is the start of their end. A risk I must take." She took a final bite of an apple and dropped it on the ground. From the spot where the core landed a tree sprouted. Within what Eir thought was a blink of an eye, it grew to a sapling and blossomed. Frigg shook the small tree and a serpent dropped down from its branches.

It started to slither away. "Lilith, where are your legs and arms?" Frigg chided and put a foot on its middle, pinning it in place. She then took a breath. "I, the Assented, Mistress of the Valkyrie will decide the fate of the Norns. The vigil has ended. You, queen of the night, will destroy the Norns for your freedom. Do you acquiesce?"

The snake tipped its head from side to side and hissed.

"Very good. But don't dally." Frigg lifted her foot and the snake disappeared into the grass.

Frigg came closer to Eir. "Knowledge is freedom." She laughed sardonically. "A journey littered with the remains of its own consumption. We must hope the fourth's thread is enduring."

Frigg started to a copse of small trees at the centre of the glade.

Eir took a few steps to follow her.

"Bring your body," Frigg commanded.

Eir backtracked to find it lying on the grass where the spontaneous apple tree had grown. She was uncertain how to retrieve it.

Frigg laughed. "Just drag it, child. It will want to be with you."

Eir tugged her own body, with a sustained swish, through the dew-covered grass.

They arrived at the edge of the copse, and Frigg picked up Eir's body delicately in her arms.

She followed Frigg between the young saplings that seemed to slide out of her way on expanding turf. She glanced around. The trees had multiplied and aged. *A trick of my spirit eyes?*

The thicket became woods, and the woods became a forest. Birch, willow, and pine got older the deeper they went. The trees grew thicker, taller, and sparser until all were left behind and they stood in a field of wild wheat. Dispersed between the long stalks, lilac flax blossoms poked through, their colour as gemstones woven into a dowdy kirtle.

Something rustled nearby, and Eir ducked behind Frigg. A deer leapt away with only the back of its white tail visible on each hop as it cut a path through the crop.

The ground inclined gently to a flat meadow. At the centre was a great hall. A thin ribbon of white smoke curled from its roof.

The distance across the meadow to the hall was greater than she had expected. When she stood close to it, she understood why. The hall was colossal. Each ancient timber that supported its roof were the thicker than ten of her own home. Carved into the wood were more runes than could be read in a lifetime.

Many of the runes she didn't understand, and she only recognised a few fragments of ancient sagas. She tried to decipher a line as they walked passed. *Hocon the feeble cowered in his hall.* She had heard of Chieftain Hocon from tales around her village's hearth. But in those tales, he was strong and heroic.

"My Lady, what do the runes tell?" Eir ventured to ask.

"The history of our people . . . This is my hall, Sessrúmnir."

Once inside, Eir froze and feared to move. Four orange eyes, owned by two snow-white lynx with black spots, stared at her. Each was the size of a bear, while being lean and muscular. They sat to attention with their front paws together.

The cats moved aside as Frigg walked past. Eir uncertain if she could be harmed, followed Frigg's footsteps while warily watching the cats.

The interior of the hall was unlike any she had seen. Mosaics covered the floor, depicting battles against unfamiliar beasts. The walls were too distant for her to discern any details, but she could see they were covered by dusty tapestries. She recalled when her father returned from Danelagh, the great island of Anglo-Saxons, he told her about a place called Jorvik. It had many ancient ruined buildings left by warriors from the south. They were built of cut stone with pictures made from tiles. Eir wondered if this was how those places would've looked.

They stopped halfway down the large hall. Ahead, Eir saw the flickering glow of a fire.

Frigg called out, "Bygul, Trjegul, come here!"

One of the cats emerged from the shadows, startling Eir. "That cat scared the life out of—" *My life is already absent.*

The other lynx appeared. Frigg shepherded them to stand next to each other and flung Eir's lifeless body across their backs.

"To the hearth," she ordered.

The cats moved forward as one. Eir's damaged corpse dangled over their sides with its hair dragging on the floor.

Frigg gripped Eir's arm, then her shoulder and touched her cheek firmly. "Your soul is hardening. We must be quick. You cannot stay like this, or you will return as dust. Walk close to me but keep focused on the fire ahead."

As they walked, Eir felt a sensation of danger and glanced behind her.

Frigg grabbed Eir's chin with strong fingers. "Look forward, my cherished. I don't think it will intercede just yet."

"What won't?"

"Look forward," Frigg repeated in a whisper. "Be brisk. Once we are beside the hearth, it will stay at a distance, until it has reason to do otherwise."

"What is it?" Eir asked.

"A Norn."

Eir trembled. The Norns were the three beings who decided the destiny of mortals and gods.

They marched towards a round central hearth. It covered a circle that was the breadth of a sheep-shearing pen, but only a single fire burnt at its perimeter. Next to the fire, three large tables were turned on their sides. They were twice as high as Eir and created a walled space by the hearth.

A hall within a hall, Eir thought. It struck her that the small furnished area was the only occupied part of Frigg's home. The rest was dark and foreboding.

Eir could hear a strange noise as they got closer to the fire, a raspy squashed repeating vibration. Something was snoring near the fire. Frigg lifted Eir's body from the cats' backs and lowered it onto a bench. She pointed, and the cats took up a position to guard the entrance of the makeshift room.

"What will happen now? I need to get back."

"Yes," Frigg smoothed. "Be patient. Sit."

Eir sat on a wide bulbous log covered in a thick grey hide next to the fire. She couldn't feel any warmth from the flames, but it gave her some comfort and she tried to relax.

The log moved up and down in time with the snoring. A loud grunt sounded and Eir was thrown to the ground.

Frigg doubled over and laughed uncontrollably. "Hildisvíni! That's no way to treat a guest."

Eir scrambled to her feet and found herself face-to-snout with a boar the size of an oxcart. The boar examined her and extended a large pink tongue over its nostrils. It seemed to smile, exposing stubby, worn teeth.

"Don't worry, he's too old to hurt anyone . . . and drunk on mead by the look of him. Go back to sleep, drunken old boar," Frigg ordered.

Hildisvíni took two unstable steps and collapsed back down.

Eir brought her hands to her heart, expecting to feel it pounding after being shocked by the great beast. She felt nothing and wanted to cry. *Crying without a body wouldn't help.* She pushed her will to the forefront, her courage and conviction. *I'm going to leave this place to help those I love.* Her thoughts sheared, as wind on the crests of relentless waves. *I will be disobedient to my own death.*

Frigg moved a pelt to reveal a chest made of a single block of yellow pine. She lifted the hinged lid and removed a leather purse. She pulled a necklace with an amber pendant from it.

"Come here," Frigg beckoned.

"No. What are you doing?" Eir bit her lip; she shouldn't have spoken to Frigg in that manner.

Frigg smiled. "Good, you are wilful. The brave ask questions. The wise listen to the answer and ask a new question." She placed the necklace around the neck of Eir's body.

"This is not something I would normally do, but I cannot be sure Lilith will do as I've commanded. And I don't want a Norn to be able to control your fate. Even if I persuade them to send you back, I don't trust them to keep you safe." Frigg sighed. "So, we will fool them." She took hold of the amber pendant and cradled it in her palm. "This is my necklace, the Brísingamen. It will heal your body and prolong it." She dropped it against the motionless chest.

Eir went to stand next to Frigg but found it difficult to bend her knees. There wasn't any pain, just a sense of the movement needing as much strength as she could exert. She watched as the wound on her skull reversed and recovered its shape. She gasped as her body began convulsing. Its back arched, arms flailed, and the mouth gaped. Her body's head turned suddenly towards her. Its eyes flung open and it tried to reach out just before it collapsed, motionless.

"What's wrong, what's happening?" Eir screamed.

"Calm yourself. It's to be expected. Let things settle for a moment."

One of the lynx, apparently bored of standing guard, padded into the snug. The cat brushed her head against Frigg's back, and Frigg in turn stroked her neck. "Bygul, back to your duties." The cat stretched out her paws, lowered her head, and yawned before finding a spot to rest. Frigg laughed. "I see sleeping comes first. The priorities of cats can never be understood."

"I must go back!" Eir was beside herself with fear and anger.

"First, we must bind your soul. Not to your body but to the necklace. If we bind it to your body, the Norns will be able to control your fate. But if we bind your soul to the necklace, when needs must, they can be separated, and you can return here, where"—she gave a short chortle—"you can start afresh." She stroked Eir's lifeless cheek. "Just know that when I bind your soul to the necklace, it will be unnatural and your manner will remain as it is now."

"I understand." Eir didn't, but she was desperate to be whole again.

"I don't think you do. You will age slowly and stay young at heart. And, if you are joined in this way, there will be no means for you to die whole in Midgard."

So be it.

"Learn, my child. When your body eventually fails, you must return to me, or your soul will be entombed in Brísingamen. There it will be free to be harvested by any of the Norns' servants. And they will be waiting to catch it."

"Fine."

Frigg nodded slowly. "Very well. Just come back here when your body tires. I will create an integument for resumption."

"I don't understand," Eir stuttered.

Frigg pulled a slender knife from her waist. The blade reflected no light, and without hesitation, Frigg cut off the tip of the ring finger from Eir's corpse.

Unlike the wound on Eir's head, the finger didn't repair itself. The skin just grew over the stump. Frigg carried the severed finger to a dais. She pulled an old tapestry off its top, sending dust into the air, and heaved open a lid, then slid it with two hands just wide enough to reach inside. Eir forced herself to move closer and looked inside too. It was actually a sarcophagus, and inside lay a brilliant fleece of silver and amber.

Frigg folded the corners of the fleece back, carefully positioned the fingertip underneath, and covered it up. "It won't take long, a few hours perhaps, and then you will have a replacement." She smiled. "Once, there were many of these. Used so warriors could fight again in Odin's spectacular battles. So, here, your integument, under an Osiris Fleece, will remain unchanged, ready when you need it." She shoved the lid back and replaced the tapestry. "Now we must bind you, and hastily, by the look of it." She danced quickly back to Eir's body and cupped the amber pendant again. She sang and her melodic voice reverberated in the space of the hall.

> *Fearless heart, o'child.*
> > *Fearless thought, be proud.*
> *Never bound, by trave.*
> *Never found, their slave.*
> *Fearless desire, my kin,*
> *Only your steps you walk in.*
> *Calm spirit, rise above.*
> *Calm seas, carry my love.*
> *Fearless heart, o'child.*
> > *Fearless thought, be proud.*

"You know the song?" Frigg asked.

Eir was rigid and couldn't get any words out.

With tears, Frigg touched Eir's soul. For a moment, Eir's view of the hall changed. It became more distant and a cloudy orange. She shook and gasped for air. Her vision had been restored but she was laying down. She jolted upright and clenched her knees.

"You are born again, my cherished." Frigg kissed Eir's forehead and helped her to sit.

"When . . . do . . . I . . . go . . . back?" She huffed out each word.

"Breathe slowly." Frigg comforted Eir until she had her breathing under control.

"I'm alive?"

"You are whole, in a manner." Frigg's face darkened, and she whispered, "But now, to go back, we must placate ourselves to the approaching Norn and ask for a weave with a new thread."

Eir closed her eyes tightly and gritted her teeth. *I must save Kari. I must save the children! I must revenge my death!*

Frigg pointed into the dark hall. A contrast in the gloom moved towards them. "They come to every birth to decide one's destiny, for better or worse." She hugged Eir as her face hardened. "They have the most incongruous sense of humour. But to *Helvíti* with them. They won't be able to control your disconnected soul."

The Norn moved closer in a pool of darkness that was clinging to its silhouette. The great cats bounded over the partitioning-table walls and disappeared in the opposite direction.

From where she stood, Eir couldn't make out any details of the Norn. Its image was distorted, like a reflection on rippling water. She felt sweat form on her forehead.

Frigg walked into its camouflaging shadow of the Norm. She engaged in an incomprehensible discussion, which lasted so long Eir's knees and hands shook and she feared she could bare no more of the Norn's presence.

The discussion finally ended and Frigg looked deflated. She glided over to Eir, ran her hand along Eir's shoulders, and stepped behind her to whisper in her ear. "It will do what I've asked. You can return."

The tall, grey wisp appeared for an instant. It was nude, and too slender to be human, only partly revealing itself Eir dared not look at its face, if it was a face. Its skin was criss-crossed with cicatrices. She could feel its gaze and glanced up to see it bow its head and then its body, curling and collapsing into the indiscernible shape that rotated and flexed until a human-height cylinder of wavering light was left in its place. Eir recognised the distortions. It was her village, the spot where she had been killed.

Frigg let out a sigh of relief and looked around as if checking that everything was where it should be. She called for her cats. They raced back and circled her, sniffing, and then sat at her feet. "Good, little has changed . . . But it will be impossible to know for sure."

Frigg pulled a feather from her garment and handed it to Eir. "Take this and keep it safe. Touch it to your lips when your body is at an end. It will cause your wings to appear. And they will bring you back here. Then you can be reborn."

"My wings?"

"Yes, you are a Valkyrie now. But there is no time for questions. You must join your thread before it moves into the present."

Eir watched as the small feather in her palm hardened into solid silver. She carefully pushed it into her pocket and buttoned up the flap.

"Use your time in the careless, mortal Midgard well. Reduce the suffering. Too many are dying needlessly." Frigg embraced her. "When your body is spent, come back to me. I will miss you. You must go, now."

Eir rested her head against Frigg's chest, then pulled away and darted into the window that would take her home. She turned back to look at Frigg.

"Will I see you again?" To her ears, her words were muffled as if she were underwater.

"Perhaps, child, when the Norns are destroyed, we can spend time together."

Eir wanted to ask more. She felt a jarring against her head that then faltered, replaced by a burrowing pain near her eye. The shadow of a wing blocked out the sunlight, while within the same moment, she saw a woman being pulled off her.

Eir's Return

EIR SQUINTED AGAINST the bright rays of the midday sun. She tried to condense all the messages from her senses into something she recognised. She rolled over and pushed herself up onto her hands and knees.

Waiting for her strength to return, she looked to the right and saw Kari stirring on the ground a few feet away. *I'm going to be sick.*

A pair of wet deerskin boots appeared in front of Eir. She stared at them for a moment, confused and nauseous. Behind them, the mast of a longboat protruded above the slope that dipped towards the shore.

The owner of the boots spoke her name.

Eir tried to raise her head and reply, but something was stuck in her throat.

The voice of Rancor, her uncle and captain of the returned vessel, demanded her attention. "What is going on here?"

Eir tried to breathe but couldn't. The lump in her throat was blocking her airways.

"Your kin is possessed by Pesta," Ragnvi said. "She has brought the plague here and is making our children sick."

Eir gagged and then vomited. Out slipped a fat slug the width of her mouth and coated in bile. It landed on the ground with a repulsive plop. The crowd gasped and recoiled in shock.

"What demon of Helvíti is this?" Rancor stammered, stumbling while drawing his long knife from his belt.

Eir glanced up and saw Ragnvi's shock turn to a sly grin. "You see! She carries the plague. Pesta's spawn, she must be destroyed."

The slug floundered and flapped as a fish out of water. It elongated and scales appeared, texturing black skin. Inner eyelids blinked, and a striped tongue flicked to taste the air.

Rancor kicked at the creature, missed, and knocked Eir into Kari, who was sitting and rubbing her forehead. He kicked again and this time the aim was true. It sent the snake flying into long grass.

"You must kill her before another appears!" Ragnvi ordered.

Eir scrambled to her feet and yanked up Kari.

Rancor hesitated and lowered his knife. Eir was not sure he would kill her, but she frantically looked around to take in her surroundings. She needed to know which way to run.

She was shocked to find herself in the exact same situation, but only moments before her death. *Frigg sent me back. Kari is alive. I'm alive, not dead! But I'll be killed again!*

A woman screeched, "Kill her, she has brought plague to my child!"

"Do it, my love." Ragnvi nudged Rancor forward.

Eir heard the words but didn't understand their significance. *Your love? He's not your love. You want my father as your husband.*

Events of the previous day flooded back. *It was you.*

Kari rushed in front of Eir and knocked aside Eir's wavering hand as she tried to point at Ragnvi.

"You poisoned the children," Eir said hoarsely. But she couldn't be heard over the din as others now called for her death.

Rancor's expression became grim and determined. He raised his knife and stomped towards her and Kari. Her legs wouldn't budge. A trembling whisper escaped her lips. "I'll die again."

Rancor fell to the ground with a thud. Standing in his place was Ylva, gripping a heavy branch. Ylva dropped the makeshift weapon, raced between Eir and Kari, and grasped their wrists as she went past.

"Run, idiots!" she yelled.

As they fled, Eir glanced behind her to see Rancor being helped up by Ragnvi, while the rest of the villagers stood by, seemly unsure what to do.

Eir was at Ylva's heels as they raced around the corner of the smokehouse, then through a small pen, knocking over the low willow fence and releasing a flock of squawking geese.

"Faster, turtle!" Ylva screamed over her shoulder.

Eir spun around to see Kari trailing a few feet behind. She waited then grabbed Kari's hand, pulling her towards her father's longhouse, now just two dozen strides away. They darted through the hanging pelts that covered the entrance, and once inside, Ylva tugged on a thick oak door.

Eir doubled over, trying to catch her breath. Her legs shook from fear and the effort of running to the hall. She placed her hands on her knees to stop from falling.

"Help me. It won't move!" Ylva yelled.

Gathering herself, Eir went to help. She gripped the edge of the door with Kari, and they shoved it closed. Ylva slid a thick iron bolt, locking the door.

"You're safe now," Ylva said.

Eir touched her own face. She expected to find it swollen from Ragnvi's death blow, but it felt normal. She looked over at Kari. She was pale and an angry welt showed on her forehead.

"How are you feeling?" Eir asked.

"Fine." Kari's face was tight and her jaw clenched, while her body was rigid.

Eir had known Kari all her life, and knew she always put on a brave mask to hide her pain.

She turned to Ylva. "Why did you help us?"

"Why wouldn't I?" Ylva sounded annoyed. "You didn't bring the plague. Ragnvi poisoned them. She was trying to poison you. And tested her poison on Halvard's boy. That's clear to any imbecile."

Thuds sounded on the door and Rancor told them to come out in a muffled voice.

"What do we do?" Eir asked.

Kari gave a helpless shrug while Ylva seemed to be glancing around floor of the hall.

"We should wait for my father's return," Eir added.

"That won't be before they set fire to this place," Ylva said, gesturing upward.

Eir looked up at the thatched roof. "*Skit*! We need to get out of here."

"Be calm, child." Ylva spread out her arms. "Where are we?"

Eir took a breath. "In my father's great hall."

"And what does Ragnvi want?"

"My father as her husband."

Ylva hit her forehead with her palm. "No, child."

The banging on the door continued. "Shut up!" Ylva yelled in its direction. She opened her hand. "She doesn't want your father, but your uncle. She wants your father's sheep, ships, land, and his wealth." She counted on her fingers. "She wants this hall. But she knows your father won't give those to her. So she schemes with Rancor. She hopes to make this hall her home." An odd expression formed on Ylva's face. She reached towards Eir's neck but then pulled her hand back.

Ylva squinted at Eir. "Where did you get that?" She pointed to the necklace.

Eir looked down and lifted the amber pendant. "I—I'm not sure." Frayed images of her time in Asgard raced back.

"That is Frigg's necklace. Isn't it?" Ylva asked.

"Yes."

"What happened?"

"I don't know. It's all muddled up." Eir tried to put the events of her rebirth in order.

"Finish my words, child. She gave me the necklace so I could . . ."

Eir rubbed her temples. "So I could come back. I wanted to save the children before more died." She threw her arms around Kari. "I thought you were dead." Tears ran down her cheeks.

"I'm not," Kari said. "And no one has died."

"I don't understand."

Ylva laughed bitterly. "Ragnvi can't even make a good poison."

"What about Halvard's son?" Eir rubbed her temple in puzzlement.

"Your medicine helped him. I spoke to Gjertrud this morning. He was better," Kari answered.

Eir nodded, immensely relieved. "Why wasn't I told?"

"Gjertrud didn't want anyone to know and have him taken from her again."

"But she told you?"

"Yes, well, as a *thrall,* I learned to keep my mouth shut."

Eir hugged her again.

Voices came from the other side of door, too many to discern until Rancor's voice sounded clearly. "Come out or we'll burn you out!"

"It's a shame this whole village is so full of fools," Ylva muttered, "that they would burn Frigg's child."

"Frigg's child?" Kari asked incredulously.

Eir listened to the tirade of insults coming from outside. "I need to end this." She steeled herself and went to unbolt the door.

"Stop, don't open it," Ylva said without her usual venom. "If you go out, they'll rip you apart and feed your lungs to the caribou." She pulled Eir away from the door. She held Eir's forearm so tight that it hurt. "Half of them out there think you are the bringer of death, while the others harbour jealousy of your looks. It's time you grew up."

Ylva released her grip and brushed aside a loose strand of Eir's hair. "I knew both your mothers," she said in a hushed tone.

"What are you saying?" Eir's voice trembled.

"Too much." Ylva sighed. "You are half ascended. When you weren't accepted into Asgard, Frigg gave you to me. I was—Well, I have no use for a new-born. Your mother, here." She pointed at the dirt floor. "Desperately wanted a child . . . You are of the goddess Frigg's womb and that of a mortal man."

Eir gaped at her, shocked. *No more! I don't want to hear this. Where is my father—?*

A hand spun her around and she looked into Kari's intelligent brown eyes. "What happened? You need to explain this to me."

"I will, when I understand!" She raised her eyes and saw Kari's wound. She touched Kari's injured forehead as her anger left her. "I'll need to get some kelp to reduce the—"

"Come out now!" Ragnvi shrieked, sending icicles down Eir's spine.

"Brother's whore." Ylva snorted at the door.

Eir gasped at Ylva's vulgarity and stared at her. Ylva shrugged, turned, and walked to the hearth in the centre of the hall. She picked up the end of a burning split log and threw it upwards with both hands. The log embedded itself into the underside of the reed roof. The dry thatch smouldered, then burst into flames.

"What are you doing?" Kari shouted.

Ylva turned and marched to the rear of the chamber. "It's time to leave."

Wads of flaming reed cascaded down from the roof and landed in small fires across the hall.

Ylva wandered back and forth in a small area, inspecting the ground.

An ember smouldered on Eir's garment and Kari flicked it away. "*Skit*, that old witch is as mad as a hare. We have to get out of here."

Eir felt numb and didn't know what to do. Kari took her hand and led her to where Ylva scraped in the dirt with a stick.

Kari stared in disbelief. "Fire is falling on us, and you are drawing."

"This is the way out, stupid. Just help me clear it."

Kari dug into the dirt with her hands, until they hit a wooden surface. Ylva scraped clean a square with the length of her stick, revealing a trapdoor.

The roar of the fire had changed, causing Eir to look up. The flames were no longer in isolated pockets, but an inferno of red and orange covered the majority of the roof. Smoke hadn't yet started to fill the space below as air was drawn upwards.

"Here! Help me pull." Ylva freed a large iron ring and Eir and Kari grabbed the ring and pulled on it. The trapdoor wouldn't budge.

Kari mumbled a Christian prayer with the cross of her necklace between her lips. She bent down and frantically scratched at the edge of the trapdoor with a sharp flint stone. "Try now!"

They strained at the rusty ring. The trapdoor flung open with a whoosh of dust, and Kari fell backwards.

There was a sudden shutter, and Eir flung her head around just in time to see the beams of the roof collapsing. She leapt aside as a billow of heat, smoke, and sparks blasted towards them. A large pine timber hit the floor almost on top of Kari.

Eir grabbed Kari's arm while Ylva took hold of Kari's ankle and they dragged her away from the flames. At that moment, a strong downdraft funnelled thick smoke and heat into Eir's face.

"In!" Ylva screamed.

She shoved Eir and Kari into the space under the trapdoor, jumped in, and pulled it closed. Above them, Eir heard the thunder of collapsing beams and rafters.

FRIGG, DEEP IN thought, stroked Bygul between her ears. The lynx stiffened, seemingly sensing her mistress's unease. The clatter of claws on tiles preceded the arrival of Trjegul. Trjegul was Bygul's sister and larger in stature. She appeared from the shadows and padded wearily towards the hearth.

"Any luck?" Frigg asked. The great cat slumped down by the glowing embers, blinked both orange eyes, and went to sleep.

"I see you've had none." She sighed. "Where is that forsaken creature? It should be killing Norns!"

Frigg sat and folded her cloak around her. She bowed her head and with her eyes closed, she shuddered. "There is no avoiding it." She stood. "I have not seen Lilith since I released it. And now, it is nowhere to be found." She tapped her forehead. "Lilith must have escaped with Eir . . . Is this what the Forth intended?" She paced and shook her head. "Or have I simply done the Norns' will again?" She twisted a handful of her hair against her skull in frustration. "This will change everything. Lilith will cause the mortal world to consume itself." She rolled of her eyes. "All that it knows will corrupt and compel everything to extinction."

Frigg started to pace. "Lilith may cause the Norns to abandon their realms and start again. Purging all life. Maybe the Fourth can help."

She stopped in front of the cats. "Which one of you will go and keep Eir safe?"

Bygul turned to Frigg, but Trjegul lay motionless. Frigg was uncertain if Trjegul was ignoring her or asleep. Bygul moved forward to rub a cheek against Frigg's shoulders and back. With her delicate frame, Bygul was Frigg's favourite. Where Trjegul was stocky and ill-tempered, Bygul was agile and placid. They both had their uses, and in truth Trjegul endured the bulk of Frigg's errands.

"My devoted, I don't want either of you to go. But I cannot leave the hall with Lilith's whereabouts unknown, and old Hildisvíni's fighting days are long over." Frigg wrapped her arms around Bygul's neck. "You must go."

Tears filled her eyes. "I will miss you terribly." Bygul's purr echoed into the darkness while Frigg clung to her.

"Go now." Frigg watched with sorrow as Bygul strode out of the hall without glancing back.

A Missing Longboat

EIR SAT IN darkness. She listened to her own breathing and watched illuminated tendrils of smoke descend between hairline cracks.

Kari spoke first. "That would've been a lot easier if you set fire to the roof after we opened the trapdoor."

Eir laughed hysterically. Her relief at getting away from the heat and flames meant she couldn't control her emotions.

"Possibly," Ylva said, joining Eir's laughter.

"Why set fire to the hall at all?" Kari asked.

There was a subtle tremor in Kari's voice that caused Eir to quiet.

"To distract everyone, of course, simpleton."

Something's wrong. Eir reached out to touch Kari. At least she thought it was Kari; she could only make out the outline of shapes in the pitch-black. "Is something wrong?"

"No," Kari snapped.

"Are you hurt?"

"I'm a sunny day."

Eir knew something was seriously wrong. "Ylva, we need to get out of here."

"Stinking fish gut, yes," Ylva said, impatiently. "You're in front, get going, *semi dea.*"

Eir felt along the wall and found a gap below waist height. Tentatively, she ducked her head into it. *A tunnel.* "I found a way out. Follow me."

Eir started to crawl but her knees pinned her apron-skirt to the ground, straining the broached shoulder straps.

Smoke caught harshly in her eyes, nose, and throat.

"Get a move on, Eir!" Ylva said while coughing, and she pushed Kari, who in turn bumped Eir, causing her to fall on her face.

"I can't, my clothes." Tears slipped down Eir's cheeks.

Ylva sighed in annoyance. "You have to think when there is a problem. Not just bawl like a baby."

Eir snuffled and wiped her tears away.

"Gather it like me, at your waist. Use the twine from your hair and tie it around the bunch," Kari said softly. "So it's knotted at your side. Understand?"

Eir nodded into the dark and bit her lip to draw up her courage. She sat with her head bent against the tunnel's ceiling and twisted up the linen to free her knees. She then wrapped the lace from her hair around the gathered folds and tied it in place.

"Ready," Eir said and crawled forward in darkness. She shuffled slowly along, fearful a shaft would appear and swallow her up. "Where does this go?"

"To the shore. It's so a cowardly chieftain could escape to his ships." Ylva cleared her throat. The smoke was making her cough again. "It's finally being used after all these years . . . I wonder if it's blocked?"

Eir stopped crawling. "You wonder if it's blocked. *Helvíti*, Ylva! If we are trapped in here we'll be smoked like herring."

"Then keep going. The daughter of Frigg won't get stuck or smoked like fish." Ylva then grunted, "And go faster. You're making me hungry."

"Quit pushing me," Kari said sharply to Ylva. "Go ahead, Eir. We can't go back. I'm right behind you."

Eir thought how brave Kari was. She started to hum a song for strength and put a hand forward.

Ylva swore and complained that sharp rocks were jabbing into her knees. "What's that you're humming?"

"I don't know." She had to think where it came from. A flash of Frigg singing in that forsaken hall came back to her.

The tunnel started downward, but continued in a straight path. The ground became softer and they had to breach roots. But still there was no light. Eir slowed to a halt.

"Do you want me to go in front?" Kari asked.

She was unsure. In her head, she had been replaying the encounter with the goddess Frigg in the planes of Nifelheim, and the serpent she disgorged. She reflected on the events of her death. *No one alive should be able to recall one's own death. Should they?* The complete darkness of the tunnel was separating her from anything real. And she felt like she'd been in this place before. She had thought the same thoughts and felt the same feelings.

"Lie down. I'll go in front," Kari said. Eir flattened herself and Kari climbed over her to take the lead.

Kari moved quickly, and this helped Eir focus on her efforts to keep up. Ylva was quiet and sounded out of breath but didn't fall behind.

Kari increased her pace. "I see light ahead."

"Thank Odin," Eir said.

"Thank Frigg," Ylva corrected.

Pinpricks of light filtered through at the tunnel's end. Eir waited as Kari tried to pull the rocks free and then, instead, kicked them outward, opening a hole. Eir watched as Kari shimmied out and then enlarged the gap for Eir and Ylva to get through.

Once outside in daylight, Eir took a moment for her eyes to adjust. She stood, arched her back, and stretched her limbs. They were on the shore. Maybe three hundred paces away, the longship, *Frihet*, sat on a muddy bank of a wide estuary. Over her shoulder, inland, a voluminous plume of grey smoke, from the fire at the great hall, filled the north-eastern horizon. It blew in their direction, creating an eerie fog.

Eir turned and screamed Kari's name.

Ylva silenced her with a hand over her mouth. "Control yourself or we'll be caught and burned as well."

The back of Kari's head had been scorched such that only a few ragged ends of her hair remained. Her neck was also burnt, showing raw skin and white blisters. Eir sidestepped Ylva and spun Kari to examine her more closely. *It's not that bad, Kari's woollen tunic must have protected her.* There was thick blister along Kari's neck, but nothing deeper. *It must have touched embers on a rafter.* Eir pulled Kari to a nearby tidal pool. She got her to bend down and then splashed the ice-cold water onto the burn.

"That stings, and you're getting me wet," Kari complained, trying to stand.

"Stay still." Eir yanked her back down.

Ylva tapped Eir's shoulder. "Do that later, we've been spotted." She pointed over the crest of the shore's bank to four men who were running through the smoke towards them.

Eir stood with Kari, but not before she grabbed a handful of Ulva seaweed. She handed this to her. "Hold it against the burn. And don't be stubborn! It'll help."

Kari took the seaweed and held it to her neck.

Eir quickly scanned the bay, looking for her father's boat. But the waves were empty. *Where is he? Where's his ship?* She felt like crying again, but remembered Ylva's words. *Think!* She took a handful of her hair, twisted, and clenched it against her forehead as she tried to decide what to do. *I don't know! I don't know—but Kari will.*

"Kari, where should we go?"

"We have to go into the sea or we'll be killed. We can't run faster than them and there is nowhere else to go."

"But the water is icy cold. We'll drown!"

Kari pointed at the *Frihet*. The ship had been left unattended and wasn't fully stowed. The sail, although lowered, was still attached to the yardarm, and the sheets flapped in the offshore wind. "No one is there. The fire must've led them away."

Ylva chuckled. "As I expected."

Eir looked at Kari. "We just take it?"

"Yes."

Eir saw the reason in this; no one would be able to reach them once they were out in the bay and there they could wait for her father's return.

Eir was surprised when Ylva hugged her. "The tide is leaving and soon the *Frihet* will be beached."

"You are not coming?" Eir asked.

"No, I'll stop the idiots catching you." Ylva pointed to the group of four men who were so close that Eir recognised their faces. She thought they had been loyal to her, friendly even, but their grim expressions caused her gut to turn. *They will kill us.*

"Please come with us, Ylva. They'll hurt you!"

Ylva smiled warmly, before letting it drop back into a frown. "They won't harm me. They think I'm a witch. Besides, I hate everything to do with the sea." She hugged Eir again. "They're getting close. Safe travels, daughter of Frigg." She scampered up the bank and walked directly towards the men.

"Come on. We have to get to the boat before they do!" Kari pointed to another group; the crew was returning to the ship.

Kari nimbly scrambled across the rocky shore as Eir concentrated on her feet. *Large stone, flat stone, jump water, wobbly stone, and another.* They finally leapt on to a stretch of sand and darted towards the longboat.

Shouts came from all directions, as they raced at full pelt. Eir's lungs burned and she felt her heart race faster than it ever had. Kari spurred ahead and reached the boat first to pull herself up and over the hull. With strength she didn't know she had, Eir's arms hauled and feet scratched until she rolled into the boat. There, Kari was frantically trying to pull up the yardarm and raise the sail. "Help me!"

Eir took hold of the halyard with Kari. She pulled as hard as she could but the sail would not budge.

"What are you doing?" a voice came from behind them.

Eir twisted around to see Knud standing with his thumbs in his belt. He was a stocky boy and a year younger than her.

"Are you alone?" she asked.

"Yes, the others ran to the village when they saw the fire." He looked puzzled and embarrassed. Eir knew he liked her. He was always fixing things for her or bringing her new stools he'd made. She had so many that, on a few occasions, used them to revive the fire in the hearth.

"We need to get the sail up. Help us."

He seemed unsure, but Eir knew he wouldn't disobey the chieftain's daughter.

All three pulled on the halyard, and the yardarm with sail attached was raised. The westerly wind caught the sail and it flapped around the mast.

Knud blinked. "The wind is the wrong way for the boat. Why do you want the sail up?"

Eir jabbed him hard into his shoulder and spun him around. "Get out. Push us free!"

"It's not going to move. It's too heavy and there is little water."

"Get out and push!"

He jumped into the chest high water and leaned his weight against the prow.

"Stop, Knud, what are you doing?" someone shouted. Eir looked to see that a dozen or more men had arrived on the beach and were running towards the *Frihet*.

"The sheets!" Kari yelled. "Pull the ropes attached to the sail!"

Eir didn't understand but followed Kari's lead, looping a rope connected to the right bottom corner of the sail around a cleat. Each time a gust eased, she pulled in the slack, tightening until the sail no longer flapped. Kari had done the same on the left side.

The ship seemed to groan in pain. The wood creaked and ropes winced under tension.

Kari kicked at a man's fingers when they gripped the side and he to let go with a yelp.

A sudden gust of wind caused Eir to stumble backwards as the boat lurched forward, sliding down the slick bank into the receding tide. Eir glanced back to see that Knud had fallen flat on his face into the mud. Other crewmen ran past and tried to catch the ship, but they soon found themselves waist-high in the frigid water. She watched as the men backtracked to the shore. They stood with their hands on their hips, yelling at her and then laughing while pointing towards the boat.

The sail filled from the reverse direction and the mast divided it awkwardly into two billowing sections.

"They expect us to drown." Eir felt her anger well up inside her.

"We will! We are sailing backwards." Kari took hold of the rudder and tried to turn the craft. A wave broke over the stern and flooded it with water.

The extra weight caused the stern to bottom out on a shallow bank and the ship began to pivot. A gust then caught the side of the hull and accelerated the twisting of the craft.

"We are going to capsize!" Kari yelled. "The ropes!"

She darted to the sheets and untied one. The sail flapped and the *Frihet* started to right itself, but it turned further until they were sidelong to the waves. Kari released the other sheet. She then grabbed the first and leapt over the benches to cleat it correctly at the boat's aft. The wind caught and it pulled the ship further around.

"Eir! Again, tighten the other rope! But here, at the back!"

Eir was already carrying the rope from the front to rear and then pulled tight. The ship performed a full turnaround and the stern broke free of the bank. *Frihet* now raced quickly in the right direction with the wind.

"Praise the gods!" Eir said as she came to stand by Kari at the rudder. "I've never seen a boat turned like that before!"

"I didn't think it would work," Kari said and then looked down. Water sloshed around their ankles. "I need to bail out the water. Steer for a bit."

"I don't know how."

"Just hold it straight."

Eir nodded and took hold of the rudder.

Kari, at the mid-section of the boat picked up a bailer and started emptying out seawater. Eir watched, wishing she could help. It wasn't long before Kari put the bucket down, with only a small pool left, and came sit beside her.

Eir looked to the shore as the *Frihet* raced towards open seas. The faraway figures turned and headed back to the village.

"Do you think we will see my father's boat?"

"At least we won't freeze or go hungry," Kari said, ignoring the question. "Plenty of food still onboard." She picked up a discarded tunic and passed it to Eir. "Put this on."

"I'm not cold."

"You must be. Please put it on."

But Eir wasn't. Something had changed and she no longer felt the chill of the air. She wondered if the necklace might be affecting her. "All right, but you need one as well."

Kari found a leather jerkin on a forward bench, wrapped it around herself, and returned to Eir.

"Why didn't you answer my question about my father?" Eir asked.

Kari wouldn't look at her.

"Kari, please."

"He won't be coming back—we won't find him," Kari said in an ominous tone as she gripped Eir's hand.

Eir hung her head so her nose disappeared under the collar of her tunic. "They never sail alone. Do they?"

Kari shook her head. "No. Never."

Eir was quiet for a long time. This was something she'd dared think about when she saw only one mast above the shoreline. But she knew. They always sailed as a pair. If Rancor had come back in the *Frihet* without her sister vessel, it meant the boat and her father were lost.

"Where should we go?" Kari asked.

"It doesn't matter. Not anymore," she said to the wind.

THAT NIGHT RAGNVI was content. She was pleased with the events of the day, despite the setbacks. The hideous Eir and a foolish slave would die at sea. But more importantly Rancor had done as she had asked. He had sent his own brother to a watery grave so he could share her bed. He would be the chieftain and she his wife. How easy it had been to rid herself of the tiresome suitor and witch of a daughter. She frowned, considering the fire, which was still burning, destroying the great hall. Its destruction was annoying and the loss of both longships was unexpected. It would take a year to replace them. But the price wasn't too great to finally hold power.

Rancor would do all she asked. He was simple and easily manipulated by temptation. Ylva was a different kettle of fish. She should be punished for her involvement or even banished. Ragnvi bit a fingernail and considered this. *Dare I?* She shook her head. Ylva was a thorn, but she mostly kept to herself. *It'd be better to try to control her and learn her secrets.*

Ragnvi climbed into the bed beside the sleeping Rancor. *Besides, she speaks to the Norns. Being able to influence them would be absolute power.* She revelled in her cunning and fell sound asleep. She dreamt of her children being lords, and her children's children being kings. But in the night, she woke; something felt wrong.

"Rancor, get up." She shook Rancor, who just grunted.

She moved her feet to rise and as she did, her foot touched something cold and damp under the hides, then a thud sounded on the floor. In the darkness of night, she thought it was one of Rancor's leather boots. She picked it up, and it uncoiled. She opened her mouth to scream, and the serpent darted inside.

Rancor stirred and sat up. "What's wrong?"

Ragnvi gave a muffled choking gasp, her hands at her neck. But then she went limp and her arms fell to her sides. She didn't turn to Rancor but spoke in a level, melodic tone. "Nothing, my love, go back to sleep. All is as it should be."

Serpent's Tale

August 2013, London

IT WAS MONDAY morning and the Knightsbridge Hotel was busy with guests. Freya spotted Karen and went to sit beside her in the lobby.

"You look tired," Karen said.

"I didn't sleep well." Freya's complexion was paler than usual, and she'd hoped Karen wouldn't spot her fatigue.

Karen watched Freya as she lowered herself onto the sofa. Her expression showed concern for an instance, before returning to a back-to-business veil. This suited Freya; she didn't want to talk about things.

"We don't have to do anything today after your appointment," Karen said.

Freya was quiet for a moment, then turned away. "I wish I hadn't agreed to this."

"It won't take long and afterwards, you're free for the next few days," Karen reassured her.

She faced Karen. "You can't change things. You know that, don't you? They have already been decided years ago."

Karen stiffened and blinked rapidly. She opened her mouth to say something as a member of the hotel staff placed a tray of tea and cakes on the low coffee table in front of them. Freya raised an eyebrow, questioning. She hadn't asked for anything and was wondering if Karen had. Karen gave a small shake of her head.

The auburn-haired woman serving the tea must have seen their puzzlement. "Tea and coffee for you."

"We didn't order any," Karen said.

"It's complimentary."

"Why?" Karen's tone was suspicious.

"Charlotte, right?" Freya asked the woman.

Charlotte smiled. "Yes," she replied, her cheeks flushing slightly. "I noticed you didn't take breakfast and thought you might like some."

Freya's mood lifted. She stood and hugged the hostess. "That's very thoughtful. Thank you!"

"Um, okay . . . It's, I mean, you're welcome," Charlotte stammered. She gave Freya a blinding smile, lingered for a second, and then disappeared.

Freya sat back down.

Karen stared at her with one corner of her mouth upturned. "What was that about?"

"I spoke with her earlier this morning, when I was getting a coffee."

"Earlier?"

"Yes. Five thirty, I think."

"Well, you must have made a big impression on her."

"She is just being helpful."

Karen handed a cup of tea to Freya. "Lena called. She's insisting you come down for a week next year."

"Sure, I want to see her. She must be seventeen now?"

"Yes, I think so."

The tea and cakes reminded Freya of a small café, a magpie, and an embrace. She felt a pang in her stomach. "Has Jade answered my text?"

Karen checked her phone. "No, just the one from Sunday, where she says she wishes you had a phone."

Freya ignored the dig. "Can you text her for me?"

Karen rolled her eyes and mouthed, *Get a phone.*

Freya mouthed back, *Nooo.*

Karen laughed and she crafted a message dictated by Freya: *Hei, Jade. It's me, Freya. I'm free from this afternoon until Friday. Then off to US of one A. If you're available, I'd like to meet up. P.S. What life form has your salsa become?*

Karen placed her phone down on the table. "Okay. Sent."

Freya nodded, and Karen picked up her tablet and dragged her finger across the screen. "Looks like your Jade did well. I don't see any news about . . . What the—?" She clunked the tablet down on the table and grabbed her phone.

Freya didn't change her expression. She felt unwell and didn't want to engage with whatever had enraged Karen.

"Of course she's not answering," Karen muttered. She quickly made another call. "Hi, Joyce, it's Karen" " . . . Yes, I agree . . . Yes . . . Go ahead and take legal action. Can you text me the number for the paper? I will call them now."

Karen put her phone down. She turned to Freya, opened her mouth, but took a deep breath instead.

"I take it you saw something in the news you didn't like?" Freya wasn't really interested but made the effort anyway.

"Don't worry, I'll handle it." Karen's phone beeped with a text, and she started to make another call.

"You know, there is no point in legal action."

Karen looked at Freya intensely and snapped, "Don't talk like that."

Karen's phone connected and she brought it to her ear. "Jade Platt, please," she said in a level and completely controlled voice.

This was not the first time she and Freya's legal team had aggressively stomped on any media invasion into her life. The call lasted a few minutes and her ears perked up when she heard Karen say, "Yes, of course. I'll let you know if we hear from her," just before ending the call.

"Who was that?" Freya asked.

"Max McKenzie, acting chief editor of the *United Herald*, and as I understand, recently appointed."

"Did you speak to Jade?"

"No, she resigned yesterday."

"What? Why?" Freya sat up straight, scooted to the edge of the sofa, and turned to Karen.

"It was hard to get the full picture. But she went head-to-head with the previous editor about him publishing the story about you in today's paper. It sounds like she quit over it."

"Oh no . . . That's my fault."

"No, honey. How can it be your fault?" Karen touched Freya's arm. "Apparently, the newspaper's board sacked the existing editor this morning."

"Can you contact her?"

"I just tried. I'll try again in a bit. Alright?"

"I guess so," Freya said, anxiously twisting the ends of her hair.

Karen scrutinized her tablet again. "I can't believe reporters write this rubbish."

"Do I need to see this story?"

"No, you don't."

Freya glanced at the screen over Karen's shoulder. "My hair is a mess. Jade looks nice, don't you think?" She frowned when she caught some of the words with the picture. "You can't think Jade had anything to do with this? This would've upset her."

"No, no . . . I don't think that. This is a *Freelance Press* photo."

"Meaning?"

"They must have licensed the picture to go with this story."

Freya nodded her understanding. "What does it say? I can't see from here."

"God, it's just rubbish, suggesting, well, that you're a harlot amongst other things." Karen turned off the tablet. "It's a good thing they got rid of the editor, but I still want his slimy ass in court."

Freya sat back, still twisting her hair. "I don't know what *harlot* means."

Karen picked up her teacup. "Someone who sleeps around."

Freya faked a laugh. "Wish that was true. I could do with a good night's sleep."

"Honey, it doesn't mean *sleep*, sleep—"

"I know."

Karen packed up her things into a tan leather briefcase. "We better get going."

Freya stood. "Can you try Jade again?"

Karen reluctantly tapped in Jade's number. There was no answer.

YALE GARRETT SCRATCHED his hipster beard and pushed his glasses back in place on the bridge of his nose with one finger. He shoved his laptop to the side of his desk, and in the vacated space dropped a thin, leather-bound book. The evening sun in Santa Clara was too bright even with the tinting on the windows of his corner office. It was a large and austere space, a relic of the past when businesses didn't fit onto a smartphone. He liked his persona. The image was young, smart, in vogue, and intimidating.

He clicked a button on a remote. Aluminium blinds folded shut and automatic office lights, in balance, brightened. He opened the book and ran his fist down the binding to flatten the title page.

"This is an original, right?" Yale asked.

"Certainly," a man with a heavy French accent answered.

"Not a fake?" Yale noticed the quill-written ink on the title page.

"Sir, this is my field of expertise. This is the last one of three known to exist. And if I'm not mistaken you already own an edition." The man's voice was edged with dampened anger.

Yale lifted the corner of his mouth just slightly. He was pleased that he had rattled the man. "Yes, I do. But this one includes the markings."

"And as result, is the most valuable."

Yale looked at him. "How much?"

The man cleared his throat. "Three million dollars."

"Ridiculously expensive."

The man's face turned a dark shade of purple but he kept his cool. "Mr Garrett, the price is fair. I suspect I don't need to inform you that a fifteenth century, first edition of *The Canterbury Tales* sold for five million dollars at Christie's last year."

"Yes, I know. I collect the odd book or two." Yale grinned. "But I gathered you paid a lot less at Sotheby's last week."

The man shrugged. "Commerce doesn't favour those with necessitousness."

Yale laughed. "That's very astute of you. And words you should take heed of. Or perhaps, simply not use." He walked around the desk and sat on its top. He swung his dark blue Chucks in the direction of the man. "Okay, sure. Three million."

The man nodded, and Yale sprang off the desk and shook his hand. He then picked up his phone and rapidly typed a message with both thumbs.

"Nancy will organize payment for you. She is outside and just to the left of my office." Yale directed the man to the door and shook his hand again. He then gave his best spurious smile. "Thank you for your business."

"A pleasure," the man said, and left the office.

"Tedious," Yale mumbled while he reached into his minibar. He pulled out a can of Dr. Pepper and opened it, took a sip, and returned to the ancient book.

Nancy burst into his office. "Yale, really? Three million for another drab book? That's a huge amount."

Yale swallowed a burp. "Nah, it'll be worth ten times that in fifty years."

"Fifty years?" Nancy stared. Her dark brown skin and goddess-braided black hair gave her the look of a warrior. And right now, she appeared to want to dispatch Yale. "No corporation invests that far ahead. It's hardly a Jasper Johns. Wouldn't it be better to focus on more of his work?"

"Why don't you speak your mind?"

"I just did."

"I was being sarcastic."

"You need to work on that. And I get we need to put some of our surplus cash into physical insurable assets, but books are a pain to value and need special storage."

Yale smiled. "I agree, but these books are just an interest of mine, not really corporate investments."

Nancy raised a hand to her mouth and gasped, "Oh! You mean it's a personal purchase? I made the payments from the company's account." She turned quickly and headed out of the office.

Yale, laughing, intercepted her, and gave her a firm shoulder hug. "It's fine. It's the same difference." He went back to his desk and leaned over the book. He took another sip of his soda and a drop fell from the rim onto the page. He brushed it away, smearing a finely detailed illustration.

Nancy called to him from his office door. "Your stockholder's meeting starts in fifteen minutes. The car is waiting. With the traffic now it'll take twenty—"

He didn't bother to make eye contact. "I'll teleconference in."

"Yale, they're expecting you in person."

"I'll teleconference in to it," he said in a firmer voice.

Nancy closed his office door behind her.

He crossed his legs in his chair with knees wedged against the arms. He twisted the book sideways and flicked through the pages, stopping where there were notes in the margins. He wasn't interested in the original Latin text; he had read it before. It was the fine black ink additions that he translated carefully. Those scrawls had been added by a foolish monk and had been used as evidence to condemn the zealot for heresy ten centuries ago.

Yale expected the conspectus to be a waste of time and money. But when he saw that this edition had been sold at Sotheby's, it reminded him of his distant past. His interest was piqued at the word *annotated* in the auction house's description. He had been too late to bid on it and it took some minor hacking into Sotheby's transactions database to find the details of the anonymous buyer: a rare book collector in Paris.

He paused at page XXVII. The page, which was originally blank, had been filled with scribbles from the unfortunate monk. The words were written in Latin and Yale hoped he was translating correctly:

> *My studies indicate that Sunniva was not a Saint, but a pagan follower of the false Norse gods. This I derived from my own investigations and readings. I admit to have not visited the Monastery at Selja, my own bones too weary to undertake such a journey; but I have studied the acta sanctorum in great detail and attest to anomalies in the hagiography.*
>
> *It is said that Sunniva arrived by boat from Ireland where she joined the monastery on the Island of Selja. She became known for her miracles of healing. I see no evidence of an Irish origin. The miracles of healing, however, have many collaborating accounts.*
>
> *We are told she feared the intentions of the pagan King Haakon and took shelter in a nearby cave. The cave was blocked by a miracle of our Saviour; whereas years later the great Christian King Olaf Tryggvason found her unblemished body within. This preservation having led to Sunniva being canonized.*

Her relic I have seen, in the cathedral of Bergen. It is perished and morbid; and my conscience cannot accept it as being her. With assistance, I was permitted to inspect the body at length; a described disfigurement of Sunniva was absent. An account of an aide to the great King Olaf Tryggvason, tells a different tale to the writings. It imparts how hearing of the fate of the angel Sunniva, the King, methodical in his excavations, removed the rocks from the cave. There Sunniva lay placid, pristine and unblemished in the gloom. It was said she was perfect in every regard, except for the absence of a fingertip on her left hand. The relic in Bergen has all fingers intact.

This in itself may not warrant my doubt, but the account of the monk Knud, in the King's service, also enlightens how the great King Olaf Tryggvason noticed she was wearing a pagan necklace and feared her preservation was not the work of God. Knud's journal also goes on to say that Sunniva was a pagan chieftain's daughter named Eir and not from Scotia.

From here the threads in the tale are lost; and I cannot hold my words against hearsay. But the monk suggests that the great King Olaf wanted this sleeping beauty as his own and a substitution was made.

Yale turned forward a few pages to find the ramblings didn't continue. His phone flashed a message.

He replied, *Okay, Fredrick, I'm joining.* Fredrick was the CFO and Yale knew he could get away with being late. He scraped his teeth on his knuckle while thinking. He closed the book and picked it up.

His phone flashed again. *Get on the f***ing call!*

He slammed the book onto the desk, opened his laptop, and joined the investors meeting. The conference room's camera displayed the backs of balding heads, and he sighed. *Nothing changes despite my efforts.*

"Hello, everyone, sorry for keeping you. I had a few issues dialling in. And my apologies for not being able to attend in person. I'd really have loved to be there with you."

Yale waited for people to chime in; a number agreed there'd been issues with the conferencing system recently.

"I'm all yours. This is your meeting." He paused, while counting off two seconds. "But before we start, let me talk about our last fiscal year and the hundred billion dollars in revenue." He paused for another moment. "Or, maybe I should talk about the double-digit year-on-year growth for the last decade."

Yale continued after the clapping and cheers subsided, while in parallel, his thoughts drifted back to page twenty-seven. *I don't remember a deformity. But the time period matches and the monk had confirmed her as Eir, Frigg's daughter.* He let others speak while he googled the location of Selja. A number of matches came up. Selja was a small island in Norway.

"I agree completely, Fredrick," he interjected, without having heard what the CFO said. "But I want to discuss an alternative that I believe will continue our unprecedented growth. Since you are the experts, I would like to bring to your attention opportunities in the Nordic region." He then made the rest up. It had a great deal of merit; he knew how to shoot fish in a barrel. He waxed on about investments in renewable resources, moving away from fossil fuels and how this could be used to promote the company's image. After he was done, he sat back and let the others debate the potential. The group readily agreed to expand the business and set up an office in Oslo. *Good, a convenient base to investigate Selja from.*

When the call ended, he touched his smartwatch: 8:32 PM, thirty notifications, and six voice messages. He picked up his drink and took a slurp. He used his left hand to push his chair away from the desk and spun around.

As the office door, windows, desk, and walls spun past his eyes, he thought out loud, "What if? What if this Saint Sunniva was Frigg's daughter? What was she like?" He tried to recall her image. *Beautiful, of course. Blond, blue eyes, average height, and strong sense of purpose. But, it was so long ago.*

He gripped the desk, jarring the chair to a halt. *Blond, Norway. Royal?*

He flipped open his laptop, remembering a news story when he was browsing in bed last night. He checked his search history and brought up a web page for the *United Herald*. The link was broken as it appeared that the article had been removed. He did a Google search using the paper's tagline for the story: *Rykkel Scandalez Liaisons?* There were many matches. The same story and image had already proliferated across the web.

He examined the clearest instance of the picture carefully. Miss Rykkel was kissing a woman with short, dark brown hair. He ratcheted up the zoom level. Her left hand was on the woman's shoulder. He could clearly see the ring finger was missing part of its distal phalanx. But more telling was the amber necklace she wore. He remembered its glint in the sun the day of his escape.

"Holy shit indeed." He grinned, pushing against his desk with both feet and zipping across the room on his chair.

A Folded Page

JADE WANTED TO get up, but her impulses couldn't trigger physical movement. She lay on the floor against the wall and managed to turn her head, exposing indentations on her cheek that were created by the carpet pile.

The curtains were drawn, and she guessed it was ten in the morning. *Come on, you useless shit.* She tried again to push herself up. Sertraline was taking its toll. The antidepressant just filled her with fatigue and did little to reduce her anxiety and dark thoughts.

When the weariness hit her, she'd decided to lie down behind her sofa. It seemed a safe place. She didn't want to accept a status quo; repeating a serial of nightmarish spirals. What others considered normal was for her a path through flames. Besides, her bed scared her. It was better to stay up, hoping to feel different. The desperate need for comfort kept her awake. But without it, and not for the first time, she curled up on the floor at four in the morning.

"To hell with this," she seethed and finally pushed herself up with concerted effort.

Anyone observing would have thought she was drunk as she staggered to the bathroom. She filled the tub to near overflowing, slipped in, and dunked her head under, so the rim of her lips was above the surface. She stayed in the water until it was tepid, before using a burst of willpower to get out, dress, and search for her phone. Her mattress was bare, the linen in a twisted bundle on the floor. She rifled through the sheets and her phone thudded on the carpet. She picked it up, headed to the kitchen, and plugged it into the charger.

She thought about Freya. The day they spent together, the awful story in the paper, yelling at the editor, and then quitting her job. "Brian—What a shit." When fatigue filled her again, she paced from the small kitchen area to the end of her lounge and back. All the time her mind replayed events of previous days, months, and then the moment a year ago when she nearly died.

"Caffeine. I need a coffee."

She filled an orange chipped cup with black coffee. It was the one her mother had given her when she was eighteen, and its colour mocked her mood. Sara's baby was wailing in the flat below. She wanted to put her cup down, but couldn't, as a wave of weariness caused her to lose concentration. She closed her eyes and all her strength ebbed. She fell with the cup still in her hand.

SOPHIE WHACKED HER spoon onto the plastic tray of a highchair. Next, she threw it, and it travelled with a dollop of baby food to hit Sara square on the nose.

"Now hush, Sophie," Sara told her screaming daughter.

Sophie was in a rage and swept her chubby arm across the tray frantically, knocking her bowl of food onto the floor.

She stopped crying for a few seconds and it appeared to Sara that Sophie was admiring her handiwork. The bowl was upside down on the lino floor, its contents spread in all directions. Then she wailed again.

"Ssh. You'll annoy the neighbours," Sara said, struggling to keep her cool.

The two-year-old strained on her harness, screaming at the top of her lungs.

"For heaven's sake, darling. Stay put while I clean up."

Sara went to the sink for a cloth and the room grew suddenly silent.

She looked over to make sure Sophie wasn't holding her breath and turning blue. *Not blue. Good. What's she pointing at?* Outside, a magpie was perched on the windowsill. Sara smiled, thankful for an interlude to the tirade. Then it flew away and Sophie waved her hand.

"All gone."

"Yes, bird all gone," Sara said.

There was a loud thud from the ceiling above her. "God, what was that!"

"SO WHAT ARE your plans today?" Freya asked before unwinding the curl in her Danish pastry, tearing off a segment, and popping it into her mouth. The pastry was fresh and she wanted to eat it slowly, rather than just stuff it in.

Karen took a gulp of her tea. "You mean while you're swanning around Kensington High Street?"

Freya nodded.

"Working, of course."

"What work?"

"The worst kind. Legal shizzel."

Freya laughed. "What? What is this *shizzel*?" She dissected the remainder of her pastry.

"S-h-i-t. I'm going to talk to the new editor of Jade's paper."

Freya felt a morose flood of emotions fill her, and after a long pause she asked, "Have you heard from her?"

"No, honey."

Freya looked away. *I don't understand. Why hasn't she got in contact?*

"Listen, I'm sure she'll be in touch. She might just need some time. She just quit her job; she's gonna want to sort things out." She squeezed Freya's shoulder. "You should think about yourself for a change."

Freya didn't want to go there, not back into that discussion. *You don't understand. I was thinking about myself!* She decided to change the subject before Karen dove deeper and reminded her yet again about her current circumstance.

She gave a long sigh. "So, anyway, why are you seeing the editor?"

"I want them to do a story about the Foundation. You know, as an apology. It's going to be better than going down the libel route."

"Yes, that sounds like shizzel." Freya flicked her hair and pushed her chair away from the table. "I should go see if Jade's at her apartment."

Karen gently touched Freya's hand while shaking her head. "Stay. Spend time with Georgia. This might be the last—"

Freya glared at her and closed her eyes for a moment. "Okay. You are right." She sighed.

Karen tried to look cheerful.

Freya drew her hand over her face and took a moment. "Do you have a pen?"

Karen dug through her handbag, and then emptied it onto the table one item at a time.

Freya watched in fascination as Karen extracted a bursting purse, tattered address book, tissues, moisturizer, various articles of makeup, insect repellent, calculator, painkillers, and a worn pocket-sized English-Norwegian dictionary. At the bottom was a pen, and she handed it to Freya. Karen replaced all her items and put her handbag back on the floor.

"Do you have a piece of paper?" Freya asked.

Karen rolled her eyes.

"It's fine," Freya said in a monotone. "I'll write on my hand, then you can take it with you. Do you have a hatchet in your bag?"

Karen stared at her. "I'm never sure if you are being serious with that accent of yours." She picked up her handbag. "Do you want paper or not?"

"No to your or not. So yes."

"You're in an odd mood today." She retrieved her address book and ripped out a blank page, then handed it over.

Freya wrote only a few words, then folded the small sheet. "Here." She passed over the pen and note. "In case you see Jade or maybe someone in her office who can give it to her."

Karen took the note and put it in her purse. She checked the time. "I better go. I will see you later, honey." She stood and kissed Freya on each cheek and pointed across the room to a smartly dressed woman in a business suit beside the entrance to the café. "Miss Kapoor, from Special Protection Branch, will be assigned to you while I'm out. Enjoy yourself."

THE TAXI PULLED into the short crescent in front of the *United Herald*'s headquarters, and as Karen prepared to pay the driver, she remembered Freya's note. After paying, she walked up the steps to the entrance and unfolded the page. The note was a simple request:

> *Come to New York with me. Please.*
> *Call Karen if you can come.*
> *Freya.*

She held the note between her thumb and forefinger, trying to decide if she should destroy it.

What is Freya playing at? She'll break her heart.

She returned the note to her purse and pushed through the glass doors into the lobby. She was greeted straightaway.

"Hi, I'm Max McKenzie, acting chief editor."

"Hi." She shook Max's hand. "Thanks for seeing me at short notice."

She was pleasantly surprised. She knew the newspaper would be laying on the charm to appease her, in the hopes of avoiding a libel suit. But this new editor seemed genuine and his casual good looks put her at ease.

"Not at all. It's important for me to correct this issue as soon as possible." He led her to a pair of small sofas tucked behind two large Yucca plants in the corner of the lobby. "Can I get you a tea or coffee?"

"No, thanks." She sat down on the sofa with care. She was wearing a new navy-blue skirt, which felt tighter than when she had first tried it on. She crossed her legs and straightened her suit jacket.

Max took a seat opposite. "So, tell me more about your proposal and how I can help. Again, I'm sorry for what happened."

Karen nodded. "If we can agree on an apology and the feature article, then that will help to rectify things."

Max nodded. "I'm sure we can. I've some details in the email you sent me, but do you have a brief for what you'd like to see?"

"No . . . I don't have a brief, but it's pretty straightforward."

Max sat ready to listen, pinching his clean-shaven chin.

Karen smiled. "Basically, I'd like a piece about the Harmoni Foundation. Freya is the chairwoman. Have you heard of it?"

"I'm sorry, no."

Karen rubbed her knuckles along her jawbone with her wrist facing outwards. Max's focused attention was refreshing. *He's handsome*, she thought. She gave her head a little shake, to refocus. It had been a long time since she had considered such things. Her job and her devotion to Freya had been singular. "All right. It was founded in 1929. It supports humanitarian activities globally. There are a number of scholarships it funds for gifted underprivileged students." She paused, thinking about what else to describe. "It also provides funds to charities involved with disaster relief efforts. Many different things; it would take a while to go over them all. If you can assign a journalist, then they can interview Freya for the details. That would be better than running through it all now."

"Just to make sure, Miss Rykkel is currently chairwoman?"

"Yes. But she plans to step down. This is why we're trying to find new patronage and chairperson. Namely the Prince of Cornwall, but he hasn't committed to the position." Karen's phone buzzed and she ignored it.

"Do you need to get that?" Max asked.

"Yes. I should check." She reached into her bag.

"Jade Platt would've been ideal for the assignment." Max sighed. "But as you know, she resigned and I've been unable to contact—"

Karen turned her phone towards Max so he could see the screen. The name *Jade Platt* was displayed.

Max raised his eyebrows in surprise as she answered the call.

"Karen Felds . . . No . . . it's okay . . . Why, what's wrong?" She frowned.

Concern was evident in Max's face, and he moved to the edge of the sofa.

"Do you want me to call an ambulance? . . . Is there someone else I should call? . . . All right, I'll come over . . . I know the address . . . It's fine, I'll be there shortly."

Karen grimaced as she put away her phone. She looked at Max. "Apparently Jade collapsed. Her neighbour, Sara, found."

"Christ, is she okay?"

"She is confused but okay. Sara doesn't want to leave her alone. I better go over and see what the situation is." She stood. "Apparently my number is the only one in Jade's contact list, so Sara called me."

"God. I can go. I know her well," Max said, rising. "Just need to tell the office I will be out."

"We can both go," she said.

Max typed a text message on his phone. "Okay. Ready."

Karen started towards the main entrance and Max followed. "What else did the neighbour say?"

"Just that there was a bird in her window, then she heard a noise and went up to check on Jade. When Jade didn't answer she let herself in and found her unconscious on the floor."

Max flagged down a taxi, and when they were underway, he asked, "She hasn't intentionally hurt herself, has she?"

Karen blinked and stared at Max. "Don't think so. Would she?"

Max tipped his head back and frowned. "I'm worried about her. She's been pretty low." He cleared his throat. "She went through hell in Syria. She is lucky to be alive."

Their cab pulled up in front of Jade's building fifteen minutes later.

Karen squeezed Max's wrist. "Let's see how she is."

The door to Jade's flat was opened by a young woman with a baby positioned on her hip. Karen thought the baby might be a girl but wasn't sure. She had never been good with the whole kid thing.

"Sara?" Karen asked.

"Yes. Thanks for coming." Sara hesitated. "You're Karen, right?"

"Yes, that's right. This is Max, a friend of Jade's."

Max gave a reassuring smile. "Thanks for calling."

They entered the short hallway and went into the open kitchen area.

Sara looked towards the lounge. "She is resting on the sofa. I keep checking on her. I'm pretty sure she's sleeping." She adjusted the baby on her hip. "I asked if I should take her to the hospital but she wouldn't let me. I wasn't sure what else to do."

"It's fine. You did great," Max said.

"I really need to change Sophie. I'm just one floor below, apartment four. I wrote my phone number down. It's okay if I leave?" She pointed to a slip of paper on the kitchen counter.

"Sure, go ahead. Thanks so much for helping," Max said.

Sara gave a little wave and said to her daughter, "Come on, stinky. Let's get you changed," and left the apartment.

Karen crouched next to the sofa. She wasn't sure if Jade was asleep. "Hi, it's Karen. How're you feeling?"

Jade opened her eyes, blinked, and quickly sat up. "Karen?"

"Yes, and Max is here."

Max stepped forward. "Shall I make some coffee?"

Jade nodded, rubbing her neck.

Karen sat beside Jade and put her arm around her. *Heck, she's just skin and bones.* "Honey, what happened?"

Jade lowered her head. "Fainted, just stupid really . . . I had doubled the dosage of my meds." She turned away from Karen, then looked down. "I guess I shouldn't have without talking to a doctor—" She closed her eyes. "Very tired," she mumbled.

"Why'd you change your dosage?"

"I wanted to see if it would help speed things up." Jade closed her eyes and dropped her head.

"Come on, rest." Karen helped her to spread out on the sofa. She was going to ask Jade another question but she was out like a light. "Max, I'm going to phone Freya's doctor and ask for advice."

"Okay. Anything I can do?" Max fidgeted and put his hands in his pockets.

She touched his arm. "See if you can find the medication she's taking."

At Jade's desk, Karen made a call. "Hello, Dr Sorenson . . . This is Karen Felds . . . No, Freya's as well as to be expected . . . Actually, I'm calling about a friend of Freya's who collapsed today." She looked up as Max appeared from the bathroom with a small packet of pills, which he handed to her. "She said she'd doubled the dosage of her medication . . . I have them here, 100mg Sertraline . . . I don't know . . . Yes, sleeping . . . But she's very thin . . . Okay, ten tomorrow morning. Thanks. Bye." She looked up at Max. "She thinks the dosage is wrong and doubling it made things worse. She said to let her sleep. But she needs to continue her normal dosage tomorrow."

Max sighed with relief. "Okay."

"I've arranged an appointment for her in the morning. It'll be with Freya's doctor."

"In the UK?"

"Yes," Karen said, hesitating, but then decided to explain. "Dr Sorenson has always been Freya's doctor. London is a good central location for Freya."

"Freya also lives in London?"

"No, but Dr Sorenson has been her specialist and Freya trusts her. So she comes here when she needs to."

"Specialist?"

Karen could see Max's investigative instincts were kicking in, and it was time to put an end to them. "You ask a lot of questions."

Max leant against the desk. "Sorry, old habit."

"It's okay." She found herself looking at his hand and noticing no wedding ring. She guessed he was mid-forties, perhaps a few years older than her. "I'll take her to the appointment tomorrow."

"I can take her, if you need—"

Karen put her hand up. "It's not a problem for me."

He seemed relieved.

Karen's phone rang in her hand. She answered it. It was her superior calling. Normally, she had a fixed time to report in, but her boss had provided concerning information. *Like bloody busses: none, then three turn up at once. Like I don't have enough to deal with.* She frowned and put her phone in her handbag. *Why now is someone spending a fortune on ancient texts about Saint Sunniva?*

She looked up to see Max watching her.

"If you need to go that's fine. I can sit with her," he said.

She smiled, liking that he had noticed her need and put her first. "Don't you have to get back to your office?"

"I'll have someone bring over my laptop. It'll be fine."

"Thanks. I do need to deal with a few things." Karen stood and hoisted her handbag onto her shoulder. "Let's talk tomorrow."

"Sure."

"I'll ring you." Karen paused and then having decided, left Jade's flat.

She stopped at the curb and dug into her purse. She removed the small folded note Freya had written, crumpled it up, and threw it into a bin as she headed towards Holborn Tube station.

A Rescue

One year later, July 2014, London

"GO," MAX SAID from beyond her office door.

Jade looked up. It was nearly seven p.m. and everyone was busy with the final proofs for tomorrow's edition.

"You promised you'd go in my place. And take tomorrow off," he said with a smile.

She closed her laptop, stood, and grabbed her coat and camera case. "I don't know why you don't send someone else."

"Because," he said, leaning against the doorframe of her office, "I need someone who can tactfully represent the paper."

"Anyone can do that. And I don't need tomorrow off."

"Look, you're the most tactful person I know. Besides, it's just a few hellos." He moved to one side, allowing her to pass. "I'll keep an eye on tomorrow's edition. And seriously, I don't want you in the office this weekend. If I can't persuade you to have a week off, at least take the weekend. You've been doing seventy-hour weeks for months now."

Jade sighed.

It was bizarre that Max had asked her to take his place when he had given her the role of copy editor for the paper. Friday was the most critical day for the weekly edition. But she knew why he was asking her to take some leave and it wasn't about work. She had been completely avoiding her personal life. And maybe he was right, but she wasn't sure what she would do with the time off and feared having to face herself; it was still a lot easier to act behind a professional persona. Although medication organized by Freya's doctor had helped, she was not the Jade from a few years ago. She had yet to look at the pictures from Aleppo to see if Aaina had been killed in the explosion. She daren't think about what they depicted.

Hell. Her face tingled and her chest tightened. Tears welled, and she wiped at her eyes; her emotions were still not under control.

But she was grateful to Max and didn't want to upset him. Max had eased her back into work. First a few hours a week and as time went on, when she became more confident, he offered her a senior position. She initially refused, but now was comfortable with the role.

Jade felt both their contributions had resulted in a marked change to the fortunes of the paper. They no longer produced dailies but instead just a Saturday edition. All other content was posted on a revamped website. In the space of ten months the circulation of the single weekly paper outstripped a month of the old dailies. Remembering all that had happened last year, she reined in her protest about attending the royal charity event.

As she walked out of her office, Max said, "No camera. We want to build relationship with the royal family. It's an opportunity to show we're not just about snapping compromising pictures. The royal press offices in two countries are still distrustful of us."

Jade jerked to a halt as a memory of Freya surfaced. She had not heard from her since that day at the museum almost a year ago. The time after was a blur and it took many months for her mental state to settle down. Dr Sorenson had prescribed some new medication to help her deal with anxiety, and when Jade was well enough to make contact, Karen was no longer answering her text messages.

"I'll leave the camera at home," she told Max without looking at him and stepped out into the corridor. She darted through the open-plan office, crammed with busy journalists at their workstations.

Max caught up to her and touched her shoulder. "Wait." He looked unusually nervous.

Jade paused in puzzlement, her eyes not quite meeting his. She pushed her fingers through her hair. She'd let it grow long and it was now just touching her shoulders. "What?"

He hugged her. "I'm sure an employer isn't supposed to do that. But it's from a friend," he stammered.

He had never done that before. *What on earth is this about?* It wasn't an unpleasant hug; overly firm, but at least it wasn't sickly soft. It was definitely embarrassing, in front of all of her co-workers.

"Good luck." He patted her on the shoulder, turned quickly, and retreated back to his office.

An hour later, Jade crossed the Thames using the footbridge near Embankment Tube station. She'd first gone home to change, but now, she cursed herself. She had put on her old faithful, but tattered ankle boots without thinking.

Shabby chic, she told herself, but could not shake her feelings of being conspicuous. She wore a tailored dark blazer, one she normally reserved for funerals, and a pair of ill-fitting navy chinos. The chinos were the first thing she found in her wardrobe and she'd hastily put them on. They had been a gift from Rachael, her first serious girlfriend. She had met Rachael at Oxford and graduated together. It was Rachael who'd persuaded her to sell her mother's home and buy the apartment in Holborn.

Jade didn't like the chinos, and after a year living together, Rachael didn't like her. At that time, she'd just started her job as a freelance photojournalist and met Max.

She ducked as a pigeon, moving out of her path, took flight. She puzzled over how her thoughts, left to their devices, always ended up in the past.

Why did I agree to this? The chinos were too loose around her hips, and not for the first time, she stopped and reached under the hem of her white blouse to pull them up. When she spotted a discarded shoelace on the pavement, she picked it up and weaved it through two belt loops. She drew it together and tied it tight. The hem of her blouse concealed the makeshift belt. She felt marginally happier after that.

She finally arrived at the Southbank Centre at nine p.m. The gala was by invitation only, but even with all the pre-event checks, it still took fifteen minutes to get through security and into the fourth-floor function room.

After a coat check, the space opened up into a contemporary ballroom. To one side, a bar ran along its length. An inch-thick frosted glass counter was lit with tungsten spotlights and accented by blue LED lights. The effect gave a club feel to the event. Opposite, a narrow terrace overlooked the Thames. The large room contained soft seating areas and open spaces for mingling. Stands of elaborate summer bouquets helped to bring an element of elegance to the otherwise hard-edged avant-garde design.

Jade hadn't been to one of these events before. She'd been briefed that it was a simple matter of introducing herself to the Prince of Cornwall. Her job was to be a visible representation of her own newspaper's donation. *Just make small talk for a moment. Mingle with the other guests and then get the hell out.*

She recognised the prince across the room, easily spotted by the orchestrated queue of people filing past, greeting, and chatting. A waitress interrupted her, offering a choice of drinks from a silver tray. When Jade declined, the waitress told her she could order from a wider selection at the bar. The tray started to tilt in Jade's direction and she grabbed its edge, levelling it.

"God, I almost spilt those on you. Sorry, I'm not very good at this," the waitress said.

"You're doing fine."

The waitress smiled. As if sharing a special secret, she leaned in and said, "You know, you can even order flaming cocktails at the bar if you like." She turned and continued on her rounds.

Rehearsing what she would say, Jade headed to where the prince stood. A feeling of being watched caused her to look to her right.

She stopped in her tracks and her whole body tensed.

Freya's blue eyes cut into Jade and she froze. Her mind raced and she could no longer discern individual thoughts.

Freya stormed towards her with arms at her sides and hands clenched. Despite Freya's obvious anger, Jade couldn't help but notice how breathtakingly beautiful she was. Freya wore a white lace evening dress and had her hair up in a French twist.

Jade just stared. Her emotions were spinning like a roulette wheel, and she waited for the marble to find a slot. Freya thumped her firmly on the collarbone with her palm.

"You didn't answer my note," Freya said in a slightly slurred voice laden with a Norwegian accent.

"I—"

"Why if you didn't want to come with me, you do not just say it?"

Jade was at a loss. *Why is she angry?*

"You read my note and never contact me. Not even for goodbye." Freya raised her hand again and Jade put hers up defensively. But instead of another thump, Freya slipped her fingers between Jade's. Their intertwined hands lowered together.

"What note? You never gave me one."

Freya squinted in puzzlement. "What? Wait—You mean Karen didn't give it to you?"

Jade shook her head.

Freya yanked her hand free from Jade's and glanced around the room in a rage. "Where's that liar?"

Jade tried to calm her. "Freya, I'm sorry if I didn't contact you. I wasn't well. I didn't want you to see how I was. I never heard from you. I just assumed you had things to do."

Freya had arms bent against her chest, and Jade put her arm around her to stop her darting off. Freya went still then leaned into her and held her close.

"Take me away from here," she whispered in Jade's ear. Her breath was perfumed with the sweet smell of champagne.

Jade's heart pounded a million miles an hour. Her whole being wanted to obey, protect her, and escape with her. *Things can't just happen like that.* She glanced up and noticed the prince watching, and a number of security agents were taking an indiscreet interest. *Bloody hell.*

"Freya, everyone is staring."

Freya sighed and pushed herself away. Now at arm's length, she looked at her, side-on. "Take me away without anyone noticing." She put on a cordial expression and walked back towards the prince and a young man who stood chatting with His Highness.

YALE WATCHED THE two women embrace as he spoke with the Prince of Cornwall. *Sunniva's lover? Intriguing.* He corrected the position of his spectacles while inwardly congratulating himself. It took the trivial fact of a missing fingertip and the luck of a single photograph to find the Valkyrie he first used to escape from Asgard. *But where are her wings? And if she has them, why is she still here?* The last question gave him pause. *After all this time, I should go back? I have achieved so much.* He frowned. *But this won't last another century.* He sighed. It was wrong to consider a different fate. *No, I must go back and avenge my unjust sequestration.*

As Freya approached, he posed himself in the style of a fashion model: a leg bowed, the foot vertical and balanced on pointed toes, pushed against the arc of the other, fingers of a left hand gripped the rims of two champagne flutes, while his right hand stroked a short, dark beard.

Yale seamlessly continued his conversation with the prince. "I understand your concern about accepting the chairmanship of the Harmoni Foundation. I don't see how you would have time to perform the role as well as all your other critical responsibilities." His words were lavished with precise diction. "Which is why, if I may, I'd like to make a proposal."

Yale could see the prince watching Freya.

"What's your proposal?" the prince asked.

Freya stopped in front of them. "What are you two talking about?" She smiled.

"You, of course," Yale said, handing Freya her glass of champagne.

Freya laughed. "I cannot think of a more important subject."

"Indeed. Nor one more arousing," the prince said and smiled at her.

Yale felt the conversation had taken a wrong turn, so he steered it with purpose. "To be specific, I was discussing leadership of your foundation, Miss Rykkel. I believe I might be able to assist with the problem of finding your replacement."

Freya took a sip of her drink. "*Hvordan?*"

Yale smiled to himself. "Sorry?"

"I mean, how?" Freya shot him a frustrated glance.

"I'll offer my services as the new chairperson and we would cordially invite His Highness to act as the patron." Yale turned to the prince. "Is that something you would consider?"

The prince nodded his assent and turned his attention to a pair of women who curtsied in front of him. "Please excuse me."

Yale bowed and watched as the prince was escorted to another group desiring his presence. "He has a short attention span. So it looks like we have a solution. Shall we proceed on that basis?"

"Yes," Freya answered, but Yale noticed her searching the room.

"You have lost something important?"

"No. No—I just need to wait."

"Not too long I hope. Can I get you another drink while you do?"

Freya eyed him suspiciously. "Is this how you acquire businessesss?" She slurred the last word.

Yale laughed. "What do you mean?"

"Getting them drunk, then having your way."

Yale grinned and shook his head. "No, greed is a much better tonic for inebriating corporations."

"*Hva treet er grådighet fra?*" Freya was mumbling now and Yale was enjoying his advantage.

"I don't understand." But he had. He gently touched her forearm. "You know you are remarkably attractive at this level of insobriety."

"Don't you dare try to flirt with me." Her words sounded prepared and were sharp and clear.

"I wouldn't dream of it. Let me get you some water." *Well, I would dream of it, but bedding a drunken saint won't help my reputation.* He walked over to the bar and asked for a bottle of San Pellegrino with two glasses of ice.

Leaning at the other end was the woman he had seen with Freya. She was slowly turning a plastic stir stick in a glass of Pimm's and lemonade.

Let's find out more from this mysterious little darling.

Before he could act on his thoughts, a woman stepped in front of him.

"Yale Garrett? I'm Karen Felds, Miss Rykkel's personal assistant. It's a privilege to meet you." The woman extended her hand.

Yale shook it. "Nice to meet you as well."

There are moments like these when it is quite tiresome to not be my epicene self. He put on his most charming boyish smile.

"I understand you're interested in managing the Harmoni Foundation."

"Correct. I would like to offer my services as chairman," Yale said, scratching the annoying bristles under his chin.

"That's great news. It's an honour to have someone of your calibre interested in the position."

He hid his boredom and waited for the preamble of ass-kissing, which usually followed a new introduction. Being CEO of the world's seventh most successful company had its drawbacks. When no fatuous praise was spewed out, he took the time to re-evaluate Karen. She wasn't all she pretended to be, and Yale decided her beeline to introduce herself had deeper motives. The bulge a pistol on the left side of her blazer was a giveaway. *But which agency do you work for?*

The fire alarm sounded.

"Shit," Karen muttered, disappearing in the direction of where Freya had been standing.

Yale watched nonchalantly as fire wardens directed people to the exits. *Damn, this beard is itchy.* He scratched while noticing the undercover agents guiding the prince out. But more hilarious was Karen, darting back and forth trying to find Freya.

In the mass of people exiting the main entrance, he saw a blonde-haired woman in a white lace dress just leaving. Yale grinned as Karen darted after her. *Maybe it's her. Maybe it's not.*

The evacuees started to thin out and a warden came over to Yale. "This way, please, Mr Garrett."

"Yes, of course."

He passed the spot where Freya's friend had stood. On the bar was an extinguished flaming sambuca. The cocktail had not been drunk and pieces of a melted plastic stirrer bridged its rim. Yale looked directly above the cocktail. Black soot marred a device on the ceiling. The drink had been precisely positioned under a smoke detector.

Creative, he thought as he was led out of the building.

JADE NAVIGATED FIRE stairwell of the Southbank Centre in the opposite direction to everyone else. She held Freya's hand firmly as they climbed the stairs. At the top they pushed open a fire door to the roof.

Freya's disguise had worked. Before the alarm sounded she had led Freya to the toilets where Jade had arranged a dress swap. The young woman with blond hair was more than happy to trade her off-the-rack black party dress for Freya's expensive designer original. As an additional ruse, Jade asked them to swap hairstyles. All they had to do was wait for the smouldering drink Jade had left on the bar to trigger the detector. It went off just as Jade was zipping up the back of Freya's replacement outfit.

Outside on the rooftop, she led Freya to the edge of the building. From there, Jade could keep track of the events below and know when the coast was clear. Around them, the London night skyline glowed with its mixture of ancient and modern. The Parliament buildings dominated the view, partially obscured by the London Eye as it rotated slowly. To the east, the seventeenth-century dome of St Paul's shone a brilliant white. Festival lights ran along the banks of the Thames, and passenger boats silently drifted in the black water.

Freya's new dress was skimpier than her old one. The thin shoulder straps and plunging V-neck design would have fitted Jade much better, but instead it failed to contain Freya, who was still catching her breath. She laughed and beamed. "You're pretty amazing!"

Before Jade could reply, Freya kissed her. Her free hand pushed into Jade's hair, short round fingernails flexed against Jade's nape, and succulent lips shared secrets never spoken. The kiss was edged with the euphoria of freedom, the surroundings, and Freya's warmth. A feeling which she had assumed was in the past had returned, but with an intensity and depth as never before. She couldn't believe she'd met Freya.

When the kiss ended, Freya turned around. She leaned into Jade and guided Jade's arms to encircle her shoulders. Something pressed on Jade's wrist. She had to think what it was. It was the pendant of Freya's necklace.

Freya had tipped her head back, tight against Jade, and Jade could see a reflection of London mirrored in her eyes.

"I'm sorry I was angry with you," Freya said.

Jade could feel the vibrations of Freya's voice in her chest. "I'm sorry too. I should have done more to contact you."

Freya nodded. "Ten months. That's a long time."

"Sorry."

"Why did Karen lie to me? That's not like her." Freya rubbed her eyes and snuffled. "I don't want to think about it. I just want to get away from—If only for a moment." She twisted her head towards Jade. "You need to tell me how you have been. I want to know everything."

"I will, but later, okay? I—I want to get you out of the cold."

"I never feel the cold, so don't worry," Freya said with an undertone of sadness.

A moment passed and Jade waited for Freya to say something. She was not sure what was going through Freya's mind and she was afraid to ask. She sounded so desperate.

"Can we go now?" Freya asked.

Jade looked down at the promenade below. People were being led back into the building.

"Where?"

"Does it matter?" Freya asked, exposing her neck again, allowing Jade to kiss it.

"No," Jade said softly. *Not if I'm with you.* She wasn't brave enough to speak those words.

"Good," Freya laughed and then spun out of Jade's arms. She yanked Jade back towards the stairwell door. "Take me to St Pancras."

A Sacrifice

AT MIDNIGHT THEIR taxi pulled up outside St Pancras station. The international train terminal was still busy with travellers. Freya and Jade made their way inside, where it opened into a vast arched space. They strolled along the wide terrace overlooking the shopping arcade and train platforms.

Arm in arm, Jade was pressed close to Freya. The princess, at least that was how Jade liked to think of her, was barefoot, carrying her shoes by their straps hooked in her fingers. She stopped short and Jade was wrenched backwards. To the left, a larger-than-life-size bronze cast of a man and woman kissing caught Freya's attention.

"One day, I hope we are as acceptable," Freya said. She then pulled Jade forward. "Come on, Enkel, we have a train to catch."

Jade warmed to the nickname. She liked having a past with Freya; it felt solid. The start of a foundation only they shared. She didn't mind that it meant simple.

In the main thoroughfare, Jade offered her jacket. Too many people were staring at Freya.

"Please put it on," Jade begged. "You're practically naked."

Freya gave her a mischievous smile, reached for the coat but allowed it to fall through her fingers. "Oh." She bent down to pick it up.

Freya must have noticed her dumbfounded gawk and beamed the biggest grin imaginable. She slipped on the jacket. "My work here is done." She spun on the spot, in the manner of a fashion model, making the concourse her runway.

Shaking her head, not quite sure what to make of it all, Jade stayed put. *She's still drunk. At least I hope she is.* Something in the back of her mind wondered if Freya was manipulating her to some end. *No, stop that. Freya is just Freya.*

Freya yelled back, "Come on, old person, we'll miss our train."

In the ticketing area, with the prospect of a real journey, more doubt crept in. Jade's logical mind forced her to consider the situation, while her heart fired a relentless stream of conflicting messages. *I was just supposed to say some hellos.* She pushed the question away. Her nerves started to cause pins and needles in her face and she didn't want them; there was no rational reason for them.

Freya eyed a computerized ticket machine with suspicion. "Can you tell it we want to go to Nice? That's in France," she said, like she was talking to a country bumpkin.

When Jade had finished working the screen, Freya asked, "Um, I have nothing with me."

"You want me to pay, you mean?" Her words came out awkwardly, implying she didn't want to. But really, she was feeling nervous. She was forgetting something obvious and it was bugging her.

Freya shrugged. "Yes. I'm sorry, I don't normally need money. I will pay you back." She blushed slightly. Jade couldn't remember ever seeing Freya blush and felt bad for causing the embarrassment.

"It's okay." Reaching into her handbag for her wallet, Jade tried to keep her qualms away. She wasn't going to risk a full reality check and falter. This, here, with Freya, was where she wanted to be; in some kind of incredible dream.

With tickets in hand and the train leaving in a few minutes, they made their way through security. At passport control, Jade stopped. The customs man stared at her and waved her forward.

"Wait!" She pulled Freya to one side. She was trying her hardest not to swear while frantically searching through her handbag. Relief washed over her when she pulled out her passport.

"Do you have a passport?" she stammered, panicked. *God, I just bought those tickets without checking.*

"I don't need one," Freya said.

Jade's anxiety came crashing home. "You need one." Her hands trembled. *I need to go home. What was I thinking?*

Freya cupped Jade's jaw as their train's imminent departure was announced. "*Min frelser*, don't worry. Honestly, I don't need one. You have a lot to learn about me."

The tone of Freya's words and her touch allowed her to calm down; the high-pitched buzz in her head started to subside. "My job—I don't know what I was thinking."

Freya brushed the hair above Jade's ear. "It's the weekend. Are you working tomorrow?"

"No. My boss is covering for me. But I'll need to be back for Monday."

"It's short, but it'll be fine. You can travel back Sunday. Does that work?"

"Yeah." *She's right. I can just return early Sunday. Even get a flight if I need to.*

A middle-aged man allowed them to rejoin the front of the queue, to the exasperation of his wife. Freya walked up and spoke to the official in French. After a moment, out of nowhere, an armed police officer appeared. The officer escorted them to the platform and then to Jade's surprise boarded with them. Once they were seated, Jade noticed that the officer had discreetly taken a seat at the far end of their carriage.

FOUR HOURS INTO the journey, Jade sat with her back against the window, watching the view of Paris recede at two hundred miles per hour. The carriage was silent; there was no clatter from the tracks, no squeaks of couplings, no roar from the locomotive, or even mumblings from fellow travellers. There was only a gentle background whoosh as Paris faded away and the glow of the metropolis was replaced with moonlit fields of sunflowers.

Freya was asleep with head was on Jade's shoulder. Her knees were bent and her feet were against the aisle-seat arm.

Jade placed her jacket over Freya. Her desire to keep a vigil was overwhelming, and she was content to just listen to Freya's rhythmic, slow breathing.

A young Italian couple, sitting opposite, were reading e-books. The ghostly light from their devices lit up their faces, creating menacing spectres. She stared at the man for a moment. He reminded her of someone, his olive skin, dark hair, and earnest expression. But she couldn't place the face. She looked at his partner and to Jade there was a mismatch; she wasn't the right woman. But she couldn't think why she felt that way.

The silence was disrupted when Jade's phone beeped. Without disturbing Freya, she read the new message.

Karen: Is Freya with you?

Jade debated if she should respond. She'd hoped to talk with Freya about it when they'd boarded, to understand what had happened with Karen, and more importantly, what was going on between her and Freya. Freya promised this, but the princess, if she was one, had fallen asleep. It seemed the longer she spent with Freya, the more the questions stacked up.

Another text message appeared.

Karen: Please just confirm she is safe.
Jade: Yes. She's with me.
Karen: Can you ask her to tell me her plans?
Jade: She's sleeping.
Karen: Please wake her.
Jade: She's kind of angry about a note. I'm not sure I should.

This reply went through many revisions before she decided, To hell with it, and sent it.

Karen: Ah, you could be right. You're on a train to Nice? When do you arrive?
Jade: Yes, 7:36 AM.
Karen: Okay. Tell her when she wakes that I'll have Henri meet you. I'll catch up with her later, x
Jade: I will.

Jade had decided against adding an *x* to the end of the message. It didn't seem appropriate somehow. She put her phone back in her bag. She was puzzled by the exchange; apparently, Freya's great escape wasn't secret. Oddly, this reassured her. She wasn't doing something completely crazy and forbidden. Feeling more relaxed, she closed her eyes and fell asleep, allowing Freya's warmth to engulf her.

Her mind, as it always did when she slept, relived events in Syria, but this time it wasn't the dream of Aaina. It was something she'd refused to remember; a sacrifice too great, which had twisted her soul.

A SIREN OF terror blocked her thoughts, intense white burnt her eyes, and fire filled her chest. She was alive. Senses wound down and fragments connected to the correct cognitive channels. Background voices, shapes of moving figures, the smell of blood, dirt, and diesel, all flooded in at once.

"Get an IV in before we go," one voice said in an Italian accent.

"Trying to. It's hard to find a vein," a different voice said. All around was the noise of vehicles driving off and Arabic cries for assistance. "Got it."

A voice called from a distance, "No more, we have to go! They'll loop back soon. Leave now!"

Her whole body shifted, before sensing the spinning of tyres on gravel. A shadow moved over her. *A man?* Jade wasn't sure. The shadow deepened until all was black.

Fingers pulled at her eye and a flash. Time had passed but how much she didn't know. She gripped a wrist of the hand that held her head still and jerked to sit up. A pressure forced her down.

She wanted to scream, *Let me go!* Thoughts changed to words. "Bastard! Get off me!" She thrashed, swinging wildly at the person who held her in place. Then the searing pain hit, numbing her mind, tensing all muscles, immobilising her completely. "No . . . no!" she whimpered and started to cry.

"Calm down." The same woman's voice she'd heard before, called to someone else. "*Paolo, assistenza!*"

"It's okay. Stay still," the woman said.

A short olive-skinned man was beside her.

"Where am I?" Jade's voice trembled through tears. Waves of pain cascaded through her chest. The man did something to her and she felt it instantly; muscles that had been drawn to a breaking point relaxed. The pain receded. But relief only made room for fear and a torrent of tears.

"Your name is Jade?" the woman asked.

Jade struggled to understand the question.

"A journalist." The woman was reading her ID. "English."

Jade could only nod. Her mind grasped at threads, but it was impossible to follow them. She felt exposed as terror ripped through her. In all her days on assignment in the most dangerous places on earth, she'd never felt it before. But now it consumed her and she tried to flee. She made an effort to sit up but was too weak. The woman applied a pressure to her shoulders and she collapsed down again.

"Jade, stay still. You're safe. I'm Dr Rosa Mirante, with Médecins Sans Frontières."

Packages were dumped on Jade's chest, and Rosa picked up one and opened it to pull out a pair of scissors.

"You're in a temporary triage unit, not far from where you were hurt. Near Bustan al-Qasr."

Jade turned her head to one side, trying to focus. She was in a classroom. Except there were no desks and all the windows were broken. A blank chalkboard ran along one wall; it was riddled with bullet holes. On the floor people sat or lay. Medical workers moved between them, administering first aid. At least she assumed they were medical workers; none wore any uniforms or insignia to indicate their affiliation. Bodies were motionless on the floor, with cloths or scarves draped over their heads.

The doctor started to snip through Jade's shirt and jacket, cutting the tape Nizar had strapped around her.

When the doctor had finished cutting, she opened a packet containing a sterilised field dressing. She peeled back Jade's blood-drenched shirt. "Oh." She turned to locate someone. "*Paolo, mio caro. Correzione, Jade Platt, una donna.*"

What seemed like hours but were only minutes passed as the doctor cleaned the wound and applied a temporary dressing to the bubbling hole in Jade's chest.

"You have a collapsed lung from a ballistic trauma," Dr Rosa said without emotion.

Jade took in the information and allowed her eyes to close as something was inserted into her chest. The anaesthetic was doing its job and she drifted into unconsciousness.

Gunfire, not distant, but here!

The deafening shots were followed by yelling and screaming. Jade rose onto her elbows. Her torso was bound in a tight, new dressing, while her head pounded with dull pain.

Five men stood just inside the entrance to the classroom, armed with Kalashnikov rifles. One was firing a pistol indiscriminately into the ceiling. He was yelling, while dangling a damaged camera in an outstretched arm.

Dr Rosa Mirante was at the front. Her hands were open, asking if she could help and what did they want. Others of her team had moved to block the men from the injured in the room. Trying to appease them, Rosa said, "This is a hospital, we are caring for these people. Let us do this."

The man ignored her. He spat as he spoke. "Where is the journalist?" He shook the camera then released and dropped with a clunk onto the floor.

"Please, we are only—"

He pointed the pistol directly at Rosa. "Quiet!"

Without hesitation, he shot her at point-blank range. Screams echoed through the room.

Paolo was behind Jade and he cried out in sobs, "*Amore mia! Amore mia!*"

She couldn't allow this to happen and tried to yell out that she was the journalist, but Paolo covered her mouth with his hand while pushing her firmly down, his forearm pinning her chest.

The rebel leader turned back to the medical workers. "Give him up!"

Everyone had their hands in the air, pleading and praying. The rebel shoved his pistol into his belt and signalled to one of his comrades. The man to his right threw over a grenade. The leader unpinned it and held the mechanism static. "*Where is he?* Bring him here now or all will die!"

Jade struggled but was too weak and couldn't fight the pain caused by the pressure of Paolo's arm. From the corner of her eye, she saw a needle being injected into her. "No!" She tried to scream through Paolo's fingers. The sedative took effect in a few seconds.

She could only watch Paolo as her vision blurred.

He walked towards the men and stopped in front of the rebel leader. He spoke clearly with courage. "I am the journalist."

JADE WOKE TO find someone poking her shoulder.

"Billets, s'il vous plait."

Gathering herself, she stared at the robust, plump train official. The ticket inspector stared back with little grace. Jade pulled tolerance from a reserve she thought was empty. "Sure," she whispered, passing over the tickets. The emptiness inside engulfed her; Freya's seat was empty. She was gone.

Black Eyes

FREYA RETURNED TO her seat with two coffees and a small white paper bag containing croissants. She'd expected to find Jade still asleep, but instead, she sat in silence with her head leaning against the window. Her eyes flicked rapidly, focusing and refocusing on the landscape as it raced past. The rising sun filled the carriage with a deep orange.

Something is wrong. A taste of worry dried Freya's throat.

Jade's face was absent of all emotion. Her eyes were dull and haunted. Even in the morning glow, all her colour had drained away.

After placing the disposable coffee cups and bag on the table, Freya shifted along the seat until she was pressed next to her. The couple who had been sitting opposite had vacated their seats, perhaps also breakfasting. She put an arm around Jade and without a word, drew her close. "Do you want to talk about it?"

Jade shook her head.

"That's okay. Sometimes talking doesn't help." With her free hand she pushed a coffee towards Jade. "Do you take sugar?" Freya didn't wait for an answer. "I think I remember you do."

She is so like Kari. Unwilling to ask for help. Slow, constant reassurances would bring her back. There were no timescales to heal the mind; perhaps that was why few dared its undertaking. Over all her years, she had walked with countless damaged souls.

She guided Jade's hand around the coffee cup, pushing her fingers to clasp it. "Here." She kissed Jade's cheek and then prepared her own coffee. Glancing back, she was pleased to see Jade drinking.

They sat in silence until the pervasive hue transitioned to yellow. She suppressed her own fears and tried to make small talk.

"I miss my cat," Freya said. She still had her head against Jade's shoulder, and when Jade said nothing she lifted it and asked, "Do you have a pet? And I don't mean a genetically engineered one made from months-old salsa dip."

Jade blinked as if stepping into a bright light. "What?" She stared at Freya for a moment but then turned back to the window.

"A pet? Do you have one?"

"A goldfish," Jade eventually answered.

"That's a pretty stupid pet."

"Is it?" Jade made eye contact with her.

"Well, it will sink for a start and pirates will steal it."

"Freya, what are you talking about?"

"Your fish made of gold."

"It's not made of real gold."

"Oh, is it made of fool's gold?"

"No, Freya, it's made of fish."

Freya nodded slowly. "Not sure I've eaten goldfish before."

"Huh? Why would you eat it? It's a pet."

"What do you do with it, then?"

Jade looked stumped. "I feed it."

"So it gets bigger. Ah, now I understand. Then you eat it?"

"No."

Freya hesitated. "Does it do tricks?"

Jade shook her head. "It just swims around."

"Okay, I think I will stick with my comment. It is a pretty lame pet."

"I like my fish. I've had it since college. Anyway, my fish can't be lame. It has no legs."

"It can be, when you compare it to my cat."

"My goldfish is much better than some mangy old cat."

"Oh, my God. I can't believe you just called my cat mangy." Freya feigned shock. "My cat would eat your lame fool's goldfish in the blink of its eye."

"Fish don't blink."

She crossed her arms. "A stare, then, of its unblinking, pointless eyes. Bring your fish to Norway and we will see who is battered."

Jade laughed. "Battered? What, in some epic cat and fish battle to the death?"

"Catfish? I thought you said you had a goldfish. No swapping. Unless you are chickening out?"

"No, I will stick with fish. Chickens don't have much stamina."

"Whatever. Chickens, mutant salsa creatures, goldfish, catfish. It doesn't matter. My cat will have them all for dinner. Bring them all to my home and I'll make the popcorn."

"You're going to eat popcorn while my fish beats your cat?"

"I think your English is not so good. You have fish and cat the wrong way round."

"I went to Oxford. My English is fine."

Freya poked at Jade's chest with a threatening finger. *"Min gaupe vil vinne!"*

Jade raised her eyebrows. "What did you say?"

"Do you agree?"

"No, since I don't understand Norwegian."

Freya made a fist. "There is only one way to settle this."

"You're going to punch me into submission?"

Freya rolled her eyes. "That wasn't what I was thinking. But it's an idea. No. I think a game of knuckles, instead."

"Knuckles?"

"Yes, it's simple. Touch your fist to mine."

Jade tried to do what Freya asked but had her thumb under her fingers.

"You can't even make a fist right. Look, like this." Freya took Jade's hand and folded her fingers. "There. Now touch knuckles together. I go first."

Freya twitched her wrist, then moved her hand quickly to hit the top of Jade's.

"Ouch. What the hell," Jade said, half laughing.

"So I win that point and will continue until I have hit five times. If I miss, you go."

Freya didn't miss and after five quick hits, Jade took her hand back, rubbing it.

Freya fluttered her eyelashes sympathetically. "You need to be quicker."

Jade laughed. "I have no idea what you are doing."

"Okay, you start now."

Jade was a lot quicker than she expected. Freya tried to pull her fist away, but Jade was too fast. It was obvious that her final attempt was an intentional miss. But also, she wasn't hitting very hard. *Kari used to make my hand red and sore.*

"Can we stop now? I don't want to hurt you."

"Sure." Freya sat back in her seat. "And don't worry, it didn't hurt. You weren't hitting very hard. But it means I win five to four." The cheer of victory from Freya caused heads to turn. "So finally, it's agreed that cats are better than some dumb-ass fish."

"Fish don't have asses."

"Ssh." Freya put a finger on Jade's lips. "Stop and keep what dignity you have left." She leaned in and kissed her.

Freya was pleased the conversation and game had distracted Jade from her dark thoughts, but Jade's emotional state was worrisome. She knew from

Karen that Jade had been injured on an assignment. "Not another lost puppy," Karen had told her.

Why'd Karen lie to me about giving Jade my note? A year lost; there won't be enough time now. She's pretty much condemned me. A wave of melancholy washed over her.

There is no way I can get her strong before I'm . . . worse than dead. She recognised the familiar core of her desperation.

Why have I been given such an unjust fate?

The doughy croissant didn't appeal to her and she dropped it back into the bag. She leaned into Jade without thinking. Having her close, a familiar face, helped her. Jade was so like Kari. It was like Kari was there with her—a wounded and world-weary version. *I should stop comparing them.* A wave of sadness flooded forward from her depths as she remembered her last moments with Kari.

She bit her lip and cast her eyes down. Her vision blurred and she blinked. She wasn't sure what triggered her tears. Was it her anger at Karen's betrayal? Remembering Kari from long ago? *Or am I feeling guilty about how I'm manipulating her?*

"Sorry." She yanked a napkin out of the paper bag to wipe her eyes, but only smeared her mascara. "God—" She brushed away another tear. "That wasn't supposed to happen."

"What's wrong?" Jade asked with concern.

Freya attempted a laugh. "Nothing, I'm just being silly. I'm hungry."

After a moment, Jade said, "We can go to the dining car. We have time."

Freya nodded, still wiping away tears, but putting on a brave smile. "That would be nice." She put down the napkin. "Do I look too underdressed?"

Jade wrinkled her nose and brightened.

"What? Why are you staring? Do I have black eyes?" Freya tilted around Jade to try to see her reflection in the window. But it was too translucent.

Jade nodded. "In that dress and with those eyes . . ." She stifled a laugh.

"What?" Jade's show of emotion was contagious and Freya grinned. "What's so funny?"

"You look like a Swedish porn star for pandas."

Freya widened her eyes. She wouldn't have expected Jade to say such a thing and burst out laughing, startling the passengers in the adjacent seats. "I can't believe you just said that! Wow, well, it's good to know I've another profession I can turn to." She pretended to be outraged but couldn't stop her fits of laughter.

Jade put her hand over her mouth and she mumbled through her fingers, "Jeez! So sorry I really don't know why I said that. It was way out of line. I shouldn't have."

Freya nudged her shoulder. "You're wrong." She took Jade's hand. "And don't be embarrassed. If it's something you are into. I don't mind—"

"Heck, Freya, no, that's not—No way."

Freya blinked away some more tears, smiling. "Come here, you big dope." And she pulled Jade in for a hug. "I think we better stay here," she said seriously. She didn't tell Jade she was worried someone might take a picture of her while she was in such a state. "We'll have to eat these horrible things. Panda porn stars need lots of energy." She tipped up the paper bag and the croissants bounced onto the table without making any mess.

THE TGV ARRIVED on time at Gare de Nice-Ville. It was just before eight in the morning, but even at this time the contrast between the air-conditioned train and the heat of the southern maritime sun was palpable. Jade guessed it was already in the high twenties. She looked down at her attire. *Why the hell am I always wearing the wrong thing?*

Freya seemed to know what she was thinking. "We'll need a change of clothes. Then we can do some sightseeing. I want to show you some places."

As they exited the Louis XIII-style station, Freya's attention was drawn away from her to a man in his mid-forties leaning against a light blue Mercedes. He was stocky and wore knee-length cargo shorts and a Souleiado red-and-yellow short-sleeved shirt, which looked more like a pyjama top than the expensive regional fashion it was. Standing next to him was the border-control police officer who'd boarded the train with them in London.

"Henri? What is he doing here?" Freya muttered.

Jade put her palm on her forehead. She'd forgotten to tell Freya about Karen's message. She was relieved when Freya smiled, walked towards the man, and hugged him. "I didn't expect you here. I wasn't supposed to visit until Monday." They spoke in French, but Jade was able to understand.

Henri laughed. "You're in France. You should always expect me." While holding Freya's hands, he stepped back to look at her. "Well, Freya, I think you have surpassed yourself this time. What are you not wearing?"

"It's for a new movie career I'm expanding into," Freya declared without batting an eyelid. "Jade says there is a big demand in China."

Henri looked at her, dumbfounded, but didn't request an explanation. "Sounds intriguing." He turned to Jade.

"This is my friend, Jade," Freya said, switching to English.

"Ah, the renowned photojournalist. Miss Platt, it's a privilege to meet you. I'm Henri Lachance, an old friend of Freya's."

Still cringing at Freya's previous remark, Jade stepped forward and shook his hand.

"Yes, you're a very old friend," Freya said. "Don't shake too hard, his hand might fall off."

Henri smirked and then spoke to the officer who was still standing close by, trying to look all official while sweat beaded on his forehead. "*Vous pouvez vous en aller. Merci,*" Henri said, patting the officer on the back. The officer nodded, then tipped his head to Freya and headed back into the station.

Henri's car was causing traffic issues. A gendarme was stopping vehicles from entering the drop-off lane where his Mercedes was parked.

How does Henri know my name and profession? It's because it's his job . . . Shit, I'm such a dunce. She clenched her jaw. How many of their interactions had been watched by a member of some security agency? *Shit.* She shifted and felt like a fish out of water. A hot fish being poached in heavy slacks, a long-sleeved shirt, and scruffy old boots.

"Give me a second," Freya said to Henri and led Jade a few steps away. She put an arm around her and whispered in her ear, "Is something wrong?"

Shaking her head, she said, "I just realised you have security people escorting you everywhere."

"Yes. They are an ass pain. But Henri is loose about things. He is also a nice person. Does it bother you?"

Jade wasn't sure how to answer. It bothered her a lot, and really, she felt like getting back on a train to London.

"Jade, it bothers the hell out of me. So I don't blame you. I should've said something, I suppose. I was trying to be free for a bit." Freya sighed. "In truth, I hate it. But there is not much I can do about it. Times have changed and everyone is in my face all the time. So you have to decide if you can put up with it." Her voice was harsh and she started to turn away.

It must be hard for her. But this was not enough to explain why Freya looked like she was about to bolt.

Jade took Freya's wrist and pulled her closer. "I'm sorry. I'm being an idiot."

"I'm sorry too. I just get so frustrated. I have so little time with you. I don't want things about me to scare you off."

"They won't," Jade whispered and slipped a hand around to touch the soft skin exposed by the open back of her dress. She leaned in and kissed Freya, while keeping her eyes locked on Freya's, which changed from being dark and moody to surprised.

"You know that's the first time you kissed me, rather than the other way around." She yanked on Jade's arm, bending her forward. "Let's go. Change of clothes, then eat, then I don't care. I will show you some places I love. And don't worry about Henri. He will give us some space for sex."

"What did you say?" she whispered as they arrived at the car.

Freya punched Jade's shoulder. "The panda stuff you like."

"Freya!"

She winked at Jade and then at Henri.

"Don't worry, Jade, you'll get used to not understanding her." Henri laughed. "Breakfast at my home?"

"Yes. I'm starving," Freya said.

Jade smiled. "That'll be great."

"You don't have any bags?" he asked.

Freya shook her head. "We do need to change, though."

"I'm sure my wife"—He looked at Jade—"or Lena can lend you something." He opened the rear door of the Mercedes for them and waved to the gendarme diverting traffic. The officer saluted back and moved a traffic cone to open the station's drop-off lane.

Once inside the car and ready to go, Henri turned to Freya, tugging on his seat belt. "Belt up, Freya."

"You are so bossy," Freya said.

They drove along an ultra-clean boulevard lined with palm trees. To the right was a pebbly beach and beyond, the Mediterranean Sea rippled with cat's-paw swirls from a gentle wind. The sun was low, spreading a broad reflection, making it hard to look in that direction for too long. It was clear why the region was called the blue coast. Freya intertwined her fingers with Jade's as she spoke in French to Henri.

Jade was no longer translating, content to just be in Freya's world. She sat close, watching a powerboat race across the bay.

Freya rolled down the window, ignoring Henri's protests about the air conditioning. She pointed, extending her arm out, and told Jade about different landmarks as they drove along. It was called the Baie des Anges, the Bay of Angels, she told her. "Supposedly, when Adam and Eve were expelled from Eden, angels showed them this bay. And it was the first place where they sought sanctuary."

The story reminded her of how Freya told her facts, from the past, in the British Museum. If she'd learnt anything about Freya, it was that everything she did or said, as bizarre as it might be, was leading to something.

She returned her focus to Freya. She watched, mesmerized by her blue eyes as they flashed between the Côte d'Azur scenery and her. Apparently, at this moment, a real angel was showing her this sanctuary. *All she needs is wings.*

Enfin

JADE PUT HER hand against Freya's sleeping head, holding it still as the Mercedes bounced along the gravel drive. They'd been travelling for two hours when the car pulled into the gated entrance of a traditional Provençal farmhouse.

"Henri, is this your home?" Jade hated not knowing where she was. She'd been following the GPS screen in the front of the car. But Henri had switched it off when they left the autoroute.

"Yes."

"Where are we?"

"Just twenty kilometres north of Le Lavandou."

"Le Lavandou?"

"It's an old fishing town on the coast. Between Saint-Tropez and Toulon."

"I don't know it."

"It's beautiful, not spoiled by money as much as the others along the Riviera."

Henri stopped the car at the side of an eighteenth-century rectangular two-storey dwelling. It wasn't much to look at from the back; thick walls were rendered in grey concrete. Small windows with iron bars overlooked a yard of brown sunburnt grass. A broad roof made of mixed yellow and red clay tiles inclined along a low apex with a central chimney.

Freya woke, still groggy. She smiled at Jade and whispered, "Thanks."

"For what?"

"Looking after me, like you always do."

Jade hadn't realised that was what she did. *I've not been so close, so quickly, to anyone else. Why doesn't that worry me? Maybe because I've nothing left to lose.*

Outside the car, Henri turned to Jade. "You're my honoured guest, so don't be afraid to ask for anything you need." He patted her firmly on the back.

Freya called out, "What about me, am I chicken liver?"

Henri laughed. "I'm still mad at you for staying away for so long."

A petite woman raced towards them. She looked to be in her late forties with dark, curly hair and suntanned skin. "Freya!"

The woman was speaking too quickly for Jade to understand, as she embraced Freya and kissed both her cheeks.

"My wife, Elise. Italian," Henri told Jade as if it explained everything.

Jade couldn't help but smile.

"Are you well?" Elise asked Freya.

"Fine, thanks."

There was something in Freya's tone which pricked Jade's ears. Freya had answered the question in the same way Jade did. It was a question Jade never answered directly.

"I'm sorry for being a few days early," Freya said.

"Don't be silly, you're always welcome." Elise backed up and inspected Freya. She put two fingers on her lips briefly before smiling again. If she was going to comment on her attire, she'd decided not to.

"This is my friend Jade from London," Freya said.

Elise nodded, glancing from one to the other. She darted over to Jade and kissed her cheeks. "It's nice to meet you."

Henri, gesturing with his hand, indicated they should round the corner to the front of the house. After a few steps, the space opened up into a provincial courtyard and garden. The difference between this and the back was as an oasis in a desert. The house was painted a terracotta red. Full-length windows with lavender shutters extended along the upper storey, while the lower was separated by three sets of double doors with large glass panes.

An ancient plane tree provided shade. Roman pots planted with citrus trees, alba roses, and palms were positioned between the doors. Behind the courtyard was a pool surrounded by old fruit trees. And, at the far end, an immaculate vegetable garden; plants drooped with tomatoes, beans, and aubergines.

Under the plane tree, a table, covered with a flowery red cloth, was set out with yellow plates and cups, adorned with a cherry motif.

"Elise, they have brought nothing with them. Do you have something they could change into?"

She turned to Freya. "I think there are still some of your clothes in the guest room. Will you be staying here with us?"

"I think so, if that's okay? But Jade has to go back tomorrow." Freya looked over to her.

"Of course it's okay!" Elise practically skipped on the spot. "Let me show you what we have of your things." She turned to Jade. "I'll wake Lena. She should have something you can wear."

"Please, you don't need to wake her."

"Nonsense, you'll be too hot in those English clothes." Elise linked her arm into Freya's. "Lena's your size. She's slender and elegant like you."

Jade had never considered herself elegant, more like clumsy and gaunt.

Elise, with Freya in tow, headed towards the open double doors. When they didn't turn back to her, Jade took this to mean she should wait.

"They might be a while." Henri put his fingers through his thick hair. "I bet you're desperate for a coffee."

THE SUNLIGHT WAS creating dappled shades through the broad leaves of the old plane tree. The temperature had risen considerably, causing cicadas to start singing. The large insects, hardly ever seen, clicked in the background, sounding like a chorus of birds with buzz saws.

Freya was hunched forward, biting into a tartine covered with homemade apricot jam. She glanced at Jade with smiling eyes.

Jade thought Freya never looked more beautiful. Her blond hair was haphazardly heaped, held with a claw-clip. This exposed her swan-like neck and the perfect angles of her jaw. Contrasting shadow and light danced across her flawless skin. She'd already caught the sun and her high cheekbones were tinted pink. Freya wore a fifties-style white cotton dress with wide shoulder straps. A strip of light blue buttons extended to its waistline with the top two left undone. To Jade, she was like an iconic film star, snacking between takes.

"What?" Freya whispered, her mouth half-full with its corners upturned.

"Nothing."

"Do I have jam on my face?"

Jade shook her head, smiling.

Freya scrunched up her nose and winked at Jade. She then turned back to Henri. "So, how is Lena?"

"Much as the last time you saw her. She is, shall we say, a teenager. And as most today, just wants to be somewhere else, plugged in, or asleep," he said with a sigh.

Elise gave him a dirty look before adding, "She is up and will join us soon."

"She must be tall now?" Freya asked.

"Yes, a good ten centimetres taller than me," Henri said.

Elise stood. "I'll get more coffee." She then disappeared into the kitchen.

Henri was silent until Elise was out of earshot. "But between us, she is difficult. Not focused and moody. It's hard for us to give her advice." He sighed. "We are part of the problem in her mind. I was hoping you,

Freya . . ." He glanced at Jade. "Or perhaps you, Jade, can have a talk with her. She's, well, not sure how you say this in English, *Elle cherche des poux à tout le monde.*"

Jade leaned towards Freya. "What does that mean, looks for lice?"

"It means she has a chip on her shoulder," Freya said. "She was adopted by Elise and Henri when she was six. She comes from a difficult background." She turned back to Henri. "Is she still interested in photography?"

"Very much so."

Out of the doorway a tall, slender teen with long straight black hair appeared. Dressed in ripped skinny jeans and a dark three-quarter-length-sleeve T-shirt, she looked at Freya and Jade blankly. Her lashes were extended with copious applications of mascara, while a thick layer of concealer covered patches of acne. Headphones dangled from an iPhone in her hand.

It was a mystery why she didn't just melt in the heat, Jade thought.

Elise followed behind with more coffee and a bowl of peaches, whispering something in Lena's ear as they approached.

At the table, Elise introduced her. "Freya is here, and her friend Jade. Please take a seat, *ma chérie.*"

Lena nodded at Freya and said to Jade, "*Ravie de vous voir.*" Her tone made it obvious she wasn't enjoying herself.

"It's nice to meet you too," Jade said.

Lena sat down. She glanced quickly at Freya and Jade before moving her attention to her phone.

Henri, apparently sensing an awkward pause, started a conversation with Freya, leaving Elise to talk to Jade.

"Lena left you some clothes in the guest room," Elise said while topping off Jade's coffee cup.

Jade waited to get the teenager's attention, but when Lena never looked up, she simply blurted out what she wanted to say, while hoping her French wasn't too rusty. "*Merci pour les vêtements. Je suis dans un sac de couchage.*"

Lena raised her head. Her expression was puzzled and amused. "*Sac de couchage?*"

Jade shrugged. "Yes, I feel like I'm wearing a sleeping bag in this heat."

Lena smirked and put in her earbuds, returning to her phone.

"Lena, please! We have guests; stay unplugged for a bit," Henri called across the table.

Lena ignored him for a few seconds but then removed her headphones.

Elise's smile wavered, but then she turned to Jade. "So, what do you do?"

"I'm an editor for a newspaper in London. Before that I was a photojournalist."

"What paper do you work for?"

Jade told her, but Elise was none the wiser for it. She seemed desperate to carry the conversation forward, while giving Lena an exasperated look. "A photojournalist sounds very exciting. It's something you are interested in, Lena, isn't it?"

Lena glanced down at her phone, seemingly having not heard the question.

Elise turned to Jade. "Why did you go from being a photographer to an editor?"

Jade paused—there was no easy way to answer this. She considered making something up, but decided to tell the truth. "I was injured on an assignment in Syria a couple of years ago. A lot of people died." A wave of emotion rippled through her. This wasn't something she normally revealed to strangers. She wasn't seeking their sympathy. She just felt the need to stop keeping it to herself, and for whatever reason, it felt safe to do so with Freya beside her.

"Oh, that's terrible," Elise said, and at the same time Lena leaned forward, her grey pupils finally visible behind her lashes, as her eyes widened.

Freya took Jade's hand and added, "She is very brave."

The teenager stared at Jade and then went back to her phone, tapping on the screen at an impressive rate.

"Well, it sounds like you deserve a break. I wish you could stay longer. Let me show you your room, then you can change."

"Wait," Lena said as Jade was about to stand. "You are Jade Platt." It was the first time she'd spoken in English and her words were softly accented with French vowels.

Jade nodded. "Yes." *Where this was going? She must've googled me.*

"*Enfin.*" Lena leaned forward across the table, holding out her phone so Jade could see. "These are yours?"

Jade glanced at it. Displayed were pictures she had taken as a war correspondent in Syria. She shrank back into her chair and crossed her arms as a wave of pins and needles rippled across her face.

"*Merde. Désolée. Je devais être sûr,*" Lena said, leaning back.

"Lena! Your fucking language. Speak English, we have guests," Henri joked, but it fell flat.

Freya slid an arm around Jade's shoulders and whispered into her ear, "Something wrong?"

All Jade could do was give a small shake of her head, trying to prevent the panic attack from escalating.

"I'm here." Freya gently rubbed the back of Jade's neck, and the simple touch helped reduce Jade's fear. She looked up to see Lena watching them. The teenager was very hard to read; her face nearly expressionless.

"I want to show you the garden," Elise said. "A grand tour so to speak. But first let's get you changed."

Jade stood abruptly, knocking back the chair. She was trying hard to fight the instinct telling her to flee, which was driven by phantoms she couldn't even name.

Freya stood with her and started to collect the dirty plates from the table.

"No! You are a guest. You'll do nothing but relax," Elise said and took them from her. She started towards the house, carrying the plates.

Without having noticed her leave her chair, Jade could see Lena was already in front of Elise, disappearing through the door.

Freya moved behind Jade and wrapped her arms around her. "Are you okay?"

"Fine, thanks."

"Is that 'fine' I'm not telling you how bad I feel, or 'fine' I like it here?"

"You help so much, but, well, I'm afraid to feel more . . . It's so I can survive when this is over."

Freya placed her cheek against Jade's. "You know, it's easier to live through sorrow if you have gathered joy along the way. And, just so you know, I don't want our time to end."

Jade wanted to say more, but Elise was signalling her to come inside.

"You go get changed. I want to speak with Henri. See you in a bit, okay?"

Jade nodded.

"And put a swimsuit on underneath. I have plans."

FREYA WALKED NEXT to Henri down a dusty lane that cut through an olive grove where untended grass grew between the trees. She paused to look at him. She'd known him for twenty years, since he was first assigned to her as a young agent from the Direction de la Protection et de la Sécurité de la Défense. And whenever she was in France, he would appear, doing his job to ensure her safety. Twenty years was long enough to get to know someone, but not long enough to be ready to say goodbye.

Henri pointed to a stone building. "I've been working on something for you." He bowed his head but then raised it confidently. "I also need to talk to you."

Freya frowned. His tone told her it was not going to be a casual conversation. He'd kept much in confidence and always bent the rules for her. But she was wary now. Karen's actions weighed heavily on her. *Is Henri going to be the same? When I'm gone they will have their families, jobs, and allegiances. That's what they'll be thinking of now.*

She adjusted her sun hat as they walked. Crickets hopped around her feet and she brushed one off her calf.

They arrived at a turning space in front of the garage.

"Let's sit a moment," he said, pointing to a low, stone wall.

They sat down on the wall under the dappled shade of an old olive tree.

"So this is official business, then?" Freya asked.

She had switched to speaking in Provençal, the ancient regional dialect of Occitania. She had forced Henri to learn the language after a heated argument when they first met, refusing to have anything to do with him until he mastered it. She remembered how stubborn she was then; unhappy that someone different had been assigned to her. She hadn't expected him to learn so fast and when he did, he had earned her respect.

"*Comtessa*, I just need to ask these questions. They're on the record, so to speak." His tone was apologetic.

"Okay."

"I'll start so we can get it over with. Do you have any children, partners, or others who could legally inherit? This is specific to France."

"No."

"The registry of assets, land, properties you provided, is it complete?"

"For the record, yes." She knew why he was asking these questions. Like in Norway, she owned a considerable amount of land in France that was, in fact, not constitutionally part of it. Unlike Monaco, Andorra, or Vatican City, the Baux region had always been treated as part of France for the last four hundred years, even though she legitimately possessed the title, as a result of the end of the male bloodline. The French government was hoping to rectify this after her demise. They wouldn't be able to if someone else inherited it. Freya had made no commitments one way or another. This was not out of spite but because she didn't want to plan for her death. "This was discussed already."

"Please bear with me. So, in the off-the-record answer, is there anything the government needs to be aware of?"

"No." She laughed despite her mood.

He looked at her, but she wasn't going to elaborate. "Okay. We move on. Any change in the prognosis?"

"No. They now say three months." Henri was asking these questions like he was reading from a script and it was very annoying. She was managing to keep her voice even. It was Henri's job, and out of respect she was enduring the apathetic fact-finding.

"I apologize, Freya. These questions have to be asked in person. Just two more." Henri rubbed his neck and cleared his throat. "Between now and the next three months, do you plan to marry?"

Freya stared at him. "That's a hell of a question."

"Again, it has to do with concerns over possible benefactors."

"I've no intention of taking a husband."

"That wasn't what I asked. But I'll take that as a no."

"You will take it as I answered and record the date, time of its delivery, and duration," she fumed.

"Of course." There was concern in his eyes and Freya remembered this was Henri and not some faceless bureaucrat. "These are all questions of national security. If I didn't ask them someone else would. And they'd explore the answers in more detail."

She understood. He was putting her first. Doing this to avoid a much more formal and insensitive probing at some future date.

She nodded. "Continue."

"Have all possible solutions been explored?"

"For the record, yes." She stared at him with a blank expression then scratched her nose.

He touched her shoulder, blinking rapidly. "You're saying there's a possibility?"

"Is this a Henri question or Ministry of Defence?" Freya gazed at a ladybird that had landed on her hand.

"It's off the record," he said softly. Lines edged his forehead.

She went quiet, watching the insect as it walked along her fingers. Its world turned upside down as Freya rotated her hand. But it never fell off. Always climbing back to the part facing the sun.

"There is."

"Thank God." He gripped her shoulder firmly. "Explain, Freya. Please. What is it?"

Freya lifted her hand and let it drop quickly, causing the ladybird to fly off.

"You should ask, who is it?" She thought back to breakfast and how Jade looked at her. She loved those brown eyes.

"Who?"

Freya patted his hand on her shoulder.

"I think," she said softly, "it's Jade. But there is so little time now."

"How so?" he asked earnestly.

She stood and stepped out of the shade. Her necklace reflected the sun, scattering amber dots of light onto the ground in front of her. "I know everyone is desperate for a solution. But I don't want every government's best self-serving smart-asses breathing down my neck for the three months I have left. I don't know what is possible and what is not. And thanks to Karen, there is a very slim chance now."

Henri joined her. "Is there any way I can help?"

"Just do what you've always done for me. Give me some space. If it's not possible and all I can do is help her, spend time with her, then that will have to be my lasting happiness." She was struggling to maintain her composure. "Now, show me what is in this workshop of yours." She wiped away tears while heading towards the sun-bleached double wooden doors.

Sly Fox

THE DOORS TO the dilapidated garage swung open on squeaky hinges. Henri stepped in and flicked on the lights. Workbenches ran along the wall with tools neatly arranged on their surfaces. In the centre was a mid-sized vehicle covered with a dust cloth.

Freya was puzzled. She knew Henri worked on classic cars as a hobby, but it wasn't something she was interested in.

He slowly unrolled the cloth, exposing a fully restored red convertible. "Do you recognise it?"

Freya walked slowly around the car.

"It's your 504," he said.

Freya stopped, her hand on the driver's door. "Huh?"

"Your 1968 Peugeot. I restored it."

"It is? That was green. And I crashed it."

"More than once I was told." Henri laughed.

She walked around it quickly now, trying to recognise the car. "This can't be it. It wasn't as nice as this."

Henri opened the door for her.

She smiled at him and sat in the driver's seat. Running her hands along the steering wheel, she asked, "You're sure this is mine? It was written off before you were born. How did you get it?"

Freya played around with the buttons and then turned the wipers on momentarily, forcing Henri to move his hand away from the top of the windscreen.

"A year ago you asked me to fetch documents from your Les Baux house. Your elderly neighbour, Madame Debussy, let me in and told me a few tales. One was about your driving." He laughed. "The car was in a collapsed barn. A grapevine was growing through it. It's true a lot has been replaced."

"It was green, but this is red."

"I changed the colour when I resprayed it, to match the flag of Occitania."

"Oh." Freya was still unsure. She played around with the channel selectors on the analogue AM radio. She then opened the glove box. Inside was a pair of Oliver Goldsmith sunglasses. She picked up the glasses and looked at them. "Well, this isn't mine."

Henri looked disappointed. "You're sure this is not your car?"

"It's my car. But the glasses are Audrey's." She got out, hugged him, and smiled. "Thank you. I can't believe you've done this."

"I'm relieved. I thought you could use it while you are here."

"I will." She got back in, threw her sun hat on the narrow rear seat, and then looked up at him. "Come on."

Once he was in, she started the engine and ground the gears.

"You need to use the clutch," he said.

"What?" She tried again. The gearbox screamed as spinning cogs were remorselessly jammed into each other.

He grimaced at the noise. "The pedal there." He pointed towards her feet. "Oh."

They stalled more than once, kangarooing out of the garage, and then finally, they were moving along the lane back to the house. Freya turned to him. "I do need a favour." With her attention on Henri, the car veered into the rough grass at the edge of the narrow track, just missing an old cherry tree. "Can I use your sailboat?"

Henri took hold of the steering wheel and turned the car back on course. "If we survive."

JADE GLANCED OVER to see Freya plough over a plastic lawn chair in a red convertible. When it didn't look like she was going to stop, Jade leapt out of her seat. The car halted just a few inches from the garden table.

Henri got out and drew the back of his hand across his forehead.

"Henri has fixed my car," Freya called as she leapt out.

Jade was wearing a pair of beige shorts, a loose white round-neck top, and sandals Elise had lent her. Through the crochet lace fabric of the shoulders, a one-piece swimsuit was visible.

"Did you get a chance to talk to Lena?" Freya asked.

"Just a bit."

"She's quiet." Freya's hand found Jade's. "But very bright. Like you, I suspect, at her age."

Jade tried to think of herself when she was a teen but found she couldn't remember. She rubbed her temple. She couldn't recall anything of her schooling. Her doctor had told her the injuries from Syria might have affected her memory, but this was the first time she found it failed her completely. She reached back in her mind to before that, to her mother.

She tried to replay the years before Syria, time with her mother, days out in London or with Rachael in Oxford. None of them seemed to contain any discussion of her childhood. And across them all there had been no father figure. Like a song she couldn't remember the words to, she gave up, hoping they would come to her later.

"Are you ready to go?"

"Sure. Where?"

"A picnic. On my second-favourite island." Freya released Jade's hand. "Wait here a moment, I need to talk with Lena, and I'll get the things for the trip."

By the time Freya returned, Henri had cleared up the broken chair and backed the car away from the table. He handed the keys to Jade. "Don't let her drive," he whispered.

"I heard that," Freya said, putting her hands on her hips and allowing a backpack to fall to the ground. "I've not driven in a while. But I'm sure I'll get the hang of it."

Henri grimaced. "Let Jade or even Lena drive you around."

"Lena can drive?" Freya asked incredulously.

Henri nodded. "She is over sixteen, but she has to be accompanied by an adult."

"I'm an adult," Freya said.

Henri burst out laughing. "Are you sure?"

Jade snickered, holding back her amusement.

Freya squinted at her. "You are both now in my bad books." She then yelled at the house, "Lena, you're driving!"

Lena popped her head out a bedroom window and then ducked back in. A minute later she ran out of the front door. "*Quoi, vraiment ? Je conduis ?*" She pointed at the car.

Jade handed her the keys.

Lena let out a squeal. "*C'est trop cool.*" She climbed into the car and adjusted the driver's seat position.

"You need your swimming things," Freya told Lena.

"*Merde!*" She jumped out of the car. "One minute," she said before running back into the house.

Elise appeared and handed a cloth bag to Jade. "I made a picnic for you."

"Wow, thank you." Jade smiled and her tummy warmed at the act of kindness. "You're not coming?"

"No, it will be too hot for me. I'll spend the day in the garden."

"It's okay if Lena comes?" Jade asked.

Elise smiled. "Of course, I think it will be good for her to spend time with you two. But she burns easily, so keep an eye on her. She isn't well suited to this climate."

Henri approached Jade and whispered into her ear, "Let me give you my number."

Jade unlocked her phone and handed it to him. When he passed it back, he said, "I'll be in the area, so if you need me, just ring."

Jade nodded. She knew how things worked. Henri was Freya's security in France as Karen was in the UK. He would be tracking them somehow.

"Hurry up already. Let's go!" Freya yelled.

JADE WAS SURPRISED that the car could do a hundred and forty kilometres an hour and was grateful when Lena parked up. She got out and stretched. The rear seat, even for her, was very narrow and her muscles ached.

"We need to run," Lena said, pointing at a passenger ferry which sat with its engines idling at the quay. Before they set off, Lena had changed into shorts and a black tank top. She slung her backpack onto her shoulder. "We need to catch it. I'm not going to the island on anything smaller than that."

Freya turned to Jade. "Come on, slowpoke!"

She took Jade's hand, and they darted to catch the ferry, manoeuvring around parked cars, leaping over curbs, negotiating bollards and other tourists. They were able to reach the ferry just as two men started to lift away the gangplank. They returned it back into position after succumbing to a flash of Freya's smile.

The ferry was full and Lena found a space in the shade of the vessel's canopy, sitting on a crate containing life jackets, which was dead centre of the deck. Jade and Freya leaned against the railing, arms interlocked as they watched the different boats in the busy harbour. Once out into the deeper blue waters, Freya pointed towards the islands ahead of them. "There are four islands here. The first is a nudist colony. Are you okay with being naked?"

Jade was pretty sure she wasn't. Partly because she didn't want to be nude in front of other people but mostly because she didn't want anyone to see the scars she had across her torso.

"No. I don't want to do that." Jade felt like pulling away and a tension built up inside her.

Freya put her arm around her waist. "Don't worry, we're going to the last island, called Port-Cros. It's a nature reserve, rather than a naturist reserve."

"Hey, look!"

They turned, and Lena took a picture before they had a chance to protest. She was using a small digital camera. "Stay still for a second." Lena took a few more. "Okay good. Thanks."

Jade hated having her picture taken, a hypocritical trait given she spent so much time taking pictures of others. She realised she didn't have a single photograph of Freya. Not even from the fashion show where they first met. "Can you send me a copy of that, Lena? It's great."

"Okay, but what's your email?"

Lena dug through her backpack, found a pen and paper. "Write down your home address as well."

Jade wrote on the pad and handed it back.

It wasn't long before they approached the first drop-off point on the island of Le Levant.

"Naked people!" Freya yelled and pointed at nudists on the quay. She seemed to be purposely hollering and nearby passengers laughed.

Struck by how wonderful Freya was, not just on the outside but the inside as well, Jade found her normal reserve dissipating with the warm breeze off the Mediterranean Sea.

"Freya." Jade put an arm around her. "You know you are just crazy."

"Well, if I'm not crazy now, when am I supposed to be?"

Jade leaned her head against Freya's shoulder. "I'm wrong you're not crazy. You're . . ." She tried to think of a word to describe her but couldn't. "Perhaps impossibly dazzling," she whispered to herself, but with Freya close enough to hear.

Freya smiled and blushed. "You always surprise me and now I can't think what to say." She stared at Jade for a moment, then whispered, "You know, you've not asked much about me. I keep wondering when you will."

It was true. There were many anomalies about this woman; things that didn't fit. But she didn't want to question someone who offered so much. "I don't want to be a journalist when I'm with you."

Freya half smiled. "Then, I guess, I'll need to get you drunk and then spill the beans."

Jade resolutely resisted asking, "What beans?"

THEY ARRIVED ON the crab-shaped island of Port-Cros at mid-afternoon. Jade scanned the area. When she realized she was looking for sniper vantage points, she put her hands on her hips and shook her head in annoyance. *Will everything be tainted by the past?*

With the exception of a few modern fibreglass boats moored in the harbour, the place looked like it hadn't changed in the last fifty years. To the left, hidden behind palm trees and a manicured mature garden, was a grand hotel. It reminded her of a plantation house in the southern US, although the roof was made of terracotta tiles. To the right was the village. A row of two-storey buildings ran along the crescent of the port. A couple of shops and an empty café offered some shelter from the rays of the sun. In the background, the island's Napoleonic citadel rose above the village, while beyond this were trees that marked the start of the nature reserve.

"So where do you want to picnic?" Lena asked Freya.

"Let's walk to La Palud beach."

Lena nodded, taking the lead.

They soon passed all signs of civilization and followed a trail along the northern coast.

"Let me take that." Jade reached for the beach bag Freya was carrying.

"It's okay, I'm stronger than I look."

"How long does it take to get there?"

"As the crow flies, who knows?"

"What about as we walk?" Jade asked, if only to see what Freya's response would be.

"We are already there."

Jade laughed. "I thought I was starting to understand you."

Freya stopped and turned to her. "That isn't clear to you?"

Oh no, she's testing me again. Jade tried to work out what she meant as they continued along the trail, side by side. "I guess I wasn't specific as to the 'there' I was talking about. You're taking advantage of that, maybe referring to something else?"

"Not really. It's just that people always ask how long it takes to get somewhere as if the important thing happens at the end, and they forget about the moments along the way."

"Oh, I see. You think the journey is as important as the destination."

"Not quite." Freya bumped Jade's shoulder. "A 'there,' which is the destination, should not be a distraction or an excuse to delay making the most of now. A 'there' which is us, you are already at. You cannot separate living from the journey, since you always arrive with yourself."

Jade put her arm around Freya's waist. "Um, well, actually I was just worried about how long you'd have to carry that bag for. But I know what you mean."

Freya laughed. "And I'm just wondering why you haven't kissed me properly yet."

"I didn't want to assume . . . You're a princess."

Freya stopped and put her arms around Jade's neck. "First, I'm not a princess and second—just do it already."

As the softness of Freya's lips pressed and played against hers, something happened, if only for a moment: Jade's constant loneliness ebbed.

Lena walked around them on the narrow path. "*Alerte! Une ado!*"

They separated and Freya took her hand. "Now that's done, let's get a move on. This bag is heavy."

The path sloped upwards and they were now at a much higher elevation. They could see the island, with its cover of dense green pine in its entirety.

Lena was busy snapping pictures. A few were of Jade and Freya, with Jade trying to avoid being in the frame.

"Tu es un hypocrite," Lena mocked Jade. She seemed to be enjoying herself.

"Yes I am." Jade laughed. She picked up a pine cone and chucked it at Lena.

"Now you have a big problem." Lena put her camera in her backpack and collected a number of the egg-sized cones. She then threw them at Jade, who returned fire.

Freya seemed content to just laugh at the antics, which they stopped when a pair of professional beachgoers attempted to pass them.

"I'm really sorry about the behaviour of my children," Freya said to the couple.

Once the slap-faced pair were out of sight, Freya took a bottle of water out from beach bag, removed the lid off, and slung the contents at Lena, who sidestepped the stream. Freya turned and shook the remaining liquid at Jade, soaking her.

"Now behave or I'll do that with the rest of our water."

"*Tatie*, you're crazy. That's our only water," Lena said.

"Oddly, I've also told her she was crazy today," Jade said.

Freya pushed past them. "Maybe I am insane and you're just my delusions. Think on that, bitches."

Jade and Lena stared at each other as Freya marched ahead. Lena circled her index finger around her ear, then pointed it towards Freya as she marched away from them.

Jade nodded. "We better catch up." She pulled her wet shirt away from her body to help it dry. "She has all the food and water."

"*La vache!*"

THE COVE WAS small and at the boundary from beach to forest, the sand spilled between brush and scrub oak. Other than a small dock, no structures could be seen. Two people sat in the sun, and Jade recognised them as the couple who'd passed them on the trail. Jade, Freya, and Lena opted to spread out on the sand, under the shade of two young umbrella pines.

They ate saucisson sandwiches and peaches that Elise had given them, before being content to just relax in the heat. Lena spent twenty minutes applying sunblock. Her pale skin was testament to her diligence. Freya lay on a beach towel with her back pushed against Jade and her sun hat over her face. Jade removed the hat when she thought Freya was asleep. She didn't like not being able to see her face. She knew why. *So many bodies stretched out. Faces covered.* The association, although ridiculous, given the circumstance, still nagged at her.

As time passed, a small group gathered at the water's edge next to a pile of diving masks, snorkels, and fins. A woman in a green swimsuit handed out the equipment.

"Do you want to go snorkelling?" Lena asked.

"I better stay here with Freya."

"She'll be fine here."

"Lena, can you keep a secret?"

"Well, yeah."

"I can't swim."

"No one taught you?"

"No. You can go. I'll keep an eye on your stuff."

"I don't like getting wet, but I'll check out who's there. Back in a bit." She leapt up and darted off to where the guide was preparing to take a group out into the marine nature reserve.

Jade looked down at Freya. An ember within Jade's chest started to glow. The inviolable connection that began the first time they met was much more now. She felt its pull as it stretched out from her. It was a rope bridge crossing a chasm. Offering a path to a haven she didn't deserve. She contented herself with listening to the wind, waves, and chatter from the snorkelers as they prepared.

Freya woke ten minutes later and sat up on her elbows.

"You must've been tired," Jade said.

"Yes, I hardly sleep at night. But it's only when we've been together that I can sleep properly, so I'm taking advantage of you." She half smiled.

"Why don't you sleep?"

"I thought you weren't going to ask me questions?"

Jade shrugged. "I'm concerned. It's a different kind of question."

Freya grabbed a handful of sand. "I have nightmares. Same as you." She let the sand fall away, until none remained. "I don't mean we have the exact same nightmares."

Jade frowned. "How do you know about mine?"

Freya brushed a finger along Jade's jaw. "Well, I'm not completely a dumb blonde."

"No, you're not."

"Are you saying I'm mostly dumb?"

Jade laughed. "No!"

"So, you think I'm completely dumb?" Freya teased her and picked up the last bottle of water, opened it, and held it ready to pour over Jade's head.

"Freya, put, the, water, down," Jade commanded, as a police officer would order an armed assailant.

"You will be damned by my water for all eternity." Freya started to tip the bottle.

Jade took hold of her wrist. "That's the last of the water."

"Indeed. The last."

Jade held tight and with her other palm covered the opening so no liquid would leak out.

Lena appeared and picked up her T-shirt and pulled it on. "Is that the last bottle?"

"Yes!" Jade grunted, "Put the lid on, while I—"

Freya twisted her, freeing the neck of the bottle for a moment and releasing a few sloshes onto the sand.

"Quickly!" Jade said.

Lena found the lid. Jade removed her palm, and Lena twisted it onto the bottle. She stepped back.

"Stop!" Jade said. "Your weapon is defused."

Freya let go of the bottle and stared at Lena, then back at Jade. "You cheated. You got someone else to help." She grinned. "You cheated." She fell forward, pushing Jade onto the sand and kissing her. "You're now officially promoted to *Slu Rev*. It means sly fox."

Lena sat down. "You two are idiots," she said and then took hold of the water bottle and tucked it in the side pocket of her own backpack.

THE SUN WAS lower and trees no longer offered shade. Still on the beach, Freya sat with her legs crossed and drew in a notebook she had borrowed from Lena.

Jade scratched her nose.

"Hold still or this will be ugly," Freya said.

Jade smirked. "Then it will be more realistic."

"Stop talking like that." Freya had her tongue out, concentrating on shading something on the page. She stopped drawing and closed the pad. "We better get going."

"Hey, let me see." Jade leaned over as Freya opened it again. "Freya!" She put her hand over her mouth and then spoke through her fingers. "I thought you were drawing me."

"I like looking at you, so I let you think that," Freya said in a subdued voice.

There was no question that Freya was a talented artist, but the picture was foreboding. A dark landscape with black clouds contained a bolt of lightning, drawn using the white of the paper, while detailed hills made of odd toppled stumps filled the background. Jade gasped. Those weren't trees but corpses, charred and burnt, in piles to form mounds. She'd seen so much horror in Syria, but the gruesome nature of the picture caused her throat to tighten. What shocked her more was the figure at its centre. It was an angel of sorts, without wings, being pulled apart by a grotesque demon.

"Why did you draw this—?"

"It's a dream. It's not quite right, but close enough."

Jade put her arm around her waist. "This dream keeps you from sleeping?"

"Yes."

"Is that you in the centre?"

Freya nodded and then pointed to a thumbnail-sized area in the foreground, which was left blank. "It's not finished." She looked directly at her and their eyes met.

"What should be there?" Jade whispered.

"A person. She never reaches me. Each time closer, but never close enough."

A shadow was cast over them and they turned towards its source. Lena stood in front of them with her hands on her hips. "Can we leave now? I don't want to burn."

"We can," Freya said, reaching a hand out to Lena. "Pull up the old person."

Lena laughed. "Come on, *vieille Comtessa.*"

Flying Colours

FREYA TOOK A step back from the ledge. Below, anchored at the heart of a cove, was a wooden yacht, its painted hull reflected in the aquamarine sea. At the end of the cove, on a stretch of sand, a dinghy rested just out of reach of the waves.

Henri had done what they had arranged earlier in the day, moving his boat from the port to its prominence between the cliffs. She looked at Lena, who was taking a picture. Freya pulled her cover-up over her head and slipped off her sandals, revealing a white bikini. She bent down, grabbed Jade's foot, lifted it, and removed her sandal.

"What are you doing?" Jade asked.

"Taking off your shoes." She repeated the process, leaving Jade barefoot.

"Why?"

Freya straightened and took Jade's hand, holding it tightly. "Ready?"

"For what?"

Darting forward, she pulled Jade over the ledge and into the water that looked to be five meters below.

The sea was warm, and after a few seconds Freya broke the surface to hear Lena screaming. "*Elle ne peut pas nager!* She can't swim. She can't swim."

In the buoyant sea, Freya treaded water. It was crystal clear and she watched Jade clumsily find her way upwards. Jade surfaced, splashing frantically next to Freya, who grabbed her under her arms.

"I have you. Stay still. You can practically float here."

Jade gasped for air and Freya held her, slowly kicking.

"You're safe." Her mouth was against Jade's ear.

Jade nodded, still breathing hard but no longer moving her arms or legs.

"See, it's okay."

"Yeah," Jade said breathlessly.

"Lena, get the dinghy on the beach!" Freya yelled up to her.

Lena flicked her hair over her shoulders and crossed her arms.

"Lena, the dinghy!" Freya yelled again.

"Okay already!" Lena screamed back and slowly collected their things.

"Kick with me. A big kick like a pair of scissors." Freya encouraged Jade to move with her. Backwards, they swam as one to the anchored yacht. A hook-ladder was attached to the stern, and Jade grabbed it when they were close. Once on board, Freya watched to see how quickly Jade recovered from the ordeal.

"I guess I should've said I can't swim." Jade was bent over with arms crossed against her knees.

Freya shrugged. "No. I already knew. I heard you tell Lena." She sat opposite and twisted her hair into a single braid, wringing out seawater, and then allowed it to unravel on her left shoulder. She had seen Jade despondent, confused, and, during a panic attack, terrified. But she'd never seen her angry, not even annoyed. When Jade didn't respond straightaway, Freya anxiously twisted her pendant between her fingers. *Maybe I went too far?*

"You knew?" Jade finally said, tilting her head up towards her. "And you pulled me in anyway?" She wasn't angry, just confused.

"Do you know how to swim now?" Freya jested.

"No!" Jade shook her head and gave a quick laugh in disbelief.

Freya shifted around to sit next to Jade and put her arm around her. "You might need some more lessons."

She snorted. "Really? I don't think so."

Freya rubbed Jade's back in small circles against the fabric of her one-piece bathing suit.

"So why'd you pull me in?"

Freya shrugged and pursed her lips while raising one side of her mouth. "I wanted to see what would happen."

"Like if I would drown?"

"No, I wasn't going to let you drown. At least not without me. Your father never threw you in a pond so you could learn how to swim?" Freya fiddled with the pendant again.

"No, I never met him."

"Well, he should have. Then your girlfriend wouldn't have to do it." Freya pushed on Jade's shoulder.

"My girlfriend?" Jade smiled. "I won't live long with a girlfriend like you."

Don't say things like that.

Freya was silent for a moment and turned to watch Lena clumsily rowing the small tender towards them. Oars were going back and forth in all directions, but she was managing to close the distance between them. She returned her attention to Jade. "You know, I'm pretty sure our hearts have seen the same things." She pushed her hand into Jade's short hair. Her trimmed fingernails glided through wet strands. "Can I ask you something?"

"Yes."

"I was wondering why you didn't panic. I mean . . ." Freya paused; it was a sensitive topic. They'd not discussed anything personal yet, at least not so directly. "Like at the café or train station?"

Jade took a moment before answering, her eyes fixed on a point on the steep cliffs of the cove before finding Freya's. "I guess I didn't have time to think. But you were there so I felt safe. I mean, I somehow trust you, which is odd given you just tried to drown me."

Freya laughed. "That's good, but maybe you just want someone to trust."

"I don't trust anyone normally, so I don't know why I feel different about you. Even though you're very unpredictable."

Freya nodded, her eyes now locked on to Jade's.

Jade moved an arm around Freya and slid her fingertips across the bare skin above Freya's bikini top. "You're consistently inconsistent. I kind of love that about you. But maybe we can avoid cliff tops."

"No cliff tops. I will ensure to make a note." Freya tilted closer to Jade, her voice a husky whisper. "Do you have a pen and paper in that suit somewhere?"

"Don't think so." Jade was an inch away, her cheeks flushed.

"Maybe I should check." She flicked her tongue along the top of her lip.

"Freya . . . jeez."

Parting her lips, Freya tipped towards her, toppling like a tree, and captured Jade's mouth. Jade quivered when she gently slid her hand to cup her jaw, fingers caressing the soft area below Jade's ear.

"Stop with those *réanimations* and help me out of this hell-fucking dinghy!" Lena yelled as the dinghy thudded into the hull.

JADE BROKE AWAY first, flustered and breathless. *My God.* "Wow," she whispered, gathering herself.

Freya's eyelashes fluttered and Jade refocused, noticing how Freya's chest heaved slowly with deep breaths.

"*Enculer!*" Lena swore as the dinghy moved out from under her. "Help!" She was trying to transfer their things into the yacht.

Lena threw Jade the rope that was attached to the dinghy. "Tie it!"

"Where?" Jade asked.

Freya was still sitting and pointed to the butterfly-shaped bracket at the end of the stern.

Jade did her best, but after looping it around, she wasn't sure it would hold. She looked back to Freya, who had her eyes closed with her head drooping.

"Are you okay?" Jade asked, still holding on to the rope.

"Yes," Freya said and made an effort to get up and help Lena step on board.

Lena darted towards Jade and undid her attempt at tying. "Like this, a figure eight, then under. You should tell people you can't swim."

"Freya already knew."

"Oh. Okay. Well, you try the knot now," Lena demanded.

Jade untied the rope, and this time duplicated the knot.

Lena glanced around. "Where's she gone?"

The companionway to the cabin was open. Jade slipped down a short ladder into the space below. For an old boat its interior was very modern. A small kitchen with a stove and sink was to the right, while a fixed table was to the left. She walked along the narrow passageway, passing the WC and storage compartments.

"The sails are here." Freya sat on the forward berth and beside her were two large sail bags. A blanket was wrapped around her shoulders.

Lena was behind Jade and took hold of the first bag. She pulled it along the corridor and then pushed it out into the cockpit.

"I'm going to lie down," Freya said.

Jade sat next to her. "Are you all right?" She brushed her fingers along Freya's forehead, then around her ear.

"Just tired."

"Should I call Henri to pick us up?"

"No. I will rest for a bit." Freya gave a forced smile. "We've done so much today." She lay down, curling up on the two triangular cushions that formed a sleeping area at the prow.

I should check in with him anyway. Jade stood, then hoisted up the other sail bag and went to find her phone.

Lena was on deck waiting for her. Jade dropped the bag and found her backpack. She held up the dripping backpack and frowned.

"Sorry. I don't know how it happened," Lena said. "It was dry when I passed it over."

Jade opened it and pulled out her phone, then shook water from it. The LED flash was on and the screen was black.

"I'm sorry."

Jade put a hand on her shoulder. "It's not your fault. Do you have yours?"

"I left it in the car. I had my other camera and well—"

"You didn't want it to get wet?" Jade laughed.

"Yeah."

"It's okay. It's not your fault. I'm pretty sure Freya dunked it."

"Why would she do that?"

"I think she just wants to get away from everything for a bit."

"Yeah, I get that . . . Oh, I have your shirt," Lena said and then retrieved it from her backpack before passing it to Jade.

"I guess we sail back." After pulling on the shirt, she looked around and realised she didn't know where to start. "Is this Freya's boat?"

"No, my fake dad's."

"Henri? You call him fake dad?"

"Yeah, why not? Don't you have fake parents?" Lena's tone was cutting and sarcastic.

Jade decided now was not the time to discuss Lena's relationship with Henri. But it was evidently strained. "Have you sailed before?"

"Yes, but I prefer not to. But why don't we get the ferry? It's bigger. Safer."

"Pretty sure we missed the last one. Anyway, Freya's resting." She looked at the two sail bags. "You're okay to sail?"

"If we must." Lena crossed her arms tightly around herself.

"Have you gone from here before?"

"From the port. Henri made me come with him."

"How long would it take to get back?"

"I don't know, three hours, maybe longer. Felt like days. But it depends on the wind. We could use the engine."

"That would be easier."

Lena turned to the control panel for the inboard motor, which was on the lower left-hand side of the cockpit. The key was there and she twisted it to the On position. Next, she pushed the green Start button. After four attempts, it still wouldn't start. She checked the panel again. "*Merde*. I don't understand. There's fuel." She tried two more times. "Double shit, start!" She tried once more.

Jade stifled a laugh; it was funny hearing Lena's delicate vowels being used in English swear words.

"*Pas bien*," Lena said when the inboard failed to fire after cranking it for at least a minute.

Jade leaned around her and tapped the fuel gauge, only because that's what everyone seemed to do in this situation.

"I don't want to try more. We need the battery for lights." Lena pulled a hair band off her wrist and tied her hair in a ponytail.

"I can ask Freya," Jade suggested.

"We shouldn't wake her."

Jade was a little taken aback by the force of Lena's response. "Okay. I guess, then, we sail."

Lena stood still and Jade realised she was waiting for instructions. "Lena, just tell me what to do and I'll do it. You're in charge. Okay?"

"Like I know."

"You sailed with your dad."

Lena bit her lower lip. "Okay. We need to fit the sails. Bring the small bag to the front."

They hoisted the sails, with only a few difficulties, and then were underway. Jade was surprised how able Lena was. She definitely knew more than she'd let on. To Jade, the mechanics of sailing were straightforward; it all made sense. It was the terminology that she was not familiar with, and it didn't help that Lena used English as well as French words.

After they left the shelter of the cove, conditions changed. Waves, that looked to be the height of a person, caused the boat to tilt and roll.

"I don't like this," Lena said with a tremor in her voice while clinging on to the handrail by the central hatch.

"We're doing fine, relax. It doesn't seem that hard."

"Just don't sink us." Lena slumped into a cockpit seat with arms crossed.

They followed the shoreline of the island and once past the harbour, turned north towards the mainland. After an hour, Jade went to check on Freya and found her still sleeping. On her way back she decided to use the stove and boil water for two cups of coffee. While pouring the kettle she noticed the marine radio to her right. She turned it on and climbed out to the cockpit, carrying the cups.

Jade sat opposite Lena and handed her a coffee. "I didn't know there was a radio on board."

Lena bit her lip. "Um. Sorry, I forgot about it."

"Don't worry. I should've known." Jade took a sip of her coffee. They were travelling with the wind and the direction of the waves. The sailboat moved smoothly along the troughs and peaks.

An hour passed and the sun was low on the horizon. It would get dark soon. The air had cooled, just enough to change how things smelled; ozone and salt cleared Jade's mind. She thought about Freya's behaviour today and wondered why she didn't just ask things, but instead she seemed to be testing her, seeing how she coped in different circumstances. *Maybe it's just her way. She's very different.*

"Is there something wrong with Freya?" Jade blurted out, realising it was a question she hadn't asked Lena. The teen was quiet long enough to worry her. "Lena?"

"I'm not supposed to say."

Jade rubbed her forehead as the muscles in her body tightened. *Again, I'm in the dark.*

"Well, you're her girlfriend," Lena finally said. "So I guess it's okay."

In truth, Jade suspected it wasn't. But she needed to know. "Sure."

"Last year, she was here in the spring. She was ill. So they called for her doctor to come here."

"What was wrong?" Jade's said quickly in high pitch.

"I don't know. I don't know medical words."

"Was it something serious?" She tried to clear the lump in her throat. "Tell me."

"Yes, it is." Lena's formed a pained expression. "Look, I shouldn't have said anything."

Jade drew her hand along her face and stood. "I better check on her."

"You're upset. I guess you really love her."

Jade swallowed. *Why would she say that?* Her mind raced through all the moments she'd had with Freya.

A MAN STOOD on the first breakwater. He was a small speck in the dark grey of the granite boulders.

Jade recognised the red-and-yellow shirt. "Henri!"

Lena's eyes followed the direction Jade was pointing in, and she appeared immensely relieved he was there.

As they watched, he turned and made his way back towards the quay.

In the shelter of the breaks, where the sea was still, they had lowered the main sail, continuing to move forward just on the jib.

No other boats were entering the marina as they passed jetties where luxury yachts and powerboats were moored. The restaurants on the harbour edge were full. People were strolling along the promenade or looking out to sea. A small group was gathering, watching their approach.

"*Merde!* Don't they have something better to do," Lena muttered.

"Just ignore them."

"They want to see us sink. No one comes in on a sail. It's too hard to control a boat this size here. *Oh putain de merde.*"

Jade put her arm around Lena's shoulders. "We can do this."

Lena stared at Jade with her jaw clenched. "I'm sorry for yelling. This is hard for me."

"Show me where the berth is."

Lena gestured to an empty space at the far end of a pontoon near the sea wall. This was close to the point where the tourists were watching their approach.

"We have to turn at the right time and let the jib go so we slow down. It's impossible. We won't be able to see around the jib," Lena screeched.

"You steer. I'll go up front and tell you when to turn."

At the bow, Jade crouched. The crowd was bigger and a few people were filming on their phones. She spotted Henri's fancy shirt moving through the spectators as they glided by a grand three-storey cabin cruiser.

Jade was trying to judge their speed and distance. They needed to make a left turn; too soon and they would hit the boats before the gap to the berth; too late and they would collide with the sea wall to the delight of the onlookers.

"Now?" Lena yelled.

With just two boats remaining, Jade waited one second more. She then waved and yelled to Lena. The yacht made a slow left turn. And an instant later, Lena released the sheet on the jib so it flapped; it was no longer powering them forward.

Jade scampered back to the cockpit and took over, hoping she'd judged it correctly. Lena gathered a loop of rope attached to the stern, preparing to jump off when they were close to the jetty. All they could do was wait and see if they would clear the million-dollar yacht in the adjacent berth.

Everyone was silent as their bow slid past the stern of the neighbouring vessel with only inches to spare. Their speed slowed and they slipped perfectly into the gap. Lena leapt off and hooked the line around a large cleat, then leaned and held the rope tight. The boat continued to move forward against the jetty, but then, taking up the tension and fighting the friction around the cleat, it slowed. Lena shifted herself with the rope, decelerating it to a stop. A few people in the crowd clapped.

Jade jumped off and secured the bow just as Henri arrived.

He was smiling and approached Lena then hugged her. "Very impressive."

Lena gave a smile of relief, relaxing for a moment, before pulling away.

Jade came over to them and put a hand on Lena's back. "Awesome, perfect."

"Yes, very good, Lena, well done," Henri added.

Jade heard a confused voice from behind them.

"We made it back?" Freya stood in the cockpit, a blanket loosely around her shoulders, and Jade thought she looked very Cytherean.

"Of course," Lena replied.

"Well that's not much of an adventure. I was hoping to be lost at sea."

"Not funny, Freya," Lena retorted.

Henri raised an eyebrow.

Jade knew there was a truth in Freya's words. She wanted to be free.

Affirmed Commitments

DINNER WAS UNDER the stars, lit with lanterns and candlesticks. Jade listened to the now familiar hum of the *cigales* and spoke with Lena about how she got started in photojournalism. Lena was boisterous, making jokes with Henri, exchanging English swear words.

However, it was apparent Elise had lied. She'd not spent her time in the garden but in the kitchen. The meal was a banquet fit for a king . . . or a comtessa. Jade had heard Lena call Freya this.

"Does *comtessa* mean countess?"

"Yes, in Occitan," Freya answered, without making eye contact. She seemed deep in thought, staring into the darkness of the garden.

"Occitan?"

Freya turned to her. "It's an old language of the southern parts of France. Some call it Provençal, but there are different dialects." She flicked her hair away from her face. "Why do you ask?"

"Lena called you it before. I was just wondering. Your royal status confuses me."

Freya managed to smile. "Well, it confuses me too, and it really doesn't matter." She rubbed her eyes and sighed. "I lie. It does matter. Ask me tomorrow, okay? It'll take a while to explain. I need to go to bed."

Freya kissed Jade's cheek, said goodnight to the others, and walked wearily into the house. Jade wanted to go with her, but they'd been given separate rooms.

She took another sip of the Kir Royal she'd been nursing. It was too sweet for her palate and really she didn't feel like drinking. She was worried about Freya. It didn't seem right to just ask her what was wrong, especially if she didn't want to tell her.

When everyone was ready to turn in, Elise showed Jade to her room. It was lit by a soft low-wattage filament light bulb. The high ceiling and fleur-de-lys wallpaper made it feel like a room Voltaire might have occupied while spending hours writing letters on the small roll-top desk in the corner. Jade pulled the duvet and sheets off the bed, creating a makeshift mattress on the floor between the bed and the wall. The habit was now ingrained; she would feel safer there, less exposed.

In the early hours, the mistral, the north-westerly wind of Provence, rattled the shutters. It was still very warm and Jade dozed with just a sheet, and her forehead pressed against the skirting board.

The hinges on her bedroom door creaked.

"Jade?" Freya called out softly.

She went still and held her breath. Freya wouldn't be able to see her, hidden where she lay. She didn't want to call out and admit to Freya how she slept at night.

"Jade?"

The door creaked again as it was closed. Jade had a fraction of a second to decide. Yell out for her and have her discover she was still unbalanced, or let her leave. If they were to be more than lost souls, she'd have to expose herself completely.

"I'm here."

Footsteps padded to where she lay on the floor.

Jade pushed herself onto her elbows to see Freya crouched at her feet. Her golden hair was loose about her shoulders. Her eyes jerked rapidly before focusing on one point.

"There you are. Can I?" She started to crawl forward into Jade's safe place.

"Wait, I'll move onto the bed." But it was too late. Freya was already slipping beside her under the sheet.

"I'm sleeping here with you," Freya said, forcing Jade to turn on her side to make room. She put an arm around Jade.

"This'll be uncomfortable for you," Jade said.

"It isn't."

"You're tired, you need to—"

"I just need this."

Jade went quiet and felt Freya's breath against her neck.

As Freya's breathing slowed, Jade relaxed. It was strange, the effect Freya had on her. *Why does it feel like . . . ?* She found the Welsh word. *Hiraeth resolved . . . a loss found?*

"Freya?"

A moment passed and Jade felt a soft kiss on the back of her neck. Butterflies rose from her depths. She shuffled her fingers in Freya's hand. "Freya?"

"Shh, I'm sleeping," Freya mumbled.

"Sorry."

Another kiss. "What is it, *søta?*"

"I—" The shutters rattled in the wind. "It's just . . . I want to spend more time with you."

Freya nuzzled against her. "I want that too," she whispered, a slight tremor in her voice.

She gathered her courage and said what she'd wanted to say since they'd gotten back. "I care about you. I want to know what's wrong. I—"

A gust of wind travelled around the courtyard. Chairs toppled, clattering over the gravel, and the leaves of the plane tree, outside the window, rustled, as if a spirit were climbing through them, racing between the branches. The linen drapes billowed high into the room.

Freya simultaneously squeezed with her hands, arms, and legs and held Jade desperately tight. When the gust diminished, she slowly released her.

"I don't want you to ever leave me alone," Freya whispered, trembling as the wind blew again.

Jade tried to reach back to touch her, but Freya held her too tightly.

She knew what she had to say, for both of them. "I won't. I promise."

The drapes dropped, and as quickly as the wind had started, it was gone. A bird cried in the distance, and slowly other noises of the night joined its call.

Long, slow kisses moved along from the back of Jade's neck, sliding across her cheek, before finally, Freya's lips found hers. Their bodies slid together, Freya shifting on top. They faced each other, pressed together in the small space.

There was enough light for Jade to see her eyes. Their noses touched. "You'll stay with me?"

"As long as you want me to."

Freya pushed herself up to sit on Jade's hips. She pulled off her cotton nightdress. She wrapped the sheet around her bare shoulders, snuggled back into Jade, and covered them both. "This is long overdue," she whispered in a sultry tone.

They shared a kiss in the dark, with a view of the pellucid stars, and after, more.

IN THE MORNING, Karen arrived in a rental car and was at the table in the courtyard, sipping a cup of tea.

Jade had been avoiding her and offered to help Elise with breakfast.

"There is nothing to do. Sit down. I'll get you a coffee. Henri has gone to get bread. He'll be back in a moment," Elise said as she placed cutlery on the table.

"I can help," Jade offered again.

"No. Just relax."

Jade was about to tell her she would stay longer, but Elise had darted off into the house.

With no other choice, she lowered herself into the seat opposite Karen.

"Hello, Jade, it's good to see you again. How are you doing?"

"I'm fine, thanks."

"Listen, before Freya appears, I need to talk to you. Can you walk with me? It concerns you and Freya."

Jade's body went rigid but she forced herself to respond. "I'd rather not."

Karen frowned and blinked. "Oh, well, it's important. There are things you don't know about her, and the more time you spend with her, the harder it'll be for me to make sure she gets the help she needs."

Jade frowned; she hadn't expected Karen to be so direct. "So you're saying I'm bad for her and we shouldn't spend time together?"

"In a way, yes. She's really not that grown-up, you know. Not emotionally. She escapes into fantasy, not facing things. She's doing that with you, but I need her to focus on her health."

Jade clenched her fists under the table in an effort to stay calm. "Can you explain her health to me? I'd like to understand." Really she wanted to say, *Go to hell*, but that wouldn't help. As a reporter she'd learnt how to put emotions aside in order to get answers.

"I'm not at liberty to tell you that."

"Freya is important to me and—"

Karen raised her hand. "Listen, the longer she spends gallivanting around with you, the harder it's for me to persuade her to see the specialists she needs. "It is critical we try everything possible. Not just for her."

"So you're asking me to leave?"

"For her sake, yes."

Jade leaned forward. "For her sake I'm staying. This conversation shouldn't have taken place without her. You're making decisions for her." She sat back and let her emotions fade. She pulled her phone out, as a distraction, but remembering it was dead, she pushed it back into the pocket of her shorts.

Karen's face was flushed. "Okay. To a degree you're right. But you don't understand. I've known Freya all my life. It will be impossible—"

"That doesn't give you the right to manipulate her for your own agenda. These are her choices. Let her decide. She is a grown woman, after all."

"In her head, she's not," Karen muttered.

Jade tried to untangle the inconsistencies in what Karen had just said. *You're at least fifteen years older than Freya. How can you have known her all your life?*

"Good morning," Henri said from across the table as he put down bread, croissants, and then a pitcher of water. Looking at Jade, he asked, "Did you call your office? Are you able to stay longer than just today?"

How can I trust you two when you're not even asking Freya what she wants? You're supposed to be protecting her.

As Karen opened her mouth, Jade interjected, "Yes. As long as Freya wishes." She looked at Henri. "If that's okay."

"Of course," he said, glancing between the two.

Jade stood. "Please excuse me. I need to check on her."

KAREN WATCHED JADE go back into the house.

"Something wrong?" Henri asked.

"I seem to be annoying everyone." She sighed. "I don't think it's wise for Jade to spend time with Freya. I didn't last year and I don't now. She is a distraction and Freya will hide there rather than continuing to explore every possibility for a cure."

Henri pulled a chair out and perched on its end. "Do you know Freya thinks Jade can help her?"

"No." Puzzled, she tilted her head. "How?"

"She's not said, but she blames you for not giving her enough time with her."

"I don't mind taking the blame for everything if it helps keep her alive. But that reporter is too broken to help."

Henri shrugged. "I think you need to give Jade more credit. Freya shines when she is around her." He paused and gave a half smile. "Have you seen the NIS document about Freya?"

"Yes, of course."

"What clearance level?" Henri asked.

"ND-05, but not higher."

Henri nodded slowly. "Then I know a bit more than you. But you would have read that there are things only Freya understands that we must be humble to."

"Maybe, but I don't believe everything in that document. It reads like it was crafted by NIS to justify our own existence."

Henri stood and placed a hand on her shoulder. "Trust Freya's judgment, and by implication, I think you should also trust Jade." He turned and headed back into the kitchen.

EVERYONE EXCEPT FREYA was seated for breakfast in the shade of the plane tree. Jade hadn't told her about the conversation with Karen. Freya was tense this morning and she didn't want to add to it.

Lena surprised everyone by getting up early and was now chatting with Jade.

"Can I borrow your phone at some point, Lena? I need to call work."

"Yours didn't dry out?"

Jade shook her head. "No, I tried to charge it with your charger, but nothing."

"Let me see." Lena reached out and Jade handed it to her.

Freya arrived and sat in the chair beside Jade. Freya glanced at her and smiled warmly before staring at Karen. "I wasn't expecting to see you until later in the week," she said in a tone close to being hostile, leaning possessively towards Jade.

Karen's face dropped. "No. Well, we've some business with Yale Garrett to finish off and he agreed to meet us in Cannes tomorrow. We have to start the legal process and sign things over."

"I forgot about him." Freya rolled her eyes. "He's two-faced. Is there no one else?"

"He's the best person for the position. We need to resolve it. You can't ignore everything."

"I can ignore him."

"He's an expert in investments. We're lucky to have him interested."

"Fine. Why not. But that letch, leech, both apply, can come to Les Baux. I'm not going to him."

Lena gaped at Freya's outburst. She was still holding Jade's phone and looked concerned.

A mobile beeped and Karen looked down at hers, as did Henri.

Freya stood up and snatched the phones from Lena, Karen, and finally Henri, stacked them in her hand, and dropped them in a pitcher of water.

"Are those boxes more important than flesh and blood?" She spun away, knocking her chair over and stormed off towards her Peugeot. Jade stood up first and darted around the table to go after her. Henri and Karen also rose from their seats.

"Stay here," Lena snapped at them. "Leave her alone. She just wants Jade."

Jade touched Lena on her shoulder as she went past. She scampered to catch up with Freya and pulled her into a hug as soon as she was able to get a hold of her.

"You can't just run away," Jade said softly.

"Can't I? Why not? It's worked for the last thousand years."

Why is she exaggerating? A sudden wave of fear passed through Jade and the words burst out. "Don't run away from me, please!"

Freya's expression softened and she coiled around Jade, pushing her head into Jade's neck.

"I won't. We promised remember?"

Jade felt tears moisten her eyes. She knew this was no longer a friendship or a partnership of need. She was falling in love with Freya and there was no going back.

"Besides." Freya leaned so she could see Jade's face. "I wouldn't get very far without you. I need you."

"You do?"

"To drive."

Jade smiled and tears wet her cheeks. "Just that?"

"No. I also need you so I can live."

Floating Feather

TO THE WEST there was a storm. A dark band of clouds met the sea, extending across the entire horizon. It appeared as if night, in the form of a great turbulent vapour, was spreading towards them.

In the opposite direction was a different day. The sun was shining, the sea docile, and at that moment the longboat glided with grace through the waves.

They'd been following the coast south, seeking a place to land, but after three days had seen nothing but forest. Eir had just woken and was retying the braid in her hair when she noticed a pair of square sails on the horizon.

"Look," she called to Kari.

She darted to the port side and leaned over with her hand shielding her eyes from the sun. Two longboats were far off in the distance.

"Steer towards them."

Kari shook her head. Her eyes were dark and her nose was pinched white by her compressed brows. "I've been watching them for a while. They're following us."

"They will help us."

"They won't."

Eir looked again and could see that both ships were fully manned, with carved beast-heads on their prows, while the banner of a raven flew from atop the first ship's mast.

"They will take this boat, then take what they want from us."

Eir knew Kari was right. These warriors were out for plunder and pleasure, heading to or returning from raids on Northumbrian monasteries to the southwest. She went to stand beside Kari as she steered the boat. "We'll outrun them."

"The *Frihet* is too slow and they know it." She glanced at Eir, then tipped her head down. "We're an easy catch."

"No! This is a good boat. She is fast."

Kari pointed towards the ships. "See the size of their mast against the line of rock on the shore?"

Eir nodded.

"Each time I check, the sails are getting bigger against the coastline."

"And that means?"

"They are getting closer. They'll catch us long before nightfall."

Eir was now afraid and wrapped her arms around herself. Without the dark to hide them, there would be no escape. "What if we sail to the shore and run into the trees?"

"They are much nearer to the land than we are. They'll cut us off before we get there."

Kari put an arm around Eir and pulled her close—an unusual thing for her to do. Normally it was Eir who annoyed everyone with her hugs.

With tears in her eyes, Kari whispered, "When they're close, we'll jump—"

"No." Eir shook her head in disbelief. They would die after a heartbeat in the frigid waters.

"I'm sorry. I failed you. It will be a better fate." Kari shook as she cried.

Anger swelled up in Eir to the point where she wanted to set the sea on fire. She was fed up with the talk of fate, of destinies, death, and all of these being decided by those abominations, the Norns.

"To *Helvíti* with that. No one will decide our fate, no man, no god, and no Norn!" She pulled on the tiller, turning the *Frihet* west and into the storm.

A PLUME OF sea and foam sprayed over the bow of the longboat as it crashed through the crest of a hill-sized wave. Kari held fast, steering the *Frihet* as best she could through the storm. Squalls were followed by sleet and then curtains of icy rain. It was near dusk, but the only luminance was from chains of lightning escaping clashing clouds, which fought as great black bears above them.

Eir was green and low in the boat, groaning, her arms wrapped around Kari's calves. She was reconsidering if drowning would've been better. The *Frihet* shuddered over another monstrous wave. *I don't want to be sick again. Please, Rán*—She was about to ask for deliverance from the goddess of the sea but now considered cursing her. Rán hadn't kept her father safe. Frigg, her own mother, had delivered her back to exile, and Odin, *well*—Eir decided it wasn't prudish to curse them all and tightened her grip around Kari's legs.

"It's best if you stand up. Look at the sea . . . You'll be worse down there," Kari yelled against the noise of the storm.

She didn't want to move. She'd already thrown up three times, and each time reminded her of the snake that had stowed away in her belly.

The next wave was bigger than the last, and when the small longboat almost keeled over, saltwater flooded the hull up to their ankles.

"You have to bail or steer," Kari yelled.

Eir looked up at Kari's determined expression. Kari's singed dark hair, damp from the spray, ruffled in the wind. Eir felt ashamed and forced herself to rise.

"I'll bail."

She navigated the rowing benches with a wooden bucket in hand, scooped up the water, and poured it over the side. The sea temperature was near freezing but something was different about her body after being reborn: she no longer felt cold. Well, she did a tad, but it didn't bite her flesh the way it used to. She dumped another bucket over the side and paused to retch.

Checking progress and deciding that, in fact, none had been made, she dropped the pail, leaving it to float in the sloshing pool they now carried.

With the gunwale as a guide and shifting arm over arm, she struggled back to the stern. "Why are these waves getting bigger? The wind has died down." She gripped the tiller with Kari, helping her steer.

"Because of that!"

"What?" Eir yelled.

Kari took hold of Eir's chin and pointed her head in the direction she was looking.

As they climbed a trough, suddenly right in front of them, dark rocks loomed, tall and jagged with breaking white sheets, which blasted upwards to fall as spindrifts of rain. The roar of the war between wave and rock was deafening as the *Frihet* plummeted down another near-vertical drop.

Eir braced herself, wedging her feet against the bench in front of her and lying with her back against the one they should've been seated on. The longboat was no longer in contact with the water as it hurled down the seemingly endless face of the breaking wave. She took hold of Kari's tunic and twisted it around her hand. Then the bow dove as a great cormorant into the depths of the freezing sea.

EIR LOWERED KARI'S limp body until it lay on the sand, just beyond the flotsam of the *Frihet* and in the shelter of two boulders. Kari was blue and unmoving. She leaned over her, saltwater dripping from her clothes and hair. With an ear on Kari's chest, she listened. Her heart was still beating deep below her frigid husk.

The sea hadn't felt cold to Eir when the *Frihet* broke apart. She kept a grip of Kari, pulling her to the surface, then grabbed on to what remained of the hull. Wave after wave crashed over them, and they twisted and rolled under their wake. When they eventually surfaced again, Eir could see the shore. With the strength she had left, she pulled Kari out of the water and onto the planks she'd been clinging to. Exhausted, with an arm around Kari, she held on until they were knocked into the surf. There, she was able to drag Kari's still form between the rocks and onto the sand.

Eir hoisted Kari up into a seated position as she inclined against a boulder. Trying to keep her warm, she wrapped her arms and legs around her, but knew it would be impossible with no shelter, fire, dry clothes or hides to cover them.

Kari's head fell to one side and Eir lifted it and tucked it into her neck. "You mustn't die," she whispered as tears streamed down her face.

Where she was pressed against the rock, something jabbed into her hip. Searching, she found a sharp object in her pocket. She reached in and tried to fetch it out. It was caught in loose threads, and she ripped it free. It was grey in the dark light and she turned it, unsure what it was. Her fingers curled, about to flick it away, then with eyes closed, she remembered. *Frigg's feather . . . My Valkyrie wings.*

Weariness overwhelmed her. Forcing herself to stay awake, she raised the silver feather to her lips. The broach disappeared as a sensation spread to her cheeks and her shoulder blades. She couldn't fight the fatigue any longer; she rested her head against Kari's as the howls of the wind were silenced, surfaces were made soft, and the rain deflected. She slept enshrouded with Kari in a warm cocoon of white feathers.

YLVA STOOD ON a slope, watching the two longboats row into the bay. The long grass was wet and had soaked the hem of her *hangerock*. She'd left the path to get a better view but now cursed being sodden.

A week had passed since Eir and Kari's escape. *This isn't a good omen. Do those animals have Eir as a captive?* She cleared the mucus from her throat and spat.

"This body is getting too old for this."

Bygul was beside Ylva and tipped her head up towards her.

"Don't you look at me like that," Ylva said.

A raven glided low, following the lay of the hill, then landed on Ylva's head before leaping onto her shoulder.

"Get off, stupid thing." Ylva swiped at it, but it only hopped over each swing. "Off now. You'll soil me." The bird jumped onto the great cat.

Ylva burst out laughing. The lynx blinked; the raven was perched just between its ears. "A nice hat you have, Bygul." She put her hands on her hips, still laughing. When she finally stopped, she spoke to the raven. "Is she there or not?"

The raven cackled.

"On the longboats, bird. The big logs in the water with men."

The raven fluttered its wings and squawked.

Ylva tried to hit it, but Bygul lowered her head. "You dimwitted windbag. A girl with hair of straw."

The raven bobbed its head in one direction, then the other, crowed defiantly, and then chattered as if telling an epic tale around the hearth.

"Mighty Mercury, give me strength. I don't need to know how many good rookery trees you flew by."

The bird gave a few more clacks of its beak, bowed its head, and folded a wing to form a curtsey. It then flew off.

Ylva sighed. "My weary legs." She started down the hill and then turned to Bygul, who had not moved. "And why are you late? If you'd come a week ago and told me Lilith was here, I could've done something different. As it stands, a new thread must be started with limited possibility of success."

The lynx just stared at her before yawning.

"Boring you, am I? Come on. We have to find her before Lilith does. I can't take on that thing myself. Why the *faen* did Frigg let it escape to Midgard."

Bygul shrugged one shoulder.

She inspected the animal carefully. "You don't say much, do you?"

Bygul flicked one ear.

"Be like that, then, flea food."

Ylva turned and developed her stride into a steady pace. "I knew that whore Ragnvi was not being her usual *skit* pile." She continued to curse and mumble all the way down the hill, past the village, and along a cart path. The trail weaved through thick forest pines as it headed south. Bygul followed more than a few paces behind with her ears folded back.

RAGNVI GREETED THEIR guests. She offered a low bow while giving a sidelong glance to Rancor, who was standing tall and trying to look fierce. It had taken Lilith a few days to work out who was important and who was not, tapping into Ragnvi's knowledge as it merged with her body and thoughts. But as the odds would have it, the only people of interest had fled the day Lilith had arrived.

This was rather annoying. Lilith wanted to find out more about the girl it had escaped in. There was no way it was going to do Frigg's bidding without enjoying some freedom first. Killing Norns would be a near-impossible undertaking.

Should I move again? To another? It decided not to. It liked a challenge and although Ragnvi came with many inherently misguided disadvantages, it was silly not to leverage her capabilities, rather than risk a less-able host.

A barely concealed laugh escaped from Ragnvi's lips as she watched the posturing. A self-proclaimed king, of some falsely claimed land, had come to the small village with an entourage of immoral hedonists. *Aristippus would be proud? Disappointed?* Lilith was not sure which. *Proud.*

King Haakon Sigurdsson stood in front of them, his gold armbands glinting in the sun. Ragnvi smiled at him and feigned being suitably impressed.

"Greeting, Lord, welcome to our hall," Rancor said.

Ragnvi frowned at Rancor and shook her head. *You mean that pile of burnt timbers?*

He seemed to get her gesture, but how, she couldn't fathom; he was as dense as rock.

"I mean welcome to our hamlet. Our hall caught fire."

"Yes, I know," King Haakon said. He flicked his long, wiry red braids over his shoulders. "We've seen the smoke for days. It's what led us here."

"You are most welcome to our food and shelter and I offer you my home," Rancor said while going down on one knee.

The king snorted a sardonic grunt.

Ragnvi knew the truth; King Haakon could take what he desired. The village had no warriors, not even longboats anymore. For all intents and purposes, all Haakon could see was now his.

"Have you travelled far?" Ragnvi asked.

"No." Haakon paused to scratch his beard. "The seas are foul and our journey cannot be done. It'll be best if we winter here."

Rancor drew in a quick breath, and seemed lost for words.

Ragnvi knew speaking for him would tarnish Rancor's reputation, so she dove right in. "You're very welcome to stay," she said in sultry tones.

Haakon raised an eyebrow. "Good." He turned to his men and said loudly over their mutterings, "We will wait until spring before returning to Trøndelag. So don't *skit* in your own bed."

The next day, Ragnvi sat next to Haakon, refilling an ivory cup with ale. It was ridiculously small, but valuable; the constant refilling meant Haakon wouldn't know how much he'd consumed. It could've been worse, she thought. They could have gone on the rampage. As it was, they seemed content to take three of the largest longhouses, eat everything on offer, and get drunk.

Lilith topped off Haakon's cup again. It was hard to make conversation over the din of his men. *Such a foul bunch of children.*

Haakon explained he'd been battling the Christian Danes to the south and this hadn't gone well. He was heading back home to regroup, but hampered by early winter storms, which had plagued them since leaving Kaupang, they decided not to risk the journey further.

"I'm as brave as any, but I'm no fool." Laughing, he put his arm around Ragnvi, as she filled his mug again. "But I won't go against Ægir's rage." He belched in her face before leaning back. His laughing continued. "Unlike those fools who headed into the storm." He slapped the back of the warrior to his left. The man turned and grunting in agreement.

"What fools?" she asked.

"Whelps, facing Hel now. We would've caught them, but they chose a coward's death."

"Whelps, sire?"

He was drifting off. "*Já* . . . Impressive though for only two to sail such a . . ." He fell asleep, and Ragnvi allowed his head to fall onto the table.

She'd have to find Ylva and ask her some questions. Ragnvi's mind had told Lilith that Ylva was important, perhaps even had powers. But the witch had disappeared. She had been the one who helped the two who burnt down the great hall and took the longboat. But it wouldn't be easy to find Ylva. Most treated Ragnvi with a cold disdain. They seem to be protecting Ylva and the fugitives. Lilith suspected one of the two who fled was the girl it had escaped with from Asgard. *She'd be useful to find, if Frigg endowed her with wings.*

Lilith, using Ragnvi's hands, helped King Haakon up. "Come, Lord, to my bed." He represented power, and that was a fine thread to weave with.

YLVA LOOKED THROUGH the gloom and down the path as it curved into the mist-laden forest. Someone was following her.

"Come here. And stop sneaking around back there."

There was a snap of a branch underfoot and a sapling quivered twenty strides away.

"For Odin's sake, come here. Or I'll send my *gaupe* to eat you."

Bygul sat and then lay down.

"Get up, stupid animal. Look hungry and tough."

Bygul started to groom herself and purred.

Ylva nudged Bygul with her foot. "Little use you are to me."

A young man stepped out from the trees at the edge of the path. He was stocky with broad shoulders.

"You're Knud, son of Eric. Come here. If you're going to travel with me, then you must do as I ask."

Ylva held an arm out, pointing ahead of them to an outcrop of rock between the firs. "Make a fire there." She kicked Bygul. "Get up and follow." Once Bygul was back on her feet, seemingly unperturbed, all three strolled to the outcrop. Ylva turned to the boy. "Help me up there, then."

Knud was hesitant but let Ylva grip his shoulder as they climbed the incline to the flat perch. At the top, she sat and waited expectantly. "Get a fire going. I'm cold."

When the flames were tall and dancing to music unknown, she let her hood drop, releasing her black-and-greying hair.

She was impressed. *Perhaps not a boy anymore.* He'd lit it quickly and gathered an enormous supply of dead wood that would last through the night. He was also prepared. A satchel, which he kept close to him, was stuffed to the brim with food and tools.

He offered a smoked herring to Ylva; she raised one eyebrow but didn't accept it. He presented it to Bygul, who took it from his hand and ate it in one gulp. Knud provided another one, and the lean cat got up, and moved to lie beside him, and devoured the morsel.

Ylva laughed. "So it's like that, is it? Traitor."

A wolf howled in the distance and Bygul's ears moved in the direction of the sound. The fire crackled and sparks rose with its smoke through the pine trees.

She'd been waiting for Knud to speak first, to ask her a question or make a demand, but when he didn't, she was even more impressed. She lay down with her back to the fire and before going to sleep, she told him, "Keep the fire burning." After the hoot of an owl, she added, "Eir is five days away as the raven flies. And that is never straight."

Angel's Tears

"FATHER! FATHER!" OLAV squealed like a suckling piglet being taken from its mother. "There's—" He was out of breath from running. "At St Michael's cove." He bent over and rested his hands on his knees. "An angel!"

Father Arend put down his basket of goose eggs. "Careful what you say. Remember the dead seal you thought was the body of Christ?"

Olav turned red. "But this time it's so." He straightened. "I was walking along the shore." He panted. "Between the rocks on the cove. Wings of the purest white."

"It's just a bird. An albatross perhaps." Father Arend turned away.

"*No.* She is much bigger."

He looked back in surprise. "She?"

"Yes, with hair of gold."

Father Arend rubbed his chin. He doubted Olav had ever seen a woman. Or knew what one looked like. He tried to clear his throat, but a croak turned into a fit of coughs. Wheezing, he said, "Show me."

KARI WOKE TO three wide-eyed monks, inches away from her face, gawking at her.

"What the—?" She tried to jerk back, but there was something soft and warm behind her. She turned her head to see Eir. They were both wrapped in a great cloak of feathers.

"Perhaps the angel is healing him. Do you see his wounds?" A monk was pointing at the burnt skin on Kari's neck, his fingers just inches from her skin.

"Don't touch me," Kari snapped. She was about to tell them she wasn't a boy when Eir stirred.

The monks moved away and whispered between themselves.

"Eir, wake up." Kari touched Eir's face, noticing a mark just below her cheekbone: a feather tattooed on her skin. "Wake up," she said, more softly this time and pushed at the cloak to find that it tightened around her. She then realised, *They're wings.*

Eir opened her eyes. "Kari?" She hugged her, squashing feathers about Kari's face.

Kari sputtered. "Not so tight."

"Oh, sorry." She loosened her grip.

"Shh." Kari looked at the men. "Monks," she whispered.

"Boy, come here," the older one called to her.

Eir half smiled. "They don't see so well, do they?"

"No, blinded by their robes, I guess." Kari brushed a hand softly against Eir's wings. "Why do you have these?"

"My mother gave them to me. I'd forgotten about them."

"Boy, come away from her," the monk yelled again.

Eir opened her wings, and they both stood. The monks gasped, rapidly praising God, while crossing their chests and falling to their knees.

Kari felt like she might faint, but managed to stay upright.

"Why are they doing that?" Eir whispered.

"They think you're an angel." Kari looked up and down Eir and blinked. "Are you one?"

"Don't be silly." She grinned at her. "But they can think I am an angel, if it helps us." She paused, staring at the tops of their bald heads as they bowed towards her. "Odd bunch. Get them to stand," she told Kari in a hushed voice.

"You don't need to kneel," she said in a commanding tone.

All three rose. One covered his ears, another covered his mouth, and the last his eyes.

"Look away, it's disrespectful," the one who couldn't see said.

Eir glanced at Kari and tried not to burst out laughing. "They are children. We need a story for them," she whispered into Kari's ear, causing a tingle to be sent down Kari's neck, distracting her from the queasiness of her stomach. "I'll stay silent and flutter my wings and flick my hair."

Kari nodded and tried to look serious. This wasn't hard given how ill she felt. "We've escaped from pagans to this shore." She spoke clearly and hoped she sounded like Rangvald when he spun tales around the hearth.

Eir extended her wings fully to the exclamations of the monks, who dived down onto their knees again.

Kari's jaw dropped at the sight of her. "You are an angel," she muttered on a long exhale and started to kneel as well. Eir hooked the radius of her wing under Kari's armpit and pulled her up.

"Stop that," Eir said between gritted teeth. "You know who I am. Don't change that, ever. Or I'll be truly lost."

Kari nervously tugged on the burnt hair at the back of her neck. "I won't. I'm sorry."

Eir managed a half smile. "I am too." She folded her swan-like wings around herself. "Tell them to look. I'm hungry."

The sun broke through the clouds and a ray of light shone across the rocky inlet.

"Raise your heads," Kari told the monks.

They slowly did and as their eyes met Eir's, the morning sun spread across her, causing her hair to gleam. She flicked her hair and turned her chin upward and to the side as if gazing into the heavens.

"A vision from God!" the older monk called.

Eir perfected her angelic visitation by arching her wings into the shape of a heart.

Kari let a few moments pass. She was also in awe and needed time to find her words. The scene had given her an idea.

"Her name is Sunngifu. She is from the sun, and we now seek refuge."

The older monk, with his voice wavering, said, "An angel from our holy son, Jesus Christ our Lord. We are your humble servants." He bowed his head but looked up again as a ripple of wind ruffled Eir's feathers.

Kari rubbed her forehead in disbelief. *Sun, not son.*

"I am Father Arend." He moved his hand to the left, then to the right. "This is Brother Bernard and Brother Olav."

Father Arend coughed after each sentence, and Kari took a small step back from him. She remembered she was supposed to be a boy and lowered her voice. "I'm Alban of Scotia." She'd given the name of the first man who held her as a thrall in Scotia. She must have been four years old back then. Memories before this were only of somewhere warmer; she couldn't remember her mother's face. "We've been forced to flee from our native land by a chieftain who desired Sunngifu."

Eir glanced at Kari quizzically as if to say, *Where on earth is this going?*

The monks looked shocked.

"We need food and shelter."

"Of course, let us help you," Father Arend said. "God has delivered you to our fair island and we offer our devotion. Blessed is our Father."

The monks practically fell over themselves while attempting to lead the way from the cove.

Finally, proceeding in an orderly fashion, with Kari and Eir walking slowly behind, they progressed along a well-trodden path. The land was rocky with few trees. Goats grazed on lush grass, with the sound and smell of the sea as their milieu.

The path inclined upward and it was possible to view the full extent of the small island. Its main feature was a tor rising at its heart. To the east, with coastal detail blurred by mist, the mainland could be glimpsed across white-capped waves.

Eir was struggling; her wings were dragging on the ground.

"Do you want me to hold them up?" Kari asked.

"No. But I want to take them off."

"Do you know how?"

Eir shook her head.

"We'll try later."

The wind was blowing Eir's dark blond hair, sending it forward over her eyes.

"Wait." Kari touched her shoulder, took hold of Eir's hair, and formed it into a single braid. With nothing to tie it with, she threaded it through itself into a loose knot. "It'll do for now."

Eir smiled back a thank you. "How is your burn?" Eir touched Kari's neck. "It looks better, but you have a blister all the way across. Your hair won't grow back there."

Kari shrugged.

"Does it hurt?" Eir asked, seeking her eyes.

"It's fine. I'm just tired."

Eir's expression showed concern, and then she turned her head, checking where the monks were. "We better catch up. I'll cut your hair so it looks better. It'll have to be short, and that will help with our story."

"That doesn't matter."

"You'll look handsome as a man." Eir laughed.

"I'm glad you find me funny," Kari said sardonically.

"I'm sorry. But I'll like you being a man."

"Why? So I get to die fighting raiders when they come?"

"I wasn't thinking that." Eir blushed.

They stopped at a wall that ringed a hamlet of stone-and-timber buildings set in the dell of the central hill. One building lay in a different direction to the others. Kari surmised it was a chapel, as it was the tallest. The ground around the dwellings was set out into small plots, which were now barren except for winter vegetables of cabbages and turnips.

The monks were debating something and when they finished their muted murmurings, Father Arend said to Kari, "The angel's presence may overwhelm the other brothers. There is a place up by the cliff's edge. You can just see the rooftop." He pointed. "I'll take you there while Bernard and Olav fetch food and clothes."

Kari really just wanted to lie down where she stood, but managed a nod.

They followed a faint path until they came to a stone dwelling set beside an entrance to a jagged cave cut into a cliff. The rear of the building was the cliff itself, which arched in a semicircle away from the dwelling. There was little inside; just a table, a straw bed covered with an old fleece, and a few cooking items set to one side of a hearth.

The monk went and stood piously outside and Kari followed. Although she felt like death, she needed to make certain this place was safe for Eir.

"Where are we?" she asked.

"The island of Sellø. Ten days' sail from Hedeby to the south."

The answer didn't help Kari. She'd been captured from somewhere far south of Scotia when she was only a child. She knew nothing of the Northern Sea.

Father Arend must have seen her puzzled look and added, "Hedeby is part of the Archdiocese Bremen, and we are missionaries sent by the Archbishop Libentius." He coughed and cleared his throat. "But events what they are, we do little for the moment. King Haakon Sigurdsson would have our heads. We wait for the winds to change."

"Where is Bremen?" Kari asked.

"In Francia." Father Arend laughed. "You are a stranger to these lands." He fixed his eyes on her.

She could see he was looking at her neck where her ivory cross hung on its cord.

"You serve the Sunngifu?" Father Arend asked.

It took Kari a while to work out what he meant, but then she remembered the name she had given Eir. "I'm her brother. I speak for her and assist her."

"An earthly brother?"

Why did I say brother. Stupid monks and their fathers and brothers. Her mouth stayed open while she tried to think. "I . . . I mean, I am her brother not in blood but in my consecrated devotion to her as ordained through Jesus Christ our Lord." She tried to use as many long words as she could remember without fully understanding their meaning.

Father Arend nodded, but his expression was perplexed. "And the name Sunngifu? It is not familiar to me."

Kari realised she'd made a mistake. The name she'd given Eir was Saxon, meaning gift of the sun. Her own past in Scotia had influenced her. She gave him the Norse version.

"It's her Scotia name. Here it would be Sunniva."

He coughed, then smiled. "What purpose does Angel Sunniva require of us?"

Kari hadn't thought that far ahead and stalled. "She will tell you soon."

"Well, you and Sunniva may stay here as long as the Lord requires." He paused, looking up at the cliff edge. He then pointed. "Just don't go too close to the edge there, or into the cave for water." He waved a finger towards a small opening. "There is a spring in there, but the hilltop is unstable. It's why no one stays here."

The cliff had eroded, and Kari could see an overhang of rocks high above them. "Is it safe?"

"God will protect his messengers." Father Arend stooped devoutly and then turned. Behind him, the other monks were approaching, their brown goat-hair tunics standing out against the green land.

Olav was first to arrive, carrying two baskets containing bread, dried fish, and cheese. Bernard held a bundle of coarse woollen blankets. Full bladders of water or milk were hung over his shoulder. A new monk pushed a barrow with an iron pot at its centre. Smoke emanated from a hole in its lid. Around it, dried dung cakes were piled to be used as fuel for a fire.

Kari pulled one of the bladders from Bernard and drank while the monks watched in surprise. "Boy, attend to Sunniva first," Father Arend berated her. He then had a fit of coughing, which seemed to last forever.

Inside, after the hearth was lit, Kari dismissed the monks and sat beside Eir. She handed her bread and helped her drink water before eating herself. They said nothing and when most of the food was gone, she searched the baskets again. At the bottom of one, wrapped in a fine cloth, were four brown ovals the size of chestnuts. They looked like large beetles with their legs removed. She bit one. It was sweet, tasting of honey. She handed two to Eir. "Eat them."

Eir seemed lost in dark thoughts. Kari took one of the ovals out of Eir's hand and pushed it between Eir's lips.

As she chewed, Eir's eyes grew big. "Hail Ægir! This is delicious." A moment later she popped in the second one. "Any more?"

Kari handed Eir hers.

Eir lifted her hand to put the last one in her mouth. "You've not had any."

"I don't like them," Kari lied. "Anyway, I must look after you first."

"That's stupid. You're more important than me."

Kari shook her head in disbelief. "How is that true? You're a chieftain's daughter, daughter of a goddess, so Ylva said. And, you have wings. And now you're an angel. Odin himself is less."

Eir blinked. "I'm none of those."

Kari lifted some of Eir's feathers, then let them snap into place. "What are these, then?"

"Stupid things from my so-called mother. She didn't explain them to me at all."

"You want to try to take them off?"

She sighed. "In the morning, I can't think now."

"Why did your mother—Frigg? Give them to you?"

"Yes, yes, the goddess Frigg, and I've no idea. She told me to use them before my body died. Which I don't understand. She said I was a Valkyrie, but the wings are idiotic things that get in the way."

"They kept us warm," Kari muttered.

Eir hadn't seemed to have heard her and she'd become melancholy, with her head and shoulders dropping. "I've failed everyone. All I do is cause death and sorrow." She pulled her knees up against her chest and then gathered her wings around her, forcing Kari to move out of the way momentarily.

"I've taken you from your family, your future husband, and now you must share my curse." Her face was turned down, hidden in her wings, and it looked like she had no head.

Kari rubbed her eyes. *Why is she saying this?*

Eir started to cry. She popped her head up, every now and then, so she could wipe away tears. "Angels aren't supposed to cry. Are they?"

"I guess they do."

"I don't want you to be part of what the Norns inflicted on me," Eir said, her voice filled with anguish. "You shouldn't have come with me. You should go back home."

Kari knew exactly what her fate was, and Eir was wrong. "My place is with you. I'm not going anywhere."

"You must go back. You were to be wed. Your mother and father."

Kari rarely got angry, but she was now. "Now stop it. Stop!" Her words and frustration flowed out in a torrent. "My *víkingr* mother is not my mother. You know that. I was brought to your village a slave. And I don't want to wed some smelly oaf of a husband so I can milk his goat. My place is with you. It always has been."

Kari stood and went to the hearth to throw another dried dung cake onto the fire. So much had happened so quickly over the past few days that she no longer understood what Eir was thinking. It was true that she missed her *víkingr* parents; they were kind to her, but Eir was her friend and had been since the day she arrived. Kari was only seven years old when they made her work the fields. Slaves who didn't work weren't worth their food. Those that did became *karls*, given small parcels of land to farm, or in her case, adopted to replace a lost child. The first time they met, Eir pushed her into a puddle, then laughing, helped her up. Her blue eyes and blond hair had captivated Kari and made her a *thrall* again. Kari knew she would always serve her. Being with Eir was the difference between a spring morning sun and a midnight winter sea.

The short blue-and-orange flames danced across the surface of the dried dung. Kari twisted to look back at Eir and was awestruck. Her thoughts had allowed the familiarity of Eir's image to recede. When she saw her again, the contrast of her pale skin, golden hair, and white wings against the grey stone and grim light was mesmerizing. She truly looked like a fallen angel.

"I'll find somewhere better for us in the morning," Kari said.

Eir looked at her. "You don't need to."

"Are you still hungry? I'll get more food and water—" Kari turned away and busied herself with the unnecessary sorting through and folding of the bedding the monks had left.

"What is wrong?" Eir asked.

She held a blanket against her chest. "You'll send me away." There was a slight tremor in her voice and she was annoyed she'd failed to conceal it.

"No. I won't. I'm sorry I said that . . . Just come and rest." Eir stood. "Here." She guided Kari's shoulders to the bed.

Kari lay down and Eir covered her with the blanket and added the others on top then patted the thick stack. "There are much too many of these."

"Eir." Kari smirked. "I can't move."

"I don't want you to. Rest now." Eir laughed.

"You're not sleeping?"

"I'll explore. I want to see where we are."

Kari tried to push herself up. "I'll go with you."

"Rest, you're nearly dead. Anyway, I'm going to gather some herbs so I can make you a paste for your burn. At least I can be useful that way."

The warmth of the bed and Kari's fatigue won out. "There's a knife by the hearth. Take it with you," she said drowsily.

"I won't be long."

Frigg's Purpose

IT WAS A silver darkness; moonlight lifted shadows across undulating fields. Blades of grass merged into clumps of grey and black, while rocks hid their precise character. Eir had travelled some distance from their dwelling, and in field, she attempted to fly. All she'd managed to do was land on her face or leap into the air without staying aloft. After more grass stains and mouthfuls of dirt, she decided her wings were just for show. She sat in a big heap of feathers on the ground, thinking. *Perhaps they only work in Asgard. But how would I get there? A Valkyrie should be able to travel between the worlds.*

She looked up at the moon and yelled at it, "How do I take these damn things off?" Then, putting her elbow on her knee, she rested her chin in her hand. *There has to be a way.*

Eir pinched at the raised surface on her cheek, trying to pull out the hard insert from under her skin. But it only made it sore. Her mother hadn't told her much about the silver feather. *I should've asked more questions.*

She brushed her fingertip along the line of the shape inside her cheek, and after the third stroke, something fell into her palm. She lowered her hand carefully and saw the silver feather. Her cheek was now smooth to her touch; the feather had been removed. She stood and spun around and around, like a dog chasing its tail.

"No wings. No wings," Eir sang, happy for the first time in many days. To have control of something, to be able to decide for herself what should be, was a small victory against the gods and the Norns, and in the crescent of the new moon, she laughed and frolicked as a dancing wolf.

"Who's there?" Eir turned around slowly, scanning the shadows. She sensed that something was watching her. Dropping low, she drew Kari's knife.

A raven squawked and she gasped in surprise. *It's the middle of the night. Not a time for ravens. This is a bad omen.*

She spun and spotted it perched on a rock. A thought of Kari with cold blue skin made Eir shudder. *Is something wrong? I shouldn't have left her.*

The bird answered, shook its head, and tapped its beak on its stony perch. It took a few steps before taking flight. The raven's wings moved in broad strokes. It circled, landed, and took off again. Eir understood; it was showing her how to fly. She needed to have the space to make deeper strokes with her wings. She stood and touched the feather to her lips. When her wings had fully reappeared, she walked over to a ridge on a steeper part of the field. The raven had followed, flying the short distance and landing on a stone close to her feet.

"Well, if it works, I can fly with you," she told the bird. "If it doesn't, I'll have a broken neck. And it'll be your fault." She stepped backwards from the edge to get a run up. "Just so it's clear. I don't want to break my neck."

She darted forward with her wings spread out, counting down each step: three, two, one. Then there was nothing under her feet. She flapped down as far as she could and the tips of her wings touched the ground. She then drew them in slightly and brought them back up until they almost made contact with one another behind her shoulders. Repeating the strokes, she careened downward, following the lay of the land, but this time staying just above it. She almost collided headlong into a stone fence but rose on a gust of wind.

In the darkness she could see just enough to be enthralled by the incredible view. Travelling with the wind, she stayed aloft with little effort. There were gentle changes in pressure under her wings, which she compensated for with minor adjustments to the tips of her primary feathers. She rose higher, following the currents of air. The feeling of absolute freedom allowed her mind to drift and become clear. Two images painted themselves; the first was of the goddess Frigg, curled up on a chair in her empty hall, and the second was of Kari, upset and afraid. She let them sit side by side, holding on to both. The visions merged and Kari stood before Frigg, angry and yelling at the goddess. In this image, Frigg spoke to her. "One day, Kari, you will return."

A gut-wrenching drop caused Eir to gasp. She shook her head to come to her senses and then concentrated on the landscape below.

It was time to get back to Kari, but Eir had already lost her bearings.

"This place is not that big; you'll find your way back," she tried to reassure herself.

She tilted her body in the direction of the shore and to the cove where the monks first found them. She flapped harder, fighting the wind. The sound of the crashing waves had led her to the jagged coastline.

A noise reached her, not the hoot of an owl or the bleat of a goat, but a word on the wind. It was her name being called.

A figure, off in the distance with a torch held high, appeared, rising from a depression formed by a stream bed. As Eir got closer, she knew who it was, or at least who it wasn't. It wasn't a monk. This person had a full head of hair. Then, recognising the thin shape and the way she walked, Eir dove downwards towards her. An important detail popped into her head. *That stupid raven didn't teach me how to land!*

Misjudging the distance to the ground, she tried to correct this by opening her wings fully to slow her descent. She crashed into Kari, knocking her over and sending the torch spinning into the air.

With Kari pinned under her, Eir raised her head and shoulders but couldn't get up.

After Kari had caught her breath, she blurted out, "Eir! I thought you had left me." Her words hinted at fear changing into relief.

"No. I'm sorry."

Kari wriggled, trying to free herself, but Eir still pinned her to the ground, her wings outstretched like a dead seagull's. "I don't think I like you having wings. You're dangerous and you fly like a whale."

"A whale. Not a hawk?" Eir teased.

"You're as heavy as a whale as well. No, maybe a walrus," she groaned.

"Hey, skinny fox, watch what you say."

"Better than a fat walrus-angel. Get off me."

The dying flame of the torch was reflected in Kari's eyes. "Maybe I'll just stay put here and sleep like a walrus." Eir tried to push herself up with her wings, having forgotten for a moment that she had arms.

"We're in a field. Walruses sleep on sand." Kari half smiled.

"You're too clever for me." Eir noticed moisture under Kari's eyes. "You've been crying?" she said softly.

"Smoke from the torch." Kari turned away. "Get off now."

Tucking in her left wing while shoving with her right hand, Eir rolled off Kari. She was silent for a moment, lying on her side, feeling the wind ruffle her feathers. The torch went out and she pushed herself up. Then she offered Kari her hand. "You mustn't worry like that."

Kari rubbed her eyes on her sleeves. "It's hard not to."

Eir swallowed. Her heart panged and she wanted it to stop before she was reminded of how empty and lost she'd felt when she thought Kari had been killed by Ragnvi.

"Hey, watch this," Eir said, brushing the feather under the skin of her cheek three times, then catching the silver relic as it fell away.

Kari gawked as Eir's wings withdrew until they were completely gone. "You got them off."

Eir spun around, showing that the wings were truly gone. Kari stopped her and touched the back of Eir's tunic. "They ripped through your clothes. I'll need to sew these holes."

Eir waited as Kari tucked in the torn folds. "At least I can take them off."

"Yes, thanks to your Odin. Now monks and *karls* may travel safe at night without fear of being squashed."

"Very funny." Eir thumped Kari's shoulder. "Come on, let's get back."

"Yes, whale bird."

"Hey. I'll make a mighty Valkyrie someday." Eir took a step forward. She was unsure and turned to go in the opposite direction. "My bravery will be told in great halls across the land." She stopped again and went to the left. "I will be known as heroic Eir, the merciful *læknir*." She paused and bit her lip in confusion. "Which way?"

Kari laughed. "You mean Eir, the lost walrus?"

Eir punched Kari's shoulder again.

"It's this way," Kari said and put an arm around Eir's waist.

STILL TIRED AND in a sombre mood from last night, Kari couldn't shake the lingering feeling of saudade. It had kept her from sleeping and she'd lain awake until the dawn light, spreading from gaps underneath the door and between the window shutters, dispelled all darkness. She got up and fed the fire.

The monks had been generous, bringing more food and asking about their well-being. She sent them away, but they would be back, expecting miracles from the angel.

Eir stirred, stretched, blinked, and then smiled while rubbing her nose with the back of her hand. "What are you cooking? It smells amazing."

She didn't want to talk.

"Kari, I have an idea."

"Sounds dangerous."

"You haven't heard it yet."

"Does it involve your wings?" Kari muttered.

"No . . . well, kind of."

Kari passed over a bowl of *skause* and a piece of rye bread. She waited for Eir to eat before taking a portion for herself.

"I'm not starting until you have some. We are friends," Eir said, her bread poised to scoop into thick mutton-and-vegetable stew.

Using a wooden ladle, Kari filled another bowl from a cast-iron pot heating on the hearth. She sat beside Eir and started to eat.

"Wait!" Eir screeched.

Kari had taken some onto her bread and was chewing slowly.

"Where did this come from?" Eir's hands were trembling.

"Father Arend brought it with Brother Olav for our day-meal."

"Stop! It could be poisoned."

Kari carried on. "It's not. I'm still alive."

Eir yanked the bowl from Kari's hand and stew slopped onto the floor. "Don't! It's like the children. I should've made sure it wasn't poisoned. Ragnvi could be here." Her face was pale and her eyes wild.

"*Fagr minn*, it's fine. I already tasted it ages ago." Kari took her bowl back.

"But it could be—"

Kari put an arm around her. "It's not poisoned."

Eir seemed to gather herself and then said quickly, "I don't want you to taste my food ever again. And you must eat after me." She took a big mouthful of the stew.

"You said we are friends, so we should eat at the same time."

Eir pursed her lips but then took another scoop of the stew. She turned to Kari and said with her mouth half-full, "You know, I'm not sure we are friends."

Kari creased her forehead and turned to her. "Why?"

"You call me 'my beautiful,'" she said after swallowing her food.

Kari squinted slightly. "So?"

"Lovers say things like that."

"And?" Kari frowned, slowing her eating. "It's not bothered you before."

"You don't need to get upset. I like it when you say those things to me, and I don't want anything to happen to you."

Kari was quiet for a moment, wondering why Eir had brought up the names of endearment. "We will get a cat or boar to taste our meals."

"Yes, that's a good idea. Maybe Frigg trapping my soul was not such a bad thing."

Kari spat out her food and turned to scrutinize her directly with her mouth open in shock. "What do you mean?"

Eir said nothing and looked down at the table.

"What did you do?"

"I don't know, but I had to. I thought about you and saving the children. My body wouldn't take my soul, so the necklace. She gave me wings. Then I flew and . . . I mean last night I did. I knew I didn't want a husband, not even Knud. I couldn't let you die. I don't really know what I've done. I had a dream after flying and—" She was talking quickly, and Kari put a hand over her mouth.

"Slow down."

The room fell silent except for the crackle of the flames and pops from the boiling stew. Kari kept her hand in place until Eir's breathing relaxed. "Tell me again, but not like a berserker, all right?"

Eir nodded.

Kari moved her hand away.

"I bound my soul to this necklace and I became a Valkyrie so I could come back and save you and the children from Ragnvi."

Kari frowned. "Back from where?"

"Nifelheim."

"You came back from the dead?"

"Yes. To save you and—"

Eir was still speaking, but Kari couldn't focus on her words. She found it hard to believe in these pagan gods, but she'd seen and heard so much that there must be some truth in their sagas. Eir would never lie to her. But even if it were true, why would Eir give up the feasts in the halls of her gods for this world of hardship? "Why did you come back from your heaven?"

Eir twisted her head while it was still bowed. Only one eye was visible behind a dangling lock of hair as she whispered, "Isn't it obvious?"

Kari stood, crossed her arms, and started to pace.

Talking again, Eir was jumping from one topic to the next. Kari returned her attention to what Eir was saying. "My mother, Frigg, made it possible. You know her hall is empty, no one is there. Even the—"

"What do you mean, trapping your soul?" Kari backtracked.

"Well, bound to the Brísingamen." She pulled forward the pendant of her necklace. "She told me I must stop the suffering and help others."

The thought Kari had pushed away popped back into her head. *She came back from the dead for me?*

"Now, listen to my idea," Eir said.

She gave her soul to save me? Oh my Lord, what have you done?

"We can set up a home here. I'll be a *læknir*. People would travel here to be helped, and we can use our craft. As I always wanted you to, I mean, you can be my apprentice. If we must, I can try to be a Christian. We can stay together and do as my mother wanted . . . Do you hear me?"

This was all the work of Eir's pagan gods, her mother Frigg, and the Norns of fate. Tales about those had been spun around the hearth of the great hall, but perhaps this could be undone if Eir became a Christian. She turned to walk the length of the room again and a hand hit her chest hard, stopping her in mid-step.

"Stop that pacing. You're such a stubborn goat. Did you hear what I said?"

Kari closed her eyes and everything washed away. Eir was here, that was all that mattered.

"Kari, answer me. Do you like my idea?"

She opened her eyes. "I like all your ideas, except, mostly I get hurt at some point."

Eir laughed. "Yes, that's how it has to be. Good, then I'm glad we agree." She beamed.

"I can't believe you gave your soul for me."

"Of course I would. You stepped in front of that stone for me."

"But your soul. I don't know what to think."

"You always think too much. Stop with all that stupid thinking." Eir twisted a knuckle against Kari's skull.

"Ouch! Hey." She grabbed the wrist of the offending hand. "I've stopped thinking, already. But you mustn't give up your soul again. Maybe the idea of becoming a Christian would get it back."

"It's possible I suppose." Eir turned, trying to get out of Kari's grip.

There was a knock at the door, a rasping cough, and then a reverent voice came from behind it. "Boy Alban, is the Angel Sunniva awake?"

Kari froze, as did Eir. Then in a deep voice, Kari called out, "She will see you in a moment."

"*Boy Alban,*" Eir whispered, half laughing with a hand over her mouth. "You're so handsome."

"Be serious now."

Eir took hold of Kari's hand and spun around behind her. "I am." She laughed.

Kari responded by putting a foot behind Eir's, stepping in front of her, trying to trip her, but Eir shifted in the same direction and they fell backwards onto the dirt floor.

"Is something wrong?" Father Arend's voice came from behind the door again. Then a sequence of disgusting hacking coughs.

They held in their laughter as the coughing continued.

"Our first task is here." Eir's expression changed to focused determination.

"What task?"

"That monk's cough."

Mirrored Night

THE LAST DAY of their journey started much like the first. Ylva rose to see the fire still burning. Her bones were extra heavy in the morning dew.

"Winter's coming," she muttered.

Bygul had vanished and Ylva suspected the lynx was hunting, knowing it would catch up to them later along the road.

The young man had said little during their travels and Ylva was grateful. The last thing she wanted was mindless chit-chat, but today he spoke. "Is it much further?"

Ylva bit back her normal reaction to questions; he had earned her manners. "By dusk we'll be at Seljatún. There you must get a boat for travel to Sellø. We won't be welcome in the day, so we'll wait until it's dark."

Knud nodded. "And your pet?"

"I can't speak for her. Come on, we can't be late."

Under pink-and-orange clouds tinted by the setting sun, they arrived at the first homestead in the village of Seljatún. It was a low circular building with a grass roof, and it appeared empty. Ylva suspected its occupants were at the village's great hall. Two goats greeted them and then followed.

Just when Ylva thought she would have to give the goats names, they darted off and leapt over a stone wall.

Ylva turned to see Bygul approaching.

"There you are, mangy cat. Little use you'd have been if bandits came to take me."

The cat blinked both eyes and carried on padding towards them.

Knud laughed. "I doubt anyone would try that."

"What do you know? I was a beauty in my time."

"You still are," he said.

Ylva opened her mouth about to speak, but then closed it swiftly. She was old, truly ancient. She ran her thumb along the line of her jaw before curling her index finger onto her chin. *What does that idiot know?* But she was curious. It'd been such a long time since anyone had said something like that to her. "Are you drunk? Or just blind?"

"Neither." He appraised her for a moment. "You're strong, tall, your face shows determination, and your eyes, wisdom and kindness. You are as a mighty hawk."

Ylva wiped away a smile. *Perhaps he is dense. That won't bode well.*

"A hawk might not be right," Knud said, "but I cannot think of anything else."

"You're a strange one. I'm three thousand winters old."

Knud shrugged. "It doesn't matter. I look at things. I like faces. Yours I'll remember."

"Well, look again. There is no kindness in the present."

"It is what I see."

"Enough of this." She knew that Knud worked as a carpenter in the village. He'd made most of the wooden stools and he carved images into the beams on the longhouses. *He has an artist's eye. Perhaps that is why he is so besotted with Eir.*

They carried on down the path but turned when they saw people ahead. The town was a trading port, and there were several longboats hauled up on the shore. They weaved past fishing nets drawn out on racks for repairs. Gulls called and flew from their perches as they passed.

Ylva shivered. The sea was one of the few things she feared. *I'm not going. This is something I won't do. The boy can bring her to me for the deed to be done.*

She tugged on Knud's sleeve and pointed. "Go find a small boat, anything will do. Then signal to me as a crow would. Everyone will be eating now, so be quick. If you're caught you're dead. Or maybe you will just lose your pretty eyes. In either case, I won't know you." Perhaps the threat was over the top, but she needed him to be fast and careful.

Knud nodded and disappeared towards a pair of jetties, which extended far into the bay.

Ylva sat on a smooth log at the edge of the tidemark. The stars were out and she counted them; not all, only the important ones. *By Odin, I wish there was another way. This thread is so long and painful. But there's no other that endures.*

She was about to go and find Knud when she heard the sound of a crow in distress. Following the cries, she found Knud pushing the prow of a small crabbing skiff into the water. Bygul was standing by Knud and leapt into the boat when she saw Ylva.

"Good," she told him and patted him on the back. "Get in, then. I'll push off."

Knud didn't move. "You're not coming?"

"No!"

"I won't find her without you."

"Of course you will. It's a small island. Now don't be an ox's turd, get in." Ylva pointed at the boat.

"I don't know the way."

"It's there, right in front of you, across the bay." Her hands shook as she gripped the side of the boat, ready to push it into the cold sea. Bygul leapt out of the skiff and came around behind her. "Get back in, Bygul. And boy, when you find Kari, bring her back to me before sunrise. Oh and tell Eir—"

The lynx nudged under her bottom, lifting her feet off the ground.

Ylva screeched, "Owwee, stinking—stop shoving me!"

"Bygul thinks you should come," Knud said.

Ylva tried to stay planted on the ground.

A noise came from behind them. They turned to see two men with torches coming down the bank and onto the beach. "You there, stop!"

Ylva heard a sword being drawn. Bygul flipped her, head over heels, into the small boat. "*Skit* mounds of Nifelheim! Damn you. Stink cat from Hel!" She tried to stand, and the boat jerked forward as Knud pushed it into the water. She fell backwards. "Knud, you toad's fart!"

But it was too late. She no longer had both feet on the ground.

Knud jumped in and took the oars. He put all his strength into the strokes.

The men on the shore threw stones that whizzed by them, just missing Knud.

Ylva ducked down against the stern, her whole body trembling. Below them was nothing, a void, a black endless depth none could escape from. *Only the insane travel in these infernal tombs.*

The bombardment from the shore stopped, but Ylva was too afraid to move and all she could do was watch as Knud rowed. It seemed to her that he was a great bird, flapping its wings and dragging her off into a mirror of night.

"Are you faring well?" he asked.

"No, foul fowl," she said. Bygul moved closer to her and nudged her face. "That's not helping, hellcat."

Knud laughed. "We'll be there soon."

She stayed curled up on the bottom of the boat. Then after what seem like a thousand seasons, she heard the keel slide onto sand. She hauled herself up, grateful of Knud's steadying hand as she climbed out. As soon as she did, a raven landed on the prow of the boat and Ylva paused. "Wait over there, boy."

Knud reluctantly moved out of earshot.

Ylva spoke with the bird after it squawked at her.

"Yes. Yes. I'll send her, tomorrow. Now get lost." She started to turn away but the bird clacked its beak at her.

"Just keep her unchanged. I'll create a new thread when I need her."

The raven hopped and squawked a long monologue.

"Sow's tits, you are annoying. Shut up already. I'll give her something so she won't remember. It is too long anyway; her mind would fade. Now pass the words back to Frigg, and no embellishing them with endless details of dead foxes you have eaten on the way."

The raven bowed. It actually crossed its legs and lowered its beak.

Ylva tipped her head in turn.

THIS WAS A fool's time to be out and Kari wanted to head back. She walked slowly along another stream bed in the dark, trying to find the last plant. She had gone far to the east side of the island to find sneezewort, a daisy-like flower which grew near fresh water streams. Winter was coming and she needed to find what she could before snow covered the land, but it was getting too dark to continue.

She turned and made her way back, following the rim of the butte that dominated the centre of the island. She put her hands in her pockets to keep them warm. One contained a small bundle of dates wrapped in a fine cloth. This reminded her of the encounter with the merchant earlier in the day.

THE MERCHANT'S SKIN was tanned and his beard was black, braided into thin strands. Each braid ended with a bead of jade, glass, or amber.

Father Arend introduced her. "Brother Alban, this is Waelise. He comes here every month."

Kari peered up at an unfortunate view of Waelise's groin. He was standing above them on the short primitive jetty to which his boat was tied. Leaping down onto the muddy beach, he splashed Kari and then offered a low bow.

Waelise straightened and turned his attention to Father Arend. "So, Father, how many manuscripts do you have for me this time?"

"Where's the proof you delivered the last?"

Waelise laughed. "You have little trust in me."

"All men can be corrupted by greed." Father Arend crossed himself.

"Men of your God especially, I venture." He grinned. "You need not worry. Your books are of no value to me. Wool, knifes, skins, and cheese offer more profits. Those I can trade in Hedeby for cloth from the southeast."

He chuckled. "And cloth I can sell for silver to your bishops." He hit Father Arend hard on the back. "And I've more dates for you to flavour your mead. You won't believe where they've come from."

A heavy-set woman stepped off the boat and approached. Her red hair and rosy cheeks gave her away as being Scotian, from a land far to the west where Kari had once been enslaved. Shifting from one foot to the other, Kari was reminded that she was an outcast. She looked like no one else; not even people from Scotia. She was thin, small-chested, and dark in complexion with deep hazel eyes. It was no wonder she was thought to be a boy.

"Good day, Father, are you keeping well?" the buxom woman asked.

"I am, Maddie, and God's blessing upon you." Father Arend beamed.

But Kari could see something behind the woman's expression. *She's putting on a brave face? Why?* Her eyes were bloodshot and her freckles appeared as flecks of burnt oats, against skin whiter than it should be.

Waelise clammed up when Maddie spoke, but then whispered to Kari, "My wife . . . Never marry a Scotian with red hair." He elbowed Kari in the ribs and laughed, going quiet when Maddie glanced his way.

"Is your wife in good health?" Kari whispered.

"The gods wanted our child. Seven days ago it was born without life."

"I'm sorry."

Waelise dropped his eyes and he crossed his arms. "It was our third taken." He sighed. "My wife believes it's the cold that killed him. She wants us to head south." He turned, climbed onto the jetty, and scurried back to his boat.

Kari watched as the monks manoeuvred two wide handcarts onto the beach and positioned them against the side of the dock. They were pushed by monks she'd not seen before. The beds of the carts were now level with the planks of the jetty. *Where do these monks come from? Are they breeding them somewhere?* She suspected that was unlikely. One cart was stacked with baskets and clay jugs, which she guessed were filled with ale, while the other contained wooden barrels. The island was so barren, she wondered how the monks were able to make such things.

More handcarts appeared, but these were empty. Waelise whistled and flicked his fingers towards his men on the boat. Her question was answered as bundles of reed and oak slats were unloaded and rolled onto the empty carts.

Waelise slapped one of his men on the shoulder as they went past him. "Bring His Holiness's chest."

The man fetched a small wooden chest from the boat and placed it onto the nearest handcart. Father Arend approached the chest and waved to Kari to come and stand beside him.

"Brother Alban, you may see this." From around his neck, Father Arend removed a cord with a small key and unlocked the chest. There was a single parchment inside and a small book. He picked up the parchment and broke the wax seal. After spending some time reading the densely written page, he paused to explain. "This is from the archbishop in Bremen. He has some news of the new pope, Gregory the Fifth. I hope His Holiness is not as corrupt as the last, and there is news of the godly King Olaf Tryggvason, who fights pagan kings in the name of Christ. Praise be to God." He wiped a tear from his eye. "And we have an angel here who has cured my cough. So many miracles, thank the Lord."

He scanned the parchment again. "The archbishop wants twenty copies of this prayer book by spring." He examined the book briefly. "Winter is coming. We'll need more candles. Brother Alban, would you like to learn to be a scribe?"

Kari didn't need to think about this. "I can't. I must tend to Sunniva."

"You won't be able to live with her once you become a man." He patted Kari's shoulder.

I don't plan on growing a beard. She wondered how much longer Father Arend would think she was a boy.

He took a sealed letter from his pocket and placed it into the chest. "I have said nothing of you and Sunniva, since I believe you're correct, that if I were to divulge that she is truly an angel from our Lord, she would be taken from us to be delivered to the pope. That is not our Lord's purpose." He took hold of the cross around his neck and kissed it. "God's will be done."

Kari had been surprised by how easily the monks had accepted the story she had spun. But the more she thought about it, the more she wondered if it was a story at all; it felt like the truth. Eir was an angel and was performing God's will. Helping others was surely that. The absence of her wings was easily explained; that in the mortal world they could be concealed. This also wasn't a lie. As for miracles, well, Eir had stopped Father Arend coughing, alleviated Brother Olav's toothache, and cured an elderly monk's blindness. The last seemed to surprise Eir as much as anyone else. She had mixed up a concoction from garlic, onion, and the bile of a goat's stomach. She let this sit before pouring off the clear liquid and telling the old monk it was holy water and he should drip it into each eye. After three days there was a noticeable improvement and he could make out shapes. Kari had never seen a man cry like that before.

"DAMN!" KARI'S FOOT went down a rabbit hole, bringing her thoughts to the present. She cursed again and after pulling it out, continued in the dark. She picked up her pace but then froze.

Orange eyes of a great beast stared back at her. Drawing her short knife, she took a step backwards. The creature licked its nose. Kari could see its long fangs. *I'm dead!*

She was about to turn and run, if only to live a few more moments, when a hand gripped her shoulder.

"Bygul. Stop causing everyone to soil themselves. Prowl louder. Or I'll get you a bell."

Kari knew the voice and spun around to see Ylva. With her knife still held in front, she caught her breath. "I should've known this would be of your making." She pointed towards the creature. "What is it?"

"Frigg's cat. Now put that pointless knife away."

"Stay back, witch. I don't want anything to do with you."

Ylva chuckled. "Why so angry? What've I done?"

"This is all your fault."

"What is?" Ylva moved a step closer.

Kari waved her knife. "Stay away! You—You allowed Ragnvi to attack Eir! You trapped us in the hall and burnt it, and me. Then left us with only the *Frihet* to escape in. And now you show up with that beast. You're not going anywhere near Eir."

Ylva pondered, scratching her chin. "Very well, that's mostly true. Now put that knife away before my cat eats you alive."

The fearsome feline yawned and looked to one side as a figure approached.

"Knud, is that you?" Kari asked.

"Yes." He stood by the beast.

"Stay back," Kari yelled.

Knud scratched Bygul's neck. The creature purred, a noise so loud Kari could feel it in her chest.

"She won't hurt you. She's friendly," he said.

"I don't care. It's not going anywhere near Eir. Nor are you, witch. You wrecked everything."

"I'm cold and tired, and you're wrong; this is better for Eir," Ylva said.

"Better? Better than her village, home, and friends?"

Ylva sighed. "I thought you were clever. Her family is dead, her village is now in the hands of a king who would've taken her for his pleasure. Her home is slept in by an entity so old and unpredictable that it was imprisoned for a thousand winters, and as far as I know, you are her only remaining friend."

Is this all true? Frustration, rather than fear, caused her to tremble. Ylva was right. Kari knew it. She had no one to blame.

"Kari, my feet hurt and the wind is blowing right through me. I won't harm Eir."

Kari let out a long breath. "All right." She pointed at the cat. It had stopped purring and was sitting to attention with ears twisting. "That thing is harmless?"

"It's just a big kitten." Knud rubbed the animal's cheeks with both his hands. It seemed to smile at this.

"Can we go before winter covers us in snow?" Ylva pulled her cloak tight around herself.

Unsure, Kari tugged at her short hair that Eir had cut the day they had arrived, removing all the singed ends. "Do I have a choice?"

Ylva put her hand on Kari shoulder. "If you love her, no."

Blinking, Kari wondered what Ylva meant. "Come. This way." She started towards the cliff where their dwelling was nestled.

After a few steps, Ylva whispered to her, "You should tell her. Tonight."

A Stilled Present

BEFORE KARI HAD a chance to open the door and enter their dwelling, the latch jerked back and the door was flung open. She was pulled inside. Eir's arms were wrapped around her and thick golden hair tickled her face.

"By Odin. Where have you been?" Eir said, pressing her cheek against Kari's.

"I'm sorry."

"You mustn't stay out so late."

Kari reached into her pocket and retrieved the date palms, then handed them to Eir. "A present." Crossing her arms, she waited for Eir to unwrap the silk cloth which protected the fruits.

"You didn't need to get me anything." She beamed at her.

Kari smiled back at her, but was then shoved aside as Bygul wedged her head and whiskers between them.

"What?" Eir's jaw dropped. "What is she doing here?" She gasped as two more arrivals stepped through the doorway. "Ylva. Knud."

"See? She is fast." Ylva gestured towards Kari. "You, Knud, are slow."

"I was waiting for you," he mumbled.

Ylva went straight to the fire. "Knud, stoke this up. I'm as cold as ice."

"Hello," Knud said, before heading to the hearth, where he threw on the last of the dung cakes. "I'll fetch some wood." He headed back outside.

"How did you find us? Is that one of my mother's cats?" Eir took Kari's hand and she leant against her.

"Birds have eyes," Ylva said without turning away from the heat. "And yes, she's Bygul."

"She was larger when I saw it in Asgard."

"Maybe you were smaller," Ylva muttered.

Eir laughed. "Maybe. It's good to see you, Ylva. I'm happy." And she was. Kari hadn't seen Eir like this since before Ragnvi had dug her claws into Eir's father. She was almost bubbling over and it appeared she might burst.

"Let the merriment commence," Ylva said sarcastically, but a marked inflection hinted at an undercurrent of amusement.

"How are the children?" Eir asked.

"Safe. But let's talk later, I'm too cold." Ylva was warming her hands; her fingers were practically in the flames.

Bygul turned a circle, her tail brushing Eir's face. Then she lay down in the centre of the room.

"I knew you wanted a cat to check for poison, but really, Kari, did you have to take one from the gods?" Eir whispered in Kari's ear and then turned. "Let me get you some food."

"Open your present," Kari said.

Eir folded open the cloth to find the dates inside. "How did you get these?" Her blue eyes searched Kari's.

"I just promised to help the monks. That's all."

Eir took one and popped it into her mouth and then nodded, leaned in, and hugged her. "Thanks," she said with her mouth full.

"Some hospitality for your guests, Eir. Where are your manners?" Ylva snapped.

Eir released Kari and offered Ylva a date.

Ylva took one, inspected, sniffed, licked, and then put it in her pocket. "Is that all you have?"

"No." Eir laughed. She fetched a lump of cheese, the remains of a leg of mutton, and the day-meal bread. "Where is the—?" Kari handed her the knife from her pocket. "Thanks." Eir gazed at Kari for a moment, before returning to dole out the food.

Kari put her hands in her pockets and shifted from one foot to the other. *How can anyone be so beautiful? I have to tell her.* She took her hands out, crossed her arms, and then a moment later uncrossed them.

Eir put the knife down and moved to Kari, lifted Kari's hand, and held it up to her chest. "Is something wrong?"

"No. I'm good, truly."

"I was worried about you."

"I'm back now." Kari paused, remembering what Ylva had told her. "I missed you. Ylva scared me, and that oversized cat."

"Did it? Is that why you are so jumpy? Wait—Are you hurt and you're not saying?" Eir took hold of Kari's chin and bent her head one way and then the next. She started to spin her around.

"I'm not hurt."

"What is it, then?"

"Well . . . I . . . I have to tell you something." Her voice was just a whisper.

"Tell me what?" Eir's blue eyes searched hers.

She was afraid of the words. Her hands trembled and Eir gripped them tighter. They were words she wasn't sure should be said; not how she meant them. *But they are true. And cannot stay hidden forever.*

Knud pushed the door open, holding a bundle of thin fence posts. He skirted around the two, embarrassed, and hurried to the fire.

They separated, and Kari thought that maybe Eir already knew what she was about to say.

Soon tall flames heated the room and Ylva cheered. "Very good, Knud, very good indeed."

At the table, Knud told them of the events in the village, including the arrival of King Haakon. He explained how he had followed Ylva, presuming the elder was travelling to find Eir, and he'd come to help. Kari knew the truth. For many seasons he had wanted to make Eir his wife.

"You'll need to become a monk if you stay," Kari said to Knud.

His face dropped.

Kari felt a tapping on her knee. She turned to Eir, who whispered, "Hold my hand." Kari entwined their fingers under the table so no one would see.

Speaking as if to a gathered clan, Eir told of how they had arrived on the island. "So, then Kari, who is always clever, came up with a tale to tell the monks, and made me an angel called Sunniva. They gave us shelter and food. But I don't wear my wings anymore as it upsets the monks. They tend to fall about themselves, hurting their knees, but also, she doesn't like me wearing them, either. She says I fly like a walrus."

Kari half listened. She was tired.

"So I had an idea. I could be a *læknir*, as I had wanted to be at home. Well, Kari is a *seiðkonur* at finding the herbs I need, and if people are sick they come to us and we tend to them. She is so smart, she even tricked the monks into thinking she's a boy, and they call her Brother Alban." Eir laughed and squeezed Kari's hand.

Kari was glad her cheeks couldn't be seen in the dark, but as hot as she was on the outside, her tummy warmed to Eir's praises.

Knud looked at them, his eyebrows scrunched and lips pursed. "Wings?"

"Be cautious who you tell," Ylva said from beside the fire. "Your wings are precious and powerful."

"I know," Eir said.

Ylva hunched towards the fire. "Fetch me some hides. I need to sleep."

Knud collected some from near the door, after Eir gave him a nod, and passed them to Ylva.

Kari was also very tired and feeling sick because of it. She closed her eyes for a moment and opened them to the sound of Eir saying, "Come, sleep now." Eir led Kari to the straw bed they'd been sharing for warmth since they first arrived. Nuzzling up to Eir, she fell fast asleep.

Before dawn, she woke and was unable to drift off again. She kept an eye on Ylva, who lay in a heap of coarse blankets.

The shadows faded slowly, and at first light Ylva eased herself up, like a giant spider slowly rising after pretending to be dead. She shuffled over to her, leaned down, and whispered, "Come, we must talk." She then went outside with Bygul following.

Kari didn't want to go. She didn't want to have anything to do with the elder, who'd always been terse and dismissive. She knew Ylva was a witch. She'd seen her kind in Scotia, by the standing stones on the hill. But if Ylva wanted to speak to her, there would be a dark reason, and it would involve Eir. Witches only ever offered insight into misery.

Kari lifted Eir's limp arm and slipped out. Immediately, she felt the loss of warmth and raced to put on her *skikkju* to keep warm. She trod softly towards the door but stopped halfway, looking back at Eir. A shudder rose up her body, chilling her from the inside. She tiptoed back, bent over, and kissed Eir's hair. "I love you," she whispered. She kissed her again. "I won't be long."

Kari made her way outside to find Ylva waiting. Ylva turned and headed along the edge of the stream that flowed from the cavern close to their dwelling.

The spring ended in a still pool and disappeared underground. Ylva stopped and sat on a low, flat rock. She beckoned to Kari to do the same with her feet dangling over the dark water.

"Why are we here?" Kari asked.

Ylva tucked her black, greying hair around her ear. "Eir's mother, Frigg, has started something which requires our attention." She spoke softly and with guilelessness Kari hadn't heard from her before. "Yours and mine." She rubbed her running nose with the top of her hand. "Frigg has released an entity as old as time. It travelled with Eir and is now here."

"A what?" Kari asked.

"Just listen. Its name is Ereshkigal or Lilith. The Queen of Night has many names. But really its name doesn't matter. It can take any form by subsuming another. Right now it's with Ragnvi."

The sun was not yet casting light on their perch, and Kari shivered. She couldn't shake the tension from her chest. Even though they'd been gone less than an hour, she already missed Eir dreadfully. She then remembered how pleased Eir had been with the present.

"Are you listening? There are things to tell and to be done." Ylva gave her a look that made Kari's heart sink.

"Speak quickly or I'm going back."

Ylva took a moment, bending her fingers and stretching them. "Lilith cannot be destroyed, so we must let it be, until the weave is right. Then you must help it. This will be the thread that is best for all."

Kari hated how Ylva always talked about the ending, rather than about the steps to get there. She took a deep breath and tried to stay calm. "Speak clearly."

"The balance was broken. Lilith had tried to correct this but was punished for acting as a Norn when it was just a servant. Then a lie was told, and until it is disbelieved, Lilith will be twisted towards it. It is not an evil thing, but it will always go towards the brightest light, and with the flame now being violence and power, that is where it will dwell, fuelling it. If it had Eir's wings, it would be able to call on others beyond this simple plane and in a short period make all of it its own. Even without the wings, it will influence this world at a pace that will be destructive."

Kari put her head in her hands. "I don't understand." She rubbed her face. "Just tell me what must be done."

"Hand me the cross about your neck first," Ylva said in a matter-of-fact manner.

"Why do you want it?"

"Just give it to me. Then I'll show you what must be done."

Kari fished out the ivory cross from her cloak and lifted its cord over her head. She handed it to Ylva, who bunched it up in her hand and placed it beside her on the stone.

Ylva sighed. "You must save Eir and help Lilith. But not now." She looked at Kari. "I am truly sorry, child."

"When, then?" Kari was consumed with dread and her voice trembled. *What is this witch saying.*

"A when that is past your present lifetime."

Kari grunted out of frustration, "You're talking in riddles." She pushed herself up to stand. "Only birds understand you, I'm going." Slipping her hands in her pockets, she turned. Ylva wrapped her long bony fingers around Kari's wrist, crushing it.

"Let me go!" Kari tried to pull free.

Ylva yanked her and shoved her towards the edge of the stone on which they stood.

Kari tried to weave out of the forward motion, spinning on her heel, but Ylva had put her off balance. She tried to grab Ylva's sleeve, at the same time Ylva propelled her towards the pool of water.

"I am sorry," Ylva said, giving a final thrust, pushing Kari into the ice-cold water, like she was a broken whorl.

Kari screamed as she fell backwards. The water was frigid beyond any she'd experienced. She thrashed frantically with arms splashing and legs kicking, trying to grip the slippery edges, but she couldn't. There was nothing underneath her. She was being dragged down by the water drawn into her clothes and boots. She popped her hand above the surface and she was able to get two fingers onto a fissure at edge of the pool. All her strength had been taken by the cold, and her numb fingers slipped. She sank, and when she could no longer hold her breath, her lungs exploded in pain as they filled with water.

A TENDER CIRRUS snapped inside Eir's mind, causing her to wake suddenly. She rose on extended arms and mapped out the room. Only Knud was present, snoring in the corner.

"Knud!" she yelled. "Knud!"

He jumped to his feet in a start, patting his waist. "What?" He took two steps and grabbed his knife from the table. "What is it?"

"Where are they?" Eir flung open the door and raced outside. She scanned the landscape but didn't see them. Returning inside, and near to tears, she knew something was wrong; a discord pumped through her veins. "Where?"

"I don't know." He stood still, rubbing his neck.

"Something has happened." Tears rolled down her cheeks. "Find them!" She whirled around and pulled out the silver feather from her pocket. After touching it to her lips, she didn't wait for her wings to fully realise before darting through the door. Feathers slammed into the frame as she took flight.

Eir circled over and over again, but Kari was nowhere to be seen. She'd also not seen Ylva or Bygul—only the monks and their stupid goats. Panic made it hard for her to think. *Kari wouldn't just go!*

She flew low along the shoreline as it started to rain. Her eyes blurred and she wiped them clean. Again nothing. She turned inland towards their home, retracing Kari's possible movements.

Where the fresh-water stream disappeared underground, she spotted it. On the ground, a shard of white against the grey basalt slab.

Homing in on it, she approached the ground to land. Her speed was too great, even with her wings at full-braking stretch. She slipped on the wet expanse, fell onto her front, and slid along the ground. With grazed knees and hands, she scrambled to her feet. The rain was heavier now and she took a few steps before crouching and picking up the ivory cross.

Eir bowed down. Her wet hair hung in cascading sheets. Rain splashed off her feathers, and she held her hand on a bent knee. Kari's crucifix dangled from her fingers. *She is gone. I've lost everything.*

A Toll

THE TWO MONTHS after Kari vanished were the worst Knud had ever experienced. Eir's total devastation knew no bounds. He shook his head, remembering it took a week of constant persuading to get Eir to come away from the edge of the pool where she huddled. But even after he had searched the water with poles and hooks, no body was found, and Eir still wouldn't leave.

The monks brought her food that she didn't eat, while Knud had come every day to try to get her to leave the spot. Against the blue-grey sky and charcoal slab, she had become an armature on which her wings were hung.

It wasn't until a hailstorm had pummelled the land that Eir finally retreated to her dwelling.

Knud tried to remind her that Kari could still be alive, but Eir didn't accept this. He also knew it was unlikely. The witch must have killed her. Why, he didn't know, and as much as he desired to have Eir as his own, he desperately wanted Kari to be found alive. He feared for Eir's sanity.

Each day, they walked around the island's coastline, looking in the ruts and cracks and hoping not to find a body.

"I don't think we should do this anymore," Knud told Eir, leaping back onto grassy ground from seaweed-covered rocks.

Eir said nothing and walked away.

"Eir, we won't find her."

Eir slid down the bank onto a small patch of beach exposed by the falling tide. She sat on the wet sand with her arms around her knees, rocking back and forth.

He didn't know what to do, and to his shame, he couldn't bear spending all day with her; being a part of her desolation was impossible to endure.

As the days went on, he spent more and more time with the monks, helping them with chores, and he was accepted into their community. Father Arend had become his friend after he repaired the monastery fencing, fetching new posts from the mainland. The priest had been persuading him to become a monk and had also spent much time with Eir, sitting quietly, whispering words of comfort.

On one visit, Knud was able to overhear. He spoke while standing, his hand on her head. " . . . live in gratitude, giving thanks to all circumstances and bring peace to your soul. Amen."

"Will she get better?" Knud asked.

"Time may heal, but I cannot know, she isn't merely mortal. I pray to God that she finds a new path. Staying in sadness will undo her." He then spoke in Latin before translating.

> *Sorrow wears like water.*
> *Sorrow tears like the wind.*
> *Sorrow cares for no one.*
> *Sorrow burrowed under the skin.*
> *A toll must be paid, sorrow takes all from within.*

He patted Knud on his shoulder. "Come and help us. Idle hands allow the Devil in."

Later that day, Knud ventured to the southern part of the island. Father Arend had tasked him with making mats to line the floors. So he had stomped through a marsh, cutting and bundling up reed.

It was getting dark. Gathering the reeds had taken longer than he'd expected, or perhaps he was just dallying. His thoughts had been drifting back to Eir and what he could do to help her. He'd finished lashing the last sheaf around its centre, while leaving others stacked up, deciding he would come back for them tomorrow at first light. He wanted to bring at least one so he could start a mat before he slept. Dragging the bundle behind him, Knud set his sight on the dominating tor and headed in its direction.

There was no moon, making it hard for him to establish the nature of the ground on which he travelled.

Suddenly, his footing subsided and he sank up to the top of his calves. "For Saint Peter's sake!" he cursed and tried to walk on, but the movement only caused him to sink further.

He stood still but was slowly descending into the saturated peat and was now up to his waist. There was no point in yelling. No one would hear. He made an effort to push forward and something bumped into his shins. A stump perhaps, he thought, but it pushed too easily.

The goo now was around his ribs.

He used his knee to ease up the object below him, hoping it would be something he could use to escape. He coaxed it until something broke the surface. He reached for it and then let go in horror, almost slipping over under the black mire.

A bubble of air caused the corpse to rise, gurgling the water around it. An outstretched finger of brown leathery skin pointed to something behind him. He could see the gaping mouth and closed dead eyes of a woman's forlorn face. The body rolled slowly towards him before the head slipped under. A strand of yellow hair was the last to disappear back into the watery tomb.

Knud's chin was under the water and he spat after taking in a mouthful. Turning in the direction the corpse had pointed, he caught sight of his reed bundle and the cord floating on the surface. He grabbed at it and pulled frantically as his nose dipped under the water. When it was closer, he was able to use the floating bundle to get his head above the surface. He stopped sinking; no longer fated to join the dead woman. He drove forward, half kicking and half walking until he was at a firm edge of the pit and able to pull himself out.

Exhausted, his chest moving in frantic breaths, he rested. He stank of decay, but he was alive. "Father Arend can get his own reed next time," he said, staring up at the empty black sky.

As he trudged back to the monastery with his sheaf dragging behind him, he felt thankful but couldn't get the image of the dead woman out of his head. It haunted his soul. Even after all the years she must have been in that pit, her blonde hair and features were preserved. What preyed upon his mind most of all was that the dead woman looked like Eir.

LATER THAT WEEK, Knud found Eir squashing a root with a stone and placing the mash into a boiling pot by the fire. It was the first time he had seen her busy and was suspicious.

"What are you doing?" he asked. When she didn't answer, he put his hand on top of hers. He knew what hemlock root smelled like. "You mustn't."

"Leave me be."

"I won't."

She turned towards him. "Leave me to do this." Tears streamed down her face.

"I won't," he said, gripping her hands.

She struggled, using all her strength to pull away.

"Let me go!" she screamed.

"I won't let you harm yourself."

She then broke down and sobbed, a heart-wrenching keening, which sent shivers down his spine. She fell into him and he wrapped her in his arms.

"There are things you can do for others. Just do those. It's what she would've wanted." His words were tender and he stroked her hair while she cried. Moments later, she let go of him and withdrew to the straw bed.

After a few weeks, Eir had somewhat improved and Knud was able to spend more time with her. They had started to sleep together, however Knud wasn't sure if Eir actually liked him or merely wanted him close by. One night after they shared more than sleep, he knew the answer. She'd made a separate bed for herself.

In the nights to come, he asked her to let him into her bed, even demanded. She rejected him and finally he could no longer face the shame of it. Heartbroken, he left her and went to join the monks where he embraced their God.

As winter ebbed, Eir started healing others and at least once a day someone would appear from the mainland after braving the storms. As Eir's renown grew, so did her unborn child, and by the end of spring she refused to see anyone.

During the new moon of midsummer she called for Knud. "Fetch a *léttakona* from the mainland. My child will come soon." That was the most she had said to him since he'd become Brother Knud.

A few weeks later, he knocked on the door of her stone dwelling, his heart filled with a stew of emotions.

"Come in," Eir said.

He entered to find her with a newborn, wrapped warmly and held against her bosom. A woman was close by, fussing over mother and child.

"A girl."

Knud tugged the swaddling away to see his daughter's face. He smiled. "She is beautiful like you."

Eir smiled back. "I've called her Caitlín. It's the name Kari had when we first met, before she was given a new one."

A wave of sadness passed across her face, and he noticed the ivory cross on a shortened cord around Caitlín's neck.

"You will keep us safe?" she asked.

Knud nodded. He'd since taken the sacred vow to God, but there was nothing he wouldn't do for her.

"Thank you. Can you take Hilda back tomorrow?"

"Yes. If there is anything you need—"

She touched the rough skin of his hand. "I'll ask."

The next day, Knud rowed Hilda back to the mainland. He pulled the boat ashore and watched as Hilda climbed up the bank and back towards the village of Seljatún.

He relieved himself while staring out to sea, but when he looked down, two sets of tracks in the wet sand caught his eye. One was a set of wide paw prints, and the other, small boots. He followed them until he came to an indentation in the sand where it looked like a boat had been launched.

He bent on one knee and examined at the prints, measuring them with his fingers. The animal tracks were too large to be normal. The others reminded him of the day he had first travelled to find Eir.

He gasped. "Ylva has returned. Lord protect us."

WAELISE LEANT AGAINST the mast with his hand down the flap of his caribou-skin breeches, scratching. He was looking forward to getting back to sea. *This place gives me the shivers!* The village reeked of danger with King Haakon Sigurdsson wintering here. *A man to be avoided. And that demented woman who's stuck to his ear.* But most of all, he wished he'd kept his big mouth shut. He scratched some more while enjoying the sensation.

"You're such an animal," Maddie told him. "Take your hand out of there."

"It itches."

"I'll cut it off, then it won't itch, for all the good it does me." And she burst out crying. "We should've headed south—" She sat down sobbing. Two of the oarsmen glanced at her.

It had only been a week since they'd lost another child. He touched the Thor's hammer relic which hung around his neck. "Don't be like that now. Maybe Sunniva will see us on this visit."

"She is seeing no one." She shuddered and bent forward.

"*Astin mín*, if she can't see us, we will head south. All right? I'm tired of this place as well. We can settle down somewhere warm." He glanced up at the two great longboats that sat close to his own wider craft. "I'm also sick of tiptoeing around our enemies here. It would be good to leave."

"Our enemies? Yours, you mean. You must learn to keep your mouth shut."

Waelise nodded. It was advice he should've taken last night.

She gathered herself, sighed, and then stood. "The tide is almost in." She went and finished coiling a rope, then moved a barrel that had been left in the way of the tiller. Straightening up, she put her hands on her hips. "What are they doing?" She was looking at the longboats as they were being prepared to sail.

He shrugged. "I don't know." He rubbed his nose and smelled his fingers.

"Waelise, what've you agreed to now?" Maddie poked him in the chest. "I told you to leave all the dealings to me."

She always knew when he was hiding something. He had no idea how. "Nothing, I just said they could follow us. We made an agreement."

"Follow us where?" She thumbed him hard and he tripped over a bench, falling onto his rear.

"To Sellø. I told them about the miracles of the angel. And, well, the king wanted to see Sunniva before returning to Trøndela. And then that woman of his, Ragnvi, wished to meet her."

"You're a fool, Waelise." She pulled at her hair. "A mad goat's fool. Do I have to cut out your tongue to teach you when to speak?"

She raged from one side of the boat to the other and then stopped in front of him. Her fizzy red hair tickled his face as she leaned over him. "Do you know nothing? King Haakon hates all Christians. He will kill all those monks, then our trade is gone."

"Ah, I didn't know that."

She grabbed his tunic and pulled on it with two hands. "We must set sail now. Anywhere but Sellø."

Through clenched teeth he tried to smile but failed. "*Pusen min*, we can't. We have a deal."

"What deal?"

"Well it's more of a promise," Waelise said meekly.

"What kind of promise?" she growled.

He answered softly, hoping she wouldn't hear. "That they won't take our heads, then piss in our skulls."

OUT TO THE north, three boats approached, their grey sails full. One was the trader's boat. Eir recognised its wide berth. The other two, she was not sure about.

"Are they headed here?" she asked Father Arend, who stood next to her.

"Sadly, yes."

Caitlín was a sleep in her arms, wrapped tightly in a seal-fur swaddling. "Trouble?"

Father Arend stroked his beard. "We will baptise your child today."

Eir tilted her head, allowing the wind to blow strands of hair from her face. "Do you know who they are?"

He gave a gentle nod and turned to towards the chapel. "Yes. The bishop warned me of this in his last letter. Come, Sunniva, let's welcome your daughter to God, before the king sends us to heaven."

"King?" Eir asked.

Father Arend walked ahead in long strides and Eir struggled to keep up. "King Haakon Sigurdsson. He has returned from Denmark and now he is here." He stopped when he saw Brother Olav. "He is no friend of Christians. Sunniva, you must hide. But first to your child." He turned to Olav. "Fetch the holy water and bring it to the chapel. Then tell the others to pray for our Lord's salvation and that of Sunniva and her child."

"Yes, Father, but why?"

"The pagan king is coming. Now hurry." He touched the man's arm before continuing to the small wooden chapel.

The christening was thankfully quick. Eir hadn't seen the ritual performed before and expected a more complicated affair. Caitlín wailed incessantly throughout the proceedings. Eir smiled at her daughter and kissed her forehead. *I guess you didn't want to be a Christian. But our gods took everything I loved away from me. And now all I have is you.*

Eir was trying to calm her by rocking her gently, when Father Arend took her elbow.

"I will speak bluntly. Lord, forgive me. King Haakon must not know you are here. He must not take you, at all costs." Father Arend's grip now hurt. "Do you understand?"

"I can use my wings to escape if I must."

He spun her around and put his hands on her shoulders. "Sunniva, if Haakon sees you he will hunt you down and know the rumours are true. His men are skilled warriors with sword, spear, and bow. You must stay hidden. If he finds out you are from our Lord—" He hesitated and swallowed. "Nothing would bring him more pleasure than to defile an angel and to do so for all to witness. He would use such an act against our true God and the Christian church . . . Dear Lord, I can hear his proclamations now."

Caitlín had stopped crying. Her bright eyes stared up at her mother. Eir shifted her in her arms, holding her tightly to her bosom.

"Go to the cave. Stay there until it is safe." He turned and hurried outside.

"Where are you going?" she yelled after him.

He stopped and crossed himself. "To do God's will." And then he was gone.

She ran as fast as she could with Caitlín bouncing in her arms. The trader's boat had arrived and was tied up to the jetty. The boats of King Haakon were also landing, but on the small sandy beach of St Michael's cove.

Running along the grazed path, along the goat's fence, she was soon at her dwelling. Inside, she grabbed a basket and filled it with bread and dried fish. She wouldn't need water as a spring ran through the cave. In truth, she was not sure she needed food; her body seemed able to cope with little nourishment. *Knud should be back by now.*

She picked up swaddling for Caitlín and a blanket. After exiting the house, she turned to the left. A few steps away was the cliff face in which her house was nestled. Cut in its centre was a lopsided triangular hole, only as tall and wide as a slim person. She stepped through it into the darkness. Feeling her way along the smooth walls of the cave, she carefully inched forward. The ground was covered with wet, loose pebbles and she cursed herself for not having brought an oil lamp, but she couldn't carry anything else. Caitlín was oblivious, fast asleep, cradled in her forearm.

Deep inside, the cave opened into a larger chamber. Using the light cast along the tunnel and with her eyes now adjusted, she looked for a place to hide. In one corner was a crevice, which she went to assess. Feeling its size, she whispered, "When we need to, princess, we will hide in here."

She put down her items, then touched Caitlín's warm face with the back of her finger. Carefully, over the unpredictable stones on the cave floor, she made her way back into the line of light from outside. She lowered herself and sat. She removed the strap of her *hangerock* and fed Caitlín while watching for movement at the entrance.

HIS MUSCLES BURNED, back ached, and the blisters on his hands had popped. Knud was rowing against the current, tide, and the wind, trying to get back to the island. When he rounded the eastern edge, he saw one craft tied to the jetty, and two other longboats on the shore, with warriors disembarking and paddling through the shallow water. He heaved on his right oar, leaving his left still, turning to land before he was spotted.

Using all his remaining strength, he allowed the boat to collide between two boulders and leapt off. As his small rowboat started to drift away, he hit his head with his fist, ran for it, and leapt back into it. *You're such a fool. You might need this to take Eir and Caitlín away.* He brought the boat to shore again and pulled it above the tide, which had just started to recede. As soon as he'd stopped, something sharp pushed against his neck.

"Was the child born?" a voice he recognised croaked.

He tried to twist away from the cold edge, but it pushed more firmly into his skin.

"Answer me."

"Yes."

"A girl?"

"Yes. Now let me go. Warriors are here. Eir and my child are in danger."

"Yes, fool, why do you think I'm here? You're always so slow."

He turned quickly away from her, feeling the knife edge pull along his neck. Touching, he found no blood on his fingers. Ylva was holding a flat stone, not a knife. She tossed it to him.

"Come on, sap for brains, we need to save your child."

The Hosts

BROTHER BERNARD FELL without a sound. An axe had split his skull in two.

"Died like a girl," a large brute of a man said as he wiped his weapon clean on the dead monk's habit.

"Fool! The dead can't speak." Ragnvi spat the words at him, but they were meant for all.

King Haakon frowned. "Know your place, woman." He swung the back of his hand at her. But Lilith didn't allow him to make contact, causing her body to jerk back and fall. Ragnvi stood and brushed herself off.

Haakon gave her a sidelong glance. "Don't mock me with your antics."

Lilith smiled from within Ragnvi. *You mock yourself, standing on your whimsical pedestal built from a single lie.*

"No, my lord." Ragnvi gave a low bow of veiled condescension. "I offer but humble advice."

He turned from her. "Set fire to the buildings. Kill who you like. But bring Sunniva to me." He turned away and walked up the slope towards the settlement.

Ragnvi trailed a step behind. "Sire, these monks have little. There is no need to burn their homes."

"Don't meddle in things you don't understand. We must stamp out this vile camp."

"You fear these monks?" Ragnvi said sweetly.

Haakon stopped. "No! They will die like swine."

"So why not let them be?"

"Because I cannot allow their weak god to take control. Behind them are rich bishops who build their power by controlling kings and countries. They want us all to bow and kiss their fat fingers. No, all must die."

"And Sunniva?"

His laughter echoed up the hill with his stride. "She'll be shown how feeble her god truly is." He grinned. "Her miracles won't save her from the company of my men."

"My lord." She kept her voice even and disinterested. "Sunniva may have something of value. Let me question her before your men fatally whore her. I assume that is your intent?"

He shrugged. "A message must be sent." He stopped to put a foot on the bottom rung of a wooden fence, surveying the landscape.

"You will allow me to speak to her first?" Lilith wondered if the venture had any merit. *If Sunniva is a Valkyrie, it will be worthwhile. If not, then it's time for a new host and not this churlish fool.*

Laughing, he glanced at her. "You have the tongue of a serpent. Perhaps it may at last be useful."

CROUCHED BEHIND THE remains of a stone wall, Ylva popped her head up and glanced around. An instant later, she ducked back down. "You need to be quick now." She poked Knud's shoulder hard. "This is a problem, since you're the slowest thing I know."

She was about to push his shoulder when he caught hold of her wrist.

"Where is Kari?" he asked.

"Somewhere safe."

"She's not dead?"

She'd expected the question and answered truthfully. "To others here, yes. But to others later, no."

"That makes no sense. You killed her." He let go of her hand.

"No, stupid boy. I sent her somewhere safe."

"Where?"

"She is being looked after. Eir will need her later. We all will. I can't explain it any better. And stop wasting time. The merchant's going to leave when he thinks the king's boats are beached and he can't be pursued. This is more or less now. So find Eir, get your child, and flee with them on his boat."

"I have my own boat."

Ylva scratched her cheek and squinted at him. "I hadn't expected that." She thought for a moment. "No, that thread unravels. The feather must be sent far away." She stood. "Now do as I ask. I'll delay the fat merchant as long as I can."

He pushed himself up and stared at her. "And Eir?"

"You can't save both. Get your child. Bygul is here; she will protect Eir." She pushed him in the direction of Eir's dwelling. "Skiting slime-less snail, go before the moment is lost. And all moments after."

THERE WAS A subtle fleeting change in the shadows inside the cave. Eir felt a presence but heard nothing. Caitlín was asleep. Then a movement in the scant light, like a breeze flicking a candle's flame, caused Eir to tremble.

Whatever it was, it was now inside. Eir stood, and using one arm, held Caitlín tightly against her chest. She drew a knife. "Who is there?" she whispered, but her voice was trembling. *Why didn't I bring the oil lamp?*

She started to back away. It was approaching. She took another step back and stumbled on a loose stone. The cave was pitch-black, except for the small slice of light thirty strides ahead.

"Who is there?" she called again. She moved further back to find she was at the rear of the cave. Her heart raced and her mind went blank as panic set in, forcing out her rational thoughts. She slid down against the wall, curling up around Caitlín.

A low meow echoed around the cave. A wet nose nudged her neck.

She felt another nudge and a wet, raspy tongue soaked her face. "Bygul!"

Behind the lynx shadows shifted across the cave opening and harsh voices could be heard. Eir gasped and quickly covered her mouth with her trembling hand.

KNUD WATCHED TWO warriors from around the corner of Eir's dwelling. One had just killed Brother Tacitus, and another taller, wider man laughed at the deed. Both appeared to be the same age as he was, but they had arrogance about them, as if owning all and fearing nothing. They wore ring mail and bronze armbands with short knives tucked into their belts. Knud crossed himself and said a small prayer for the quiet Tacitus.

The larger man tried to squeeze into the cave entrance, but the breadth of his shoulders and chest meant he couldn't fit. "You go, Uffe."

Uffe laughed. "So you're too fat?" He pushed the larger man aside and lowered himself to fit through the wider part of the triangular entrance. "It's too dark. I need—" He screamed and gurgled, then silence.

Knud, holding a rock, crept toward the larger warrior, who was reaching into the cave for his comrade.

"Uffe, are you dead?" the warrior called into the cave.

Knud brought the stone down hard onto the man's head. The man turned, his eyes rolled up so only the white showed, and he fell to the ground, unmoving.

Knud collected the knife from the dead warrior and tucked it into his belt. "Eir, are you there?"

"Yes!" an echoed voice called to him. "Is it safe to come out?"

He spun round to check his surroundings. Flames and smoke billowed from the monks' buildings. Off in the distance he could see the merchant, his boat still at the jetty, but his sail was unfurled and flapping in the wind.

Knud's skin went cold, and prickled as a group of warriors marched up the path towards him.

"Come quickly, more are coming. The king, and I think Ragnvi is with him."

Her voice was close. "I can't get out. Bygul killed one; he is in the way."

Caitlín's wails echoed inside the cave like nothing Knud had ever heard before. It sounded like the spirit of a trapped dragon was trying to burst free from the mountain.

"Knud!"

He extended his arm to find the dead man's ankle and pulled with all his strength. There was an unsettling sound of a bone breaking as he yanked the corpse out. He looked away from the mangled remains. One leg had been bent backwards, while half the man's neck was torn away.

"Come out, Eir, quickly—" He leapt backwards at a loud crack above him. A pile of rubble and rocks tumbled from the top of the cliff. There was figure high up on the ridge, jumping on the edge of the cliff's overhang. A shower of dirt and rock fell in front of the cave's entrance.

He raced forward and pulled away what rubble he could. A hole opened and a delicate hand reached out for his.

"Help!" Eir screamed between Caitlín's wails.

"The cliff is collapsing. Someone's on the ridge causing it to fall."

He pulled away a few more stones but couldn't move a large boulder. "I can't clear it. The stone is too heavy." He gripped tightly and used his legs as leverage, but the rock was three times his size.

A yell sounded behind him. Three warriors were charging ahead of others on the slope.

"They're coming, Eir!"

A screaming bundle was pushed out of the small gap, wrapped in Eir's tunic.

"Go!" Eir yelled.

"Eir, no!"

Eir pushed her hand through the gap and took his. "Go, Knud. Save Caitlín!" Her voice was filled with fear. She released his hand and pulled it back into the cave.

Knud turned and ran with Caitlín in his arms, past Eir's house, now half-buried in rubble. Three men changed course, trying to cut him off as he raced through the long grass and down the steep incline towards the jetty.

A loud thundering followed him as boulders, dirt, rocks, and a priest fell from the heavens. Eir's home, the cliff, and the entrance to the cave were gone.

THE SOUND CAUSED Ylva to turn away from Maddie. Ylva watched, waiting for the dust from the landslide to settle. After a moment Knud appeared from out of the cloud, half running and half falling in the slick meadow grass.

"Maybe not so slow." She frowned, seeing the three men with swords drawn chasing after him. They were but fifty paces behind.

"Well, then." She turned to Waelise. "Do something useful."

"I'm no warrior," he said.

"Do you want this child or not?"

Maddie took his arm and whispered into his ear. Waelise bent down and pulled a long-handled axe from under one of the benches of the longboat.

"Come on," Ylva said, jumping onto the dock. She counted each step and stopped at twenty-two. Waelise followed and stood beside her. Two-thirds of the jetty remained before them.

Knud was closer now and leapt across a ditch towards the path, which led to the quay.

"We should meet him," Waelise said.

Ylva shook her head. "We must stay here. There, we all die. Here, only one does."

He pointed at each person including himself. "Which one?"

Footsteps sounded on the planks of the dock as Knud raced towards them followed closely by three of King Haakon's warriors.

"You have the child?" Ylva yelled as he darted towards them.

"Yes, but Eir is trapped."

Ylva sighed. "I know."

As soon as Knud was close, Ylva pulled Caitlín from his arms. She opened the tunic wrapped around the child to see her beautiful blue eyes glancing around. Caitlín was no longer crying. Ylva stroked the pale blond hair on her forehead and smiled. "She's so ugly."

The three warriors approached cautiously with their weapons drawn. Knud turned to meet their advance with his knife ready. Waelise moved beside him.

The menacing bulk of the two men stopped the warriors from coming closer. Ylva felt around Caitlín's swaddling and found Eir's silver feather. "Maddie, come here!"

Maddie jumped from the longboat and ran towards them.

The three warriors appeared reluctant to attack. Ylva knew why; the rest of Haakon's men were coming down the hill. They were waiting, rather than risking a mortal wound.

Maddie stopped next to Ylva, her cheeks flushed from running.

Ylva handed Caitlín to her. "You can feed her?"

"Yes."

"She is very special. You understand what I told you?"

Maddie nodded.

"There must be no exception." Ylva took the silver feather, and using her own finger as a guide, bent it into a ring. She pulled the crudely shaped ring off and gave it to Maddie. "Wear it, keep it safe, and hand it down to Caitlín when she is old enough. And she must give it to her daughter, and so forth. The bloodline must not be broken."

"I'll do as you ask." Maddie hesitated. "This is the right thing to do? To take her?"

Ylva tucked her greying black hair around her ear. "It is the only thing to do. Come on, merchant, it's time to go. Hand me that axe."

He hesitated, and Ylva yanked it from him.

The three who had chased Knud laughed and stepped forward. A tall, lanky man with dangling arms and a long red beard said with flying spittle, "Where do you think you're going? Wait for the king."

His companions laughed and the one on the far left said, "Come on, let's kill the pups."

No sooner had he spoken, when Ylva swung the axe in a wide arc towards the man's knee. Its iron head crashed through the joint, separating his leg in two. He toppled over and reeled on the ground as blood spilled onto the jetty.

"That's one who dies," Ylva said.

Waelise blinked in amazement and laughed nervously. "No others?"

"Only if you leave now, fool. Go!"

Knud closed the gap and stood beside her as she leaned on the shaft of the axe.

"I can't do that again," Ylva whispered to him. "Are you going with your child or staying?"

The two remaining warriors had edged away and were furtively glancing back to see how far Haakon was behind them. The wounded man was still, and his eyes stared directly into the sun.

"I must stay."

Ylva nodded. She let go of the axe, grabbed his wrist, and dragged him towards the boat.

"I must help Eir!"

"We are, *skit* for brains. Run to the boat."

Waelise had already untied the longboat from the jetty and it was slowly turning in the shallow waters of the receding tide. The wind had caught the sail and it billowed into a taught belly.

"Too slow, too slow, you're always too slow!" Ylva screamed as they sprinted towards the departing craft. The space between the jetty and the boat grew wider with each stride. "We won't make it." The two warriors were fast on their heels now, yelling insults.

Just as Ylva's worst fear appeared to be coming true, Knud put his arms around her waist and leapt with her. They flew across the breach and landed in a heap against the rowing benches as the boat completed its turn and headed out to sea.

STANDING NEXT TO Haakon, Ragnvi scraped her knuckle on her teeth while thinking.

Why was that witch there? What was the monk carrying?

King Haakon watched the merchant sail away.

"Shall we go after them?" the man next to him asked. "They'll be an easy catch."

Haakon shook his head. "Don't be a fool. The tide is too low. Our boats are beached." He turned to a man whose face was marred with scars. "We'll leave in the morning. Tell the men to set up camp."

The man nodded and went back to the larger group, leaving Haakon alone with Ragnvi.

"You won't free Sunniva from the cave?" Ragnvi asked.

"No. She is as good as dead."

"She will be martyred. Maybe even canonized."

"Perhaps, but I have those who will usurp me to kill and the Danes to fight. I cannot spend a season digging out a dead angel."

Lilith caused Ragnvi to step in front of Haakon as he started to walk away.

"Who is trying to usurp you?"

Haakon laughed. "Why? Do you plan to become his whore?"

"No, sire, I just need to know who to poison for you," Lilith lied.

He pushed past her. "Go back to your weaving, woman. We sail to Trøndelag tomorrow."

TIME HAD PASSED—how long Eir didn't know exactly—but it was more than a few days. She had felt every crack and crenature of the cave. There was no way out. The original entrance had been completely sealed by the landslide.

Bygul must be somewhere in the darkness, but the cat was avoiding her.

"I know you're there!" she screamed. But the animal didn't respond.

Her mind started to close down. With no input, it was left to spin, spiralling into a fissure deeper than the darkest ocean. Words came to her and she repeated them over and over again. Words of her own creation.

> *In the darkness I must wait.*
> *Forever alone, a deserving fate?*
> *What hideous bond holds my shadows?*
> *Merciless beings won't offer the gallows.*
> *An eidolon cursed, exiled by hallows.*

Lying down, she closed her eyes, which did nothing. Unable to die, her mind, to protect itself from madness, shut down.

YLVA WAS NOT standing by Knud so much as clinging to him for dear life. "Can't this thing go any faster?" she hollered at Waelise.

The merchant laughed. "You're afraid of the sea."

"Everyone has a fear. Don't ridicule me or I'll tell the world yours," she snapped back.

"I fear no man or god," he boasted.

"But you fear a woman." Ylva glowered at him before glancing at Maddie, who was feeding Caitlín. She was pleased that the child had been able to take her milk so readily.

After seven days they were close to the trading town of Hedeby. Ylva spoke to Knud so no one else could hear. "Boy, there are things you must do. I have done all I can. Leave your child with Maddie. They will take good care of her. You must find someone with the power to free Eir." She examined his face. There was sorrow there, but also determination. "Do you have a god?"

He was quiet for some time, but then answered, "Yes."

"Good, you'll need someone." She said nothing for a moment. "You know she is more important than you and me."

He made a barely perceivable nod.

"Your brain is still too slow, even if your legs are not." She patted his shoulder. "Go stand at the front and get ready to jump. We won't stop here."

"You're not coming with me?"

"Dimwit, I will for a short while. I need you to catch me so I don't get wet."

"I think you need to overcome your fear of water."

"Not today." Ylva pulled out a sticky brown fruit from her pocket and went to sit on the bench next to Maddie. She picked some hairs from its surface before showing it to Maddie. "Do you know where this date comes from?"

Maddie's wiry red hair was being blown around her face, and she pushed it aside before shaking her head.

Ylva sighed. "You have a child now. I ask only two things of you. These two things will keep you safe, your child and those in the weaves to come. But they must be honoured or all will be lost."

Maddie nodded slowly in time with her rocking of Caitlín.

"The loom is set. Go and settle in the place where this comes from." Ylva put the date into Maddie's hand. "Waelise, you know where this is from?"

Waelise was close by, steering his vessel. "The date is from a great distance away. South. Down endless rivers and into another blue warm sea. I've not travelled so far. It would take a season to get there."

"Of course," Ylva snapped. "You travel to Damascus. It is far. But listen. Settle to the north in the old Roman towns. Do this and you will prosper."

Maddie looked up at Waelise. "A new beginning away from the cold."

Waelise scratched his beard and shrugged. "An adventure."

"And the ring must be passed down," Ylva said, touching the bent silver of feather around Maddie's finger. "But it must be given to a certain person when asked for." She looked around; she needed to think of a name she could tell Maddie. She spotted Waelise's beard and the beads dangling at the ends of its braids. A green one caught her eye. "It must be given to a woman named Jade."

Chocolate Plan

THE CONVERTIBLE'S TYRES squealed around a sharp right turn, heading along what once was a Roman road. Jade clung on to the dashboard as Freya flattened the pedal to the floor. They had only just survived a set of descending hairpins to now dice with death at speed on the straight.

Jade leaned towards Freya. "Sweetest, the accelerator's not an on-off switch."

"It's not?" Freya dropped down a gear, gunning the car around a tractor.

The speedometer hovered around one hundred and sixty kilometres an hour. "Aren't you worried about getting a speeding ticket?" Jade asked.

"She can't get one." Lena reached between the seats and tuned in the radio.

"Why not?" Jade yelled against the roar of the wind, the engine, and the distorted house track blaring from the radio.

"She is the comtessa de Baux. It's her road." Lena shifted back into the rear seat, stretching out lengthwise. She ducked down while holding her long black hair in a bundle to stop it whipping around her face.

Jade turned the volume down as vineyards and olive groves raced past them in a blur of deep greens and silvers.

"You're royalty in France as well?" Jade asked, putting a hand on Freya's thigh.

Freya looked at Jade longer than she should have. "Oh!" She reacted late to a sharp bend in the road. The car lunged with all four wheels locked as Freya braked heavily while turning. There was the distinct smell of burnt rubber as the Peugeot fishtailed before following the road upwards. In front of them were the ruins of a Templar castle, set on top of a limestone escarpment between the scrub-covered Alpilles Mountains.

"Freya, please. We're not immortal." Jade wedged one leg in the footwell and gripped the dashboard again.

"Speak for yourself," Freya mumbled, screeching the car round another turn.

"Then you have time. Slow down."

"I don't." Freya stomped on the brakes, bringing the classic car to a near halt. She ground in reverse gear, popped the clutch, and slammed down the gas. Lena and Jade's heads were jolted around like a terrier's toy. Freya changed direction and swung the car into the right-hand turning she'd missed. The narrow entrance was to a car park positioned below a walled village.

"Thank God," Jade said when a parking attendant stepped in front of the car, preventing Freya from blasting up the lane and running over meandering tourists.

"We're here." Freya grinned at Jade and kissed her cheek. She turned off the engine and stepped out.

The car started to roll backwards.

"I don't think we can park here," Lena said, ratcheting up the handbrake.

"Just get out while you still have your soul," Jade said.

Lena climbed out over the driver's seat. "I told you not to let her drive."

YALE SAT OPPOSITE Karen at a table covered in a white linen cloth, set out for six with square blue-and-white porcelain plates. They were outside on a long and narrow terrace at the five-star Auberge de l'Ange. The air was still, and the sun would have burnt them in minutes if not for the protection of a patio umbrella.

"What time were you expecting her?" he asked, glancing down at his Rolex.

Karen offered a pseudo-friendly smile. "Twenty minutes ago, but she's usually late. Give her ten more, then I'll go look for her."

Karen fidgeted in her seat and picked up her phone to make a call. Yale half listened while looking out at the view from the terrace. A waiter was shifting the umbrella to keep the table shaded.

They were positioned high above a valley, which offered stunning views of white limestone cliffs and woodlands. The cliffs were scarred where bauxite had been mined over a century ago, while on the lower coulee was a field of sunflowers with their heads facing north, defying the urban myth that they tracked the sun.

"Are you ready to order?" the waiter asked.

"We are still expecting others," Yale answered.

The man frowned vehemently and Yale wondered where someone could learn how to do that. He'd been to Les Baux before but that was perhaps seven hundred years ago. Of course, not as Yale, and Lilith didn't bother to remember who it had been occupying back then.

Karen put her phone down. She picked up a glass of rosé wine and took a delicate sip. "I'm sorry for the change in venue, and I appreciate you making a detour from Avignon to be here."

Yale touched her hand where it lay on the table. "Not at all. This is a charming place, and what an exquisite view." He focused on Karen rather than the scenery to his right. "I take it Freya has a home here?"

Karen withdrew her hand. "Yes. She uses it in the summer."

"And where does she live?" He already knew the answer to the questions but wanted to see how Karen reacted. He leaned back. She was attractive in her own way, but not his type. Not even Lilith's type. There might be an advantage to charming her, but it was clear that couldn't be easily done.

"Norway," Karen said.

"I know the country well. Whereabouts?"

"The Nordfjord region."

"Big area." He decided to step things up a bit. This luncheon was likely to be the only opportunity he'd get to gather first-hand information from Freya's most trusted confidante. He found that meeting people in person was always the best way to assess them. "So how is it you're able to carry a firearm?"

Karen blinked but her expression didn't change.

He shifted to one side as the waiter placed a basket of bread and black olives on the table. "Come on, the weapon is easy to see. You can't just be an assistant to Miss Rykkel."

"You're observant," Karen said, glancing at her phone again.

"Let me guess. You work for a government agency. Part of Freya's security?"

"Let's change the subject to the Harmoni Foundation. I was wondering why you're so interested in the position as chairman."

Yale smiled and poured himself a glass of water. "Of course. I can't say I'm that interested. It just seemed Freya was in a bind, and I could offer my assistance. Managing investment funds is something I do in my sleep." He could tell Karen was not buying his answer. Her expression didn't changed and she stared blankly at him.

"Okay, well, if I'm truthful, and I rarely am," he joked, but she didn't laugh, "I wanted to get to know Freya as well. In business, connections in high places have advantages. I understand she is one of Europe's largest landowners."

Yale smiled, watching Karen's surprise at his inside knowledge. It had taken a lot of data mining, using back doors into local government systems to discover this fact, and in the process he'd worked out five of her aliases.

"Why do you think that?" Karen asked, while glancing towards the open doors of the terrace and the main entrance.

He laughed. "I don't think it. But I apologise, I must know everything about, well everything. It's a useful trait when managing investments. You can't predict the future if you don't know the present."

"I see." Karen's phone rang and she answered it.

Yale popped a black olive into his mouth, then spat the pit out over the balcony so it bounced off the Roman tiled roof below them.

Karen ended her call and lifted up a slim brown leather briefcase. She pulled out a tablet and a folder containing the agreement they were meant to ratify. "Freya will be here in a moment."

"It'll be nice to see her again." He stroked his short beard, wondering if he should waggle his eyebrows. "I'm surprised she's unattached."

"Look, Mr Garrett, I must insist we stay focused on the Foundation. I want to get this resolved. And Freya, well, let's say she has her mind on other things." She unlocked the tablet. "And thanks for providing the hardcopy."

"No worries." He drummed his fingers on the side of his glass. *Maybe I should find a quiet island somewhere. No . . . I've been delaying for too long.* Lilith wondered if it should subsume Karen. *No, the fact Freya is ridiculously late means her security agent doesn't have her confidence.* It was annoying to Lilith that it been rejected by the Valkyrie's body when they first met. *There was a discord there. Something incomplete. But if it had worked I wouldn't be chasing after the damn wings a millennium later.*

He sighed, and Karen glanced at him before returning to her tablet. There was no way Freya still had the wings. Everything Yale had found out indicated she was on her last legs. She needed them to save herself, and if she had them she would've used them by now.

JADE FELT LIKE she'd been spun in a rock polisher. Freya's driving, combined with the noise from the car and the radio had pounded her senses. She filled her lungs with the clean air of the Alpilles Mountains. Serenity in the enveloping heat and allure of her surroundings allowed her to relax. She looked at Freya and couldn't help but smile. *I know there are no absolutes, but she is perfection.*

Freya was in a friendly discussion with the attendant, and when they finished, the man got into their car and drove off.

"He is parking it for me." Freya took Jade's arm.

"How do you charm people so easily?"

"You should know that. You are my main victim."

"You might have to remind me."

Freya kissed her quickly. "Come on, attention-seeker. Talk and walk."

"I'll catch you up. WC," Lena called to them.

As they entered through a postern into the village, Jade noticed how many people stopped and stole glances at them. Only a few were discreet. It reminded her of a school trip she went on when she was in sixth form. The old Italian men would blatantly ogle them everywhere they went. She decided to make them her point of interest, rather than the places they were visiting, by taking pictures and asking them a few questions. It became her trip project, entitled "Famous Monuments and Perverts of Italy." Jade's language teacher at the time wasn't too pleased and he gave her an incomplete. So she published it on social media, drawing notable traffic, as well as an email request from the Italian Tourist Board to remove it.

Once inside the citadel, a path of *pavé calcaire* cut between stone buildings containing stores, cafés, and restaurants. Most of the shops were selling tacky tourist gifts, but a few offered traditional crafts. In these, the artisans themselves looked to be left over from the Middle Ages.

An elderly woman sitting outside a santon shop stood as they approached. She dropped the tiny clothes she was making for the small clay figurines and rushed towards Freya.

"Comtessa!" She bowed her head and exchanged three cheek kisses with Freya. They conversed for a few moments, augmented with smiles and nods. Jade could only recognise some of the words as they spoke. She guessed they must be using a dialect of Occitan.

When they were done, this maker of very small clothes turned to Jade. Her smile exposed a missing front tooth. She must have been in her nineties. Lifting up Jade's hand in her leathery fingers, she said, "Keep Alix safe and happy." She released Jade's hand, tipped her head, and went back to sewing a blue ribbon onto a minute red vest.

Freya faced Jade, encircled Jade's forearm with her fingers, and slid them down to her wrist. Jade couldn't read her and waited to see her intent. As Freya smiled a tear broke free.

"Are you okay?" Jade asked.

Freya kissed her softly. "I'm just so happy to be here with you. It's an old dream of mine."

"How so?" Jade asked, but Freya just leaned in to kiss her.

They separated to the sound of Lena yelling, "What are you gawking at!"

Freya and Jade looked at a group American tourists wearing the same T-shirts.

"Stop with the kissing. You're making everyone jealous." Lena shoved them with a palm on their backs. "*Marchez!* Let's get to the restaurant for the *réunion de merde.*"

Freya laughed as Lena steered them forward, forcing visitors to move out of their way. She then pushed between them to take the lead.

Brightly glazed pottery caught Jade's eye as they went by another shop. She felt the desire to get Freya a gift, without knowing why or what Freya could possibly want.

Freya took her hand and slowed her pace. It was clear she was not eager to get to the restaurant. Jade couldn't blame her; she also wasn't keen to confront Karen again.

"So you're a countess?"

Freya hesitated. "I guess I should explain that." She squeezed Jade's hand. "You will not bolt on me?"

"Why would you think I'd do that?"

"Well, I am not exactly a normal everyday person." Freya's Norwegian accent had become stronger.

"I'm not going anywhere."

"Okay, then . . . so, this comtessa thing. Well, years ago, I was Comtessa de Baux. Baux is a canton of France. It's not big, but it's pretty important. Anyway, I gave up the title, and it followed a male bloodline, until not that long ago. When that bloodline ended, the title fell back to me." She bumped shoulders with Jade. "You didn't bolt."

"No." Jade hesitated for a moment. "How did you get the title to start with?"

"That is the thing I'm worried you might bolt from."

"Don't be silly."

"For now, is it okay if I just say it really doesn't matter anymore?"

"Sure." Jade was confused, but it was clear Freya had subjects she didn't like talking about; one was her past. But Jade's journalist instinct caused her to ask more. "The old santon woman called you Alix?"

Freya cleared her throat. "Oh, a nickname from a while back."

Their hands swung together as they walked through alternating shadows and bright sunshine.

Jade wanted to learn more, so using a different tack, she focused on the here and now. "So what does being Comtessa de Baux, mean?"

"Well, it is mostly an archaic title, but I'm the landowner, although it is under *la juridiction de la République Française.*"

"Heck, you own this place?"

Freya shrugged. "Blood is thick here, so traditions are strong and go back many centuries."

"But you're Norwegian royalty as well?" When Freya didn't respond, Jade glanced to see her frowning. She realised she was crossing boundaries again. "I'm sorry, you don't need to answer. I'm being nosy." Old fears of the past had landed on Jade's shoulders. *God, why am I drilling her? I'm such a plebe.*

Freya stopped, turned to her, and took Jade's cheeks in her hands. "Hey, you. We are together. You can ask me what you like. Just be a little patient. I'm sometimes not sure how to answer. Or even if it's safe to."

Jade tried to nod her head with Freya holding it.

Freya squeezed her cheeks harder and laughed. "You look like a chipmunk."

"I thought I was a fox."

"You've been demoted after criticizing my driving." Freya shrugged. "Shit happens."

"You were trying to execute me in that red guillotine of a car."

"I was not. Maybe you are just too old for excitement."

They passed a shop selling Savon de Marseille, and Freya picked up a bar of the soap, sniffed it, then presented it to Jade.

"I'm not too old to want to be older." The scent of lavender tickled Jade's nostrils.

"Maybe you want me to bring your slippers and a blanket?"

Jade pretended to consider this by placing her fingers on her chin. "That does sound cosy."

Freya yanked Jade away from the display of soaps. "Now stop and give up. The first rule of being a comtessa's girlfriend is to always agree with her and praise her prowess at driving. Maybe that's two rules."

"You're an excellent driver. In fact, so good you don't really need to practise anymore."

"That's more like it! I think . . . oh wait . . . you're too clever for me." She laughed.

They carried on a few more steps, then Freya gestured to a side lane, which ran under the ruins of a vaulted arch. "Let's go this way."

"Do we have time?"

"No, but I want to show you something." Freya winked.

"Where are you going?" Lena called to them. She was ahead, but now walking backwards while still heading towards the restaurant.

"Won't be long!" Freya yelled, darting down the narrow passage with Jade in tow.

It led to a courtyard. To one side was a church, while opposite, after a stone wall, Jade could see the valley floor many hundreds of feet below.

"Beautiful, isn't it?" Freya made a beeline for the wall and leant against it. "I used to come here a lot and sit for hours."

The view cut along the narrow fields towards the Camargue and the Mediterranean Sea. Freya's hair was blowing around her face. The strands reflected the sunlight, causing the ends to glow.

Jade scanned for sniper placements in the steeple of the church and the ridge of the low cliff. She realised what she was doing and turned back to see Freya climb the on wall and swing her legs over.

"Eir, get down. It's not safe!" Jade screamed.

Freya froze, crouching on the wall like a cat caught in the act of licking butter. Her face had gone pale and her mouth gaped. She tilted her head and then jumped down onto the cobbled courtyard.

"What did you say?" Freya asked. Her legs were shaking and she took hold of the wall to steady herself.

Jade ran over and wrapped an arm around her, but Freya spun behind Jade and pressed her against the wall. She pushed Jade's head down and backcombed the hair on her lower neck.

"What are you doing?" Jade asked, completely perplexed.

"You have a scar . . ." Freya said.

"I have a few. Syria, remember?" Jade turned to face her.

"I knew it was you," she said in a trembling voice. She slammed into Jade and held her so tightly Jade couldn't breathe. She was crying, wetting Jade's cheeks.

Jade was worried for Freya's sanity; she seemed to be having a breakdown. "It's okay." She let Freya calm down in her arms. She wondered if her medical condition was affecting her.

"I didn't know for sure." Freya placed her forehead against Jade's.

"Know what?"

"It doesn't matter, you don't remember."

"Remember what?"

Freya twisted in Jade's arms and wrapped them around her. "What's your first memory?"

Lena was calling for them from somewhere behind.

"I . . ." Jade had to think hard on this. "I don't know. Actually, I don't remember anything before my seventeenth birthday, but I was told it might come back to me."

"Why can't you remember?"

"My head was hit pretty hard in Syria."

Freya frowned, turned, and pushed her fingers through Jade's hair. "It seems so. But I don't understand how you're here. It was so long ago."

Lena trotted up to them. "Karen is waiting for you, and I'm not going in by myself."

THE MEAL HAD been uncomfortable. Nothing flowed. Not the wine, conversation, or service. Jade's thoughts were also stuttering. *I don't remember meeting Freya before Somerset House. How does she know me?*

Jade picked at her lunch, feeling like an interloper. As a journalist, she'd been forced to dine in appalling circumstances to get a story. Today, in what should be affable company, she was on edge.

Lena fidgeted in her seat and picked up the bottle of rosé wine, filled her glass to the rim, and drank half in one gulp. Henri, sitting next to Karen, raised an eyebrow at this. He'd arrived late, and with the exception of small talk, had said little.

Lena lifted the glass to take another slurp, when Jade pressed two fingers on its base.

"Can you drive later?" Jade asked.

Lena's eyes brightened behind heavily mascaraed eyelashes. "Sure."

"Lena, you don't need to stay for this," Karen said.

"*Dieu merci!*" Lena said.

"Jade, you're welcome to leave as well." Karen's tone indicated it wasn't really a suggestion.

Freya took Jade's hand. "She'll stay."

Before they entered the restaurant, Freya had explained she needed to sign an agreement that allowed Yale to take over as chair of the Harmoni Foundation. Jade knew this had to do with Freya's illness.

"*Je me casse,*" Lena said and slid her chair back so quickly it made a chalkboard-scraping shrill on the tiles. She leapt up and darted out of the restaurant without a backwards glance.

After this, the topic of discussion became the Foundation. Jade listened while picking the label off a Perrier bottle with her fingernail, creating a decimation of paper fragments on the tablecloth.

"I don't understand why this is taking so long," Freya complained, taking a pinch of the ripped-up Perrier label and sprinkling it on Jade's shoulder. "You are making confetti, for a wedding?" she whispered to Jade.

Jade hid her laugher behind a tight smile, but some must have escaped through her eyes.

"You know in Las Vegas"—Freya cupped her hand over her mouth, directing her voice to Jade—"Elvis is alive, and he can marry you as you drive through. Ten minutes tops." She punched Jade's shoulder, clicked her tongue, and winked.

"That's not very romantic," Jade whispered back.

"Elvis not romantic? You philistine. That's it, it's over." She laughed, brushing the confetti from Jade, like she was clawing away a horde of spiders.

"Can I have your attention?" Karen reprimanded as if they were schoolgirls.

Yale chuckled. "I want to sit between them next time."

"Joyce, please continue." Karen turned her propped-up tablet to face Freya.

Freya's lawyer and a woman whom Jade assumed worked for Yale were on a conference link from New York.

"Freya, we have to make sure the governance is contiguous," Joyce said. "Are you happy with the altered clauses?"

"I prefer the original Santa," Freya said seriously.

Yale smirked. "Me too, with the green coat." He signalled the waiter and ordered a Coca-Cola.

"Joyce, just run through the changes," Karen said. "They've had too much sugar."

Yale got up and leaned with his hands on the back of his chair. "We could just sign it in principle. I don't have a lot of time. Let's worry about the details later."

The suggestion set alarm bells ringing in Jade's mind. She never trusted anyone she couldn't read. Well, Freya was the one exception. But this Yale appeared aloof. It was like he was playing a game and everything around him was inconsequential. Jade wondered, not for the first time, why he was involved.

"Good plan, pass me a pen." Freya reached for the paper copy of the agreement.

"No!" both Joyce and Karen called out.

Yale excused himself and walked to one end of the terrace to answer a call.

"Listen, Freya, we have to be careful. You had all the authority as the chairwoman. There is a lot at stake," Karen said.

"A lot of cake? Where?" Freya glanced around before slouching in her chair.

Karen rolled her eyes up as if trying to find the bird that had pooped on her. "God, Freya. Please cooperate for once."

"I do not think I want to."

Freya's reaction was juvenile, but she'd been acting oddly the whole day. Karen had told Jade that Freya had not grown up emotionally. At the time, she'd dismissed the comment, but now she could see there was some truth to it.

"Look, Freya, this has to be resolved. You wouldn't see the specialists I asked you to. So this leaves us with sorting out what comes after." Karen turned to Henri and exchanged words Jade couldn't hear.

Freya closed her eyes. She let out a sigh before dropping her head. Her pallor worsening before Jade's eyes.

Jade grabbed Freya's hand and pivoted towards her. "What's wrong?"

Freya spoke in muted Norwegian but then in English. "I hate this horrendous machinery that keeps the world turning. People know right from wrong. Why can't they just do it?"

"Let me help. Do you want me to take a look at this?"

Freya gave a nod.

Yale wandered back to their table and hovered around his chair.

"Yale, what are your plans for the Foundation?" Karen asked as he sat back down.

"Well, I suppose, cancel all the programmes and invest the capital in fossil fuels. Then in forty years when prices go ballistic, sell all the equity and retire to Greenland. It'll be smaller and the climate will be nicer then."

Karen and Henri turned to stare open-mouthed at Yale.

"What?" Yale laughed. "Don't tell me you've not bought land there yet?"

They continued to stare.

"Well, you should. It's a highly probable scenario. Climate change, I mean. I was joking about using the Foundation's endowment." He looked at Freya. "I'm already over-invested in non-renewables." He shuffled his chair up. "How much time does Miss Rykkel have anyway?" he asked with his chin on the table, his eyes glancing up to Karen.

"Stop!" Jade slammed her hand down, causing glasses to rattle and Yale's chin to bounce up. Everyone stared at her. "She is right here." She tried to rein in her emotions. "Karen, I'd like to review this agreement."

"That would just slow things down."

Freya sat at attention. "I trust Jade. Let her see it." She tried to take the papers from Karen, but she wouldn't let go. "*Stole på henne!*"

Henri whispered to Karen. She rubbed her temples and handed the papers to Jade.

"Give me a moment." Jade read through the dense print.

Freya draped her arms around Jade's shoulders, putting her lips next to Jade's ear, whispering as Jade tried to concentrate; Jade only half registered what she was saying.

I missed you dreadfully, when you disappeared—

Jade used her skills as a copy editor to speed read.

I don't know how I survived, all those years.

Freya toyed with the strands of Jade's hair around her ear.

Pretending in my dreams, you were near.

"Darling, let me read," Jade whispered, but Freya continued.

Now I only have your shadow and the sun is low.

Freya's breath tickled, and Jade twitched her head away. "Princess, please."

My fate is sealed without you, or do I risk your soul?

Jade felt a soft kiss on her neck as Freya's final whisper drifted away.

But even in this final twilight—Jeg forelskelse, as I did, so long ago.

Jade finished at page thirty-three, focused back to the table and felt embarrassed; everyone had been watching them. She glanced at Freya, wondering about the poem she had being whispering, and what "*Jeg forelskelse*" meant. She filed her thoughts and reengaged with the agreement.

Most of it was boilerplate, but on page thirty-three financials were listed. Jade scanned the sums. The numbers were in billions and they didn't add up until she noticed that Freya provided a third of the fund's annual income. She turned the page over to see sixteen charter items that defined how the fund was controlled. It was clear these had been edited to put more power with the board.

She tried to stay calm on the outside.

"Where did this physical copy come from?" She waggled the page in her hand.

"Yale provided it," Karen said.

Jade ran her fingers through her hair. "You can't agree to this, Freya."

"What?" Karen's face tightened.

"I'm glad this is now resolved," Freya said. "Jade, let's go."

Jade felt sick to her stomach. Freya entrusting her with a decision that involved billions of dollars.

"Freya. Be serious, this is critical. Do you know how many people have worked on this?" Karen turned to Jade. "You have no right to tell Freya what to do."

Yale lounged in his chair with his head back, tipping ice cubes from his glass onto his lips before taking one into his mouth and chewing it.

"If there is a concern I want to hear it," Joyce said.

Karen seemed to refocus. "Very well. Jade, go ahead."

Jade cleared her throat. "I would say . . . it's fundamentally flawed but if you want a reason why she can't sign it . . ." She leaned closer to the tablet. "Joyce, how many sentences are in item thirteen on page thirty-four? The one that starts with . . ." She read out the first line.

"Eleven, why?" Joyce said after a few moments.

"The copy that's here to be signed has twenty-five." She glanced at Yale, who winked at her. "They mean that the chairman can overrule the board on funding decisions. But more concerning is a proviso that Freya's estate would need to be sold to support restructuring of the fund, when Freya is no longer alive and contributing. I take it to mean that places like this"—Jade pointed towards the vista to her left—"would be up for grabs by anyone who could afford them."

"That's what we are trying to avoid." Karen grabbed the page. "It doesn't say that. The authority is kept with the board. The fund is rebalanced." Her face dropped as she read. "This is not the version I—"

"Also, the chairman and the board have first option on purchasing." Jade pointed to the line on the page. "But, I suspect, only Mr Garrett could afford such things."

The tablet squealed from the volume of Joyce's exclamations. "I've not seen those amendments."

Jade watched the screen as Joyce turned to the woman beside her and they had a conversation on mute.

Yale tapped his teeth with the corner of his glass. "Those are edits from my lawyers. They were sent by email a few days ago."

Karen went stiff, took all the papers, and aligned them in her hands, then tapped them against the table. "We must void this," she said, putting down the papers. "I don't know what game you're playing at, Mr Garrett, but this is unacceptable."

Yale shrugged. "The clauses are sensible and ensure projects are not cut. But I'm not clear why you haven't seen this version or who is at fault—"

"Not us, that's for sure," Karen interrupted.

Yale stood. "This is not something I need to debate, and I'm late." He bowed his head. "It has been a pleasure, Freya." He looked directly at Jade, seeming to size her up for the first time. He then flicked on a smile, turned, reached into his pocket, pulled out a pair of headphones, and walked out of the restaurant.

KAREN WATCHED HIM go. God, if Jade hadn't checked it.

She sighed. "This is my fault. I'm sorry I kept you, Freya. I didn't know he would—"

"It doesn't matter," Freya said before turning to Jade. "Let's go. I'm not feeling well."

Jade stood immediately, offering her hand to Freya, who took it and rose slowly, then went to stand behind Jade.

Karen watched as they exchanged whispers. *They're like lovers.* She gasped at the realisation. Jade had protected her, and now the two were huddled together. *When did I fall so far from her grace?*

Henri stood and patted her on the shoulder. "I'll report in. Then we can go to Freya's."

"You think we are still invited to stay?" Karen asked.

Henri shrugged. "She just doesn't want to deal with these things. Let's discuss the fallout in the car."

Karen watched him go. She put her head in her hands and rubbed her temples. It was part of her training to question herself. *Why did this go wrong? Why have I failed her so badly? But also, when in the hell did I start putting my job before her?*

Who was she kidding? She just didn't want to face up to losing Freya and she was focusing on the wrong things.

JADE FOUND LENA in a small square near the entrance to the village. She was perched on a rectangular plinth, sitting cross-legged while eating a chocolate crêpe. The stone was as tall as Jade and might have supported a cross in the distant past.

"How did you get up there?" Jade asked.

"I had some help." Lena pointed to three teenage boys sitting in front of a pâtisserie. "We can go?"

"Yeah," Jade said.

Lena leapt down and they walked toward the car park. Freya looped her arm around Jade's.

"Are you feeling better?" Jade asked.

Freya nudged Jade to the left so she almost collided with a young man taking a picture.

"Your walking is as dangerous as your driving." Jade laughed and nudged her back, causing Freya to collide with Lena, who was trying to offer her some of her crêpe.

Freya halted briefly and held her hair out of the way as she took a bite.

As they continued through the packed lanes, Jade's thoughts went back to lunch, and she wondered if she would see Yale so she could kick him in the balls. "I can't believe the nerve of Yale, trying to sneak in changes like that."

"He wasn't."

"Sorry?"

Freya stared at Jade for a moment. "I deleted the email he had sent to Karen."

Jade stopped. "You did what?"

"A few days ago. It's not hard." Freya put on the voice of a cartoon mouse. "Scroll, scroll, 'Revised contract from Yale the leech to Karen,' touch, delete, gone."

"Um . . . so, that's why Joyce and Karen hadn't seen it. You deleted it."

"That's what I said, wasn't it? I know my English can be ignominious. Anyway, she should not have lent me her phone. She knows I hate those things."

"Wow." Jade let out a small laugh. "You're tricky. But why did you do it?"

Freya lifted one shoulder and let it drop. "Everyone thinks they have something to lose unless they control my affairs. It's been like that forever. So I let them. It keeps them out of my hair, but then I have to undermine them at the last minute." She bit her lip while looking into Jade's eyes. "I always have an escape route planned. It's how I survive."

Jade grinned back. "Do you have an escape route for chocolate?"

"Huh?"

Jade rubbed off a smear of chocolate from Freya's cheek.

"Oh . . . yes, of course." Freya's eyes were smiling. "You're part of my chocolate-removal plan . . . and my not being-trapped-in-hell plan."

Jade was not sure what she meant by the last comment.

At the car park, they waited for Lena, who'd insisted she go with the attendant to fetch the car.

"Can I ask you something?"

"No," Freya said. "Ask me anything."

Jade tucked Freya's hair around her ear. "Can you tell me what's wrong with you?"

Freya rubbed her eyes and slid her hand onto her cheek. She looked like a child with a toothache. "You know, I've played out that conversation over and over again and it never ends well. When I think—" She frantically waved her hands around her face, then stopped. "There was a bee."

A sinkhole developed in Jade's stomach. She wondered if there had actually been a bee or if Freya just needed a way to avoid giving her an answer. *Is she ever going to share anything important with me?*

Freya took Jade's hand. "A bee might be a good way to explain. Why do you think that a bee does what it does every day, tirelessly without question, never stopping or giving up?"

It was a good question. "I don't know, because it needs to feed the hive, I suppose. If it didn't it wouldn't exist."

"That's a logical reason, but not one filled with life." Freya looked beyond Jade at the vista of ancient mountains. "The point of me asking was not to find an answer. It was to make you understand that you don't need to ask why everything does something. You just need to embrace it as part of moments in your life. Well, that is how I look at it. But I was never one for logic."

They swivelled their heads to see a convertible coming up the steep hill to where they waited.

"You're letting Lena drive instead of me?"

"Well, I want thousands of moments with you. If I let you drive, we might only have one."

Freya fluffed Jade's fringe. "You say the sweetest things, *ma belle*." She gave her a quick kiss. "But I'm afraid"—she grinned—"you've been demoted to hamster for not letting me drive."

"A hamster . . ."

"Yes." Freya poked Jade's chest.

"That's pretty bad, isn't it?" Jade gave Freya a sideways smile.

"Oh yes, but you only have yourself to blame."

The car roared past them and it seemed Lena wasn't going to stop, but she pulled up just beyond where they stood and beeped the horn.

Freya jumped back, taking hold of Jade's forearm. "The youth today have no respect for the passed," she yelled in the direction of the car.

Lena beeped the horn two more times.

"Come on, thousand moments girl," Freya said. "Let's go make some."

"THAT WAS FUN," Yale said on the phone while waiting in a queue at Nîmes Airport. He'd called Nancy in New York as soon as he was in the terminal building.

"You have a warped idea of fun. It seemed like a waste of time to me and I don't understand why they didn't have the revised version," Nancy said.

"Ah, well, it doesn't matter. They wouldn't have agreed to it."

"What? So why are we putting effort into this—No wait . . . This isn't another one of your personal conquests?"

Lilith laughed. "You could say that."

"Jesus, Yale, even you can't charm a lesbian to the dark side."

"And you're case in point." He laughed. "But you misunderstand. This isn't about sex."

"Okay, good, no new lawsuits coming our way, then."

"Afraid not."

"So why are we messing around with this Harmoni Foundation?"

"I needed to see who Miss Rykkel's people were and how they operated."

"Oh, great, so you're being your usual troll self. Why?" She dragged out the last word.

"Let's just say it's to do with a long-term investment that's about to expire."

"That sounds better. If there's a bonus in it, I'm in."

"Listen, have the MR team create a profile and update stream on the Jade woman. What's her last name?"

"It's Jade Platt. She's a photojournalist."

"You know her?"

"Only from when I worked for the Freelance Press. She's impossibly brave and sexy as hell. She went low-key after being injured on assignment."

Yale moved forward in the queue, sliding his cabin bag with his foot. "That fits. When are you flying to London?" he asked, while smiling at the man checking boarding cards.

"Well, I'm booked for Thursday, for the meeting with Dranic Energy. You need me to change my plans?"

"Come a day earlier. I'll sort out a room for you at the Park Lane Hemmington."

"Okay, but why?"

"I'll need your assistance with Miss Platt, since I'm no longer in her good books."

But I am in their God books.

After the call was finished, it scratched his beard, knowing it wouldn't have to do that for much longer.

Somerset Girl

A THICK CLOUD of chalk dust followed the classic Peugeot as it drove alongside sparse fields of grass and young cedars. Jade sat, folded into the rear bench seat, with Freya's head resting against her chest. They were en route to Freya's home in the mountains, and Jade could smell rosemary, thyme, and lavender in the air; a combination that was accordant with the floral scent of Freya's hair.

Jade tried to untangle her thoughts, but they were tied in a Gordian knot and she had no sword to cut it free. To her, Freya was like a land flooded so only the peaks of the mountains were visible; it was impossible to imagine what was submerged below.

She needed to phone Max and ask him for some time off. She wasn't sure how that would go down, but it really didn't matter what the answer would be.

The radio was playing a British indie track and Jade was drawn to the lyrics.

> *There's markings, on your upper thighs.*
> *Those markings, express your inner eyes.*
> *If you let me, I'd make you my own.*
> *But when I ask, you keep us alone.*
>
> *I lost you, while I was standing there.*
> *I told you, while you were unaware.*
> *My ocean, caused me to forget,*
> *I found you, as your summer sets.*

Jade remembered Freya as a bundle of white feathers in the courtyard of Somerset House as the chorus kicked in.

> *In reverse spotlight, I lament in helpless hindsight,*
> *And I pretend I'm with my Somerset girl.*
> *In a world that isn't, I forget the bars of my prison,*
> *And I pretend I'm with my Somerset girl.*

Lena parked in front of a dilapidated farmhouse overlooking a small unpopulated valley.

Freya hadn't stirred and Jade brushed her cheek. "Wake up, sleeping beauty."

KAREN SAT IN the passenger seat as Henri drove, listening to the car's speaker phone.

"This is very disappointing," The commodore's harsh voice boomed through the vehicle's audio system.

"Commodore, all is being done to resolve the situation," Karen said in an even tone.

"Look, I have the offices of two governments asking for updates. They're viewing it as unacceptable that we've not yet been able to secure Sunniva's land. We need results."

Karen clenched her jaw. She hated how the commodore always used Freya's historical name, Sunniva, rather than her present-day one, making her a thing rather than flesh and blood.

"As I recall," he continued, "There were two steps. First, put in place a new charter and chairman for the Harmoni Foundation, and second, ensure Sunniva's land falls under national ownership when she dies. Can you explain why you've made no progress?"

"Sir, you have to appreciate these are not easy topics for Miss Rykkel. We've been exploring all possible cures first and we'll continue to do that." Karen muted the call for a moment to gather herself. A tear had broken free.

Henri handed her a tissue from the central console. "I can answer if you want."

She pushed his hand away. "No, I'm dealing with it." She returned to the call. "Getting Freya to accept her condition and even cooperate has been difficult. And since Mr Garrett didn't work out, I'll have to revisit the issues of the foundation once she has settled back in Norway later this week. It'll be easier there, without the distractions."

"Distractions? What distractions?"

"She is currently . . ." Karen tried to find the right word, but then gave up. "She's spending time with a reporter, Jade Platt."

"What? A reporter. Why are you allowing this?"

"I haven't been. But Freya has her ways—"

"Hold on. What paper does she work for?"

"The *United Herald.*"

In the background, Karen could hear the commodore asking, someone new called Fredricks, for a profile of Jade.

The phone went quiet as Henri pulled into the car park of a small grocery store, and it was a couple of minutes before a boyish voice reeled off a stream of information. "Jade Platt, female, British, twenty-eight, copy editor for the *United Herald*, in 2013 was a photojournalist for the same paper. Prior to this she was a freelance war correspondent for three years. An Oxford graduate with a first in English Literature. No father on record. Mother registered as a missing person in 2004. Notable Events: July 2013, injured on assignment in Syria. Rescued with MSF hostages after ransom was paid by the Harmoni Foundation. But, more interesting is the fact that there's no data before 2000, other than a birth record."

"Sir, I looked at this a year ago. She's no threat, except possibly to herself," Karen said.

"Is this a false identity?" the commodore suggested.

"I considered that. But I don't think so. It looks like a pre-Internet black spot, that's all."

"There should be something more than just a birth record. Fredricks, take a look. And Henri, Karen, get this assignment resolved by next week. There can be no more pussyfooting around. I'm keeping the bureaucrats at bay for now, but soon I'll have to give them direct access."

An image of an ill Freya, withering in government offices, being forced to sign away her rights, her legacy, and what was left of her life flicked into Karen's mind. Freya would never agree. It was a miracle at all that she'd given concessions in the distant past. She knew it would be hard to keep the officials away; both countries could lose significant percentages of their GDP if things weren't handled correctly.

"Sir, it's critical they don't get involved," Henri said. "If Sunniva feels she is being put in a corner, I'm sure she will lash out by using her constitutional powers."

"We can't have her doing that. Besides, no one would accept her authority," the commodore said.

"I think, if tested, she would win," Karen chimed in.

"We have looked at that scenario," Fredricks interrupted. "There's a high probability of Sunniva dichotomizing her entitled regions into independent constitutional monarchical states and this would be sanctioned by the operating judicial systems, creating a world event without precedent."

"Fredricks, don't speak unless you simplify!" The commodore's voice reverberated throughout the car.

"She'd be successful in separating her land," Karen said.

"There's no time for her to do that," the commodore said after a few moments.

"But there's time for her to establish a consort," Karen said.

"A consort? Explain, Lieutenant."

"Sir, there's time for her to marry and have her spouse inherit, with the same privileges."

"I thought she was—"

"Same sex marriages are legal in Norway and France," Karen said.

"You think this reporter, Platt, is a possible . . . fiancée?"

"Maybe," Karen admitted.

"End it. I want the two separated." He paused. "And I want daily reports on your progress. Same time tomorrow." The call was disconnected.

"I don't think we should send Jade packing," Henri said.

Karen rubbed her temple. "I think we should, but for a different reason."

"What reason?"

"If Jade gets more attached to Freya . . ." She wiped her eyes. "Well, I don't think she'll survive when Freya is gone. She's too broken."

THE FARMHOUSE WAS small and mundane; a structure of rendered clay with weather-worn shutters that were closed on all windows and doors.

Freya went to the middle shutter, yanked it open, and folded the panel to expose a cherry wood door with peeling varnish. She reached into a crevice and retrieved a key, but then leapt back and screamed. A snake dropped from the hole and slithered towards her.

"Get it away!" Freya scrambled in the direction of the car.

Jade caught the snake by its tail and held it at arm's length. "It's okay. It's just a grass snake."

"Take it away, Kari!"

Jade walked to the edge of the curtilage, dropped it, and watched it slither into the dry, yellowing grass. She wondered why Freya had said *Kari. It likely means "quickly" or something in Norwegian.*

When Freya was sure it was gone, she jumped down from the bonnet of the car.

"A snake? You're sure?"

"A harmless grass snake."

Freya's breathing slowed. "I thought it was something else."

"A viper? They are very rare and shy."

Freya's complexion was paler than normal. "No, no. Something a lot worse."

"It's gone now." Jade went to hold her, but Freya held her hand up, bent over, and vomited.

Jade had an iron stomach; whether it was a decaying corpse or dealing with the ill, she was never fazed. She put this down to her general despondency to most things around her. She had always been disconnected from her emotions, her feelings to others. However, with Freya, her emotions flowed like a cascading waterfall. She stood beside Freya and held her hair out of the way while Freya continued to throw up her lunch.

Lena had collected two backpacks from the car and was now digging in one, before retrieving a T-shirt. When it looked like Freya was finished being sick, Lena offered the shirt.

Freya took the shirt and wiped her face and mouth with it. "Sorry . . ."

"Let's get you inside." Jade started to take Freya towards the house.

Lena stopped her. "That's not her house. It's up there." She pointed along a narrow footpath, which cut through the trees. "That's just where the key is kept."

"How far is it?"

"Ten minutes or so," Lena said.

"Can't we drive there?"

"The road has to go around . . ." Lena waved her finger at the valley and ridge behind the old house. "It takes a long time. This is shorter."

"I'm not dead yet. You can talk to me," Freya said before stooping and throwing up again. When done, she straightened and wiped her face on the T-shirt again.

Lena handed her a bottle of water, and in exchange, Freya gave her the key she'd been gripping. "In case I don't make it."

Lena put the key in her backpack and slung it onto her shoulder while Jade had an arm around Freya's waist. As they started towards the path, Freya struggled; her legs unable to carry her full weight.

"I'll piggyback you," Jade said.

Freya didn't protest when Jade bent down to lift her.

"Get Alice," Freya called to Lena, who was already ahead of them.

"Alice?" Jade asked with her arms around Freya's legs.

"A friend. She has the most beautiful eyes you'll ever see."

Jade felt a twang of jealousy, but she knew she was being foolish.

The trees offered some shade from the late afternoon sun, but still Jade was sweating with the effort of carrying Freya. Drifting into a dark mood, she started to question everything. She wondered if Freya ever intended to tell her anything personal. From last night, to the drama of the morning, they had promised to stay together, but maybe that was just an emotional spike. She tried to catch herself, remembering that Freya was okay and Alice was likely to be an ugly prune with blackened teeth from chewing cigars.

Freya was very quiet, with her cheek pressed against Jade's temple. Freya's arms tightened around her. She was apparently reading her mind.

"There won't be any room for self-doubt later."

"What do you mean?"

"You'll have to be stronger than you've ever been."

"What later?"

"After this." Freya arched her arm away from Jade's collarbone like she was a ringleader presenting the next act.

"You mean the slope gets steeper?" Jade asked.

"Put me down and take a break."

With bent knees, she let Freya stand and turned to see that her face was still pale. They sat on a nearby rock, in silence, listening to the rustle of leaves and noises from insects.

"I didn't think I would live forever," Freya said out of the blue.

Jade tried to speak but Freya put a hand over her mouth.

"I wish I'd known it was you when we met in London . . . but that's like wishing you hadn't eaten that extra donut. To fix problems not addressed in the past, you have to make sacrifices in the future."

"I don't understand," Jade said when Freya lowered her hand.

Freya closed her eyes tightly and bent forward as if riding out a wave of pain. After a moment she opened them and put on a brave smile. "I wish you could remember . . . I wouldn't need to explain and have you not believe me . . . That's another donut wish, I guess."

Jade uncurled Freya's fingers, touching each one, separating and examining them. "I wish you'd open up to me . . . That's not a donut wish by the way. It's a here and now." She was filled with anguish and tears were close by. In the last few days, she had been close to tears more times than she could remember. "Why won't you tell me? You're not well and I—"

"Hey." Freya pulled her close.

This is stupid. She is sick and I'm the one falling apart. I'm so utterly—

Freya yanked Jade's head upright and aligned it with her own. "Whatever you're thinking, Miss Platt, stop it. Because it'll be wrong."

"I'm sorry—"

"None of that." After a second, Freya sighed. "What am I going to do with you?" she said softly, looking into Jade's eyes like a doctor checking her reactions.

Whatever you want. Jade hoped that last thought hadn't slipped out.

Freya glanced over Jade's shoulder and smiled. "Alice!"

Jade turned to see the biggest eyes behind the longest lashes, topped by the bushiest ears.

Alice blinked and shuffled forward as Lena pulled on her bridle.

Jade stood and let out a cathartic yelp while helping Freya to rise. "She's an ass."

"She prefers the term *donkey*." Freya laughed. "Come on, get me on her."

Lena and Jade helped Freya onto Alice's back, almost catapulting her over the animal.

Lena handed the rein to Jade. "I'll go back to the car and get the rest of our stuff. Can you lead Alice to the house?"

"I suppose so."

Lena turned and scarpered off in the direction they had come before yelling back, "She'll only bite you if you are in reach of her mouth."

"Awesome," Jade muttered.

"Lead on, hamster," Freya commanded.

Jade tugged on the lead rope, and Alice jutted her head forward, trying to nip Jade's rear.

"What the heck!" She hopped forward, now keeping the rope at full length to stay well away from Alice's teeth.

Feeling like Joseph leading Mary to find an inn, Jade dragged the unpredictable donkey along the trail, and after ten minutes they passed between two dilapidated buildings. When they rounded the corner, Alice stopped.

Jade tried to pull her forward, but the donkey wouldn't budge. Alice made a swipe for Jade's thigh with teeth bared. Jade sidestepped the attack. "That thing's evil. What've I ever done to it?"

Freya slipped off her back and unclipped the lead rope. "She's envious. You have what she can't have." She patted Alice's neck. "Thank you. Now off you go."

"Envious?" The donkey wandered headed to stand in the shade of one of the ruined buildings.

"Mhm." Freya nodded slowly while looking Jade up and down. "You're strong and beautiful, and you're with me. So she wants to bite you."

"Great . . ." Jade offered Freya the crook of her arm.

"You should be pleased she's not my cat. Her teeth are even sharper." Freya slipped her arm around Jade's.

"Does everything of yours want to hurt me?"

"Of course, that's how it has to be." Freya gnashed her teeth at Jade.

Jade smiled. "You look silly." After a few steps she asked, "Do you feel better now?"

"A bit better. Maybe it was the car."

Jade knew she was lying. It was time to put an end to this. "How long?"

"Not far. My house is just on the other side of that wall—"

Jade gripped the side of Freya's top and spun her around. "You know what I mean," she said desperately, looking into Freya's blue eyes.

Freya blinked and shrugged.

"How long?" Jade whispered, her eyes moist with tears.

Freya said nothing for a long time, her eyes fixed on Jade's. As she turned away, she whispered, "Until this summer sets."

Hand of the Relic

SUNRISE AND SUNSET repeated until six winters had passed on the small island of Sellø. Knud waited, allowing the king to peer into the small opening. King Olaf Tryggvason had insisted he be the first to enter the cave after his men had broken through, but now he hesitated.

"Knud, go in front," Olaf ordered.

Knud hunched down and manoeuvred around of the king. His whale-oil lamp dangled from three chains held in his outstretched hand. He stepped carefully over the loose rocks until he was able to stand. The light from his lamp didn't extend far and the chamber appeared endless.

Something brushed by his leg. Raising his lamp, Knud tried to see what had gone past. The light from the tunnel entrance darkened a fleeting moment.

He paused, remembering Ylva's words. "Release Eir. She must be set free." He wondered if Eir's spirit had just flown past and escaped the cave, but then he recalled the rest of what he'd been told, and he relived that time by the river.

"She won't die, well, not like creatures of this earth," Ylva said, watching the clear, flowing water of the brook before them. "Knud." She poked his arm. "Are you going to carry me across?"

He raised one eyebrow. "No. It's time you overcame this fear of water."

He shoved her without warning and watched as Ylva fell face-first into the icy stream.

"You goat's turd!" Ylva screamed, raising herself on hands and knees. Her hair was soaked and being pulled by the current. "You . . ." She stared down at her wavering reflection in disbelief. *"Get me out!"*

She shoved herself up to stand. The front of her black woollen tunic was drenched. On the bank she raised a finger to Knud. "You're in so much trouble! That's no way to cure someone's fear." She huffed and puffed for a few more moments before growling, "Dung-pit *thrall*, build me a fire."

Knud did as she ordered, and they camped for the night. They had just finished eating a poor meal of dried mutton when he asked, "Why are you afraid of water?"

Ylva didn't answer straight away. She wore his cloak; her hair was twisted into a wet braid running down to her waist. She got up to rearrange her garment, which was drying by the fire between two sticks stuck into the ground. "Not the water, witless. My sisters."

"Sisters?" he asked, but really he wasn't that interested. Digging below the surface of Ylva gave him a headache.

Ylva spun on him. "Go back to scratching your ass and stop asking me questions."

"I never do that," Knud said.

"Picking your nose, then."

She had him there.

They'd been travelling together for more than a month, on boats, carts, by foot, and a long trip across the sea, before they arrived at the market town of Hedeby. It was here they parted company.

"Go to King Ethelred's court in Andover. Find the Scotian who makes claims on Norway. His name is Olaf Tryggvason. He'll want a saint. Tell him of Eir . . . No. I mean use the name she is known by, Sunniva. Tell him of her miracles."

"Andover?"

She paused and frowned. "You understand?"

Knud shook his head.

"Well, it doesn't matter. Just go while Olaf bows to your God."

Knud hesitated, not sure what she was saying. "Andover?"

"Yes, Andover. For *Helvíti*'s forsake. Just remember the words. Say them to the merchants at the dock." She took his hand and drew symbols on his palm. "Find a boat that will take you to Andover in Mercia." She lifted her hands and patted his shoulders. "You can pay for your journey with these."

He nodded.

"You're a good man." She then turned and walked slowly away.

Knud just stood.

After a few steps Ylva went back to him. "Some people are here to use their broad shoulders to carry others. Be happy you have purpose. Many don't. Free Eir. She has things to do."

Many years passed, and he hadn't imagined it would have taken so long to return to Sellø. Much had happened, and the death of Haakon by his own *thrall* hadn't surprised Knud. King Olaf had offered a huge reward for

Haakon's assassination. The *thrall* had come to Olaf with proof of his deed, but no silver was given. Instead, the king beheaded the slave for his treachery.

While Haakon and his thrall's headless bodies were placed on stakes, Haakon's woman, Ragnvi had disappeared. Knud had seen her for a moment at the back of the crowd, watching the spectacle. But when he looked again, she was gone.

Almost a year later, in the darkness of the cave, Knud was now squashed up next to Olaf Tryggvason. The king was a huge man with blonde hair and blue eyes. His silver-plated belt, the cross around his neck, and the golden hoop brooch that held his green cloak in place, all reflected the light from Knud's lamp as they crept slowly forward.

Knud stumbled over loose stones, almost losing his balance. When he straightened, Olaf pointed into the darkness.

"What's that?" Olaf asked.

Knud couldn't tell; in front of them was a thing foreign. A shape, as white as snow, undulated with the contour of the boulders on which it lay. Knud took two more steps and the angle of his perspective shifted. He could now see wet strands of a woman's dark blonde hair floating in a pool of water.

The oil lamp captured the beads of her necklace, sending dots of light onto the roof of the cavern. It was as if a heaven of orange stars had been released from slumber.

Olaf gasped, drew near, and knelt beside the body. "Is she alive?"

Knud licked his fingers and held them above her lips and then nose, trying to feel for Eir's breath. She was as beautiful has he remembered. Nothing of her had changed—ruby lips, straw-coloured hair, and her pale, lightly freckled skin were all pristine.

"In a trance I think. We must take her out of here—"

"Uncorrupted. Truly a miracle of our Lord. And so beautiful. She has been here six years?" the king asked with reverence.

Knud nodded.

Olaf lifted the amber necklace. He turned to Knud. "This is pagan. And she wears no cross."

"She cured the sick with miracles." He repeated what he had told the king many times.

There was desire in Olaf's eyes, and the king licked his lips before tapping his fingers against his mouth, deep in thought. "Monk, you have some work to do," he said after a moment.

"Sire?"

"She is not dead and we need a martyr. She is not a Christian and we need a saint. But she is miraculous and has a reputation." He brushed her hair from her face. "Keep everyone out until you can find a corpse. Dig up graves if you have to. But I want a body. We need a relic to replace her."

"A relic?" Knud asked.

"We will rebuild the church and make this cave sacred to Sunniva and the monks who have sacrificed themselves. A relic will bring pilgrims." The king rose and he patted Knud's head with his heavy hand as if he were a child. "This will be your church and your relic."

"But this uncorrupted one . . ." Olaf bent over to stroke Eir's cheek with his ringed fingers. "She comes with me."

Knud realised his mistake too late. By having the king free Eir, he had given birth to a martyr to God, but worse still, Olaf wanted Eir for himself.

OLAF WAS NOT someone to try to steer towards reason. He was appointed by God, so Knud had no choice but to do his bidding. A church was hastily constructed of logs floated over from the mainland. It took only a few weeks to raise, with Olaf's men doing the work.

All that time, Eir lay, unmoving in a tent from Olaf's longboat, the *Long Serpent*. They had bene unable to wake her, and Olaf called in no other to assist; he wanted no one to see Eir. Eventually he asked a female *thrall*, no older than twelve, to care for her while he assisted with the rebuilding.

Knud had been trying to buy time, hoping Olaf would leave Eir with him once the church was built. He knew where a relic could be found. The dead woman of the bog, who had saved him by pointing to the cord on his bundle of reeds. Her marshy grave was a short journey away, and her preserved body could replace Sunniva's to become the relic.

One fine morning, Olaf was sitting on a log as a *thrall* tied the straps on his leather boots. Knud approached him and bowed.

"Now that the church has been consecrated, shall we move Sunniva into it?" he asked hopefully.

With his boots fastened, Olaf stood as the *thrall* placed his great green cloak on his shoulders. "No, Father. She will come with me. You must find a body and keep it in the cave. Until then no one enters. The message will be spread of Sunniva's preservation." When his cape was clasped, he turned to Knud. "Why have you failed to find one?"

Knud felt Olaf could see through him and he was compelled to tell the truth. "I know of one . . . in the marsh."

Olaf frowned. "So why is it not here? Fetch the thing."

"I didn't want you to take Sunniva away." To his embarrassment he started to tear, and he bowed his head. "I knew her when she was with the living."

"Yes, you told me."

Her smile . . . It was like a lifetime of sunrises. He wiped his eyes and looked up.

Olaf buckled his sword belt. "Fetch the relic and others will come . . . and perhaps one day, once she has woken, and if I allow it, Sunniva will visit here." He took a step away, but then drew back and said softly in Knud's ear, "No word of this. Fail me and you fail God. And for that . . . I'll punish you."

Knud withdrew and watched as Sunniva was wrapped in white seal fur and lifted by two men onto a cart. He never told the king her real name. Was this what Ylva had expected? He wasn't sure, but he had no choice. A small part of him believed she would be safer with a king than here where any pagan chieftain could come and pillage.

Thralls pulled the cart to the quay where Olaf's boat was being prepared. Knud sat on the wet grass and stayed there until the sail of the *Long Serpent* could no longer be seen amongst the waves.

SIX MONTHS HAD passed and Olaf had been correct. Pilgrims arrived on the island. Some stayed but most came to visit the cave and see the relic of Sunniva, asking for her blessing, without knowing that the leathery corpse was a substitute. Many went to the spring, which flowed from the cave to a pool down the slope; it had become a point of pilgrimage. People would drink from it or immerse themselves in the freezing water, hoping to be cured of whatever ailed them.

Others stayed for longer, and soon the monastery was re-established, having grown with the addition of a timber hall and two buildings for monks to sleep and work in.

There had been no word from King Olaf and no visit since he had taken Eir. The only news Knud had received was that Olaf was to the north, claiming the dead Haakon's land. This made Knud uneasy. Ragnvi had been with Haakon before he was killed and had disappeared. Ragnvi would surely kill Eir if she came across her, but he didn't even know if Eir was alive or if she had woken.

He sat in the darkness of the cave, staring at the Relic of Sunniva. It was laid out on a flat stone, which with great effort, the monks had moved into the cave. He had thought wild animals would've eaten the thing, but nothing seemed to touch it. In fact, if someone approached, the air cooled and its eyes, underneath the leathery lids, seemed to follow you. He bowed his head and prayed, but his prayers were unanswered.

Where is that witch when I need her? With a twinge of shame, he admitted Ylva had filled him with more strength and assurance than his God. He'd been hiding in the Lord's embrace from the pain of Eir's spurning. Hell or not, he no longer had the Lord in his heart. The things he could see were now more real to him than those of faith. Prayers had not brought Eir back to him.

Images of Eir, her screams when being trapped, her placid form as she was taken away, broke his heart. Such evil had been done to her, and those deeds were not the work of the Devil, but of flesh and blood.

When he looked up, the arm of the relic had flopped down. It was no longer held across its chest, where he had positioned it months ago, but lay straight with the elbow locked and the hand opened. A finger was pointing across the darkness of the cavern towards the northeast. Knud leapt up and scrambled out of the cave.

The next morning, he knelt beside the pool where the pilgrims came for their cures; the same one he was convinced Kari had disappeared into. He lifted the cross from his neck, held it above the water, and was about to drop it in—but he couldn't. He no longer believed, but if he let Him go, he would have nothing.

Standing, he put his cross around his neck. Gathering his cloak against the autumn winds, he headed to the jetty through the bending long grass.

He untied a small skiff and set the oars. The sea was rougher than most would dare venture into, but he didn't care. It was time to find Eir and make her his own. A wave broke close by and spray drenched him as he rounded the natural breakwater.

Knud manoeuvred the craft towards the mainland with long pulls of the oars. He must fetch her and find their child. If the task required the blood of a king, then so be it. The hand of the relic had demanded no less.

The Burning Moon

July 2014, Château de Savoie, Provence

THE TRAIL STOPPED at an iron gate built into a wall. Freya worked the latch and pushed it open on squeaky hinges. They stepped through onto a dirt carriageway lined with ancient plane trees, and at its end, camouflaged by layers of broadleaves, a *château* beckoned.

"God, Freya, is this your house?"

Jade felt very small indeed as they got closer. The manor suited Freya to a tee. It was elegant, understated, and rustic without being run-down. A hardwood door, accessed by broad steps, was dead centre of the three-storey country home. Open shutters exposed at least twenty windows, running along the first two levels, while the highest windows were half-sized and arched.

Freya halted in the shaded courtyard. "Lena had the key."

Jade glanced around and spotted the backpacks Lena had left on a nearby metal table. She went over to them and retrieved the key, then passed it to Freya.

Freya unlocked the main door and pushed it open. A waft of cold air, filled with a heady smell of old books and musty fabric, greeted them. "My caretaker comes in every day to look after Alice, but the house is usually left shut. I need to open some of the windows."

"Why don't you sit? I'll do it," Jade said, concerned Freya still was shaky on her feet.

Lena appeared behind them, dropping two canvas bags onto the ceramic-tiled floor. She held a bunch of herbs, which she must have gathered on the way. Lavender, rosemary, sage, thyme, and a few others Jade didn't recognise.

"Do you have olive oil?" Lena asked Freya.

"In the kitchen." Freya took a seat on a cushioned settle.

"Bay leaves?"

"Think so, but Karen and Henri will be over with groceries."

Lena nodded. "Cool." She zapped down the hall.

"I'll make some tea." Freya stood and touched Jade's hand. "Just open a few windows. It's always like this if I've not been here for a while."

Jade went from room to room, twisting latches and opening windows. As she did, conflicting impressions of Freya formed from the decor. An image of a seventeenth-century duchess came to mind, the type who would be depicted on the cover of a romance novel, but then in other rooms the impression was of a scatty artist, while in a few, she wondered if Freya had a daughter. She realised she had never asked Freya about such personal things.

Most rooms seemed to have no distinct purpose and were cluttered with eclectic furnishings that fitted no particular era, although Freya appeared to have a penchant for the late 1950s. The exception was the downstairs grand ballroom. With its ornate mirrors, crystal candlestick chandeliers, and marble fireplaces, it was firmly set in the Louis XIV period. Huge paintings were concealed by linen cloths. She resisted the temptation to peek behind them.

She spotted Freya carrying a tray with a teapot and cups, and raced over to take it from her.

"I thought we could have it inside. It'll be cooler."

Freya led her to a room on the second floor and pushed the door open.

"I mostly just use this as bedroom and den . . . a boudoir, I suppose."

The room was the smallest Jade had seen in the château and brimmed with bohemian flair. It looked like a dozen gypsy caravans had collided at an oasis. White-washed walls ended on lime-green skirting boards and an elm floor, but little of the planks could be seen, since the space was crammed with furnishings.

Pushed against the windows was a raised cabin bed, only just visible behind heavy drapes depicting palm trees dripping with coconuts and bananas.

Freya went over and pulled back the curtains. She then opened the privacy drapes, allowing light to flood over the bed and into the room.

An enamelled French-style wood stove stood in one corner, while squeezed next to it was a hand-painted sideboard covered with trinkets and framed photos. An iron fireback had been wedged between the stove and sideboard, presumably to protect it from the heat.

Rainbow-coloured cushions were spread on dark purple velvet sofas and chairs that surrounded a coffee table made from a richly painted Moroccan door. Freya cleared a space, moving copies of fashion magazines from last year.

"I like to look out the window before I go to sleep, so I had the bed built there. I know it's a bit strange." Freya took Jade's hand. "Come and see."

Jade weaved around stacks of books, being careful not to knock any of them over. There was an assortment of old leather-bound texts and modern paperbacks, mostly in French or Norwegian. Jade picked up a paperback. "You like crime novels?"

"I read a lot. I don't remember details so well, so I read them again later," Freya said before slowly climbing the rungs of the cabin-bed ladder and shifting onto the single bed. The space was high enough that they could sit without their heads touching the ceiling. Freya pulled off her shoes. Jade did the same. Freya took them from her and chucked both pairs into the room, knocking over a pile of books and the teapot, which slowly glugged its contents onto the floor.

Jade started back down the ladder.

"Just leave it," Freya said.

"I can—"

"Just come up, please." Freya grabbed the side of Jade's tank top. "It really isn't important. I want you here."

Jade did as she was told. Freya shifted to the end of the bed and sat against the wall with pillows behind her. She pulled Jade against her before letting out a long breath. "Oh my God, how hard was that?"

"What do you mean?" Jade guided Freya's arm around her middle.

"It's taken like hundreds of years to get you here with me."

Jade couldn't think what to say, except, "I'm sorry."

"You're here now . . . and it's not your fault. I'm just tired." Freya nuzzled her chin against Jade's neck. "I want to sleep. Will you stay close?"

"Sure."

Freya moved one leg over the top of Jade's. She mouthed a thank you against Jade's skin before lying back, pulling Jade with her.

A windowsill had been built from the bed to the glass pane. The sill and the walls around the bed were covered in doodles. The drawings and writings were only just visible, hidden under more books, paper, notepads, pens, pencils, and paint sets.

The view through the window was of a dusty courtyard shaded by large plane trees. Beyond them was a wide, shallow valley. Jade could see a small section of the road on the opposite side, but no other buildings.

Jade noticed that Lena was outside, dragging her heel along the ground, marking a line around the house. She disappeared from view and moments later returned with a jug. Jade watched as Lena poured out sloshes of its contents every few steps into the groove.

"What's Lena doing?" Jade asked.

"Stuff" was all Jade got from Freya before she was completely asleep.

Hours later, Jade woke to the sound of a car in the distance. Dusk was dusting sunrays, bringing forth twilight. Freya was sound asleep with her arms and legs wrapped around Jade. Gently, Jade slid out. She took the few steps down the ladder but stopped to gaze in awe of the sleeping comtessa. Freya resembled a Pre-Raphaelite's notion of romantic tragedy. Her hair was fanned out in dishevelled waves, her ruby lips, just slightly parted, quivered with each breath as her chest rose slowly, then fell. Jade was transfixed. A wave of sadness swept through her. Frowning, she knocked on her skull with her knuckles. *You have to be brave for her.* She took the final step, put on her shoes, and went to clean up the spilt tea.

WITH HER HANDS in the pockets of her shorts, Jade watched as the headlights of Henri's car panned across the courtyard. Then the car stopped and she went over to lift grocery bags from the rear seat. Karen was on her phone and nodded to her.

"Thanks for noticing the problems today. You have good instincts," Henri said as they carried the bags to the house.

"It's okay," Jade replied.

"Has Freya settled?"

"She's sleeping."

"Good. She seems to be able to do that with you around," he remarked over the sound of the gravel crunching beneath their feet.

"I can't find any lights in the house."

"No, Freya didn't want electricity."

"Figures." Jade smirked.

"There are candles and lamps, and there's even hot water, although the boiler does break a number of safety regulations."

"So does Freya."

"True." Henri smiled. He took a few more steps. "Where's Lena?"

"*Je suis ici,*" Lena said from behind them.

Jade spun around and looked at Lena's feet. She hadn't heard Lena's footsteps, and anxiety moved like a blunt blade through her head. Her breathing quickened and pins and needles spread across her face. She took deep breaths to counter the panic attack, telling herself this was Lena, there was no danger, she hadn't missed anything, and no one was going to die.

But someone was . . . someone she knew she loved. *She is still here, sleeping.* If Freya was standing beside her right now, she would tell her everything was okay. Freya would comfort her. Those small thoughts helped. *Freya's close, and safe.* For the first time, she wasn't alone.

Lena's long eyelashes flickered across her grey irises. "Did I jump-scare you?"

"I just didn't hear you coming, that's all," Jade said.

"I didn't want you to." Lena took one of the bags from Jade. Walking backwards for a few steps, she asked, "What are we eating?"

"Pizza. We'll get the outdoor wood oven going," Henri said.

"Okay. Awesome." Lena gestured with her free hand. "Don't go past that line." She pointed at a rut on the other side of the car, only just visible in the twilight. It was the one Lena had made earlier with her heel, and it completely encircled the *château*. She then spun around and stomped across the gravel towards the house.

THE SUN HAD long since set, but the full moon allowed a view of the valley. Jade sat at a candlelit table, watching the flames inside a wood-burning bread oven. Henri was kneading dough on a marble top next to it, while Lena seemed obsessed with the fire and kept stuffing in more vine wood.

"Lena, that's enough. You'll set the moon on fire," Henri said. "We need stable embers to cook with, not a volcanic eruption."

Lena took a step back and looked up. Jade followed her line of sight to see flames blasting out of the chimney above them. And indeed, it did look like she was trying to burn the harvest moon. It was tinted red behind the inferno.

"That should be okay," Lena muttered and went over beside Henri, where she dipped a finger into a bowl of tomato sauce. "Needs more salt."

"Yes, but we seem to be almost out of salt," Henri said. Over his shoulder he asked Jade to fetch Freya.

Jade nodded and went back towards the house. She walked past Karen, who was carrying out plates to be set at the table. The security agent, as Jade now knew she was, had been quiet and grumpy since she'd arrived.

Once inside, Jade went upstairs. Soft orange light glowed under the door of Freya's room and when she entered, Freya was half-dressed, changing her top.

"Sorry," Jade said and started to back out.

"Come in," Freya called.

She could tell by Freya's tone and movements that she was still on edge.

"I won't be a sec." Freya was digging through a drawer. She lifted up a folded top, letting it unravel. "This is so old." She dropped it on the floor and searched for another. "Screw it." She yanked on a black mod-style blouse with a broad collar. "Is this okay?" she asked while still straightening it with her hands.

"You're always heart-stopping beautiful," Jade said without thinking. "You know we're just having pizza?" she added quickly to cover up her awkwardness.

But it didn't matter; Freya was completely distracted, raising a burning candle to search the floor. "Where are my frigging shoes?"

Jade retrieved them and handed them over. It was her fault; she had moved them after cleaning up the tea.

Freya offered an unconvincing smile and slipped them on. "Can you hand me the perfume behind you?"

After Jade gave her the small bottle, she returned to look at a framed picture that'd been next to it. Audrey Hepburn was in the photograph with an arm around the shoulders of a woman who looked a lot like Freya. The resemblance was so close that Jade lifted it and showed it to Freya.

"Is this your mother?" Jade asked.

Freya shook her head. The picture was from the early sixties, judging from the style of the clothes. Scrunching up her shoulders, Freya waited like she was about to be showered with a bucket of cold water.

Then Jade noticed it, and her mouth fell open. Freya was wearing the same top as the woman in the picture.

Freya's eyes widened and she let her shoulders drop. "It's me."

Before Jade could say anything, Freya took the picture and chucked it onto the sofa. She grabbed the lit candle, took Jade's wrist, and sped her along the corridor, down the stairs, and into the great ballroom.

Jade started to speak but decided it was best to hold her tongue. Suspicions around Freya's age were starting to solidify.

In a whirl, Freya released Jade, put down the candlestick, and took hold of a dust sheet that was covering a ceiling-height painting. She tugged hard on one corner until the sheet fell away.

"It's too dark. To hell with this." She darted towards a cleat on the wall, then frantically loosened the rope that lowered the central chandelier. She let it go and the chandelier crashed onto the floor, showering antique glass in all directions.

"Freya!" Jade yelled. The chandelier had just missed her.

"Stay put!" Freya screamed in a release of tension and picked up her lit candlestick, which she used to light the undamaged ones. Once finished, she pulled on the rope again, raising it to the sound of broken crystal clattering to the floor. Some of the lit candles fell with their broken sconce and arm, only to be snuffed out on impact. When the chandelier was at full height, the picture was illuminated.

Jade was prepared for what it would depict. Freya had been hinting at it, and all the anomalies she had picked up in conversations were leading to this conclusion, as impossible as it might be.

"Why is everything so hard?" She spun on Jade. "Look then. Also me."

Jade moved behind Freya and wrapped her arms around her as they gazed at the painting.

"You look younger there," Jade said after allowing an impossible reality to settle in.

Freya relaxed in Jade's arms. "I guess I was. They say one year for every hundred or so."

"They?"

"Norwegian government medical specialists. Old Nags, I call them."

Jade dissected the composition of the picture. It showed Freya in a lavish bulky gown of white and dark blue embellished with pearls. Her amber necklace was against pale white skin, while her hair was all yellow curls and ringlets. She was posed with her fingers on the neck of a lute, ready to play. At her feet was a large white dog with black spots. At least Jade thought it was a dog. It was hard to tell, as the proportioned of the animal were badly done. The ears were too short and pointy and she couldn't see its face.

"Eighteenth century?" Jade asked.

"Yes," Freya whispered.

"Surviving past the French Revolution. Impressive."

Freya sighed. "I have my lineage in Norway. So I went there."

"How is it you have titles in Norway and France?" Jade asked.

"Long story." Freya laughed. "You have to remember, many of the European ruling classes married for power. Once, I had to fake my own death and pretend to be my daughter to hide my youth, but this backfired and I ended up being forced to marry a duke of Provence. The man died, and I inherited his titles, which included Les Baux. When I returned to Norway, I found friends there. I confessed my nature and was accepted as a queen, but as one who must stay hidden. Also here in Les Baux, they understand my age, and they are happy to have a special secret."

Freya twisted nervously in Jade's arms. "Does it bother you?" she asked, stuttering out the words.

Jade didn't say anything for a moment, unsure how she felt about the impossible. She squeezed Freya in her arms. "I can't believe how chubby you used to be."

"Hey! That's just the style of painting back then." Freya nudged Jade's ribs. "Just be thankful I don't have a boob hanging out of my gown."

Jade laughed. She stared at the painting for a moment then answered Freya's question. "I don't know how I feel about it. I guess it's hard to believe. Do you know why have you lived so long?"

"The Nags say it's something to do with my cells. Their cycles are a lot slower than normal. Well, were. They say some animals are similar; they don't die from old age, but disease or predators. Turtles for example. Or lobsters."

Jade thought for a while. "So you're saying you're a lobster."

Freya laughed. "Yup, a crustacean with decoration."

"Decoration?" Jade kissed her neck.

"My necklace."

"Oh, yes, you always wear that."

Freya turned her head against Jade to try to look at her. "I kind of have to." She found Jade's lips and turned in her arms as the kiss deepened.

When they separated, Freya's eyes beamed and wore a matching smile. "There's a lot for you to believe and not much time."

"I'd believe anything for you."

"Hmm, well . . ." Freya gave Jade a quick smooch and took her hand. "Come on. We can talk after . . ." She lowered her voice.

Jade loved when Freya played games with her. "After what?"

"*Pizza!*" Freya yelled, laughing and tugging Jade toward the door.

Those to Come

THE NIGHT AIR was warm as Karen poured herself a glass of wine. She sat at a table beside the pizza oven. There was no wind and the candles burnt elegantly, standing tall and proud at the centre of the table. She had been worn out by the day's events and the day hadn't discharged her yet. She needed to speak with Freya before she turned in.

Freya walked across the courtyard from the house. Karen stood and pulled out one of the *fer forgé* chairs for her.

"Would you like some wine?" Karen asked. "It's very nice, a 2001 Gigondas."

"No," Freya said as she sat.

"Are you feeling okay?" Karen asked after returning to her own chair.

"Not really." Freya crossed her arms around herself.

"Cold?"

"No."

"Do you want something else to drink?"

"No."

Freya glanced towards the house, and Karen assumed she was waiting for Jade to appear. Karen straighten and waited to get Freya's attention.

"I'm sorry if I've upset you. I'm only trying to do what is best." She put her hand on Freya's forearm, then retracted it when Freya, who had been her ward for most of her life, frowned.

"You should have asked."

"Asked?"

"Asked what is best for me," Freya said in a tone infused with anger.

"I'm sorry, honey, but I'm not just thinking what is best for you. I have to think what is best after, and for so many others. The bigger picture."

Freya gripped the pendant with her arms still crossed. "The bigger picture . . ." she mocked. "The bigger picture is my damnation in hell. That's pretty damn big, don't you think?"

Karen tried to keep her cool. She'd sailed through many of Freya's emotional storms. This was one she'd weathered before. "Sweetest, I know.

I know that's what you think will happen, but you really don't know. No one does."

"I do. I've seen them, waiting for me. I see them every night. They are from Hell. I don't know why. I won't be able to get away from them." She shuddered as if the words were ice cubes sliding down her back. "They'll take me and I'll become one of them." A pained expression spread across her flawless features.

"These are just dreams of yours. You've read too much and those things play with your fears." Karen paused. "You know, it might even be a result of your condition affecting your thinking. We should talk to Dr Sorenson about that."

Freya said nothing for a few seconds then leaned forward and uncrossed her arms. "Why do you hate Jade?"

Karen let out a laugh. "I don't. In fact, I like her a lot."

"So why do you want to keep her away from me?" Freya narrowed her eyes and her blue irises could no longer be seen in the candlelight.

Karen picked her words carefully. "Darling, she's not well . . . She's dealing with post-trauma stress and depression."

"I know."

"Freya," Karen soothed, "I know she's improved a bit since I got her to see your doctor, but she is still not there yet—"

"Wait . . . You did what?"

"Not much. It was that first week, last year, after you met Jade. She'd collapsed and I went over to her flat with her boss. She needed help. It's why I didn't give her your note. She was in no state to spend time with you." Karen waited to see if Freya understood.

"Jade collapsed?"

Karen took Freya's hand. "Her medication wasn't right."

"Was she hurt?"

"No. Marianne put her on a new prescription. But, honey, she's still not stable. She's desperate for anyone who'll make her feel better and she's becoming too attached to you."

Freya stared at her with the face of a child waiting to be told everything will be okay.

"I don't think she is strong enough to fall in love with you, and then have you . . . leave." Karen let out a slow sigh. She didn't like being so matter of fact about life and death, but it had to be done.

"She is strong," Freya said, but her voice wavered.

"You know that isn't true." Karen spotted Henri, Lena, and Jade coming out of the house with the toppings for their pizzas. "You need to let her go. Giving her false security will be cruel."

"No. She knows the situation. And I need her."

"I'm sorry to say, but I think that's being a bit selfish. I know you have a right to be selfish at this point, but I don't think you should do this to her. I wish things were different."

Freya waved away a moth that had flown near the flame of a candle. Crossing her arms again, she lowered her gaze.

"I've arranged for us to go back to Norway tomorrow," Karen whispered. "I can change it, but I think you know it's the right thing to do . . . for her sake as well."

AFTER DINNER, EVERYONE was subdued. Jade had tried to make conversation with Freya but she seemed distracted. Jade studied those around her; Karen seemed intent on discovering if there was anything at the bottom of the wine bottle, while Lena sat on the counter by the pizza oven, feeding it wood from a small pile she'd collected, and Henri was nursing a drink.

Lena's fascination with flames was starting to concern Jade, and she didn't like how close she was to the oven. Jade's phobia of fire had started when she was young. She had never been able to work out the source of it.

"Lena, please move away and stop adding more wood," she said.

Lena shifted along the counter, away from the fire. She looked odd tonight, like a cat who had been spooked. Her black hair, voluminous and loose, was wild around her shoulders.

"I think I'll turn in." Henri put the top back on a bottle of pastis and heaved himself out of his chair. "Goodnight, everyone."

"I'll go to bed as well." Karen rose. "Do you need anything, Freya?"

Freya didn't answer.

"Well, goodnight, then." Karen turned and headed through the darkness towards the house with Henri.

Lena jumped off the counter and poured herself a glass of wine. It was her first of the night. "It's okay?" she asked Freya.

"Not too much. Nothing worse than a drunken teenage witch."

"Very funny, *Tante*." Lena went back to stoke the fire.

The ambient light darkened significantly as a bank of cloud hid the moon and stars.

Jade had been storing up her questions, and now seemed like a good time to set them free. "What's happening tomorrow?"

Freya avoided making eye contact with her and topped off her glass with wine.

Jade's heart sank. She sprung up and marched away from the table into the shadows. *What the hell is going on?* She continued to walk away, trying to condense her emotions.

Footsteps came from behind, and she turned to see Lena. She was holding a flaming branch.

"Where're you going?" Lena asked. She hung back for a moment but then yanked Jade in her direction. "Hey, stop!"

Why is everyone messing with me?

Lena threw the branch on the ground and pointed at the illuminated area. The branch was just a few inches beyond the rut Lena had made in the dirt earlier in the day. "You were on the wrong side. I told you about that."

"Wrong side of what? Explain this to me." Jade didn't want to yell at her, but again and again, no one told her anything.

The flames died to glowing embers.

Lena appeared unfazed by Jade's tone. "Okay. It's a protection ring. You were on the wrong side. I've got one at home. I had to make one here too, as it's too close to her time and they know of this place."

"Who knows?"

"We need to go back to Freya. It's not good to leave her."

Jade watched as the embers went black. Then the light from the fire in the oven diminished and almost disappeared.

"Let's go back." Lena took hold of Jade's shoulders and pushed her towards the vignette that contained Freya.

When they got there, the flames in the pizza oven looked like they were being starved of air. Lena grabbed the bottle of pastis and threw it into the oven, causing a ball of flame to explode out and up the chimney.

In the light from the brief flare of orange, yellow, and red, Jade saw it, or maybe it was a trick of light and shadows. It seemed to move in stuttering spasms, as if someone had edited out frames of a film. She couldn't see its edges, but long black wings were twisting and hammering like a bird against a window. What those wings were attached to wasn't normal, mythical, or even fanciful. It was a horrific amalgamation.

Within the ribs of a titanic decaying corpse, a lissom human was lashed and held in place by a chain. The human figure was female in appearance, and its woeful bald head was below the jaw of the outer abomination. A claw twisted the sorrowful subservient in one direction then the other, bending its neck at impossible angles. Jade didn't want to see any more; she closed her eyes for a second and reopened them, expecting to find the vision gone—hoping is was just a montage of the horrors she had seen in Syria, painted by the flames on the night's canvas.

For a moment longer, it was still there—wings folded in jerks of fractions of a second, missing the intervening movements. A wave of blue flame pulsed along the rachis of each feather in its wings. Then, with a snap, the monstrosity closed its wings and merged with the darkness around it, as the alcohol-fuelled fireball collapsed into the flickering embers.

Lena tossed a few more branches onto the fire, bringing it back to life.

Jade went numb as she created a layer between what she'd just seen and her emotions. It was a technique she'd learned in order to survive, and over time it became her disposition. It was a blasé indifference to events that would warp the minds of others. The most appalling things didn't scare her, and she simpered at the irony. Her fears were made inside. *How can I fear things that are already true? I did fail, and I am alone.*

She looked up, seeking Freya, who stood close to the opening of the oven and pulled Jade next to her.

"What just happened?" Jade asked.

"You ran off," Freya said meekly.

Jade decided she'd been hallucinating. The different meds she'd been prescribed to try to solve her anxiety and depression had taken a toll. She knew that. On a few occasions she became confused, even felt disembodied, and every so often she'd have sudden surges of what felt like electricity coursing through her head—but she'd never seen a thing like that before.

"Why'd you do that to the fire?" Jade asked, annoyed by the absence of reason.

"It was going out," Lena said in a matter-of-fact tone.

"And what was out there?" Jade pointed.

"What do you mean?" Lena bent over to pick up another branch.

Jade knew Lena was being evasive.

"Why did you run off?" Freya asked.

"What the hell is going on?" Jade caught hold of Lena's wrist. "Lena, don't you think you should tell me?"

"*Merde . . . non.*"

"Why not?"

"You want to be able to sleep at night, don't you?" Lena mumbled.

Jade was maxed out and needed to be elsewhere. She started back to the house, took several steps, and decided she was being an ass. She turned and bumped into Freya, who locked her arms around her.

"What's wrong, my love?" Freya said softly.

"You tell me," she blurted out, then instantly hated herself for yelling.

Freya squeezed Jade as tightly as she'd ever done. "Just come with me."

Freya took Jade's hand and led her back into the house and to her boudoir.

THE SUN HAD risen and Freya was busy selecting clothes. Jade watched, leaning up on one elbow, as the outline of Freya's figure revealed itself through her nightgown. She fluttered, recalling their night together.

She's packing!

Freya was stuffing items into a carpetbag as Jade climbed down from the cabin bed. Nude and feeling very exposed, she found her clothes from the day before and got dressed. Freya gathered an armful of random objects from the sideboard and dumped them on the sofa. She still hadn't acknowledged her.

"You're leaving?" Jade asked.

"I have to go back to Norway." Freya tucked one shoe into the bag without the other.

Jade tried to put up her defences against the fearful event that was unfolding, but they failed to rise. The scene playing before her was a complete repeat of how Rachael had left her, and it shocked her. "I thought you wanted me to come with you?"

Freya grabbed a used coffee cup, a book, and yesterday's cut-offs and jammed them into the bag. "I do, but you can't." She glanced up.

"Freya . . . ? Why are you doing this?" Jade said, crossing her arms, hot tears flowing down her face. The dots she hadn't fully connected the night before, as she'd been afraid to draw the lines, formed a picture. Freya's behaviour during dinner and her desperate passion after plotted a painful inevitability. Last night was their last.

"I . . ." Freya performed two *pas de chat* steps over items on the floor to where Jade stood sobbing. She frantically stroked Jade's face, her palms wiping away tears. "I don't want to hurt you. But I am . . . and I will even more. I did not think it through . . . It will be best for you—"

"I don't understand." Jade pulled away from Freya and bolted downstairs into the front hall, where she spotted the keys to the convertible on a side table and her backpack still on the floor. She grabbed them, went straight out of the front door, and towards the trail that led to the car.

"I HATE THIS!" Freya had tried to find Jade so she could explain, but she was nowhere to be seen. Then she heard the sound of a car off in the distance.

Freya ran into the ballroom and darted to a window. She looked out to see a red vehicle appearing and disappearing behind trees as it raced along the road on the other side of the valley.

Not sure what to do, she ran to find Karen. She wanted to scream at someone, but in her heart she knew it was too late. It had been done. She collapsed under the broken chandelier, curled her legs against her chest, and twined her arms around them.

The past in the room was scolding her. Malicious reverberations that voiced her catastrophic end were painted in the canvases around her. It was as if her story had already been told and she was a historian absorbing and lamenting what couldn't be reanimated. She was where they wanted her to be. There was no way to go back. She rocked on the broken glass spread out around her. A piece cut into her nightgown, pricking her skin. She picked up the shard and turned it in front of her. Through teary, blurred eyes she could see her reflection, stained red by her own blood.

WITH A SORE head that was in need of reviving with cups of tea and aspirin, Karen went into the kitchen. There Lena sat cross-legged on the table with a bowl of cereal balanced on one knee. Her headphones were plugged in, and she was staring at her device, scroll-clicking with the tip of her thumb. On the table next to her was a black feather.

Earlier, Karen had found Freya being Freya: an emotional wreck in the ballroom. She pulled her off the floor, heard the story about how Jade had left, corralled Freya into the shower, and stuck two adhesive bandages on her ass. Her behaviour was becoming increasingly bizarre and hard to deal with. The sooner they saw her doctor, the better. But at least she'd let Jade go. Things would now be easier to manage.

"Good morning," Karen said to Lena while looking for the kettle.

Lena took out one of her earbuds. "There's some cereal if you want some." She gestured to a variety pack with three cartons missing. "I ate most of the good ones though. Except the Coco Pops, which I'm having next."

"Tea first, I think." Karen never really understood this girl. Lena seemed such a mix of personalities. She said little, but if she did speak, it was mostly to swear or make a cutting remark. She knew that teenagers went through this phase, but Karen felt there was no excuse for it.

She topped off the kettle and put it on one of the gas rings after lighting it with a match. She watched the kettle, waiting for it to boil, but it was taking forever.

"Where's Jade?" Lena asked.

"She's gone."

Lena looked up from her phone. "Gone?"

"Yes. It's for the best."

Lena swore a string of French expletives only just under her breath.

Karen noticed the feather and picked it up. A ripple of blue moved along its length as she turned it.

Lena gripped the feather's base, keeping it still. "Don't play with that. Double shit." She took it from Karen's hand and carefully tucked it into the pocket of her red-and-green plaid shirt. "Are you an idiot?"

"Don't talk to me like that. Don't you have any manners?"

Lena sighed. "But you let Jade go, and almost—*merde* . . . Why did you let her go?"

"None of your business," Karen retorted.

The kettle started to whistle nosily and fill the kitchen with steam.

Henri came in, went to it, and turned off the gas. He glanced at them. "What are you two at loggerheads about?"

"She wants my Coco Pops," Lena lied, staring at Karen.

"Yeah, I'm crazy about them," Karen said through gritted teeth.

"Have them, then." Lena hurled the packet at Karen and then slid off the table and darted out of the kitchen.

Why was she so bloody rude?

"You like those?" Henri asked.

"Not really."

He made a pot of tea. "So, what are your plans?"

"I'll take Freya back to Norway and start the ball rolling to get Dr Sorenson to relocate." She poured a cup for Henri and herself. "Can you take us to Avignon Airport for noon?"

"Yes, of course," he said, but the corners of his mouth were not affirming. "I thought Jade and Freya were going to spend more time here?"

"I spoke with Freya. She saw sense. And, I think you'll have to collect Freya's car from the TGV station in Avignon."

"Jade took it?"

"Yes."

The wind had picked up, blowing dust in through the open window. Henri closed it and twisted the central knob to latch the two frames together. "I guess that's that, then."

Karen nodded. "Just the Foundation and her inheritance to resolve now." Her cup rattled on its saucer as she lifted it from the table.

Old Haunts

July 2014, London

IT WAS WEDNESDAY afternoon at the Park Lane Hemmington. Yale downed the sixth miniature from Nancy's minibar. Lilith reckoned that should be enough.

Earlier, Yale had booked Nancy's hotel room and checked her in, allowing him to keep one of the room keys while leaving the other at the reception desk for her to collect. The ruse meant she would arrive without knowing he was already in her room.

He turned off all the lamps, drew the drapes, and went into the bathroom so he could approach from behind. Yale was suitably intoxicated, but Lilith would control him until it was able to relocate.

Forty minutes later, the door opened and Yale heard it bash against a suitcase. Nancy cursed. He waited until she moved beyond the bathroom, then he stepped out, grabbed her from behind, and yanked her back. Before she could scream, he had his mouth on hers with his thumb stuffed in the corner to hold her jaw open. She tried to wriggle free, but his full weight straddled her body against the vanity sink. In that moment, Lilith slipped from Yale to Nancy. The fat serpent slid into her mouth and down her throat.

Yale stumbled backwards, his body floundered and he fell out of the bathroom. He tried to speak but no words came out.

Nancy looked down at him while straightening her blouse and skirt. She then stepped over him and opened the door. "Get out, pervert!"

He crawled backwards like a crab, falling, before twisting and staggering onto his feet. He swayed into the corridor and Nancy closed the door.

Lilith laughed. Yale had acted as it had expected, darting off drunk and confused. He would sober up somewhere and try to work out why he was not on the campus at Princeton and why he was ten years older.

The change was pleasant. Nancy was sharper than Yale, rounded, and more instinctive. *This'll be fun*, it thought. Lilith then remembered that this was the start of a journey to the end. It just had to create an encounter with Miss Platt and then use her closeness to Freya to find the wings.

Nancy opened her travel bag and pulled out a laptop. After connecting to the hotel's wireless network, she accessed Yale's account and the advanced research portal. Lilith was sharing all Yale's passwords with her, and she authenticated to gain access to Jade Platt's data stream. Displayed on the screen were Jade's personal details: address, education, and employment history. A section at the bottom showed live monetary transactions. She looked down the list: a TGV rail ticket from Avignon early Monday morning and then a bottle of water at St Pancras seven hours later. *The woman is here, in London. How convenient.*

JADE WASN'T SURE how she had managed the journey home. The trip seemed to go on forever. At one point, she ended up walking the lengths of the carriages, through all the automatic doors and back again. On her third lap, a conductor stopped her, hesitated, and then led her to the first-class dining car. There she was offered a table and a drink without charge. She must have looked like death warmed up to be given such kindness.

She had just enough time to shower and go into the office without being late. Max hadn't expected her back until the next day, but he took one look at her and said, "Go home, get some sleep." He knew her too well. Before heading out, she'd made a detour to the IT department. It took a while, but the IT geek managed to have her old number set to a new SIM before handing over a replacement phone.

Inside her flat near Holborn, she tried not to think about Freya; she'd done that on the train. She let the door latch close behind her and threw her keys towards the bowl where they were normally kept. They hit the rim and knocked items from her desk onto the floor.

The tin geometry case she used to hold her camera's memory chips was tipped up on the carpet. She gathered up the case and put the chips back, except for the one—the one with the smudged label. It contained photos from Aleppo; the nightmare she had revisited time and time again.

When she'd been with Freya, she didn't have those dreams, or the guilt. The interlude had weakened her; she couldn't face that place again. *I can't carry on like this. One way or another.*

Holding the small wafer between her thumb and finger, she stared at it for the longest time before pushing it into a slot on her laptop.

I have to do this . . . I'll let Aaina decide . . . My mirror. My fault. My fate.

She browsed to the folder and navigated the images within. First picture was of her colleague and friend, James. He was standing with his video camera held by his side. A handshake was being exchanged with Nazir, the leader of the small faction they'd been embedded with. Both men were now dead.

She hovered her finger over the Page Down button before hammering it repeatedly. Hundreds of shots scrolled by until the screen was filled with the same reoccurring pattern of a green pickup on its side. The thumbnails were small, and her tears refracted their images, obscuring detail as a phantom pain raced along her chest. She homed in on the first shot, then skipped forward and stopped when she saw the small girl huddled in the corner of the pickup's bed near the tailgate. Smoke from the fire in the engine compartment filled the frame.

One frame at a time. Just bloody do it.

She wiped her eyes on her sleeve with each key press.

Still, there . . . smoke thicker. *Aaina, run!*

Still there, flames. *Aaina, you must run! The sniper won't—*

Still there, more flames, looking at the camera. *God, please—*

Still there, smoke covering most of the pickup. *Aaina, run!*

She couldn't go on. She was playing a game of Russian roulette where every chamber was loaded. She slammed closed the laptop screen and put her face in her upturned palms and cried.

THE FIRST TWO days back in the office went by with every minute being tallied; they loitered as if reluctant to expire. Jade couldn't concentrate and spent most of her time avoiding Max. Her boss would be disappointed if he knew how far she'd fallen.

That evening, her flat felt like a room in a ruined asylum, with Jade as the victim and the bystander, watching herself on a black-and-white CCTV monitor, waiting for a horror to happen. She had to get out.

She showered, towel-dried her hair, and applied a small amount of makeup. In the lounge, she looked for her shoes.

"Ouch! Shit." She picked up the small object she'd stepped on. It was the ring Aaina had given her. It must have fallen out of her geometry case.

She held it for a moment, remembering the girl telling her to keep it safe. She took a deep breath and rearranged her thoughts before pushing the wide-banded ring onto her middle finger; she would wear it as reminder of her sins.

She wasn't sure where to go, but then thought about the club she used to haunt with Rachael. She felt the need to be close to something familiar.

She went to drop a pinch of goldfish food into the tank. William Shakespeare was floating on the top. Without emotion, she disposed of her friend from college and left her apartment, feeling numb again.

Orange lanterns lit Chinatown. Its grocery stores were still open and the restaurants were full. Roast duck hung in windows, but even though Jade hadn't eaten, she didn't feel hungry. She would just have a drink, then head back home, or whatever.

She stepped over a cardboard box that had escaped from its brethren near a wheelie bin. To the right, she recognised the small restaurant where she used to meet Rachael after they had started jobs in London. They'd have dinosaur soup, a rice dish, and green tea with jasmine. Well, only Jade called it dinosaur soup, due to the huge bone in the bowl. Rachael had refused to go there again after Jade lifted the lazy Suzan and a cockroach ran out from underneath it.

Why am I thinking about Rachael? She knew why; other than Freya, there'd been no one else.

Crossing Shaftesbury Avenue, she headed into Soho. The once-seedy area had succumbed to gentrification. She stopped at a busy street corner, near a newly established music venue. The Victorian building had its sash windows open and an overspill of people, with cocktails in hand, were sitting on the sills or looking in from the street. A female singer with auburn hair, appearing all the part of a tormented indie performer, was belting out a song. Jade scanned the area and spotted a cameraman filming the performance. Close by, she recognised an actress from a recent blockbuster, but no one seemed to notice her; everyone was mesmerized by the performance.

Jade wasn't keen to battle her way to the bar to buy a drink, so she got a coffee at the café opposite and just leaned against a wall, listening. She thumbed through her emails on her phone while absorbing the caffeine and music. There was one from Lena with attachments. She replied, saying thanks, and asked if Henri had retrieved the car from the station. Actually, she'd been surprised there were no calls from him. She included her number in the response just in case and pocketed her phone, not wanting to see the attachments, which she knew were pictures of her and Freya on the boat to Port-Cros.

Ten minutes passed, and the remarkable performance ended abruptly as the singer darted off the stage. Jade watched with curiosity as the actress she'd seen earlier intercepted the performer as she left the venue.

Jade turned and set off for the place she'd originally planned to go. *Maybe, I should just go home.*

The club was quiet. There were two bar areas, and she passed the busier ground floor, where loud deep-house music played, and headed up the stairs. The club had lost a lot of its charm since she'd frequented it. It used to be a women's-only hangout, where the artisan and professional crowd would meet, but now it seemed to be a place to slam down cocktails while your organs were vibrated by heavy sub-bass progressions.

She ordered a small white wine. A pierced, tattooed barmaid poured her a glass. "Have a large one, on me. Looks like you need it."

Hell, great.

She felt old. Around her, students were drinking and flirting with each other. The place wasn't full, and she hadn't come to meet someone. She never really did that. *Drink and go. Why did I come? Some random chance that you'd run into Rachael? I'm such a self-deprecating ass.*

She found a seat on a sofa next to a low coffee table, drank quickly, and was almost finished when a young woman stopped next to her.

"I know you, don't I?" Her fresh face didn't yet show the wear and tear of vodka cocktails that so many sported nowadays.

"Not sure I can answer." Jade tilted her head.

"I know I do . . . It'll come to me." She tossed her purple dip-dyed hair over her shoulder. "I'm Danny. Monday night drinking at the moment, with friends, you know, it happens." She paused, her expression now sheepish. "Thought you might want company, so hello. Do you want to join us? We mostly just talk rubbish." She laughed.

Jade smiled through her despondency. "That's nice of you. But I won't be good company and I need to go in a minute."

"Okay." She seemed disappointed, but then lit up. "You're Jade Platt?"

"Yes," Jade said, blinking in puzzlement.

"Hey, yeah. I knew I knew you. You're a photographer. We studied you in one of my classes. Your pictures are solid. Very brave to do that. I mean conflict zones. I'm doing journalism at City U."

"I didn't know I was being studied."

"Of course, you are." Danny smirked and fluttered her eyelashes at Jade. "Who wouldn't. You're like some kind of Abby Able, except like crazy brave and, well." She blushed.

Jade didn't believe the complement for a second, but it was nice to be compared to the actress, model, and LGBT icon.

"Can I have your phone for a sec?" Danny asked.

"Um, okay." Jade handed it over. She hadn't fully set it up, and it didn't need unlocking.

"My number . . . you know. So if you want to go out some time. I mean, when you feel like it. I'd love to talk to you."

Jade smiled back. "Sure."

"Picture." Danny leaned into Jade and took a quick snap on her own phone. "Can't believe I met you." She turned and completed her trip to the bar.

Jade shook her head in disbelief. *Students are studying me? Bizarre.*

She stood to leave and her phone buzzed. She was surprised to see a message from Lena.

> Kestufou! And where the f**k are you?
> Jade: Um, London. Hi.
> Lena: Je c f*ing London, where?
> Jade: Soho, at bar. Why?
> Lena: OMG! WHAT IS THE BAR CALLED?
> Jade: The Blue Candle, what's up?
> Lena: Stay there!
> Jade: What's going on?

When nothing followed, she tried to call Lena, but there was no answer. She looked up to see a dark-skinned woman in her thirties with hazel eyes. Her chic formfitting skirt and blouse showed off a perfect athletic body. Jade did a double take, recognising the face.

"I thought it was you. What are the odds of this?" the newcomer chirped.

Jade ran her fingers through her hair while she tried to put a name to the face.

"You're Nancy Coles. You were on the call with Freya's lawyer." She hesitated. Freya. Her heart dropped. The earlier uplift to her mood vanished and her mouth went dry.

Nancy touched Jade's hand. "Are you okay?"

"Fine." Jade pulled away from the contact.

"I'm surprised you remembered my name." Nancy smiled. "I'm Yale's PA. Well, ass wiper really. I didn't mean to startle you." She paused and looked around. "Are you meeting someone? I don't want to intrude."

"No, it's okay."

"I didn't want to stay in my hotel room on my own, eating stupidly priced microwaved lasagne."

"Makes sense." Jade attempted a smile.

Nancy brushed the knuckle of her index finger against her lips while scrutinizing Jade. "You sure you're okay?"

"I'm fine."

"Can I get you another drink?"

Jade blinked a number of times. *Why's she here?*

"I'll get you a drink," Nancy insisted and then sauntered over to the bar.

Jade thought about the odds of running into her. They might not be that high, if she was in central London and looking for company. Her old haunt had become a place for that.

Nancy came back moments later with two glasses of wine and sat back down. "Here you go, cutie." She tasted hers and crinkled her nose. "Wow, this is bad."

Jade straightened, trying to gain some composure. "So why are you in London?"

"Business trip. Yale wants me to tie up loose ends after the foundation fiasco."

"You know Freya was the one who deleted the revised contract."

"Oh." Nancy smiled. "Surprising. Well, looks like it's for the best."

"Why?"

"I wouldn't have run into you here." Nancy crossed her legs. She was wearing a burgundy velvet miniskirt and sheer black tights. "Actually, I got the impression you were staying in France. Yale told me you and Freya were a couple."

"I thought we were, but . . . she went back to Norway." Jade picked up her wine, took a large gulp, and grimaced. It really was awful.

"I know Yale can be a pig. He didn't mess things up for you?"

"No. Freya's not well, and . . . well, I think she didn't want me to be around when things got worse."

"Oh, that's awful. I'm so sorry. I didn't know."

Jade wiped away a tear. *What's with this crying all the time?*

Nancy put a hand on Jade's shoulder. "Do you want to talk about it?"

Jade shook her head. "No. Won't help."

"You know, maybe you should just go to Norway and see her?"

"I would, but I don't know where she lives."

"No one you can ask?"

"No. Anyway, they don't want me around." Jade wanted to go home, but Lena's last message had told her to stay put. "Sorry, I'm kind of messed-up at the moment. I'm waiting for a text, and then I'll go."

Nancy slipped her hand onto Jade's forearm and squeezed it. "Aww, why not stay for one more. I'm a good listener if you want to talk about things."

Jade glanced at her phone. *No new messages.* "Alright, one more should be fine. Let me get them."

"Let me. I'm twisting your arm. I'll pay." Nancy pushed herself up. "I always think there are times when it's best to just get wasted."

Jade smirked. "Well, just one, but I'm not sure the wine or my mood will improve."

"Let's find out." Nancy picked up her purse.

With no one driving, Jade's mind veered onto a circular track. Thoughts in the format of instamatic snaps flicked by: Freya on the boat, Freya sleeping with her on the beach, Freya in her arms. But the one that stuck in her mind's eye was Freya afraid in Jade's flat, a year ago.

Jade refocused as another large glass of wine appeared on the table in front of her. She was already feeling the first two.

"Lost in space again?" Nancy shuffled next to her.

"Sorry, my mind is all over the place."

"Then let's dull it with alcohol." Nancy raised her glass. "Cheers. To chance encounters, close encounters, or just counters where drinks are served."

They clinked glasses, and Jade took a sip. It tasted different. Maybe it was a new bottle. "I think those are inclusive most of the time."

"Sorry?" Nancy was smiling but her eyes showed confusion.

Freya would've understood.

"You used an '*or*.' I was just thinking those three things normally happen together, and are dependent on each other, so inclusive, rather than exclusive."

Nancy laughed. "Ooh, who's the cute, analytical one?"

Jade turned her head towards Nancy to find their lips only inches apart.

"And you're right," Nancy whispered. "For me they mostly are." She leaned a bit closer. "You know, there might be other things I can think of to get your thoughts under control." Her lips touched Jade's.

All the Time

JADE PUSHED NANCY away. There was no way she was going to kiss anyone, as distracting as it might be. She knew it would just feel wrong. She cleared her throat and looked away.

Nancy raised one corner of her mouth. "Sorry, I'm being too forward. Bad habit."

About to apologize as well, without knowing why, Jade heard the bartender yell from behind them. She turned and gasped.

"Lena?" Jade got up quickly and strode over to her.

The barmaid was all puffed up, her bulky arms crossed and her shoulders straight; she appeared ready to bounce Lena on her head. "Is she with you?" she growled.

"Yes," Jade said, and then whispered to Lena, taking her elbow, "Why are you here?"

The barmaid pointed towards the stairs. "You both need to leave. She's underage."

Lena took hold of Jade's wrist and hauled her towards the exit. "We're going."

Jade focused on not breaking her neck as Lena pulled her down the stairs.

Once on the street, Lena spun on her. "You're such an idiot!" She raised her fist like she was going to punch Jade, then turned, the braid of her long black hair whipping across Jade's face, before she stomped to a pillar box and kicked its innocent cast-iron shell.

Jade was shocked to see someone so young that angry. "Lena! Hell . . . Stop!"

Lena swung a punch at the defiant pillar box.

Jade stepped in front, and Lena's fist connected with Jade's head to the sound of cracking knuckles.

Lena screamed, "*Imbécile!*" while shaking her hand.

In the background, Jade could see Nancy waiting near the entrance of The Blue Candle. Lena also stared at the woman. Jade slowed her breathing in time with the throbbing pain at her temple.

"Fool," Lena said.

"Stop calling me names and explain—" she wavered.

"Your skull is made of rock." Lena cradled her injured hand to her chest. "I think you broke my fingers." She scrunched up her nose and eyes, like a cat about to hiss.

"I did what?"

Lena pointed with one of her supposedly broken fingers at Nancy. "You need to get rid of it."

"It? That's rude. Stay here. No more kicking or hitting."

"No promises. And hurry up. You don't have all the time in the world."

LILITH, THROUGH NANCY'S eyes, watched Jade head in their direction. Jade was struggling to maintain her balance. The drug hadn't worked as quickly as it was supposed to, and Lilith recalculated. It recognised the dark-haired girl from the restaurant in Les Baux. *Now that's someone with great timing.*

Jade finally stood face-to-face with her, and Nancy handed over Jade's phone. "You left this."

"Thanks. But sorry, I need to go," Jade slurred.

"Okay." Nancy wondered how far Jade would actually get.

Jade pushed her fingers through her dark brown hair, creating tufts that defied gravity.

Nancy kissed Jade's cheeks and waited until she turned and headed back to the angry girl. She brought out her own phone and checked that the app she'd installed on Jade's was working. It wasn't anything special, just a tracking programme for parents to keep tabs on their children. Jade's location was correctly displayed on the screen.

She would follow them at a distance, wanting to see if this girl would cope as Jade deteriorated. There was still a chance it could relocate if the angry girl was distracted.

JADE WAS FEELING the effects of the wine far more than she expected. "So what is this about? Where is Henri?"

They walked towards Oxford Street.

"Where are we going?" Jade stopped.

"You've been such a *le sot*," Lena said.

Lena's shape fuzzed and Jade steadied herself. *Hell, how much did I drink? It shouldn't be this bad. I can't even think . . . Wait, did Lena hit me?*

"Lena? What are you here . . . for. Where's . . . ?"

Lena laughed. "You're drunk."

"A bit, yes . . . What's going on?" Jade lost her concentration and sat on the pavement. She looked at her shoes. They weren't hers; these were stupid and small. She bent her foot towards her lap and tugged at the shoe. "*Ekki skó minn*," she mumbled and carefully inspected the twine holding it in place. She tried again to pull it off. Someone yanked her up and pushed her inside a black hut with a square door. She leaned back. "*Hvar er Eir?*" She didn't know who she was asking.

She heard *Heathrow Airport* as she drifted off.

JADE AWOKE TO her shoulder being roughly shaken.

Long, thin fingers placed a coffee cup on the tray in front of her. "Milk?"

There was a steady drone and the smell of cabbage and sweat.

"Milk in your coffee?" Lena yelled.

Jade nodded and rubbed her head, while a sachet was poured into her cup and stirred.

Two pills were placed into Jade's hand. "Painkillers. Take them."

Jade popped them in her mouth and took a drink of the lukewarm coffee.

"Were you drugged?"

Jade tried to piece together the events of the previous night. "I think so . . . Where am I?"

"On a plane to Oslo. We land in thirty minutes."

She turned back to Lena, who stared at her blankly.

"How did you—?"

"I got a train to London, found you, got you in a cab, took you to the airport, got you on the plane. Which was a total big pain."

"But you needed tickets and my passport?"

"I went to your place first, before I went to the bar. Banged on your door. Your neighbour let me in, thinking you were dead or something. She said you had collapsed before. I grabbed your passport and then found you." Lena hesitated. "Oh, and you hit your head on . . . something. And Henri, well, he doesn't know." She put in her earbuds, crossed her arms, and closed her eyes.

Jade pressed three fingers gently to Lena's shoulder and waited for her attention. "Where are we going?"

Lena opened her eyes and took out one earbud. "The moon."

"But you said, Oslo . . ." Jade drank from her cup. "God, my head hurts."

Lena's expression softened. "Freya's home. You've been going on about her nonstop."

Jade put her forehead against the cool surface of the aircraft's window. Outside, the breaking morning was painting the topside of clouds in orange and pink. The plane began a slow bank, and light reflected off its aluminium wing, forcing Jade to shade her eyes. It didn't feel like a new day, or a new beginning. It felt like an old one. She wished she could grant Freya a donut wish under a younger sun. But that was a wish for a wish, and everyone knows those aren't allowed.

LENA WAS QUIET, but that was fine. Jade was back to nursing her throbbing head with water from a bottle she'd purchased once they were through customs. The liquid did little to remove the astringent taste in her mouth, and she scraped her tongue on her teeth again.

"Do you have your driver's license?" Lena asked as they followed a yellow sign to the vehicle rentals.

She wasn't sure. She checked her pockets and found the folding wallet where she kept her Tube pass, debit card, and license.

"Yes."

"Come on, then."

They procured the rental car in English, and it wasn't long before she sat at the wheel waiting to enter their destination into the GPS.

"Just head towards Bergen," Lena said.

Jade entered the destination and waited until the system told her the driving time was eight hours.

"God, it's far."

"Just go already. What's it with you?" Lena's tone was sharp, and she pushed the knee of Jade's accelerator foot. "Drive already."

Jade pulled away and zigzagged out of the car park.

Lena's remark had upset her, and she glanced over to her. Lena was busy undoing her braid.

"What did you mean when you said, 'What's with me?'"

"You spend too much time thinking and not doing. It's like you assume there'll always be a tomorrow, another chance. Sometimes they're just gone."

The words stabbed into Jade; a spike pushing between her ribs and prodding the surface of her heart. *Freya.*

THE SUN WAS low on the horizon when they approached the exit for Bergen, and Jade needed to know where to go next.

Concealed by hood and hair, Lena was asleep against the passenger door.

"Hey." Jade gently shoved her shoulder to wake her.

Lena came round like a kitten in a basket, all yawns, blinks, and stretches. "Where next?"

Lena glanced around. "Just go north."

"You don't have a place name?"

"It's near Selje." Lena keyed it into the GPS. She looked at the screen in dismay, pinching her scrunched-up nose. "*Merde!* Another seven hours."

"We should've flown," Jade said, while indicating to overtake slow-moving traffic.

"I thought it was nearer." Lena hit the dashboard. "Drive faster."

"I can't. I'll get stopped. They put you in prison here if you're barely over the limit."

"Drive faster." Lena shrieked. "Or let me drive. Do I have to spell it out?"

"No," Jade whispered, before accelerating.

After three more hours driving in darkness, Lena's phone rang.

"*All . . . Non . . . Non, Je suis en Norvège . . . avec Jade . . . qui . . . Je suis désolée.*" She turned towards the window and spoke in a whisper. "*Oui, très mal . . . Je ne sais pas . . .*" She touched Jade's hand on the steering wheel. "Where are we?"

"Just after Sande on the E39."

The location was relayed, and then Lena spoke in hushed tones for another few minutes before hanging up.

A kilometre went by before Jade asked, "Was that Henri on the call?"

"Who else."

"Is he angry with you?"

"No. I explained, and he agreed." Lena thumped both her socked feet on the dashboard and put on her shoes. "He's sending someone to meet us."

They drove in silence for another thirty minutes, when Jade spotted blue lights flashing behind her, gaining fast.

"Shit." She'd been speeding and now slowed as they got closer.

Lena arched around and looked between the seats. "Police."

"I know."

Just as Jade expected to be signalled to pull over, the police car sped by, making her pace look like she was stationary.

"There must be an accident ahead," Lena observed.

Jade's adrenaline ebbed and was replaced with tension as tight as a bowstring. Other than the stops they'd made for fuel and food, she'd been driving for twelve hours in total and had spent every minute worrying about Freya. She turned on the radio to try to stay awake.

Ten kilometres on, a car with the word *Politi* on its door was blocking the road. Six vehicles were stopped and Jade pulled up behind the last one.

"Must be the accident." Lena lowered her window and stuck her head out, then popped it back in. "I couldn't see anything. Drive around."

"Hold on a second," Jade said as a circle of light moved erratically on the road surface. A police officer was marching down the line of cars. When he got to theirs, he shone his flashlight in her face before tapping on the glass.

"Step out, please," the officer said in broken English.

Jade did as she was asked, expecting to be breathalysed or even handcuffed, given how fast she'd been driving.

"Driver's license," he said, and she handed it to him. He then leant into the car. "You too, out," he told Lena.

While they stood together, the officer spoke into his shoulder mic. He handed Jade back her license then gestured at them. "Come with me."

Jade glanced at Lena, who'd pulled up her hood and pushed her hands into her pockets. They followed a few steps behind until they arrived at the patrol car that straddled the road.

Another officer directed her to stand by the driver's door. Further ahead they could see another police car. It was about a hundred metres away, halting the traffic in the opposite direction. In the sectioned-off tarmac, there was no accident. The area was empty.

The sound of a helicopter could be heard cutting through the silence of the night, and moments later, a light flooded the ground as it landed. Jade turned from the blast of air and pulled Lena close to shield her. Once the blades slowed, a figure jumped out and headed their way while being buffeted by the down thrust.

A woman in a navy blazer and slacks, with her black hair blowing across her face, greeted them. "Are you Jade Platt?" she shouted over the noise.

"Yes."

"I'm Special Agent Linn Nerison. I'll take you to Her Royal Highness."

"Freya?"

"Yes. Your car will be taken care of, but we must leave now."

Jade started to follow the agent then turned to see Lena hadn't moved.

"Come on," Jade yelled.

"I'm not going in that."

"You have to." She grabbed hold of Lena's wrist and dragged her to where agent Nerison stood holding the door as the rotors sped up.

"Come on. It's the same as a plane," Jade hollered.

"*Ce n'est pas!*" Lena screeched before clambering on board. "*Double merde.*"

As soon as the machine took off Linn passed two aviation headsets to them. Lena was covering her ears with her hands hidden in her cuffs. Jade pried them away and slipped a headset onto her, but she still looked very unhappy; her long hair a tangled mess, her shoulders hunched and her head bowed.

Gratitude flooded Jade when she thought about what Lena had done. "Thank you, Lena," she said in a trembling voice.

"For what?"

"Making this happen."

Jade squeezed Lena's hand. How had this young woman done so much?

It was pitch-black now except for the light from the cockpit. The luminance from the helicopter's dashboard hurt Jade's tired eyes, and she turned to look at the ground. Through the dark, as she counted the sparse pinpricks of light, a foreboding kept her chest tight, and she vowed that nothing in this world or the next would keep her from Freya.

A GREY SEA spread out below them; colour was returning to its surface as the sun broke through, searing the crests of the waves.

"Is it much further?" Jade asked, but knew the answer. She'd asked only minutes ago.

Linn pointed to the left. "You see the peninsula? There's a bay and an estuary on the other side. Her home is there."

"Can we call her?"

"We'll be there in fifteen minutes. Please wait until then."

Jade was desperate to find out how Freya was, but suspected that the agent didn't want to deal with the aftermath of any update while in the air.

She pressed her head to the plexiglass window, watching the sea and islands drift slowly past. It seemed oddly familiar to her. But only pricks of emotions and fragmented images flowed by before being lost.

The helicopter dropped as it crested the tree-covered hills, leaving Jade's stomach somewhere above. Banking, it ran along the coastline into a crescent harbour, across a wide estuary, and towards a large modern home of glass and timber. A yacht with a pea-green hull was moored just a short distance from a boathouse and dock where a cabin cruiser was berthed. They flew over the villa to a clearing just beyond.

The helicopter turned on a point and descended. The space was small and Jade couldn't believe they'd not taken out the rotor blades on the tall pine trees.

Linn opened the door. "Please leave your headsets here." She removed hers and stepped out, then offered a hand to assist Jade and Lena. As soon as they were beyond the craft, it lifted off in a flurry of dust and pine cones that were blown loose from the trees.

As they walked down the path towards the house, Jade grew increasingly anxious and picked up her pace.

"This is Freya's home?" Jade asked Linn.

"Yes, Miss Platt."

Jade started to shake; every cell in her body told her she must get to Freya. She started to run, leaving Linn and Lena behind. She could see the stairs at the side of the house. She headed straight for them, not sure where her energy was coming from.

She leapt up the steps two and three at a time, then darted onto a deck and slowed to see an open patio sliding door. Karen was standing to one side, waiting for her.

"Where—?" Jade huffed.

"Go through." Karen pointed inside.

Jade stepped past her, darted down a short hall, kitchen area, and into a spacious lounge. She scanned the room for Freya and turned a quick circle. *Why isn't she here? She would've heard the helicopter. Why's she not waiting?* Because, her cruel reason told her, she's gone. She felt her chest tighten and her legs shake.

Arms wrapped around her from behind and her knees gave way. Together, they collapsed onto the floor. Freya's blond hair touched Jade's face, and kisses with salty tears showered her lips.

"I'm sorry," Freya murmured over and over again, straddling Jade's lap, and wrapping her arms and legs around her.

With her near hysteria receding, Jade forced the strength she needed to the surface. "Shh. It's okay, I'm here."

"I . . . I need you with me," Freya said between gasps of breath.

"I'm not going to leave you, ever." She hoped Freya didn't read into her darker meaning.

Freya felt thinner. Her desperate, ocean-blue eyes were glued to Jade's. Freya blinked and tears rolled down her pale, hollow cheeks.

"Take me to my room . . . I need to tell you so much. But sleep first. You look so tired, my love." Freya pointed with a trembling hand towards a corridor that ran from the lounge.

Freya struggled to stand, and Jade supported her and helped her to the bedroom. As they shuffled down the hall, Jade knew, without question, Freya was her *raison d'etre*. A reason that had little time left.

A Future Plan

"GIVE THEM SOME time," Karen said when Linn arrived. She led her to a set of timber chairs at the far corner of the deck. Cushions hadn't been set out yet and the seats were still damp with the dawn's dew. She plopped down anyway and took out a pack of cigarettes. She offered one to Linn.

Linn shook her head. "Didn't think you smoked."

"I don't," Karen muttered. She gazed out towards the estuary, watching the seagulls standing on the roof of the boathouse. She turned and spotted Lena walking in a semi-circle around the grounds. "Must be nice to be young with so much energy."

Linn looked down towards the grassy expanse that sloped to the water. "She's Henri's daughter?" Lena was in the distance, walking in a broad circle around the garden and appeared to be searching for something.

"Fostered. A strange girl . . . Apparently, she took it upon herself to bring Jade here." Karen shifted; her bum was now damp from the seat. "I have to admit, it was the right thing to do. Freya went downhill so rapidly."

Linn scanned the perimeter, and Karen considered the young agent. She wasn't her first choice; her military background was a bit too conventional. But she was the only candidate Freya had agreed to. "You know, it doesn't matter how carefully you plan things, how perfectly you make sure things happen the best way possible. All of a sudden, everything changes and you realise you were never actually in control." She brought the cigarette to her mouth, discovering she had snapped it while talking.

"Yes, ma'am. Is Dr Sorenson here?" Linn stood at rest with her hands behind her back.

"She's asleep upstairs. But please call her Marianne."

"How much time does Dr Sorenson think Her Highness has?"

Karen jerked her head up and released a long drag of smoke. "None."

A DIGITAL CLOCK told Jade it was just after noon. She'd slept for a good six hours and was lying fully dressed next to Freya. She couldn't remember falling asleep but must have as soon as Freya had curled around her.

The small bedroom had a hardwood floor, which was covered by a fluffy white rug. Modern bookshelves lined the walls; ornaments, novels, and magazines all neatly placed. This wasn't really Freya-like, and Jade suspected that a staff member must be keeping things in order.

She listened to Freya's breathing, kissed her, and was about to whisper the three words she wanted to tell her, when a sudden sense of déjà vu hit. This situation had happened before. The fragments of a rustic room, a straw bed, and a sleeping angel coloured her mind's eye. Motionless, she waited until it passed and remembered Lena's cutting remark. *It's like you assume there'll always be a tomorrow.*

She gently stroked Freya's cheek. "Darling." She repeated it louder and kissed Freya's forehead.

Freya's eyes rolled under her lids, she moved her head, and murmured. She was pale; her rosy cheeks had lost their colour.

Her eyes fluttered open, and Jade put one arm around her. Freya was still encased in a sheet and woollen patchwork blanket.

"Sweetheart," Jade whispered.

"Morning." Freya shifted her hand out from under the covers, and they entwined their fingers. "Hmm, I slept so well," she said with a melodious tune.

"I'm sorry I woke you. I just needed to . . ." Tears pooled in Jade's eyes.

"What's wrong?" Freya squeezed her hand gently.

"I love you, so, so much. I'm . . ." She sobbed. "I'm sorry I didn't tell you sooner."

"Hey." Freya slipped her arm around Jade. "Come closer."

Jade buried her head under Freya's chin.

"I've always loved you." She kissed Jade's hair. "You won't remember. It was lifetimes ago."

Jade lifted her head. "Freya, I'm so afraid of losing you." She felt the sadness well up and override her self-control.

"Hey, my warrior . . ."

A pulse of guilt swamped Jade; she was being a coward.

"What is the best way to handle fear?" Freya asked.

"Ignore it until it destroys you . . . then you're dead or just dead inside," Jade blurted out.

Freya put her nose against Jade's. "Maybe you should try something. Yes?"

"I'm sorry."

"Listen. If you say 'sorry' one more time, I'll take you with me."

"I was coming with you anyway . . . It's not much of a threat."

"Stop it, o' dark and messed-up one. And answer my question."

All she could hear was Freya's slow shallow breathing as she tried to think. "You write down what the fear is. Then you make a plan on how to deal with it."

"That's better."

Freya was right; she needed to think ahead, and know exactly what she would do.

"But we need two plans."

"Two?"

"Yes, it's the number after one." Freya flicked the tip of her tongue twice on the end of Jade's nose. "See, two. There are two of us involved, after all."

Jade's stomach relaxed despite herself, and she smiled. "Yes, of course, sor—I mean, okay." She squeezed her eyes shut.

"So, these plans . . . Are you listening?"

Jade opened her eyes. "Yes."

"Then listen quicker. Now, the first is how you save me from damnation in Hell. I hope you have some really good ideas for that one. The second is how you survive without me." Freya pressed her fingers on Jade's lips. "No words from you. I know what you will say, Romeo. If you love me, you will make a future without me."

Jade blinked, and she felt tears roll down her cheek.

"God, sweetest, please keep it together. You have to be strong." Freya attempted a smile. "Yes?"

Jade nodded with Freya's fingers still on her lips.

"Are you ready to work on these plans?"

Jade nodded again.

"And no more talk of coming with me."

More tears rolled down Jade's face as her body trembled.

Freya removed her fingers and pushed her lips against Jade's, kissing deeply. "All right?"

"You're so brave . . ." Jade shuddered.

"Tomorrow we put our plans in action."

"I love you."

"I love you too. Now get some food. We cannot solve soul-destroying problems on an empty stomach."

Jade was up like a rocket and heading for the door.

"Where are you going?"

"To get you some breakfast."

"Sweetheart, shower first. I am pretty sure I won't die of starvation."

Jade washed and then dressed in clothes she borrowed from Freya's wardrobe. The result was a hodgepodge of expensive designer wear: jeans, tank top, and zip-up charcoal hoodie. The hoodie was a surprise as it looked more Camden Market than Harrods. But then she noticed the small Bougie Bleue logo sewn near the pocket and started to take it off.

"Hey, keep that on," Freya protested.

"No, it's too expensive. It must have cost thousands."

"Please keep it on, and it was free. Designers send me all kinds of things, hoping I'll wear them, but mostly they're too small. Anyway, hamster, everything of mine is yours."

Jade zipped it back up and smiled at Freya's comment. This was a new concept to her, sharing each other's things. "I won't be a second. I'll get you some food."

"A second is good." Freya smiled back.

Jade walked a dozen steps down the hall before entering the lounge. A balcony and stairs to the second level overlooked the space, and although the southern wall was glass, the others were made from large pine timbers carved with simple repeating patterns. A fireplace constructed from stones sat at the centre of the western wall. Long logs burnt in its hearth, and a pair of cream sofas faced each other, separated by a central coffee table.

A corner near the glass windows was set out as an artist's studio; the only part of the home she had seen that was messy. It was definitely Freya's area, with pencils, charcoals, tubes of paint, and unclean pallets spread across an L-shaped set of white laminate tables. The kitchen area merged with the lounge and included a long granite breakfast bar. The place reminded her of a ski chalet in Switzerland.

Karen sat on the sofa nearest the window and was busy typing on a laptop.

"Afternoon," she called out. She put the laptop to one side, stood, and walked to Jade. "How are you today?"

"Fine." Jade crossed her arms. She wasn't sure where she stood with Karen.

"Look, I'm glad you're here." Karen squeezed her forearm. "I'll assist you any way I can."

The tightness in Jade's chest eased. "I need to make a late breakfast for Freya."

"Let me help."

"Tell me about Freya's illness?" Jade asked, when everything was ready.

"Marianne will be down in a minute to check on Freya. She'll explain it better."

Jade frowned.

"Honey, I'm not trying to hide things from you. It's just that you'll understand her better than me. I was never good with medical mumbo jumbo. Plus, you can ask her questions that I can't answer."

Jade gave a quick nod and took Freya her breakfast.

FREYA ATE WITH a big grin, as if nothing was wrong.

"Why do you look like a Cheshire cat?" Jade was propped up next to her in the bed, sharing toast and sipping coffee.

"Because, you brought me breakfast. I love it."

"I'm glad—"

The door creaked open, but no one entered. Jade put down her coffee, and two enormous paws slapped onto the end of the mattress. A huge white-and-black–spotted beast pulled itself onto the bed.

"*Holy shit!*" Jade sprang towards the creature with her forearms held together, shoving it back. The animal continued to move forward as Jade wrapped her arms around its tree trunk-neck, twisting it away from Freya.

Freya burst out laughing. "Jade. My silly love. That's my lynx. You don't need to engage it in mortal combat. She won't hurt you."

The beast lay down with Jade attempting to flip it onto the floor. With Jade pinned, it licked Jade's ear and hair with a raspy tongue.

The breakfast tray fell onto the floor in the commotion, and Freya curled her knees against her chest, still laughing. "Bygul, leave her alone."

Jade released her death grip on Bygul's head and pried herself out from underneath the lynx. She shuffled quickly beside Freya. Her pulse was racing and her breathing hard. "Your cat? That's your cat? It's bloody huge. *Who has a cat that big?*"

Bygul blinked her orange eyes at Jade and stretched out to take up the empty part of the bed. It started a slow purr like a scooter with a broken exhaust.

"You're crazy." Freya snorted with laughter. "I've never seen anything like that. It was hilarious. Do it again."

"I was trying to protect you."

"From our lynx that is purring and would not hurt a fly."

"Our lynx?"

"Yes . . . yours too. And Bygul knows that; otherwise she would have eaten you."

"God, I thought it—I don't know what I thought."

Freya kissed her cheek, avoiding cat spittle. "It's okay, my fearless domestic-cat warrior, it's an easy mistake to make. But I think we should get you some glasses." She slid her arms around Jade. "Really thick ones." She brushed Jade's with her own and then sucked softly, encouraging a deep kiss. "Like bottle ends."

SOMETHING TAPPED ON Jade's shoulder as she stood on the deck. She'd been cursing the tranquil sea that was mocking her turmoil. *Why is my head a bushfire when reality is so hushed?*

"Hello." Dr Sorenson stuffed her hands into the pockets of her cardigan.

"Hi, Marianne." There were no kisses on cheeks or shaking of hands. Jade suspected this was a doctor thing. Jade didn't trust people easily, and her threshold for being comfortable with physical contact was worse since Syria. She would only share herself with one person, and she needed to know all the details of her illness. "How's Freya?"

"Come inside and sit down. We can talk there."

Jade followed Marianne inside and perched on the sofa, crossing her legs.

"First, how have you been?"

"I'm fine," Jade said. *One day I will start answering that bloody question with the truth—I'm drowning in a never-ending torrent of terror. But who wants to hear that?*

"You stopped your medication?"

"Yes, three months ago."

"Any headaches, dizziness, loss of concentration, blurred vision, fatigue, or hallucinations?"

"No," Jade lied. She pretty much had all of those.

"How do you feel about things now?"

"Worried for Freya."

Marianne looked older than she remembered. Her short, mousy hair now had strands of grey, and her eyes seemed more deep-set. She stared at Jade, as if trying to suck the thoughts out of her head, long enough for her to feel uncomfortable. "How much do you know?"

"Nothing."

"Well, let start with the prognosis. Are you prepared for me to be candid?" Jade nodded.

"Her condition is best described as aggressive NK Adoptive Acceleration or ANKA. The trigger is cellular flantecyclumia."

"I don't understand what that means."

"Well, Freya has an unusual cell lifecycle that is significantly slower than a typical person, but this is now returning to normal. This change means her immune system is attacking her cells. It's an awful paradox. Her immune system should have prevented the anomalous cells in the first place, but it's now killing her normal ones."

"So, it's a blood disorder?"

"Yes."

"Then it can be treated."

Marianne sighed. "There are challenges there. First, her blood is unique, so transfusions are impossible. The same applies to bone marrow transplants. And due to the aggressive adoption of her NK cells, other treatments have very low success rates."

Marianne pulled a tissue out of her pocket and handed it to Jade.

Jade wiped her eyes and nose.

"It's important that you know that Freya was in remission for over two years. But we started to see indicators of a reoccurrence last summer."

"She was successfully treated then?" Jade leaned closer.

"Yes, with extensive therapy. It surprised everyone. Freya is pretty remarkable. Since then, medication was keeping her autoimmune response under control until two months ago."

"Why not use the same treatment?"

"Freya didn't wish to go through it again, and I agree with her decision. Now with the reoccurrence, there is not much left to treat. So, well, really, there's nothing more that can be done."

Marianne's tired eyes relayed concern, and she put her hand on top of Jade's. "The rest of us have had time to come to terms with this, but for you this will be a shock and it'll take a while to cope with. Just remember you're not alone. Karen and I will always be here for you."

Jade bowed her head and then snapped it up. "Is Freya in pain?"

"I don't believe so. But she is pretty good at hiding her symptoms."

"There must be something that can be done?"

"I'm sorry. The best we can do is to help her through the time she has left. And here, there is something you can do. She has it in her head that she will be sent to some kind of Hell. I know of no one worthier of heaven." Marianne's professional persona broke and her voice cracked. "If you can help to convince her of that, it will give her peace."

Jade couldn't speak as her anger consumed her. *Why? Why now? Why was I such a mess when she needed me? Why are things always fucking twisted and messed-up.*

She shook where she sat before darting off the sofa and striding outside to lean on the handrails of the deck. She banged her head against the wooden rail until the pain stopped her.

A charged wave moved through her head, leaving her feeling like she'd touched a live wire—a side effect of an earlier prescription that she'd stopped too abruptly. The jolt made her remember the promise to Freya. *"If you love me, you will make a future without me."*

With an aching head from where she'd challenged the gods and lost, and an aching heart from where fate had dealt her sorrow, Jade spun around and raced back to Freya.

Freya looked up from the book she was reading and smiled. "Are you ready to work on our plans?"

In the silhouetted moment, the moment that was now, everything was okay.

A Proposal of Consequence

THE EVENING SUNSET flared on the window behind Jade. She fidgeted on the stool in the studio corner of the lounge. Freya had stopped mentioning plans and insisted instead that she draw Jade's portrait.

"Can we talk?" Jade asked.

Freya glanced up from her pad. "Shh. And keep still."

Jade uncrossed her legs and shifted on the seat.

"I won't marry you if you don't let me finish."

Jade froze.

Freya's head was down, and she was biting her lip while sketching with charcoal on a large ringed pad.

Jade slipped off her perch and moved quietly to Freya and then drifted behind her. With a broad smile, she asked, "What did you say?"

"Nothing of consequence." Freya was still trying to keep a straight face. She was smudging a section of charcoal with her thumb. It wasn't done, but it captured Jade in a much softer, flattering likeness than she perceived herself.

"I don't want to contradict a princess, queen, or whatever, but you suggested something rather important."

A hint of a smile broke through Freya's mask.

Jade leaned closer and huffed softly into Freya's ear.

"Stop that." Freya laughed.

Jade continued to kiss and blow.

"You minx. Stop. It's driving me crazy."

Jade put her head against Freya's back and wrapped her arms around her waist.

"I like this," Freya said, "how you are holding me."

"You can still draw?"

"Yes. I really didn't need you sitting. I know your face. It was just a way to keep you close by."

Jade smirked and squeezed tighter against Freya.

The scratching noises of Freya's charcoal soothed Jade, and she just watched and listened.

"You love me, right?" Freya asked.

"Yes."

"So, will you marry me?"

"I . . ." She tried to take in what Freya had just asked. The magnitude of it fell on her like a giant had pried up the corner of Mount Everest, brushed her under, and then let go. The person she loved was asking for her hand. It was the most joyous event that would ever happen to her. But the mountain she should be at the summit of, in shared triumph, crushed her with the knowledge that they had no future. Thoughts of a mayfly flashed through her head.

> *How long is a minute?*
> *How long is a moment?*
> *What is left behind?*

> *Bereft of purpose?*
> *Or of no consequence?*
> *Just images in a mind's eye?*
> *No. There must be a reason, no matter how fleeting, for life*
> *that passes by.*

"You're not good with answering straightaway, are you?" Freya asked in a harsh tone, while she scratched in a fury against the paper.

"Yes," Jade muttered. Her vocal cords jammed up with emotion.

Freya stopped drawing. "Yes. Yes, to what?" She turned her head to Jade and placed her forehead against hers. Her hair fell forward, cloaking their faces.

"The question where you asked me to marry you."

"I see." Freya put her pad down and drew a heart on Jade's forehead with her thumb.

Jade smiled. "That was covered in charcoal, wasn't it?"

"Yup." She held up her thumb so Jade could see, then ran it down the bridge of Jade's nose. "So . . . you said yes." Freya's eyes glistened.

"Yes."

"You need to answer questions more quickly. I could have found someone else in the time it took you."

Jade laughed, but stopped as tears welled up in Freya's eyes. "Darling!" Jade scooped her up and carried her towards the sofa. She had to use all her strength and was only just able to gently lower her onto the cushions.

Freya kept her arms around Jade's neck. "I'm okay . . . Just feeling like sugar and salted popcorn."

"You want some popcorn?" Jade couldn't think. "Let me get Marianne."

"No. I just meant my emotions are sweet and salty. Happy and sad . . . Who puts sugar and salt on popcorn anyway? It's just stupid."

Jade stood there, dumbfounded.

Freya patted Jade's thigh. "It's okay, my love. Make some green tea, all right? And please ask Karen to speak with me. Then we must talk."

Jade stood and started to the kitchen.

"You said, yes, right?" Freya asked.

"Yes. Always yes."

JADE POURED HERSELF a cup of coffee from the pot and glanced outside to the musty dawn. She hadn't yet slept. Today, she was getting married. Karen had hastily made the arrangements late yesterday. It would be a quiet affair with only those who actually needed to be there.

Henri was expected to arrive by midday, and Max was also coming. What Jade recently learnt was that Max and Karen had been seeing each other on and off.

For most of the night, Freya had explained what their marriage would mean. It was part of her plan for Jade, perhaps since the day they had first met. She was giving Jade a purpose of such consequence that she'd have no choice but to make it her future. Jade didn't think of this as subterfuge or even a burden. It felt like a gift, from the person she loved. Freya had spoken at length, detailing what would happen after she was dead. Jade thought about how desperate Freya was to ensure Jade wouldn't be afraid and formed a bittersweet smile, understanding her remark about sugar and salted popcorn all too painfully.

What they hadn't yet discussed were Freya's concerns about the afterlife. Freya had fallen asleep before they got to it. Jade felt bad about this, knowing Freya was terrified of what would happen to her after she died. On the beach, in the Côte d'Azur, Freya had drawn a picture of darkness, winged demons, and pyres made from corpses. It scared Jade that the demons in Freya's drawing resembled the one she had imagined behind Lena's circle in France.

The door to the deck slid open and Lena slipped in, bringing an envelope of cold air with her.

"Coffee?" Jade asked as Lena approached.

Lena lowered her hood. "Can I have a hot chocolate?"

"Sure." Jade smiled and set about microwaving a mug of milk. "I've not seen you for a few days."

"Been busy."

"Where?"

"Outside, while you're snoring."

"Doing what?" Jade stirred chocolate powder into Lena's cup.

"Stuff." Lena pulled out a bundle of shimmering black-and-blue feathers from her pocket. "Can you pass me some tinfoil?"

Jade took a piece from a roll in the drawer, handed it to her, and put the hot chocolate on the counter. She smiled, watching Lena as she rolled the feathers up in the foil. "You were collecting them in the dark?"

Lena passed the package to Jade. "Be careful and don't rub them in the wrong direction. Well, just don't mess with them at all. You'll need them later."

"Okay . . . What are they for?" Jade placed the shiny bundle on the counter.

"Put them in your pocket."

Jade was too tired to ask again and humoured the girl, tucking them into the front pocket of her jeans. "Good?"

"*D'accord.*" Lena turned and headed towards the stairs at the far end of the room with her hot chocolate in hand. "I'm going to bed."

"What the hell." Jade slammed her coffee down. "Your back!" She darted to Lena and grasped her shoulder. "Shit, was this Freya's cat?"

"Don't be stupid." Lena tried to pull away. Her jacket was torn with a vertical rip, which cut through all the layers of fabric, gashing her skin. The long wound was sticky with blood that had also soaked her clothes.

"Stay still. Shit, we need to get this bandaged."

Up on the balcony, Karen appeared. "What's going on?" she asked, leaning over the railing.

"Wake Marianne. Lena's cut her back." Jade pulled a stool out from under the breakfast bar. "Sit. Take off your jacket."

"Stop scaring everyone. And leave me alone."

"It's not a small cut, Lena. Sit still. Let me help you."

Under the jacket, Lena's white T-shirt was dyed with blood. Jade helped her pull it off.

With medical kit in hand, Marianne, still in her pyjamas, padded over to them. "Please turn towards the lights so I can see," she said while guiding Lena's shoulders. She opened the kit, located a pair of surgical gloves, and put them on. "It's not too deep, except in one place. How did this happen?"

"Bygul was too slow," Lena said and started to push off the stool.

"Don't be difficult," Jade insisted. "Stay put. It needs sorting. And tell us how it happened."

Lena picked up her cocoa and took a sip.

Marianne pulled out a bottle of sterile water from her kit and squirted it on the wound—the gash ran just below Lena's bra to the top. She then used cotton swabs to dab it clean.

"Given where it is, there won't be much movement, so it won't need stitches. Suture tape will do. But I need to know if it was caused by an animal. You might need a tetanus shot."

Rather than responding, Lena scowled.

"Come on, Lena, tell Marianne."

"I fell on a branch." Lena snapped at Jade. She flinched when Marianne applied antiseptic.

"Almost done. Now stay still." Marianne attached the sutures and taped three field dressings overtop.

"Don't go anywhere. I need to get a wider bandage." Marianne stood and went upstairs.

The sun broke above the hills to the south, flooding the room in hazy light.

"Where is Bygul?" Karen asked.

"She didn't do it," Lena hissed.

"All the same, I'm going to check that." Karen spun around and stormed off.

Raising Lena's chin, Jade asked, "It's just you and me now. What happened?"

Lena batted her long lashes in defiance.

"Come on, Lena, I really hate seeing you hurt. You know you can trust me. Tell me what happened."

"Your stupid feathers. One got behind me, and that dumb cat was too slow."

"What got behind you?"

"You've seen one."

Jade scrunched her head against her shoulders and crossed her arms. "The thing I saw in France . . . beyond your circle? It was real? And you're taking their feathers?"

"They've come for Freya. Because of what she is. My circle keeps them out. But you need their feathers. So . . . well, one got too close. It was quick, quicker than most."

The explanation was impossible, but she'd seen its claws and knew the wound matched. "What are the feathers for?"

Jade looked up when she heard the footsteps. Marianne shuffled towards them.

Lena lowered her voice. "A swap. Don't lose them."

Marianne finished wrapping a wide bandage around Lena's torso and put two paracetamols into Lena's hand. Lena swallowed them with a gulp of hot chocolate, slipped off the stool, and headed to her room without a word.

Marianne packed up her medical kit. "As I'm up, I'll check on Freya."

Jade watched as Marianne entered Freya's bedroom and went to wash out the cups. When she looked up, she saw Bygul being escorted to the door by Karen, one hand grasping the scruff of the cat's neck, the other holding her pistol.

"Don't!" Jade raced over and darted between Karen and the door. "Don't shoot her. It wasn't Bygul." She hadn't seen the cat since yesterday. She had a large nick in her left ear, and some fur was missing above her shoulder.

"I wasn't going shoot it. The gun is just a precaution. I don't want Freya seeing it in this state. And I don't trust it." Karen opened the door and then used her foot to encourage the lynx out. "It's clear Lena and the cat got into a scrape of some kind." She holstered her weapon inside her blazer.

"Bygul is pretty beat-up. Is there a vet I can take her to?" Jade asked.

"There's nothing close by. I'll call a vet tomorrow if she's worse. Right now it doesn't look too bad." Karen closed the door and leant against it. She had dark shadows under her eyes. "So did Lena tell you what happened?"

"No."

Karen sighed. "By the end of this day we'll need to trust each other. You'll be consort to the queen, and I'll be in your service. And what we all know will happen soon, means that you'll have Freya's title. Then we'll need each other."

"I know . . . So, okay, something strange is going on that I'm not yet prepared to explain because I can't. Lena is preventing something from happening, and she was hurt gathering feathers. I'm not sure what they're for. When I know more, I'll tell you."

Karen stared at her before nodding slowly. She reached into her blazer and pulled out a folded document. "Strictly confidential. It's time you knew. Please, burn it in the fire once you've read it." She went outside.

Jade deposited herself on the sofa and unfolded the papers. The document appeared to be Norwegian Government issue. At the top, Karen had written something in blue biro.

> *Jade, this document was translated into English for you. It's given to Norwegian prime ministers when they are sworn into office. A number of sections have been edited out. Completely confidential, but you need to know. Løytnant Karen Felds.*

Etterretningstjenesten
Norwegian Ministry of National Security
1941-10-01
Briefing: E16-SE19410123-SS
Citizen of National Importance—Sunniva
Security Level: Non-disclosure 05
Last Updated: 2013-07-08 E16.1244.RA
Restricted—Protected Identity

This document provides synopses of the Norwegian national and member of the royal house, Miss Freya Rykkel, born circa 975 AD; she will subsequently be referenced here as Sunniva. Her existence is known to the Norwegian royal house and her position is honorary, although her ancestry is monarchical. Sunniva's identity, status, and assets are confidential and a matter of national security.

The E16 special intelligence unit has overall responsibility for her safety with a full briefing of her history. Dedicated agents provide Sunniva with protection and assistance, while international security agencies are advised that she is a citizen of importance. Sunniva has been known as the following individuals (information provided by Sunniva):

Eir, 975 c. [2]—Historia Sunniva.
Saint Sunniva, 996 c.
Astrid Olofsdotter, 1035 c.
Wulfhild, 1020–71
Other entries removed, KF.
Princess Freya Rykkel, 1989–(2023)—Current identity, active from 2003.
Princess Hanne Galtung, 1999–(2043)—Surrogate Mette Lang, to start from 2023.

In conjunction with NIS, a system of rolling identity replacement has been established. Surrogates are recruited and pipelined. Once a surrogate has reached Sunniva's age, Sunniva takes the identity, and the surrogate temporarily returns to the community under a different persona. When twenty years have passed, the surrogate resumes her original identity, providing continuity from middle age. Surrogates are trained such that the transitions happen seamlessly. In recent decades, with digital photography and media intrusion it has become an increasing concern that these transitions will be noticed. As a result, Etterretningstjenesten (NIS) vigorously manages the media.

The status Sunniva commands is due to her unique position in the history of Europe and her importance to Norway. Reasons for this are enumerated below:

Land Holdings—28,542km² in Vestlanddet, Midt-Noreg, Nord-Noreg and ownership of the 373km² Jan Mayen Island. Total value in excess of 120 billion kr. Concessions made by Sunniva allow for the land to be listed and used as national holdings. This agreement and the activities involved are ratified annually. However, legal ownership remains with Sunniva. She also has holdings in France and other European countries, as well as North America. Details of assets are documented in E16-SE19410135-SS.

Constitutional Rights—Sunniva holds the same powers as the monarch with two noteworthy exceptions. First, she may exercise her rights without advice of The Council of State. Second, no provision is made to circumvent any right exercised. In practice she abstains and defers all rights to the monarchic proxy.

Harmoni Foundation—Sunniva is the chairwoman. The charity is ranked fourth worldwide and has an endowment estimated at thirty billion USD. The foundation's focus is the humanities, providing funds for relief efforts, scholarships for underprivileged, as well as research and direct action into reducing poverty. The majority of the fund comes from enterprises and investments solely owned or part owned by Sunniva.

Sunniva's physical and psychological analysis is provided in E16-SE19410141-SS. Updates were permitted on January 23, 1993 and on July 1, 2013. Her current health is poor and as a result she is not expected to require the use of the subsequent surrogate, Mette Lang.

In the interests of national security, provisions are being made to ensure all assets owned by Sunniva and her hereditary monarchical powers are provisioned in the best interests of the nation. NIS expresses concern that Sunniva's actions and wishes may not align with that of the government or the royal house. She

has within her legal right the ability to pass these to any third party she desires, prior or upon her death. A noteworthy concern is the possible existence, or potential, of a spouse or civil partner.
Document End—E16-SE19410123-SS

Jade reread the papers and then let the folds drift shut. She stepped near to the fire and dropped the document into the flames. She was getting married and it was time to get ready.

A Horror's Sorrow

THE DAKAR MOTORCYCLE ripped along a trail, which carved through the mature pines. Nancy lifted her gloved left hand to knock away a moth that had collided dead centre of her visor. She would've preferred a less bone-jarring method of transportation, but the tracking app had shown Jade located on the Norwegian coast in a great parcel of land assigned to the state forestry. There were no public roads and the motorcycle would get her the closest, as the only other approaches were by sea or air.

She slowed, pulling in the clutch and tapping down to second gear with her reinforced boot. The trail narrowed, becoming full of ruts and deep potholes. She stood on the pegs to ride out the worst of the bumps while keeping her speed high to skip over others.

After another hour, the odometer told her she was close, and she stopped and turned off the engine. Other than the sound of the exhaust ticking as it cooled, the woods were quiet.

She unzipped her jacket and fetched her phone from the inside pocket. It had a strong signal, and given the remoteness of the location, this was a clue that there was civilization hidden behind the trees.

Within Nancy, Lilith had been multitasking, considering how to approach the problem of discovering the whereabouts of the wings. Decisions were never its strong point. Having to weigh up different options was like choosing which socks to wear. Lilith could never work out why it mattered. It always decided based on what offered the most power, not on instinct or feeling. A sock was a sock. Lilith was mystified as to why Freya hadn't kept her wings safe. Her fate would be most horrid. Hel must be dancing in fits of glee at the thought of having Frigg's daughter as a Sorrow chained into one of its abominations.

"It would certainly make a magnificent butchering muse," Lilith considered.

It just needed to wait for an opportunity. If none arose, it'd have to take the Valkyrie's necklace. Hel would happily barter for the *Brísingamen* and its bound soul. Lilith hadn't forgotten the moment when Frigg attached her daughter's essence to the pendant.

A hot tub. That's what it truly wanted. Every muscle ached.

"I better get on with things. Hel can't wait," Nancy muttered before pushing the Start button on the handlebar. She knocked in first gear and sped away, throwing up clumps of mud.

She drove off the trail into a clearing filled with tall ferns. The moon offered little light, and she swung off the bike, allowing it to drop with a thud onto the soft ground. It was pretty much out of fuel, and in any case, it wasn't needed anymore—her phone told her she was a mile out and needed to head west. After removing her helm and glove, she entered the forest.

The area had been harvested in recent years, and young trees spanned out in all directions. They grew so close together that she had to push between the branches and wipe away spider silk from her face.

She broke through into an older part of the forest.

About three hundred yards in front of her, a demon stood with its back to Nancy. Its black wings were spread out to conceal its form. Suddenly, the demon thrust forward but was knocked back by an unseen force. A wave of butane-blue flames fanned out along its feathers as it hunched back down.

Lilith, through Nancy's eyes, noticed the faint line on the ground in front of the creature. Nancy circled around, such that she stayed on the protected side of the line. She crept out from behind the bushy branches of a Scots pine to see the Horror in its full tumult. With spines fused, a female Sorrow twitched within a prison of its ribs and the putrefying muscles of the host that carried it. The creature bolted forward, but again rammed into an unseen barrier and was blocked.

The Horror swung a clawed hand towards Nancy, only to have it again knocked away. The Sorrow wailed as a spasm contorted its body. Borrowed eyes of the outer Horror stared, before it spoke in a dialect Lilith hadn't heard for an era.

"*Daku sinnis. Basu mitu.*" Vocal cords visibly vibrated in the remnants of its neck.

"Shut up. Just summon your Begetter," Nancy demanded.

Lilith was having a hard time controlling Nancy's fear and wondered if she would hold out when Hel arrived.

The Sorrow screeched, its head flicking rapidly. Its pitiful, languid limbs, just skin on bones, flopped around as the Horror paced along the line on the ground. Lilith tried to recognise the enslaved creature, but she didn't look familiar. *A Valkyrie no doubt, but which one? And who created this barrier?*

A circle of fire expanded from a central point, flattening, like a wave hitting a sea wall, when it collided with the magical impediment. After a moment, the blood-red flame dwindled, leaving the ground burnt with spots of glowing embers.

An animal approached, walking on its hind legs. The dying glow of the circle reflected in a cloak of shimmering scales. Its head was that of a deer, in all but its eyes, which were small slits, hiding orbs of ice-blue. Even Lilith knew not to look beyond Hel's costume. The skin was just a facade and from a recently killed caribou.

"So you decided to summon me. Why?" The animal's mouth didn't move. Somewhere behind it Hel herself spoke.

Nancy bowed. "Yes, Goddess, I have a proposition."

The deer clapped its foreleg hooves together. "I love propositions."

Nancy's mind was on the verge of shutting down as two new Horrors appeared from the shadows, stuttering between movements with their imprisoned Sorrows screaming and writhing within the husks. Lilith directed Nancy's eyes to focus elsewhere.

"Indeed. A simple exchange. I'll give you your desire for a pair of Valkyrie wings." Nancy's words trembled with fear, even though her tone was confident and friendly.

"You don't have what I desire." The deer laughed, jumping on one leg, then the other.

"I'll retrieve it for you, since it seems your creatures cannot." Nancy waved her arm broadly along the line in the ground that had stopped the Horror from advancing.

Hel tipped the deer's head in such a dramatic swoop, it looked like it might topple off. "Why would you do this?"

This was the tricky bit. Lilith couldn't divulge that it had been released to kill the Norns. As much as it didn't want to honour its indenture, it must do Frigg's task for its own survival and the preservation of the pleasures it had grown accustomed to.

"I have a deed to complete for the goddess Frigg."

Hel laughed and pointed a hoof to the Horror on her left. "Frigg won't need your deed anymore." Lilith now recognised the jawline and strands of red hair that remained on the sunken skull of the Sorrow. Events had proceeded faster than Lilith had expected; much of Asgard must now be part of Hel's dominion if Frigg has been enslaved.

With Frigg now consumed, Lilith had another choice to make. *Do I need to still do Frigg's bidding? Nancy, what do you think?* Nancy mind, locked in a scream, failed to answer. *This is impossible. I don't know. If I don't, no hot tub, no frozen margarita meltdowns, no Jeopardy.* "No matter. I still must complete my undertaking."

"Your fatal fate, you mean?" The deer chortled while dancing a jig on the spot.

Lilith tried not to laugh. Hel was a simple creature. A servant of the Norns, and its time was nigh. The Norns were starting again, using its power to clear Asgard, then all the other planes. Lilith didn't know why, but soon Hel's demons would be in Midgard as well.

The millennia ago Norns had trapped Lilith, or Ereshkigal as it was once known, after it had conspired to undermine their weaves. The witches, in their spite, had removed Lilith's limbs before transforming it into a serpent bound to the branches of a fruit tree. Then, to Lilith's disgust, Hel was made from its own arms and legs and parts from other creatures it dare not think of.

As much as Lilith didn't want to be involved with the experiments of Norns, its own existence depended on stopping them. It would have to kill one, wait, then the next, hide, then the third, done. The fourth, it was not sure about at all. The gods and old tales only ever talked about the three, but Lilith suspected there was one more. The plaques in the old temples of the dead city of Serjilla had shown four.

"Do you want the necklace or not?" Lilith made Nancy smile but was pretty sure it hadn't come out right. Fear and smiling didn't really go together. "My Lady, there will be no Sorrow as great as Frigg's daughter."

Hel laughed, and the deer's mouth wobbled with tribulations, causing drops of blood to fall from its nose. "How do you know?"

"Frigg's daughter's soul sentenced to your damnation is a sorrowful fate. Her love taken from her. She is Eir, the Valkyrie healer. A saint and an angel, some have said. She is passion and love. There will be no greater tears. Your Horror would be magnificent." Maybe a bit overstated, Lilith thought, but it was doing a deal with the Devil and it needed to exaggerate.

A tongue protruded and licked the dead deer's lips and then slathered up the blood from its nose. "Very well. Bring it to the gate. Her mother will collect her soul." Hel burst out in a fit of hysterical laughter, bending over and splitting the sides of the deer, exposing something of the creature within.

Lilith could see the irony; it was actually pretty humorous. The mother who gave her life and protected her soul would now collect it to meet the same fate as her own. A healer, bound to a creature to perform endless acts of death, would make the power of that Horror truly remarkable.

"Where is the gate?"

"Sunniva's Well." Hel chuckled.

Lilith knew the place, and if it had its wings it would have already used the bridge to Asgard. "When?"

"Dawn after the full moon."

Nancy nodded and shook Hel's hoof. The race was now on. Lilith would have to kill the weavers of fate before their right hand, Hel, destroyed all.

Lilith caused Nancy to shrug. *All this for a soak in a hot tub.*

AT MIDDAY, JADE was taken back when hordes of guests arrived at once. The king of Norway, with a small entourage, landed on the water in a sea helicopter. Another brought the prime minister and three security agents, and finally, a third brought Max, Henri, and a rather disgruntled archbishop of the Church of Norway.

In the spacious lounge, the fire roared, competing with the cool air coming in from the open patio doors. Someone offered Jade a glass of champagne and she shook her head, too nervous to drink anything. Earlier, caterers had arrived by boat with food and were now offering snacks and drinks to the guests.

She was introduced to everyone, then finally the king. As she bowed, she realised she had never performed such an act to Freya, who was actually the true heir.

The archbishop, a tall, thin man with a greying, squirrely beard, which matched his ill pallor, thankfully took the king's attention from her.

She stayed rooted, not sure if she'd been dismissed, as a small incident of veiled friction ensued between the archbishop and the king.

"The General Synod doesn't sanction this consecration. I'll perform it, but beware, the National Council is unlikely to ratify the marriage," the archbishop said, his face screwed up like he was drinking corked wine.

The king frowned, holding his hands behind his back. "Four years ago, I agreed that the law be changed." He narrowed his eyes. "Does it really take so long for the church to align with equality?"

"The Lord's words do not allow such a union."

"Do you truly think man's transposed whispers are God's prescriptive designs?"

The archbishop didn't respond, and Jade suspected he didn't understand the king's meaning.

With the archbishop off balance, the king followed his *prise de fer*. "I would be more careful of one's own soul. Sunniva will be in our Lord's company soon. What will our saint tell Him about your pusillanimous discrimination?"

The archbishop's demeanour changed dramatically after this.

Freya appeared in a simple but delicate black chiffon mini-dress. It was decorated with pearls and green stones, which formed small weaves of flowers throughout the fabric.

Jade was wearing a dress of white macramé lace on pale yellow linen, which Freya had selected for her. The garment fitted her perfectly; it was as if Freya had planned her attire months ago. When they stood side by side, she understood the meaning of their attire. They were wearing each other. The stones embellishing Freya's skirt were made of cut jade. While, on Jade's dress, the patterns in the lace were of wings, and the accompanying belt was silver daisies with centres of amber.

Freya insisted she stand without aid as the archbishop performed a condensed version of their vows in both English and Norwegian. She couldn't get over how beautiful Freya looked, especially with her hair in a bun, exposing her slender neck; something she had never done before.

"I love your hair up. You look beautiful," Jade whispered while Karen handed a ring to Freya.

Freya smiled. "It's an old tradition to show I'm married."

They exchanged rings and the archbishop sanctioned their union.

Jade and Freya kissed to personable claps and cheers. As they nuzzled, Freya whispered, "I didn't think you would have a ring for me."

"Sorry it's so tatty," Jade said.

"It's not. It's lovely, my wife."

Hours before, when Jade was in a panic, knowing she didn't have a ring to give Freya, Lena had pointed to Jade's finger. "Why not use that?"

It was the one Aaina had given her and she'd forgotten she was wearing it. It wasn't fit for a queen, but she had no other. A dumb thought raced by. *I'll buy Freya a better one later.* But it was instantly struck down by the next. *There is no later.*

After documents were signed and pictures were taken, Freya, on wobbly feet, whispered, "I need to lie down."

Jade helped Freya to her bedroom and returned to the lounge to encourage guests to go.

The king waited after the others. He approached Jade and bowed his head before shaking her hand. "It will be a privilege to be in your service."

Jade blinked at him. "I . . ."

"If I, or your country, can be of any assistance, don't hesitate to ask." The king then turned and left with security agents trailing behind.

Someone's hand touched Jade's shoulder and she glanced to see Max standing next to her. "That goes for me as well. Not that I have any horses, or men or a kingdom."

"Thanks. And thanks for coming at such short notice."

"Karen arranged it. A bit of a surprise your sudden marriage. But not completely. It's been pretty obvious how you felt about Freya. I wish . . . well, you know."

"Yes." Jade patted his shoulder. "I better go back to her."

Marianne stood at the threshold to their bedroom. Her eyes bore into Jade; there wasn't anything left to be said. Jade went to the bed and knelt beside Freya. "How are you doing?"

"Happy, now."

"Shall I help you get changed?"

"No. Just stay." Freya brushed her thumb over the ring on her finger.

Jade climbed in beside her and put her head on the pillow next to Freya's hand. Freya gazed at her ring, and then she frowned as she turned her hand slowly.

"Something wrong?" Jade asked. "I know it's a rubbish ring, I'll—"

Freya gasped, and pushed herself upright. She wrapped her arms around Jade's neck, almost choking her.

"You . . . saved me. Kari . . . I knew you would! You found them. Oh my dear love, I love you. You have given me everything!" Freya relaxed her grip and slipped back onto the pillow, smiling, her energy depleted. "I can escape now. I can fly away." The joy stayed on her lips.

Jade had no idea what she was talking about; her nerves were on tenterhooks.

"I'll be free."

She brushed Freya's hair from her eyes. "What do you mean?"

"Just hold me." Then Freya told Jade her story from the very beginning; how Jade was once known as Kari and that they grew up together; how her mother, Frigg, had given her the wings and the amber necklace, and how she discovered she no longer felt the cold when the *Frihet* had sunk. She told how they had lived on Selje, or Sellø, as it was once called, with monks and goats, and how Kari had disappeared; how she'd thought she had lost everything she loved.

"And this ring is from my mother. It was flat before. But it is how I grow my wings. I touch it to my lips and they change into them. To remove them I just brush the mark on my cheek three times. And there is more, but I need to sleep. You know, really, I just spent most of my long history waiting for you. But there's no time to go through everything." Freya's eyes filled with tears and her breathing became shallow. "I love you, my warrior, my wife, my best friend." She released Jade's hand. "I want to see the morning."

"I'll open the curtains," Jade said, puzzled.

"No, I want to be outside on the deck."

Jade needed help, so she popped her head out the bedroom door and was surprised to see Marianne, Karen, and Lena, quickly standing from the sofa in the lounge. Their faces all dropped at the sight of her.

"Freya wants to go outside to see the sunrise. Can someone set up a chair and someone help me?"

A few minutes later, Freya was propped up on a lounger. The sun had not yet climbed the ancient mountains on the southern side of the sheltered bay, and the sky was grey, the sea calm, and a mist hovered over its surface. The timber boards of the deck were damp, soaking the knees of Jade's brushed cotton pyjama bottoms where she knelt next to Freya.

"Can you get me something?" Freya asked.

"Yes, darling." Jade's voice trembled. Freya's words sounded so far away.

"Please fetch me a hot water bottle. I'm cold . . . *Ek elska þig, Kari.*"

Jade rose and kissed Freya's forehead. Somehow, she knew what Freya's words meant. "I love you too," she said with tears. She went inside and, out of habit, closed the patio doors.

In the kitchen, Jade waited for the kettle to boil. Then it hit her: Freya didn't feel the cold.

NANCY WATCHED THE house from the trees. Miss Rykkel had been moved outside and left alone. Now was a good time. She padded up the stairs onto the deck and approached without making a sound. She put a hand over Freya's mouth and a knee on her chest, pinning her arm.

"I'm sorry, Valkyrie, but with no wings, you have something else I need."

Freya lashed out with her right hand, trying to knock Nancy away.

"That's not kind," Nancy whispered.

Freya tried to twist a ring off her other trapped hand.

Nancy took hold of the amber necklace and with one strong yank she broke the clasp and lifted it away. Freya's body convulsed. Nancy stood up and watched the death spasms with curiosity.

She caught a glimpse of a figure approaching from inside and darted out of view but turned to see Freya's last movement. Nancy watched Freya's hand, with the ring between her fingers, touch it to her lips.

Nancy turned, raced down the steps, and back into the shadows of the woods. It was too easy, too simple to destroy something so unique, but it was all or nothing. With the amber necklace pushed into a pocket, all it needed to do now was get to the island of Selja and sell an angel's soul to the Devil.

JADE'S BRAIN FELT bludgeoned as she moved on staggering feet to the glass door. Through it she could see Freya's still form; her arm dangled from the chair between folds of white feathers.

Jade yanked the doors open, tumbled out, and dropped beside her. She parted the wings to see Freya's face. She lifted Freya's hand, crossed it over her still chest, and then positioned the other in the same manner. She folded the wings together again, held them in place, and laid her cheek against the soft down.

"Safe journey, my angel."

A Misgiving

GREYHOUND CLOUDS RACED across the sky. A gravestone marked the end of Freya's days, and liquorice-hued acquaintances walked stiffly away. A muted insipidity permeated Jade's skin and condensed down to form compressing manacles that shortened each deliberated breath.

The mound of fresh soil next to Freya's grave filled her vision. She stood in a grazed glebe that was connected to the ruins of the ancient abbey on Selje Island. A stone wall navigated the undulating grounds, enclosing and ending at a square tower, which stood in the southernmost corner.

The sky and sea merged at the horizon, and the wind had picked up, blowing a light rain, which dampened faces and hid tears. Three passenger boats rocked gently in the sheltered cove where a small group was waiting on the quay.

Grief and numbness held Jade in a state of oblivion as the hem of her black felt coat flapped around her thighs. Something wasn't right. The dreadful sense of loss was smothered by a guilt, informing her she wasn't worthy of being alive. It was the same feeling she had after the pickup had exploded in Aleppo, when she'd missed the snipers in the towers, and when she'd not recognised the MiG until it was too late. She still didn't know if the girl had escaped or if her hesitation had killed her. With Freya, there was nothing she could have done to save her. *So why does it feel like there was?*

The engine of the old ketch started up in a puff of black smoke. The fifty-foot craft had a wheelhouse at its centre, offering protection from the elements. Jade didn't take shelter within its teak-framed walls but instead sat on the gunwale near the stern.

As they travelled to the mainland, conditions worsened. The boat pitched slowly in the swell, and she twisted leeward. With salty spray stinging her eyes, she gazed back to the island as it disappeared into the distance.

"Freya . . ." she whispered as a sudden sense of dread cascaded through her. *Nothing is right now.*

Seagulls followed their wake, swooping, landing, and bobbing on the waves. Their squawks overlapped with each other, sounding like hysterical moirologists. The birds expected a fishing boat, cleaning its catch at sea.

The gulls wouldn't be fed, and Jade wanted Freya back.

A vision of her mother entered her mind's eye; her long, greying black hair loose about her shoulders. Whenever Jade was procrastinating with her homework, her mother would tell her, "Don't be a dense tortoise. Get on with it." Jade would start working again and her mother would sing her a rhyme. Jade thought it was to annoy her while she tried to concentrate. Of course, the rhyme made no sense; her mother was insane.

> *Empty the ocean with devotion,*
> *Inter all Horrors within.*
> *Relentless toil to rescue a Sorrow,*
> *Ereshkigal committed no sin.*
> *Only tally after the finale,*
> *An unfledged reckoning will be grim.*
> *Let no hell be a farewell,*
> *Sisters' end to begin.*

Jade pulled the collar of her coat up over her nose. It had been Freya's, but Jade could no longer smell the scent of her perfume. On the slippery deck, careful not to topple overboard, she scampered to lean against the bulkhead and looked out over the white-capped waves, watching the misty shore slowly elongate on the horizon as they got closer. *How dismal it looks.* She closed her eyes. *What am I supposed to do now?*

FREYA'S HOUSE WAS occupied by her absence. Jade watched as Karen busied herself relighting the fire that was now just ash.

"Is there anything I can get you?" Karen asked.

Jade wanted something impossible, but instead, she shook her head. She lay down on the sofa and pushed as tight as she could against its back. She positioned one of the cushions over her head to conceal her face. In her makeshift shelter, she closed her eyes and shut out the world.

FRAGMENTS OF A nightmare dissolved as Jade woke. She was in a boat, or a house, but it was sinking, filling with cold water. Freya's wing was trapped and Jade couldn't get to her; a strong current kept her away. All she could do was watch as Freya sank below the surface. A body rose slowly in oil-black liquid. But it was a younger Freya. Her eyes were open, her skin blanched, and her head was bald. Words came from pale blue lips. *Release me.* The body convulsed, accelerating its motion, until it was a blur. And then, Jade was showered black sticky rain. The drops stuck to her clothes, hair, and skin, and their colour turned to blood-red.

Shaken by the dream, Jade sat up on the sofa where she had fallen asleep. The lounge was dark; the fire's fuel spent. Bygul lay on the floor next to her. Orange eyes blinked a greeting.

Jade checked her phone to discover it was five in the morning. She had a sudden desperate need to see an image of Freya. It was so ironic; she was a photographer, but she didn't have a single picture of her wife. Events had happened so quickly that the normal parts of life had been missed—the simple things: a lazy Sunday, a walk on a beach, or even just watching TV together. It was as if she had used stepping stones across the river of life, rather than walking through the waters in bare feet. The acid in her empty stomach burbled up to burn her insides. She was wrong; they had done all those things. Freya had made sure of it.

The email Lena had sent her a week ago came to mind, and she located it on her phone. She opened the attachments and drew in a short breath. There were pictures of her and Freya standing arm in arm on the ferry to Port-Cros. Lena had fired off the pictures in rapid succession, three identical images except for small movements. She brushed her finger along the screen, through Freya's pixel hair. She sobbed, tears flowed, and she wiped them away before focusing back on the photos.

A table lamp clicked on beside her, lighting the corner of the cream sofa.

"I'll make you a coffee," Karen said in a weary voice.

As Karen wasn't asking a question, Jade didn't look up, sliding the pictures from one to the other, watching the small changes in light and movement. Something wasn't as it should be, and she was trying to work out what was wrong with the images.

A moment later, Karen held a cup under her nose. Karen was a mess; her hair was dishevelled and her eyes puffy. Jade hadn't seen her like this before. Since Freya's death, a week ago, Karen had shown no emotion.

At least she has someone.

Max had taken two days off for the funeral and was asleep upstairs. It was clear Karen and Max were couple. They shared the same room and were always holding hands. Jade knew that Max was providing Karen with the support she needed. Jade had lost everything, and this fact meant she'd been horribly harsh to Karen for most of the week. But now, seeing the extent of her grief, she felt ashamed.

"I'm sorry. I've been so short with you," Jade said.

"It's okay."

"No. I was cruel. I thought you didn't care. I guess we deal with things differently."

"I suppose so. I was trying to keep everything together until after the funeral." Karen's voice wavered.

Jade placed a hand on the overstuffed cushion next to her. "Sit down. You're tired."

They sat in silence until Jade's coffee had gone cold.

"You know . . ." Karen stared at some point at the other end of the room. "I knew Freya when I was just a teenager." She glanced at Jade before turning away. "I couldn't tell you this before with Freya not aging." She started to cry.

Jade's heart melted. She put her arm around Karen and took her hand. "It'll be hard for a long time, but it's best to talk about things. If you hold sadness in for too long . . . it will destroy you."

Karen nodded and took a moment. "I was like her daughter at first. Then later she was like mine. Strange really. It's hard to lose both at once. I tried everything to keep her here but I suppose, in the end I failed."

Bygul stirred, climbed up onto the sofa, and took the remaining space. She settled down and stretched her paws across their laps, squashing her head against Jade's side.

"And, also I'm sorry."

"For what?" Jade shifted to compensate for Bygul's weight.

"When you first met Freya, I suggested she shouldn't see you. And even after she reminded me of my past, my cowardice, I still kept you apart. I didn't want her to get involved with you. I'm truly sorry."

"It doesn't matter. I was so messed-up then. I should've been stronger . . . I made so many mistakes."

Karen's frowned and turned to Jade. "You do know you can't expect to be perfect. We all have our failings and need to deal with the consequences. It's an endless battle, knowing what they are and trying to avoid screwing up." She gave a sincere smile and manoeuvred out from under Bygul's paws. "I better try to get some sleep," she said before heading upstairs.

Jade stroked the soft fur between Bygul's ears. The cat smelled of musty leaves and stale saliva. "You stink. Perhaps you need a bath?"

Bygul nuzzled her head more deeply against Jade.

"Cat, tell me what to do."

Bygul didn't answer, but she wasn't snoring or purring. Dawn was starting to break outside and a chorus of early birds caused Bygul's ears to twitch in the direction of the chatter.

Jade lifted her phone off the table and swiped through the three pictures of Freya again. It gnawed at her insides that there was something not right about them. She was comparing the image in her mind with those on the phone. She tapped the screen to zoom in. The hue of the amber pendant around Freya's neck was changing from one to the next. But the change was against the direction of the shadows. Enlarging the image further, showing only the pendant in the frame, Jade aligned the images, and scrolled through them slowly. Something was moving within the pendant. The reflection was too grainy to be sure, but it looked like the outline of a girl halting and then darting away.

Jade leapt up, jolting Bygul off the sofa.

"She's trapped!" Jade said, scanning the room and considering her options. Then she noticed Lena leaning against the pine balustrade at the top of the stairs. She looked like an electrocuted bear in an oversized T-shirt and flannel pyjama bottoms. On her shoulder was a backpack. She could have been going for a picnic in the woods.

Lena started down the stairs, and they met at the bottom, where Jade shoved her phone into Lena's hand. "Look. There is something in her necklace. I think it's her—"

Lena ignored the phone and pushed the backpack into Jade's arms.

"The feathers are inside. The ones you fail to keep with you, and other things you might need."

Jade stared at her. "What? What does this all mean?" She tapped on the screen of her phone.

Lena pushed her hair away from her eyes and used both hands to flick the long locks over her shoulders. She squinted into lines. "I can't tell you . . . I would be interfering with threads, and they would notice."

"Tell me what this is about." Jade tried to take hold of Lena's arm, who yanked it out of reach.

"You've got to be smart. I didn't squirrel you away for a thousand years to come back as a dense tortoise."

Jade's mouth fell open. There was only one person who called her a tortoise.

Lena sighed. "Close your mouth and don't look at me like that." Her words sounded older than her years. "You should've guessed by now."

"Guessed?" Jade muttered to herself. She examined Lena's face. Her angular jaw, grey eyes, and button nose were the same as her mother's. She didn't know why she hadn't noticed it before. "How can you be her?"

"Hell . . ." Lena curled her slim fingers into the fabric of Jade's hoodie, pulled her close, and whispered into her ear, "Now listen. You were needed for now. So I put you away and kept you safe. Then I brought you back and looked after you. I told you everything I could. Anymore, and like a spider sensing a fly in her web, the weavers would've known, and they mustn't. I must stay hidden from them."

"But you're too young to be my mother."

Lena rolled her eyes behind her long black lashes, blinked, and refocused on Jade. "I started again. You can't grow old forever." With her free hand, she tapped Jade's forehead. "If your head wasn't so protective, you would have remembered me, and I'm sorry about drowning you, and the one to come."

"I don't understand . . ." Jade muttered.

"You don't need to. There are things you must do, not for you but for everyone. So follow your instincts. This must happen now. The chance starts now; there is only a minute. Go to Freya and make a trade."

"Lena, please, tell me more."

"The birds have ears. I can't. Remember to take the backpack with you." Lena released Jade and shuffled a step away. She rubbed her eyes and yawned. "It's too stupidly early for me . . . and it's getting too late for you." She gestured towards the door, where Bygul hovered, waiting to be let out. "Looks like Bygul is going with you."

"I—" All Jade could think was that she wanted Freya back, and in her head, her wife was screaming to be released. She had to get the necklace. Everything else was too surreal to be believed. "Okay." *Hell can have my soul if I can bring her back.*

Lena suddenly shouted at her, "*Bordel de merde!* Go already."

Pea Green

"WHAT THE HELL was Jade thinking?" Karen lowered her phone and turned to Henri, who was supporting the fireplace mantel in the lounge. The call had ended abruptly and Karen knew they were now out of range.

"So where is she?" Henri asked.

"With Linn and Freya's cat in the middle of the bloody bay. They've taken the damn sailboat."

"I see."

Henri's lackadaisical response made Karen wonder if he was expecting this. "Against everything sane, they seem to be going back to Freya's grave. Jade has it in her head that Freya's spirit is trapped inside her necklace. I don't even think she was buried with it, for God's sake." Karen threw her phone at the sofa and it bounced off the cushion onto the floor. "And the good part is that Linn, in a voice message, said they are heading into a storm. We can't even go after them."

"Why not?" Henri asked.

"Until the tide comes in, the cruiser's not going anywhere."

"Isn't there a powerboat in the boathouse?"

"That old thing . . ." Karen considered the option while pulling strands of her hair through her fingers. "No, it won't have the range, and it's easily swamped. Too risky." She picked up her phone, which now had a thin crack across the screen. "I suppose this serves me right for taking a shower. I missed Linn's call and now all hell breaks loose."

Henri bent down to throw another log on the fire. "So we just wait?"

Karen started to pace while running her thumb over the sharp crack on her phone's screen, wanting to wind everything back and undo the last few years. "I'll call search and rescue and see if they can do anything."

"At least Linn is with her," Henri said.

Karen let out a slow breath. She was mind-numbingly tired. "She's green. It will be a trial by fire for her." She looked at Henri who seemed to be studying his feet. "Do you know why Jade has gone back to Freya's grave?"

Henri shook his head.

Karen turned to see Lena standing with a mug of hot chocolate in her hand. Somehow the teenager had snuck up on her without making a sound. "Does no one sleep? What are you doing sneaking around?"

Lena took a sip from her cup, leaving a line of froth on her lip. "I'm not sneaking. I'm waiting," she growled back.

"Waiting for what?" Karen asked. "Do you know something about this?"

"Nothing I can tell you."

"Look. Lives are at stake—"

"Yes, billions. So shut up."

"Lena, please," Henri said with his hands open and held out in front.

Lena stood still, unblinking. Karen exchanged a glance with Henri.

"All I will say is that Jade can do this; she proved she could." Lena frowned and took another sip of her cocoa. "Except swim . . . I kind of put that off until it was too late. So maybe she'll drown."

Henri scratched the unruly whiskers under his chin. "Drown?"

Lena uncurled a finger from the mug handle and pointed at Henri. "Well, it's better than being split in two." She then pointed at Karen. "Or eaten alive. So you better hope she doesn't drown."

"My God, you're delusional," Karen said.

"*Double merde!* Chill already. You're not going to be eaten. A shame really," Lena snarled.

"I'm surrounded by lunatics," Karen retorted.

"Nonkers," Lena replied.

"What the hell does that mean?"

"No one cares. It doesn't matter what you think. You will affect nothing." Lena reached into the pocket of her pyjama bottoms, pulled out a number of small marshmallows, then dropped them into her mug. "What is happening now is the only thread that has any chance. Just wait. It's not like you have a choice."

THERE WAS NO going back, but Jade wished Linn hadn't come with her. She didn't want the responsibility of another life when her own didn't matter. She pointed towards the momentous clouds that darkened the sea, air, and land ahead of them. "We'll hit the storm in half an hour, I think."

"Have you sailed much?" Linn asked.

"Second time," Jade admitted.

"Oh . . . is there a marine radio on board?"

"Below."

"At least we have that."

Linn pulled the zip of her bright yellow windbreaker up as far as it would go and then wrapped her arms around herself.

"There might be a warmer coat, if you need one," Jade said.

"I'm good, Your Highness."

"Please, just Jade."

Linn nodded.

A bruised band of purple clouds was forming into a great ring at the edge of the headland, and the sea darkened to such an extent that it appeared as if calm and chaos were at war. Ripples flashed across the water's surface in great gusts of rain as the forty-foot pea-green sailboat raced forward.

"You think Freya is trapped?" Linn asked.

"Yes. I hear her screaming in my head . . . even now. We have to get her necklace. Then I'm not sure. Break it open . . . I think Amber burns, doesn't it?"

"Yes. It's tree sap."

Minutes passed, and the rises and falls of the boat grew larger, until they were at the end of the headland. Beyond them was the all-consuming sea. Shades of navy blue darkened to black, while white veins of foam were ripped apart by wind and current.

As they rounded the point, the air became heavy, and Jade felt it in her chest. A downpour broke over them as turbulent waves collided with each other in a wind that had increased tenfold. The sailboat tilted dramatically and the mast and sails carved into the sea as a wall of water blasted across the deck. Jade held fast to the wheel until the boat broke through, finding that Linn was right beside her, soaked but clinging on.

"We have to let the sails out!" Jade called before she was knocked into Linn as a sledgehammer of air jolted the boat violently from the opposing direction. An enormous bang with whirling shrieks sounded, and she was flung onto the deck while a wave broke over her. She tried to scramble up but slipped to the cockpit floor as the boat lurched starboard.

In a pool of freezing water, with muscles numb, Jade got to her knees. Rain blinded her vision for a moment, and then she found herself being dragged to her feet by Linn. "The sails!"

The aluminium mast had been sheared off about three feet from its base. It was dragging in the water, held close to the hull by the stays, sheets, and shrouds that made up the rigging.

They were unable to control the boat as another wave hit them side-on, tipping it to a near ninety degrees, before it bounced back to an awkward list. "We have to cut the mast free!"

Jade darted down the short ladder into the cabin to see Bygul perched on the dining table with her claws wrapped along its edges as water sloshed all around.

Rifling through drawers, Jade found a pocketknife but nothing more substantial. She reached to open a cupboard but was slammed backwards as another wave hit. In the lull before the next, a rhythmic noise caught her ear. It was a glugging sound, and then another, closer by. *Must be automatic pumps.*

Linn shouted into the cabin, "Anything? We are going to capsize."

"Not yet!" The backpack Lena had given her hung on a hook near the pilot's area. She grabbed it as a blast of spray and water streamed into the cabin.

She feverishly rummaged the backpack, finding a large roll of bandage, pocketknife, a waterproof LED flashlight, five bullet clips, and a large box of matches in a Ziploc bag. *What the hell. Why does Lena think I need these?* She pushed the bullets to one side to uncover a thin foil parcel, which she knew to be the feathers Lena had collected, and finally, at the bottom, was a pair of wire clippers.

Water cascaded down the steps of the cabin as Jade climbed up to an onslaught of rain and wind. She handed the pocketknife to Linn, who was clinging onto the boat's wheel.

"Cut the ropes. I'll cut through the cables," Jade shouted while keeping hold of the wire clippers.

After severing a few of the loose stays that were close by, Jade stopped and cursed. "Shit. I'm such an idiot." She needed to make sure the currents didn't drive the sails down like an anchor and drag them under. It had to stay in position until the last moment.

"Leave that one." Jade grabbed Linn's arm, stopping her from cutting through a taut rope that disappeared under the waves. A torrent of seawater crashed over them, sending streams of freezing water down Jade's neck and back. Linn was sent flying over the edge of the boat.

"Linn!" Jade darted to her.

Linn hung on to the mainsail winch, trying to throw a leg back up onto the hull. Jade gripped tightly on to Linn's clothes with frigid fingers and pulled her into the cockpit. Another wave hit and she held fast, holding her breath as a flood of water broke over them. Before the next one, she got to her feet and pulled Linn up.

"You see the boards for the cabin entrance? Close it off and shut the hatch. We don't want more water down there; we need the electrics to work the pumps. I'll cut the lines at the front."

The boat shuddered when another wave hit the hull. Jade climbed onto the upper deck and then grabbed a handrail as the boat tilted again, but this time, it didn't right itself.

At the prow, much of the fittings and railings had been ripped off with the mast, but a few twisted steel stays remained. Jade clipped through them, but the last one was completely taut and slicing through the edge of the fibreglass hull. Using all the strength she could muster in her fingers, she closed the cutters around the wire. The cable flung away with the crack of a whip. The prow jolted back upright, and she scrambled to wrap her arms around the stump of the mast. The boat started to twist at the stern where the last rope held, and it sagged down, half submerging the cockpit. She felt pain, then a shearing ache across her forehead; the last cable must have caught her.

Risking slipping or being knocked overboard, Jade scampered across the barren deck and jumped into the cockpit. Linn was holding a bread knife above the boards that sealed off the lower cabin, and Jade grabbed it, ignoring the blood running through her eyebrows and down her face. She started to carve through the final rope to release the mast, and the cleat and the winch it was attached to were ripped from the hull. She was knocked onto her rear as the sailboat bounced upright. She wiped her forehead on her coat sleeve. Streaks of red, mixed with rain, ran in streams over the yellow fabric.

"Shit." She stayed put for a moment, gathering herself.

"You've been hurt." Linn crouched next to her.

"Are the pumps still running?"

"Yes. You have a bad cut—"

"Leave it." Sitting had been a mistake. Jade's adrenaline faded and now she felt nauseous as her head pounded. She pushed Linn aside and moved to the console that controlled the inboard motor, where she turned the engine switch to the On position.

"I'll send out a mayday," Linn called over the wind and rain.

"Can't."

Linn turned back to Jade. "Why not?"

Jade jerked a thumb to the mountainous waves behind them. "The aerial would've been on the mast, and we can't wait for anyone."

With a push of the start button, the engine fired up on the first crank, and Jade jammed the control lever fully forward. Back at the wheel, she turned the boat until the compass read exactly south-east. She ran her fingers along her forehead, feeling the painful gash across it. She was going to have to clean it up. "Take the wheel and keep this course." She touched SE on the compass, leaving a fingerprint of blood on the glass housing.

"I think we should head back."

"No! Keep the course."

What remained of the yacht struggled onward, climbing up and then slipping down the turbulent waves. The noise of the propeller was changing with the effort and its depth in the sea, pushing the craft deeper into the storm.

ON SELJE ISLAND, Nancy waited in a turret of the old monastery. Rain was sheeting in ribbons of heavy drops blown horizontally. She had arrived a few hours ago, having paid a local fisherman a considerable sum to risk the impending storm and drop her off without waiting. She was glad she was still wearing her motorcycle gear. The waterproof coat and boots were keeping her warm, and she shoved her hands deep into the pockets.

The structure she occupied was part of the solitary tower that stood in the southern corner of the monastery's defences. It hadn't taken much to break the lock with a pair of nearby shovels.

Rattling around inside Nancy's head, Lilith was worried for the first time in a thousand years. Things were not going as expected.

First, there was the annoying weather. It was odd that Hel would decide to meet in such conditions, but Hel was not predictable. *Has the diruodea arrived?* Lilith caused Nancy to again check the well. It was at the other end of the grounds, near where a crevice on the side of a cliff marked the location of Sunniva's cave. From it, a spring fed into a large pool that supposedly had healing powers. Lilith knew it was much more than that; it was one of the few remaining gates to Asgard, and they would need a pair of Valkyrie's wings to make the passage. A trade was required. *A goddess's soul, bound to a necklace, should do.*

"So we just wait?" Nancy said.

This brought Lilith to the second quandary. Why was this woman able to converse with it in thought? *Only Eve had been able to do that.*

"So, you think this Hel is going to show up?"

Yes, and be quiet!

"And you don't think the goddess of the underworld will double cross us?" Nancy paced while talking down towards the floor.

Shh! I'm the queen of the underworld. This Hel is a tool of the Norns.

Not many had been able to separate themselves from Lilith's control, and now as the wind and rain died down, Lilith wondered if the Norns knew of its task and were playing games. *No, they can't know of this. Frigg has sacrificed too much for that to be true.*

The rain changed to a gentle patter, and heavy drops splattered down from the lip of the deep-set window. The sound of an engine reached her ear, and Nancy stretched to look out of the turret.

A broken green sailboat limped into the sheltered waters of the small harbour.

A Foiled Greeting

THEY HAD BEEN digging for an hour. Jade worked furiously to get to Freya's coffin. Her qualms about having Linn come along had been quelled. Linn hadn't asked any more questions about why they were exhuming Freya.

The rain had stopped and the sky was now dark with belligerent clouds. "Could be worse," Jade muttered, dumping another shovel load of loose soil above her. She had removed her weatherproof coat but still wore the charcoal hoodie Freya had given her.

A thud from her shovel told her she had hit the coffin. Scraping away the remaining soil, they were able to clear its top.

"Linn, I'll boost you out, so I can open it . . . Please stay back for a bit."

Once Linn was out of sight, Jade wedged her feet on either side of the walls of the grave and reached down, hesitating, as tears welled in her eyes. "I'm sorry it took me so long," she whispered while taking hold of the rim of the lid with both hands.

"Jade, come up quick." Linn's head appeared above. Her face was drawn and contorted. "Get out now."

"What's wrong?" Jade straightened and looked up as a shower of dirt fell into her face, kicked loose by Linn's scampering.

"Please. Get out fast." Linn reached down and dragged her out.

As soon as Jade stood, Linn pulled her down to a crouch behind a large block, which must have been a foundation stone for one of the old buildings.

"Over there. Look." Linn's words were carried on her exhale as she pointed towards the cliff through the murky distance.

Jade rubbed her eyes clear. Dirt was stuck to her lashes, and she pinched it out. She registered what she saw, but it didn't provoke panic. She knew it should have; a horrific reaper, grim and aberrant, was shaking water from its wings by a pool at the lower end of the field.

Linn's voice trembled. "I don't think it's seen us." She reached into her jacket and pulled out her pistol. "What do you think it is?"

Jade took a second to perceive its form. Most of it was hidden behind large black wings made up of the feathers trimmed with the reflecting blue of a magpie.

"Take off your waterproof. It stands out," Jade whispered. She then picked up hers and threw both of them into the grave. "Where's Bygul?"

"I don't know."

The creature stretched and slowly turned in their direction.

"We should run to the boat." Linn tightened her fingers around Jade's forearm.

"It would see and hear us. And it has wings." Jade scanned the grounds. "We'll run to the tower."

They took few steps.

"Digging up dead loved ones, are we?" Nancy, in a black heavy motorcycle coat and armoured boots, stood behind them with her legs astride. Against the background of the monastery's tower, she looked like an apocalyptic movie heroine.

"What the hell are you doing here?" Jade saw what was hanging from Nancy's hand. Freya's amber necklace. She exploded like a sprinter from the blocks and knocked Nancy to the ground. Nancy rolled away and got back on her feet.

"That's some greeting." Nancy panted. "So you want this?" She dangled the necklace in front of Jade. "Well, I'm sorry, but no. I need to do a trade with that Horror."

The demon was heading towards them. Its pace was methodical, almost like it was a tourist admiring the historic site.

"You can't. Freya is trapped."

"I know. That's what the Horror comes for. Her soul."

"You can't . . ."

Linn pointed her gun at Nancy. "Give it to Jade."

Nancy seemed amused. She shifted her eyes between the gun and the approaching creature. "If I don't give this to Hel's dispatcher we will all be dead."

Linn hesitated and her hand wavered.

"Make a decision, please," Nancy said and took a step backwards.

Jade glanced behind. The Horror had vanished. The ground in front of her shook, and her vision was filled by a macabre mix of feathers and weeping flesh.

Jade fell backwards in repulsion.

Trapped inside the partially decomposed chest, a withered being convulsed and tried to reach out for her. The unforgettable smell of death burnt her nostrils as she desperately scrambled backwards on all fours. Then Linn was behind her, helping her to her feet and dragging her away.

The thing spoke with incomprehensible sounds that jarred as stone on metal.

Nancy held her ground. "So . . . no trade, then . . ." Her voice wavered.

A scream expelled from the being trapped within its body. "*Hlaupa fyrir lífi þínu!*"

"You nutcase. You see, I was right." Nancy appeared to be talking to herself while taking large steps away from the demon. "I told you this would happen." She turned and ran towards the tower as the Horror swung a great talon at her. The claw penetrated her side and she spun around like a kid's top, whirling until she fell onto the remnants of a ruined wall and was sprawled across its width.

Shots hammered near Jade's ear. Linn was firing at the creature, hitting its neck, punching out a small section of flesh.

With a single flap of its wings, the Horror leapt near Nancy's motionless body. It bent down and lifted her limp hand, which held the amber necklace, and then pulled it away. Its head turned and one eye moved without the other following.

The creature stuttered through the distance with moments missing from its movement, and in an instant, it was in front of Linn. A blade appeared, extending from its left hand, and it swung down. She seemed caught in headlights and then raised her gun to take aim.

"Run!" Jade screamed.

Linn's pistol fell with amputated fingers. The Horror caught Linn and lifted her up. A great claw of bony spindles wrapped around her waist as Jade watched in terror.

It was all happening too fast. As the creature turned away, Jade ran towards it, grabbing a shovel in her stride. Then with all her strength, she swung the shovel in a full loop at its hideous head.

The Horror must have sensed her and twitched to one side. The shovel cut into its shoulder and sliced the top of its wing, cracking a bone. It turned slowly, threw Linn away like she was a rag doll.

A surge of fear rammed Jade's insides as Linn hit the wet grass with a thud. The Horror was now focused on Jade. She couldn't tell if the thing had been wounded; it was already a walking mutilation. It attempted to move its wing to the sound of rasping bone.

The Horror screamed at her, tensing all its muscles.

Jade backed away and hit something hard. It was the waist-high stone they had hidden behind earlier. She took deep breaths, using a count of four, to try to control her increasing panic. She darted around the stone, keeping it between her and the Horror.

The figure trapped inside the Horror was now visible and Jade froze. It had Freya's features, her penetrating blue eyes, but strands of red hair rather than Freya's golden-blond. The body was white and withered, connected to the outer thing in some surgical manner. Jade focussed on what was going on between the incarcerated woman and the outer husk. The two were fighting with each other. The figure within was trying to grab the necklace from the hand of its custodian. There was a chance if she was quick enough. Anger overpowered her fear. She picked up Linn's gun and raced towards the demon, expecting it to be the last thing she ever did.

DUMB SHIT! NANCY blasted curses at Lilith, emitting the thoughts through waves of pain as her life flowed over the eroded stones and onto the grass. *I told you that thing was just going to take what it wanted.*

Being right in hindsight merits no one, Lilith answered. Thinking more, Lilith noted that Nancy had in fact been correct on every occasion since they cohabited. The question was what to do now. This was something it couldn't decide.

Nancy, we have three options. The first, I leave and you die. The second—

Nancy thrust a thought through Lilith with rapier precision. *Just pick the one where I don't die.*

That's the third. Very well.

Lilith expanded itself, consuming structures of Nancy's body. It continued until it merged with Nancy's brain, fusing her neurons with its own, and finally, they were one.

A BLADE OF thin steel raced towards Jade's neck, projected from the constructed hand of the Horror. Time slowed and she took in every movement, sound, and smell. She had seen its fingers flex before the blade appeared. Ducking, she felt it whizz past. The moving air touched the hairs on the back of her neck. She followed its arm in an arc. Its head turned with the motion of the swing. A shin moved upward for a split second. And in that small window, she stepped on its knee, leapt upward, jammed the pistol into its rotting jaw, and jerked the trigger until the gun clicked empty.

Its skullcap blew away with chunks of grey matter. The Horror started to fall; its diseased eyes rolling upwards in their sockets.

Jade dropped away from it and now scrambled to her feet, huffing, trying to catch her breath. She watched it spasm and start to tip backwards.

One of its legs snapped back to stop itself. Eyes tracked down to focus on her. Next, the bladed hand whipped down. *I failed one last time.*

A blur of black and white leapt at Jade and two powerful legs used her body as a springboard, knocking her backwards, while hitting the Horror square-on, toppling it for the first time. Wings flapped frantically as Bygul ripped at the Horror's head with her front claws and dug deep into the Horror's cheeks.

The woman caged within its ribs took hold of the foundation stone as Bygul pulled in the opposite direction. The nauseating sound of popping spinal joints was mixed with screams from the pale red-haired female figure that gripped the stone.

Bygul dragged and tore until the Horror was split in two.

Then everything was silent. Jade's mind slowed as she tried to work out what had just happened. All she could hear was the sound of the wind and Bygul's snorts of heavy breathing.

She scanned the area for Nancy, then Linn. Nancy was close by with half her side cut away. Her body was white; organs and blood were blotched over the ground. Linn was sitting up with her severed hand held tightly against her chest.

Jade pushed the gun into the pocket of her hoodie. She found her backpack before running over to Linn. She dug through the pack and retrieved the roll of bandage.

"Let me see," Jade said, slowly moving Linn's arm from her chest.

Linn's round face was as white as snow. "Don't touch it."

"It's okay. It will be okay." Jade tried to calm her, but Linn rocked back and forth.

"It hurts!"

"I have you. Okay?"

She gave Linn a few seconds before attempting to help her again. "I'm going to bind the wound so we can keep it clean."

"I don't know . . . it hurts," Linn whimpered and then allowed Jade to pull her hand away. Blood had soaked Linn's jacket and shirt.

Jade got the bandage ready. "On the count of three let go, and I'll wrap it. Okay? It will take just seconds. Then it will be done."

"I don't—"

"On the count of three."

Linn released her injured hand, and Jade wrapped the bandage tightly around the stubs of her fingers until it was completely bound.

She held Linn for a moment. From the backpack, she found the tinfoil parcel, opened it, and removed the feathers. She laid them on the grass and placed a rock on them to stop them from blowing away. She then ran over to where Linn's fingers were and collected them and packed them in the foil before returning.

Jade hesitated before saying the words she hoped to never utter again. "I have your fingers."

She opened the zip on the side pocket of the backpack to put them away.

"I'll take them." Linn reached out and took the package with her good hand.

"I have nothing for the pain," Jade said.

Linn watched her; some of the colour had returned to her cheeks. "You think they can be sewn back on?"

"It's a clean cut. I'm sure they can."

"I didn't do well, Your Highness." Linn bowed her head. "I missed."

"No. Linn . . . a bullet wouldn't have killed it . . . I fired many into its head and it still moved."

Linn kept her head bowed for a moment and then raised her chin. "Did you get the necklace?"

"No." Jade swallowed. "It will be with that thing."

Linn started to rock again. "Do you think there are more?" she whispered.

"I don't know."

Linn took in a breath before clenching her jaw in pain.

Jade scanned the area where Nancy lay but couldn't see her body. "What the hell?" *Has Bygul moved it?* She turned her head. The lynx was sitting on guard by the slender body that had been pulled out of the Horror.

"Bygul! Come here," Jade called, but Bygul wouldn't budge, only twitching her ears in Jade's direction for the briefest instant.

"I need to check things," Jade said softly to Linn.

"Do you have my USP? My gun I mean."

"Yes. But it's empty . . . No, wait." Jade pulled the Ziploc bag from the backpack and took out a clip. "Will these fit?"

Linn glanced at them. "Looks right. You know how to reload?"

"Yes. I trained before going to Syria." Jade released the clip and let it fall into her hand. She then cocked the gun to clear the chamber and replaced the clip. After pushing on the safety, she put the handgun back in her muff pocket. She suddenly felt cold and pulled her hood up. She touched Linn's shoulder and stood. "Back in a sec."

As she got closer to the remains of the Horror, she heard a voice on the wind and pulled out the gun. She took a tentative step forward. There was blood where Nancy had been lying but no sign of what had happened to her body. Remains of wings, flesh, and bones lay only a few steps away. The naked, willowy form of the woman within lay beside the foundation stone.

Blades of grass near the carcass of the woman moved in a contradictory direction to the wind. Jade tensed, flicking off the safety while walking towards the body.

"*Hálsmen minn, dóttir mín . . .*"

She heard the words clearly now, standing just a few feet away from what could only be described as road kill. A pale arm and hand extended along the ground from the emaciated body of the woman. A wiry finger pointed and tapped.

"Kári . . . dóttir mín." It spoke with motionless lips. "Kári . . . hugrakkur Bergeira . . . hálsmen minn."

On one knee, Jade leant closer to hear the mournful repeated words.

"I'm sorry, I don't understand." A gust of wind blew, and Jade held her hood, waiting for it to die down.

"Lilith . . . þú skilu . . . hálsmen minn."

The words were louder now. "My? Something," Jade said to herself.

The sound of a throat being cleared came from behind her. She turned around, her hood blocking her view.

"My daughter, my necklace," a soft mid-Atlantic accent told her. "It's Old Norse."

Jade flung her hood down. "How are you alive—?"

Nancy grinned, showing her perfect teeth.

Sunniva's Well

MIST DRIFTED PAST the ruined walls, a northerly wind bent the long grass, and waves crashed against the coastline of Selje Island.

Jade blinked. Nancy was very much alive.

Nancy tugged her motorcycle jacket around herself as she approached the remains of the Horror. "Evil wretch. How dare you." She stomped on its ribs and cracked them with the heel of her heavy boots. She continued to jump up and down, squelching flesh and breaking bones, until its cavity collapsed.

Jade had seen some pretty appalling scenes on assignment in the Middle East, but the sight of Nancy's gruesome acts caused her to turn away. She bent her head down, pushing her fingers through her hair. She was dead tired, and as far as she could tell, still in a dream. But this was not a gentle fantasy; this was a nightmarish collage of butchered reason. It took a few moments for her to gather her strength. There was no hiding anymore. She had to free Freya.

Bygul lay next to the woman who had once been prisoner inside the Horror. An emaciated arm was touching Bygul's broad paw. The lynx was murmuring soft trills and chirrups to the woman as she lay dying. There was nothing Jade could do to help. Most of her was missing.

Nancy was busy wiping her boots on the grass, when the pitiful woman spoke again. "Lilith, *koma hingað*."

Nancy went to her, knelt, and they exchanged words for a moment.

"You understand? What is she saying?" Jade asked.

"She wants the necklace."

"Why?"

"What if, instead of going 'tick' and 'tock,' clocks sounded like 'less' and 'life'?"

"Why does she want the necklace?" Jade repeated.

"Tick tock, less life, less life." Nancy's eyebrows were angled downward, her lips pursed. "It's her necklace. The goddess Frigg's. She is Freya's mother. Fetch it." She jumped onto the nearby ruined wall. The tatters of her coat flapped in the wind like a ragged flag as she walked down towards the far end of the field.

Jade looked into Frigg's deep blue eyes. *So like Freya's.* She surveyed the ground. The amber necklace was partially hidden in the long grass. She retrieved it and caressed it between her fingers. She wasn't sure, but if this was Freya's mother, then she may know how to release her.

She put the necklace into Frigg's lily-white hand and pushed her cold, bony fingers around it. Frigg stared into Jade's eyes, and she felt Freya's kinship in those azurite-coloured pools. The necklace glowed, and then burst into flames.

"No!" Jade tried to reach for it.

The scent of pine and burnt flesh was carried on a wave of heat that blasted into Jade's face as a ring of flames exploded in front of her. She leapt backwards, dived, and then rolled away from a blanket of fire that consumed both Frigg and the remains of the Horror. She pushed up as the leather on her boots shrunk, and her soles melted. She could feel the flames burning her shins, travelling under her as she tried to get up; the pain was blocking any cohesive action. Time slowed, offering no respite.

Jade's neck was snapped back, and her hoodie pulled tight under her armpits. An instant later she was being dragged away at speed. Bygul had her by the scruff of her hoodie and was sprinting away. Her head bounced against the turf; she could see flames dancing about her ankles as the ring of fire expanded along the ground.

Far enough away, Bygul let her drop. She licked Jade's neck and sat on her as if she were a captured prey. Jade shoved and managed to pry herself out from under the cat, just in time to see a great plume of orange-and-blue flame cut into the sky. She crossed her arms around herself and lowered her chin against her chest. The necklace was gone. Freya was gone.

She removed her boots, socks, and rolled up what was left of her jeans, then sat for some time, listening to the wind and waves. The cold air helped to cool her burns. She tried to remember Freya's voice, her image, her smell, but only a taunting memory of Freya telling her she needed to go on without her, added to her pain.

Linn put a hand her shoulder. "Are you okay?" Her hair was soaked and covered with mud, her pupils were dilated, and it looked like she was about to fall over.

Jade got up and started buttoning Linn's jacket. Linn wouldn't have been able to do it up on her own. This was her fault.

She turned at a thrashing sound. The noise was coming from Freya's grave.

Tips of white wings poked out just above the opening, franticly flapping against the sides, knocking dirt in all directions.

Jade gasped. *Is this true? Let it be true.*

The wings exploded out of the grave, acting as a pallbearer for Freya's cadaver.

"My God," Jade mouthed.

The effigy of an angel punched a hole of pure white into the grey sky, rising above the flames of the burning corpses. Freya was motionless with arms crossed over her chest, eyes closed, and head fixed in place. She hovered for just a few seconds before flying rapidly towards the other end of the field. All she could do was watch as Freya's wings folded and she dove into the depths of a pool.

Linn stood beside her on unsteady legs, her face expressionless.

"It's done," Jade muttered, but really, she had no idea what it all meant. She thought she would feel better now Freya was free, but there was still a nagging in the pit of her stomach. Her mind raced over the events of the day, looking for any mistakes she might have made.

Bygul nudged her back and then gave her another push.

"What do you want, cat?" She petted Bygul between its ears. "Thanks for back there. For saving my life, twice."

The lynx padded past her, stopped, and turned to look back.

"She wants you to follow," Linn suggested.

"I guess so." She wished Freya was here. Everything just made sense when she was around.

Linn pointed to Nancy, who was off in the distance. "Is she okay? I thought she'd been hurt?"

"I don't know. But I think we should stay away from her." Jade halted and reconsidered her words. She needed to get answers, and it would probably be good to start with the woman who was at the heart of what had just happened.

So she followed Bygul, carrying her boots, while keeping an eye on Linn, who marched a few paces behind.

THEY MET ON a slab of black stone next to a dark pool of water. They were sheltered from the wind by a cliff that jutted out from the land. Nancy was sitting cross-legged with her head bowed. Bygul was beside her, half-asleep, with only a glimmer of her orange eyes between her paws.

Linn was managing, but her complexion was ashen. Jade helped her sit and was embarrassed to notice that Linn had been carrying the backpack. It didn't weigh much, but still, she should have taken it from her sooner.

The stone was cold and damp when Jade lowered herself between Nancy and Linn. The discomfort would be a small price to pay to get some answers.

"So what is it?" Jade asked, sliding her hand inside her muff pocket. She gripped Linn's pistol. She didn't trust Nancy, especially after she'd drugged her drink in London and somehow stolen Freya's necklace. However, she wasn't sure this was actually the same person. This Nancy was taller for a start, and her manner brash, rather than manipulative. Moreover, her features had become angular, and new toned biceps tensed under the sleeves of her jacket.

Nancy scowled at Jade. "What do you think it is?"

"I don't know. That's why I'm asking." Jade frowned.

"It's a gateway. But there's no gate and no way. Understand?" Nancy's tone was filled with outright anger, but Jade wasn't sure if it was actually directed at her or if she was just in a bad mood.

"Okay . . ." Jade muttered. "Why did Freya go into it?"

Nancy's frown curled into tight lips and gritted teeth. "Why did Sunniva go into Sunniva's Well? I wonder."

Jade was used to dealing with difficult people to get a story, but this looked like it might be near impossible. "Can you explain—?"

Linn flopped to one side and her eyes flickered shut. Jade cushioned Linn's head in her lap and then turned to Nancy. "Raise her feet." She needed Nancy to help but was pretty sure she wouldn't.

Nancy got up slowly and lifted Linn's legs by the ankles. "Bygul, *koma vera stól.*"

To Jade's surprise, Bygul stirred and went over to Nancy, lay down, then allowed Linn's legs to be placed onto her back.

"Bygul is now a stool. Useful finally." Nancy took hold of Bygul's stubby tail and yelled into it as if it were a microphone. "Traitor!" She let go and stood. "Where is your sister, beast?"

Bygul twitched her ears and blinked her eyes.

"Useless, both of you." Nancy sighed and went to sit back down beside Jade.

"Strange," Jade whispered under her breath. Linn tried to rise, but Jade stopped her. "Stay still, Linn, you fainted."

"I think Karen will arrive soon," Linn muttered.

"She was following us?"

"She said she would come when she could."

"Okay. Now get some rest." Jade turned back to Nancy, who looked crestfallen—her arms were resting on her knees, hands dangling in front of her, and her head bowed.

"You are not the person I met before, so who are you?" Jade asked.

Nancy looked at the clouds; a frown dominated her face, and her eyes were dark. She spoke in another language. Jade was surprised she could understand some of the words, but this didn't help explain who Nancy had become.

"I am potential and disregard. I am grace and barbarity," Nancy droned on. Jade was able to translate, but the words just implied that Nancy was delusional. Then Jade made a connection as to why she understood her. Many of the syllables were common to Arabic, and she was suspicious that they had an older origin. She touched Nancy's arm.

"When Freya's mother asked for you, she called you Lilith. I assume this is Lilith from the biblical texts. Is this who you are?" Jade didn't expect the answer to be yes; still, she hoped any response would help quell the unease in her heart. *Is Freya safe? Is she alive, or has she died peacefully?*

"People give me so many names. Ereshkigal was my first." She gave a sigh. "It's too much. There is too much to answer for."

"Too much what?"

"Sin. Maybe the Norns are being merciful in what they do now."

Jade recalled the name Ereshkigal from the plaque in the British Museum. *The queen of the night?*

Jade rubbed her eyes, putting parts of the puzzle together. The annoying thing was, this was a puzzle she didn't even know she had been a part of. *Why do I know this place? It scares me.* A surge of anxiety flowed through her, pounding her head and tingling her nerves. *Breathe, slowly; you can't break down now.*

Her thoughts drifted to dance in the way her mind worked best and she forced herself to replay her past.

Sixteen. Why can't I remember anything before that? It can't be trauma . . . Lena, she was my mother. I know that to be true . . . I see her eyes, the way she talks and moves. Her temper . . . she knew what my mother called me. And that stupid rhyme. "Ereshkigal committed no sin." Were all those things just part of Lena's plan; this big thing I need to do? Freya found me. Saved me. Told me things. She was teaching me. Telling me what I must do to save her. She got me to sail so I could get here in time. What else? Made me jump in the sea when I couldn't swim . . . Why?

Jade shuddered and looked at the dark pool. She knew why. It was so she would follow.

Linn stirred.

"Jade," Linn mumbled. "Can I sit up?"

Jade had been brushing her fingers through Linn's hair unconsciously, and she felt her cheeks blush. She glanced at Nancy, who was glowering as if someone had wronged her.

"Will more Horrors come?" Jade asked.

"Thousands," Nancy answered without hesitation. "But it will be their hounds first . . . And you can't precision-bomb hordes of millions."

Panic heated Jade's insides, but she tried to keep her cool. "When are they coming?"

"An hour, a day, a couple of years. They will come unless I do the task I was set."

This couldn't be true, but Nancy didn't appear to be lying or joking. Her words were firm and untarnished.

Jade held her nerve as best she could, but her voice wavered. "Where will they come from?"

"You ask a lot of childish questions."

The reporter in her made Jade press forward. "They could be stopped if we know where and when they will start."

Nancy shrugged. "That would just be prolonging the inevitable. You forget that the weavers own mankind's fate. So annoying. Things could've been different. Fear is such a powerful distorter of the truth . . ." She dropped her forehead onto her knees.

Jade decided to let the queen of the night stew; it didn't look like she would get much more out of her.

Really, they should go back to the boat, but there were too many tendrils of her past pointing to this place. Freya was down there somewhere, under the water, and she had to go to her.

A blurred bundle of black-and-blue feathers appeared in front of her nose.

"Do you want these? I wasn't sure," Linn said, holding the bunch in her hand.

Jade took them and examined them as drops of rain lingered, then slipped off their vanes, glided over her knuckles, and ran down her sleeve. Their colours, those of a magpie, shone brighter than they should under the stormy sky.

"What do you have there?" Nancy leaned over her and then caught hold of Jade's wrist.

"Hey, back off."

Nancy knocked Jade hard back against the stone.

"Carefully, give them to me!" Nancy demanded.

Jade gasped in pain. "Why do you want them?"

"Release them slowly or I'll break your arm and stomp on your neck."

She tried to pull the gun from her pocket but it was caught in a fold. Nancy twisted her arm to the point of breaking. Jade's brain screamed, *Give her the feathers!*—but she wouldn't; they were a key of some kind. She finally freed the gun and pointed it at Nancy.

"Let me go or I'll shoot you."

"Go on, try." Nancy wrenched Jade's arm violently.

Jade flipped her body around to avoid her shoulder joint being ripped apart.

"Stop this!" Linn screamed. She was up and standing, but only just.

"Don't move or you're dead," Jade said.

Nancy took hold of the gun in Jade's hand and pointed it skywards. "Just give them to me."

A memory had clicked. This fight, this battle for the feathers, was another test Freya had prepared her for. The epic battle for the water bottle when they were on the beach in France. "Okay. Okay. You can have them . . . but you must help me."

Nancy pushed at Jade's arm and then let go, causing her to slide across the wet rock and land at Linn's feet. This new Nancy had herculean brawn.

"So hand them over and I will," Nancy said, showing no signs of being out of breath. "But be careful. Don't brush the vanes backwards."

Jade got to her feet with Linn's help. Her arm ached like hell, but she didn't think anything was torn. The pain of the burns on her legs hurt the most.

Nancy approached and thrust her hand forward.

Jade placed the feathers in her palm.

"So, are you ready to go after her? That's what you want, isn't it?" Nancy asked, showing no emotion.

A helicopter sounded off in the distance, and Linn pointed. "There. Looks like search and rescue."

Jade lifted her backpack and put Linn's pistol into the plastic bag that held the ammo clips before sealing it.

Nancy yanked the pack from Jade. "I'll carry it." She placed the feathers inside. "I hope you're a good swimmer."

"Jade," Linn called, "what are you doing?"

"I'm going with her."

"Jade! Don't!" Linn tried to grab Jade's hoodie.

Nancy had hold of Jade's wrist.

"It will be okay, Linn," Jade soothed. And before she could explain, she was being pulled backwards into the icy waters of Sunniva's Well.

A Thawing Relic

WINTER WAS SHOWING its cruel intentions. Snow had covered the route, and the wind had sharpened. Knud paused for just a moment to wrap the lambskin collar of his coat around his neck and tie it closed.

Autumn had been wasted, spent in the south on a wild goose chase, and now he headed north, confident King Olaf Tryggvason would be in the new town of Nidaros. The relic's hand had told him to go north, but he had followed the guidance of the chieftain in Seljatún to the market town of Kaupang. It had taken him two weeks to get there, and once there, he discovered it was the wrong king. The Danish warlord Sweyn Forkbeard had taken the town and was, if the rumours were true, plotting to overthrow Olaf. So, he had spun on his heels before he could be embroiled in the affairs of yet another king.

The bitter air stung the back of his throat and he hurried forward, hoping the extra effort would warm his arms and legs. A passing merchant told him he would be there by night fall. Spurred on, he followed the barely visible indentations of a cartwheels in the snow.

In the middle of the night, he arrived in Nidaros where he took shelter with the monks of the town. It was late into the day by the time he woke and went in search of the King.

In the town's newly built great hall, he found King Olaf in a good mood.

Olaf slapped Knud hard on the shoulders. "Health and happiness, Father." As he spoke, a fat, gold ring at the end of his beard swung against fine green cloth. "Give me news of how the monastery is growing under your leadership. I wish to hear the great things you have been doing in the name of our Lord." Olaf led him to a bench by the burning hearth at the centre of the longhouse.

Knud rambled on, telling all, except that he had left his monastery and that his belief in God had been lost. Both these admissions would have caused his head to be removed.

Various morsels were offered to him by an unwell *thrall*, and Knud took two strips of dried venison, ate one and put the other in his pocket.

Olaf responded with an overzealous reaction to his story. He hadn't been listening. "Well done, Father. But what brings you to Nidaros?"

This was the question he had prepared for during each step of his journey over the last months. Unfortunately, he had changed his answer multiple times and forgotten which one he meant to tell.

"I have heard rumours that Sweyn Forkbeard is plotting against you. I travelled with as much haste as I could."

Olaf frowned and stretched his hands to the warmth of the hearth. "This is not unexpected news. He's been keeping Æthelred's geld to himself."

Knud put on a worried face. He didn't really care that Forkbeard was keeping King Olaf's part of the huge taxes they were extracting from the Saxons. The games of kings were as complicated as the chess they played.

"How is she?" Knud asked delicately.

"Who?" the king asked, deep in thought.

"Sunniva. Can I see her?"

"No." He pulled at the gold ring on his beard, his eyes compressed, and when the *thrall* offered food again, Olaf knocked her away. He stood, swore, and dismissed Knud with a wave of his hand. "Go back to your island. Devote your time to God. You shall not see the true relic. She is not for your eyes."

"My Lord—"

"Go!"

Knud plodded out of the great hall.

He pulled the dried meat from his pocket and chewed, while surveying the town. The timbers of a new church, high up on the hill, were striking, while in the harbour, two dozen longboats and smaller fishing skiffs had been pulled ashore. A few buildings of different shapes and sizes filled the land. Older longhouses with turf roofs were interspersed with newer, taller structures that sat directly on the ground. Smoke from their hearths drifted slowly into the cloudless sky. He thought of Eir; how proud she was, and how cruel the world had been to her. Had he been part of her misery?

An elder with burn scars on her face approached him. "I heard you in the hall. Maybe you can help her. No others have. Come, Father." She gripped a large iron key that hung around her neck as if her life depended on it. She wore no coat and braved a short distance to a small, weather-worn hut. She unlocked the door and Knud ducked under the oak lintel into a chamber with a dirt floor. A fire smouldered, filling the room with smoke. A bundle of wool was piled high next to a bench, and the old woman went over to it. She sat, picked up a whorl, and used it to spin the wool into yarn. "She's behind the hide."

Knud pushed a thick curtain to one side.

Eir lay motionless on a narrow ledge cut into the timber wall. All he could do was stare at her as time passed, taking in her beauty. She was as white as snow but hadn't changed since the last time he had seen her so many years ago.

"How long has she been here?" He glanced at the elder who had stopped spinning. Snores came from her hunched over form. He touched Eir's forehead.

"You mustn't taint the angel Sunniva!" A voice squealed from behind them.

He turned to see a wiry monk.

"She's ice-cold." He had always tried to keep her warm by providing pelts, fuelling fire of her cottage, and making sure she had enough wood. *She shouldn't be so cold.*

"Keep away," the monk said and shoved Knud.

Knud pushed back, knocking the monk to the ground. "She needs to be warm!" He drew his knife and pointed it at the monk. "You will help me."

The monk scampered on all fours, before climbing to his feet near the far wall.

Before Knud could stop him, he monk darted to the door. Knud threw his knife and it hit the monk's neck. The monk dropped to his knees. Gargling blood flowed between his fingers where he held his neck. His eyes were wide and month gapped. An instant later, he toppled over.

Knud turned away from the dying monk's convulsions. He took Eir's limp body into his arms. Her long, golden hair cascaded down and her pale head reclined over his arms, exposing the amber necklace she always wore. He lay her an arm's length from to the fire, then used a pole to drag out embers and ash and spread them over the floor, mixing them with the dirt. He ripped the hide down and placed it on the coals.

"She should be warm," he mumbled as he lowered her on the hide. He stared at her features and wished their fate had turned out differently. Thinking back to their time together, he tried to image a world with a caring god.

He furrowed his brows, then watched in shock as colour appeared in Eir's cheeks. Her head twitched and then she slid her hand up to her face. She moved slowly at first like a ladybird in the cold, but eventually pushed herself up.

KNUD TRIED NOT to stare at Eir while explaining what had happened since she had been trapped in the cave.

She blinked and closed her eyes. Her head drooped and then rose again. He threw more wood on the fire and went over the events again.

"My daughter?" she asked.

"Ylva told me to give her away."

"I must find her." She attempted to stand but collapsed to the floor.

Knut took hold under her arms to help.

"Leave me be. I must do this alone. I must stop evil in men." Pushing her hands against the ground, she managed to rise. "There is a king in Kaupang?"

"Yes. Sweyn Forkbeard. But I don't want you to go anywhere near kings. They . . . they all desire you. You need to rest."

Eir's face was taut with grim determination. "I can't do the things I need to without taking power from kings."

Knud hesitated, trying to understand. "You want to marry a king? I don't want you to. I want you to be free."

"I am a woman. I won't be free without sacrificing most of myself."

The door creaked on its hinges, and he jumped up. *My knife. The king's men!*

A pair of orange eyes stared back at them.

"Bygul!" Eir yelled with joy.

The First

SHE WANTED TO scream, but it would mean exhaling her last breath. So Jade held it until the primeval part of her brain told her to breathe. The agony of her lungs filling with water wasn't a sensation that should have persisted, but it stayed with her in the directionless void. She still felt her heart thumping slowly in her chest. A moment later, it stopped.

She woke briefly, until absorbing fatigue prevented her from holding on to consciousness.

A focusing, from the broadest bokeh, turned into a morning of washed-out shades of blue. She sat on a rock next to a dark pool. She felt sad; there was something she must do.

Visions floated by of monks in brown hoods, a great boat that flew over and under waves, a stone hut with a warm fire, and finally, the smiling face of the person she loved.

An old woman with black greying hair took her wrist, dragged her, and then pushed her into icy waters. And again, she was sinking, drowning, and twisting in the turmoil.

She awoke in darkness, lying on harsh stone. A heavy mesh covered her. She tried to stay present but drifted again into memories once forgotten.

BURNT SIENNA CONDENSED into fields of golden wheat. Deer jumped through the long stalks, darting away from Kari as she walked within a gentle breeze. Except for an errand when she first arrived, she had lived here hundreds of years. Kari thought back, remembering the heat of the dusty land and the beautiful blue-eyed child she'd been tasked to nurture. She wished, not for the first time, she could've stayed with Caitlín. Before that, there were no memories but something nibbled at her emotions; a loss that wouldn't sharpen. She raised her head to see the dark timbers of her home in the distance before hurrying her pace.

That night, Frigg's great hall echoed with stories told by the beautiful red-haired goddess wrapped in magpie wings, laughing, and always making fun of her boorish husband. Frigg was retelling one of his hapless escapades to a raven perched on the rim of a pewter tankard.

In firelight, Kari sat and spun threads for tapestries that weaved through tales the goddess told. She felt restless without knowing the cause. She longed to be flying in the snowy mountains or lost on weald paths. Even her duties as a Valkyrie, dispatching the dead, would be a welcome change. Those nights had long past. No brave sorrowful souls arrived in Fólkvangr anymore.

One day, Kari was reading the runes carved into the beams of their hall when Frigg's melodic words sought her attention.

"Are you done?" the goddess asked.

"I just finished." Kari was proud of her accomplishment. It had taken years and she had never changed. "My lady, shall I start again? Or make another tapestry?"

"No, Valkyrie. Today, Geiravör, you are needed elsewhere."

It wasn't that often that Frigg called her Geiravör. It happened only when Frigg had an important undertaking for her.

They flew together to a cave high in the mountains. There, situated in a hollow cut into the stone, was a silver fleece adorned with amber.

"Remove your wings and hand the feather to me," Frigg commanded.

Kari did as she had been asked.

"Now open your hand." Frigg drew out her bejewelled dagger and flattened the blade on Kari's palm. Frigg bent Kari's little finger over it, slicing the tip off, as if cutting cord. She held the bleeding fist tight in hers along with the severed portion. Kari gritted her teeth, trusting the goddess would repair her.

She led Kari to the hollow and the fleece. She tucked Kari's injured hand under its heavy folds. After a sung ode, Frigg allowed her to retract her hand. To Kari's surprise her finger had been healed. Frigg carefully positioned her amputated tip under the fleece. The fleece slowly inflated, bulging at different points, until it was the shape of a body.

A woman with greying black hair stepped out from the shadows.

"It's time," the woman said and handed Kari a fetid scrap of meat. "Eat it." She looked at it unsure.

"Go ahead, you can trust Ylva," Frigg said. "As before, there is an errand you must do for me."

Kari put it in her mouth and chewed on the awful morsel.

"Good . . . It is best you forget," Ylva said, taking Kari's hand. "You will be my daughter and be named Jade. This is all you will remember."

HER HEAD BLAZED with piercing noise. Jade tried to see, but the intensity of the light stung her eyes. She sat up, waiting for the pain to recede.

A voice registered, but she couldn't make out the words.

Jade shook her head, trying to clear her mind. The high-pitched screeching was slowly subsiding. "I can't hear you."

"I said, you've been here before," Nancy yelled.

Jade blinked and her sight cleared.

Nancy was sitting close by with her top off, twisting it to wrench out water, before laying it to dry. The queen of the night then leant back on locked elbows, taking in the sunshine, wearing only her briefs. The contents of the backpack were also spread out, and six feathers were drying in the windless day.

Jade could feel the warming rays on her face. They were perched on a great ledge high above a horseshoe valley. Snow-covered mountains, much higher than the Alps, rose to capture clouds at their summits.

"What's your name?" Nancy asked.

Jade frowned. "You know my name."

"Your name!" Nancy yelled as if Jade was deaf. But this wasn't the same Nancy. Every square inch of her formidable body was muscle, toned, and purposeful. Not like a bodybuilder but a hundred-metre sprinter. Her skin appeared darker, her breasts were almost non-existent, and powerful thighs promised great agility. The contrast between her form and the vista behind her was that of a melanistic wolf in a landscape of snow.

"Jesus, stop yelling. I know my name. It's Jade." She looked down at herself and trembled. Her clothes had been changed. She wore a stained silk dress held at the waist with a perishing leather belt. She noticed clothes she had started in were also drying on the sun-baked rock. Checking her recent wounds, she found that her ankles were clear of burns and her forehead smooth without injury. She turned her hands in front of her.

"What's happened to me?" Jade asked.

"If you don't know, I'm not telling you." Nancy changed position to sit cross-legged with her arms around her knees, watching as if waiting for a performance to start.

A lace of faded red threads held the collar of her dress closed at her bust. Jade untied it and looked down at an unblemished chest. The scars from the shrapnel that hit her in Syria had vanished. But what she saw told her she was younger, by at least ten years.

Jade's head was still muzzy as she slowly got to her feet.

Nancy yanked her down by her wrist. "Sit down before you fall off the edge. It's like a five-mile drop, and I doubt you have another integument here."

"Nancy . . . Lilith, Ereshkigal, whatever your name is. Just tell me what has happened to me."

"I would rather ignore you. Answering would lead to death by a thousand questions."

Jade took hold of Nancy's shoulder and stared at her hand. *I must be about sixteen. What the hell has happened? Some kind of fountain of youth?*

The queen of the night turned towards her with a small measure of sympathy in her eyes. "For you to be here now, younger, you must've been to Asgard before."

"What do you mean?" Jade squashed her face into her palms before lifting it.

"Why don't you go to the cave? Answers are there."

Jade stood, then wished she hadn't; her head pounded. But she took the few steps to the entrance of the cave and ducked inside. Allowing her eyes to adjust, she could make out that the cavern must have been carved by an ancient river, with the oddity of a set of stone steps, which spiralled downward, disappearing into darkness.

She moved slowly around the stairs, careful not to fall into its bottomless descent. In the dimness, she could see recesses cut into the rock wall. Dusty skulls, stacked in piles, stared back at her. She was in a catacomb. One of the chambers looked disturbed; a wooden panel had been removed. A metallic fabric hung down from the opening. It was a mesh of tarnished silver threads adorned with beads of amber. At least, that was what it appeared to be. She touched it, and the heavy cloth fell, causing her to jerk backwards. A large, soft object bumped her calf. She turned and glanced down. "My God . . ." she said in a whisper.

On the ground was a naked body. The skin was white, lips blue, and a cut ran across its forehead. It was herself, and she was undeniably dead.

"THAT WAS CRUEL," Jade said in a level tone.

"To the naïve, the truth always is." Nancy was fully dressed. She threw jeans, a shirt, and hoodie at Jade.

"So I'm dead?"

"You should be, if that helps." Nancy shifted to where the feathers were lying on the ground and flipped each one over like rashers of bacon. "You had a replacement." She glanced up. "It's odd that your soul jumped so easily, since it's clear you're nothing but flesh and blood from Midgard."

Jade shook her head in confusion. "What are you talking about?"

Nancy squinted in the sunlight while looking at Jade. "Maybe you've done this before?"

"Done what? God's sake, explain."

"Goddess's sake, I suspect is more correct." Nancy smirked. "But okay, since it's you, I'll speak simply." She picked up the feathers. "It means you had a body waiting, stretched out in the cave under an Osiris Fleece. The fleece can grow a new self from a small bit of you and preserve it. So, when you died, your soul jumped to the waiting body. I carried that new you here. Then I fetched your clothes. And after a bit of warmth, presto, you live again. Lucky you. And hurray, you might actually be able to help me."

Nancy ran her finger along the side of one of the feathers, pushed the vanes apart, and dropped the bunch. They sparked, and then blue flames burst forth. "Stand back." The popping feathers set light like a roman candle.

"But why am I so young?"

"Here we go, more endless questions." Colours from the burning feathers danced in Nancy's eyes, and she shrugged. "Bad news. You must have come here when you were young, and to do that, as you're mortal, you would have died. Sorry. I guess Frigg was involved. She must have resurrected you and made an integument. I mean, a shell, a body, a waiting vessel, ready for your return. You understand?"

Jade shook her head.

"Well that's the simplest I can explain it." Nancy returned to her fire of feathers. "You know . . . Frigg was always messing around with regeneration. It's what she did for Odin, resurrecting his warriors so they could fight again. Christ, she kept me here for a thousand years stuck in a sprouting tree. Jade, don't assume a deed that is moral and just won't be punished."

The flame died down, and Nancy knelt, watching a fragment of metal form in the embers, its colour changing as it cooled on the rock.

Jade tried to fit it all together, but it didn't make sense. "I don't get it. How can I be dead in the cave and alive also?"

"I repeat. The only way you can get from earth to here is to die. The dead Jade, in the cave, must've been a previous resurrection returned to earth. I have only ever known of such a thing happening twice. Once, with a man at Easter, and the second, with your Freya."

"Freya?"

"Yes. I was there when Frigg persuaded a Norn to undo her death." Nancy looked Jade straight in the eye. "Frigg paid for that by becoming the Sorrow you torched with the necklace."

"I didn't do that." Jade's voice trembled.

"Don't worry about it. I'm sure a Norn already fated her demise by your hand." Nancy pulled her sleeve over her palm and used it to try to pick up the metal sliver. "Shit." She dropped it. "Still too hot." She held out her cuff to reveal a hole created by the hot metal. "Think of it like this . . ." She poked her finger through the damaged sleeve. "When one dies, a hole is created by the broken thread. It affects the lives of others. Nearby threads, so to speak. Over time the hole is lost as the weave tightens, or in some cases it all unravels. But the death happened and the thread ended. A Norn can repair such a hole, sewing in a new thread and changing your fate. The Norns control the threads, or instances of life. But the substance of the yarn itself, the blood of life, a soul, well, that's a different matter . . . literally."

The logic of what Nancy was telling her had substance, if you accepted a number of things—like souls, Norns, and mythical realms.

"But for you, I think a Norn must've managed your fate with undying attention." Nancy laughed. "Come on, *undying* . . . That was funny." She scooted the piece of metal around with her thumbnail.

Jade's head told her there were reasons for things, a reason she was here, and it wasn't to take shit from the queen of the night. "You will take me to Freya."

Nancy laughed. "I was going to do that anyway. She'll have gone to Frigg's hall. She is bait, and you might be useful."

"Bait?"

"To attract a Norn so it can be killed. She's Frigg's daughter. All of Asgard will be aware she's here."

"She must be so afraid," Jade whispered before slipping on the backpack. "How do we get there?"

"With this . . ." Nancy gingerly picked up the fragment of metal, blew on it, and then touched it to her lips. A pair of black wings burst from her back, expanded, and knocked Jade aside.

Nancy beamed a broad smile, like the cat that got the cream.

"Hold on to my back. If she is there, Hel's Horrors won't be far behind."

With Jade holding tight, Nancy extended her wings and walked off the end of the precipice.

They glided down with the sun behind them, riding with the thermals, while descending slowly.

"What's to the right?" As far as Jade could see, a great line of fire ran over the mountains and into the valley below. Behind it was nothing but scorched earth. There, the skies were filled with soot-stained clouds, while the land appeared as molten rock. The devastation was on a scale she couldn't comprehend. It wasn't just burning, but being transformed into a realm of the darkest imagination. She strained to see more but they were too distant to make out any detail.

"To recreate you have to first destroy. It's what the Norns do here, and then next, Midgard, your home. Earth. It's why the Norns must die," Nancy said over her shoulder, before turning to follow a river that had become a demarcation of the purge.

Minutes later, Nancy pointed. "Frigg's hall." The building was straight ahead of them on the bank of the river not yet consumed by the decimating fire.

FREYA AWOKE UNDER a fleece of silver threads and amber beads. She was in a stone coffin and pushed the lid off with her feet. Her clothes were rotten rags of silk, and they fell apart as she moved. All around was the wreckage of her mother's hall. Its massive oak timbers, carved with runes that told of the history of her people, were knocked down and lay in broken splinters. The roof had collapsed, letting in daylight. A great battle must have been waged here, Freya thought as she walked through the rubble. She found it hard to get a grip on her circumstance. Her memory was clouded; her past, as Eir, was at the forefront, and the rest, a jumbled collage. She tried to remember why she'd been given the name Freya, but couldn't.

"What has happened? Where is my mother?" There wasn't time to understand. Her survival instincts told her she needed to leave. Through holes in the wall, she could see flames cascading across the river as if the water were oil. She stepped over a fallen beam, halted, and clasped her hands over her mouth, stifling a scream. Her old self lay in a crumpled heap on the ground with wings twitching. This wasn't the first time she'd seen herself dead, but this time, she was scared rather than angry. She gathered her courage and tread closer. She bent down and parted the ragged hair, exposing the neck. Her amber necklace wasn't there.

"My wings . . ." She brushed her older self's cheek, causing the wings to retract and the silver feather to appear above the surface of the skin. She picked it up and backed away.

Something clattered onto the flagstone floor.

"Who's there?" There was no answer. "Is that great boar still here? It looked like it would live forever."

Freya made her way to the centre to find nothing but debris. Stone tiles lay scattered and piled in heaps where they had slid off the rafters. Broken wooden tables were covered in bright green moss, decaying in what used to be Frigg's snug. It was the place where she had been resurrected, and where she'd been given the necklace—the place where the Norn had appeared.

"But why am I back here?" Freya couldn't remember. Had she already been to her village? Had she seen Kari alive? "Kari, where are you?" she screamed.

A click-clack came from behind her, and she spun around. A lynx paused, one of its front paws hovering above the ground. Its head tilted and two orange eyes stared at her.

"What's your name?" Freya tried to remember. The lynx took a few more steps towards her, sat, and then licked the side of its paw. "Trjegul. That's it, isn't it?"

Freya approached, hesitated, and wondered if the cat might be considering her prey. She slowly reached out and placed her hand between its ears.

"Is anyone else here?"

A voice far behind the lynx answered, calling out her name.

A SHOWER OF dirt, broken batons, and stone shingles clattered around Jade. She covered her head and then looked up. A Horror sliced a hole in the roof and thudded to the ground, sending dust in all directions. It landed next to Freya, folding its great wings. It swung an arm and sent Freya flying. Freya hit the ground, rolling, and then stopped, unmoving. Another came crashing in between them, blades extended from worn, bloodied claws.

"No!" Jade screamed.

Both creatures turned to her. She tore off her backpack and searched through it for her pistol, yanked it out, and dropped the backpack on the ground. She lifted the gun to fire. Nancy ran in front of her, took flight, and dove into the first Horror's legs, clipping them and knocking it over.

A lynx leapt onto the other Horror's back and ripped at its head with her canines. *Bygul? No, that cat's bigger.* The screams and wails of the Sorrows trapped within the demons cut into Jade's senses, blocking her vision for a moment.

Nancy kept one Horror away from Freya, and the lynx had the other nearly in pieces.

The light faltered and Jade looked up to see a third descending. It dropped just a few feet away and knocked her as it swept around its right wing. Jade staggered as a blade swished a hair's breadth from her neck. She tripped on a broken beam and she fell backwards, her spine and head hitting a stone coffin of sorts. She raised her gun and fired. The Horror turned and stalked towards her. She tried to scrabble up, but her feet slipped as if on marbles. She was standing on another one of those meshes of silver and beads she had seen in the cave.

"A Norn! Too soon," Nancy shouted. "Jade, shoot it!"

The advancing Horror stabbed towards Jade's head with blades projecting from its fingers. She jerked to one side and felt one of them cut across her ear. She dropped the gun into her lap, grabbed the corner of the fleece, and pulled it in front of her just as the Horror thrust its blades into the centre of her chest. They didn't pierce the weave, but crushed into her ribs.

Nancy knocked the Horror to one side with a bone-cracking collision. "Kill the Norn! Before it—"

Jade could sense and then envision the dreadful thing close by; grey and sickly, hiding in the shadows, and she knew it was a Norn. There was no way she was going to give this thing a chance. She would sacrifice herself to do it. *No, I'll sacrifice this self.* All the facts Freya had told her formed a plan; she would create a way to come back from the dead.

Jade ripped off what remained of her earlobe. She shoved the sinew under the fleece, sprang to her feet, and searched for the gun.

A cloud of pure darkness moved into the space, absorbing all that was once there, encasing it in an orb that compressed and dimmed behind her. Everything she had once seen, once been part of, was now a receding speck in the distance.

Front became back.

A breath, sticky and warm, tickled her neck.

"You are not supposed to be here," a voice said.

Jade stepped forward and turned quickly. A spark of light reflected in an eye, and she felt the presence of others. Millions and millions of others somewhere behind that eye.

"Another fate for you," the voice told her.

The Purge

New weave, July 2012, Aleppo, Syria

JADE MOVED INTO position and raised her camera to take the shot. A composition that included the market with a minaret in the background had caught her eye. But something in the back of her mind niggled. James was talking with a tired, unshaven proprietor of a nearby stall. A girl with chestnut-blond hair and blue eyes called to her before sliding off the table where she had been sitting next to a meagre crate of vegetables. The girl ran over to her.

"How did you get there?" the girl asked. She was speaking in Arabic and her eyes were big with surprise. "Look."

Jade glanced behind to see herself and James jumping out of a green Toyota pickup. She turned to the girl. "Aaina, I—" *How do I know her name?*

This was Aleppo again, and that fatal day when so many had died.

In between a blink of the eye, everything shifted, like someone had fast-forwarded the world. Aaina wasn't beside her anymore, and Jade stood in the centre of the road.

The girl was back at the market stall, unwrapping a pack of chewing gum. People around her had progressed instantly, jumping many footsteps ahead. A jet plane appeared at a point in the sky.

Jade was shaking, trying to think back to where she was before. Then she remembered that grey, slender body of the Norn, and the eye that had focused on her. *Has the Norn given me another chance . . . to fix things? No. It has condemned me to repeat my heinous mistakes.*

Jade knew what to do; in her mind, she had relived that day so many times, looking for the best way out.

The sequence played. Aaina broke away from her grip, her father was shot in the road, the bomb was dropped from the plane and hit the market with a burst of noise and flame. The Toyota, now on fire, was on its side, with Aaina hiding at its rear. Last, Jade was wounded and fighting for her life. When Nizar arrived, finding her at the barrier and then taping up her chest, she changed their fate.

"Stay down. Sniper," she told him between gasps of pain.

"But the girl?" Nizar said frantically, his voice a squeal. "Her life against mine." He stood and leapt the barrier, ignoring Jade's warning. A shot rang out, echoing between the buildings, and he fell backwards in a heap.

But this time Jade stuck her head out at the same time. She saw the glint of the sun on the sniper's barrel. She ducked back, leaned over, gritted her teeth against the agony of her breathing, and pulled the AK-47 from Nizar's body. She knew every second. There was only one chance.

She'd have to aim and kill the sniper before he did the same. Keeping her head down, she raised her camera above the barrier and pointed it towards the sniper's position. After taking a number of pictures, she lowered it and examined the images. The sniper was in frame; a head just above coloured tiles on the second level.

"Aaina, I know you can hear me," Jade yelled to her in Arabic. "I know you're afraid. But listen and do exactly as I say." Forty-nine seconds left. "I'll shoot the sniper, but when you hear my gun, run to the barrier and jump over it and duck down. You hear me?"

"Yes." Aaina's scared response came after a moment. *Was it too long?*

Thirty seconds. Jade shuffled over. The tearing in her lung made it hard to breathe and she coughed up a mouthful of blood. She pushed upright in one motion, bringing the rifle's site to her eye and fired.

She had missed. A sniper's bullet tore through her. In the corner of her eye Jade could see the girl crouched down at the rear of the upturned truck. She had failed. All would now end.

A thought occurred to her. Something she'd not factored in. A new detail learnt after this time. "Aaina's ring was not a ring," she muttered through gritted teeth.

Five seconds. Ignoring the pain and faintness as her blood ebbed away; Jade pulled the silver ring out of her pocket and touched it to her lips. Dark brown wings dotted with white emerged from her back, ripping her clothes. Their bulk raised her body a foot off the ground. She commanded them to move with knowledge she didn't know she possessed, and with a strength of their own, the wings jettisoned her over the concrete barrier to land directly in front of Aaina. Multiple bullets sang past her as she wrapped Aaina in her arms and then took flight upwards into the smoke-filled sky.

Below, the pickup exploded, showering metal fragments in all directions, but Jade didn't look back. She had little life left. She landed a block away from the market and let go of Aaina, who looked back at her with moon-sized eyes and a gaping mouth. Jade's wings were half-open with the tips pressed against the ground. They were holding her upright on her knees. Jade raised her hand to her face and swiped at the imprint of the feather on her cheek. The wings retracted and the silver shard fell into her hand as she collapsed.

Her final act was to uncurl her fingers and presented the trinket back to Aaina. "Keep it safe for me," she said on her last breath.

Her death would take her back to Asgard. Her thread of time would shift to where, she prayed, a new instance of herself was waiting.

I'M BACK? ASGARD? I'm under the fleece. Reborn.

Since Nancy had told Jade about threads and the Norns, she had been trying to comprehend how such a thing would work. *Time cannot run out of sequence . . . so how did I go backwards?* She thought more on this while she lay in the dark with a heavy, cool mesh pressed over her naked body. *Although it's conceivable that you could roll back every event, every change of substance, every movement of a particle. It seems impossible, and even then, surely time would have still moved forward while things were being reversed.*

And yet she had ended up back in Syria replaying events of the past.

Nancy had told her the Norns could weave in a new thread. She took this to mean, to start someone's life at a different point. *It must be relative. If a Norn creates a new thread they can align it with others as they please. It doesn't mean I've moved back in time. Just that my time has been offset relative to others. If I died and jumped, as Nancy called it, my timeline continues from there.* She was guessing, of course. She rolled slowly under the silver fleece, stopped when her thigh hit something cold, and slipped her hand down to retrieve it.

Her fingers gripped firmly around the hilt of a pistol, and she positioned it in front of her face while wriggling out from under the fleece. Her body had been recreated from just a fraction of herself, and now it was her turn to decide the fate of a Norn.

She saw the shimmer of grey skin, contrasting in the darkness all around, and she knew she had just a moment.

The Norn approached quickly, projecting words that were felt before they were heard. It wrapped a set of cold, damp, splintered fingers around her neck as Jade pulled the trigger. A bullet exploded out of the pistol's barrel.

All sounds and movements froze. Jade reprocessed the same visual of a creature with an entry wound at the centre of its forehead. No blood flowed, and the fear in her mouth sat as a large acrid toad, waiting to escape. A trickle of red blood appeared, and then glacially slipped down the Norn's face as matter sprayed from the back of its skull. Time restarted, sound returned. Jade let out a scream, flicked her legs and feet upwards and kicked the thing away. She scampered back through the dark, before hitting something hard. Silence now, except for her breathing as she gulped air into her lungs.

A sense of euphoria washed over her. A vacuum of light imploded. She was sucked into a sharpening area of colour and texture until Frigg's hall returned all around her.

Goosebumps formed on her skin with the rush of cold air. Directly in front of her, a grey, slender thing twitched in its final throes. And against the odds, in that small moment, before the Norn had a chance to condemn her again, she had shot it. Now, it appeared to be dying. She didn't want to dwell on what she saw. It was best not to let the image linger and become a fearful scar in her memory. Some things shouldn't be seen in daylight.

Jade turned around, looking for Freya and Nancy. The three Horrors lay mutilated at various locations on the ground. She glanced back at the fleece, considering if she should take it with her. It was a remarkable device. But she could only raise half of the heavy silver-and-amber weave off the ground. *Just in case . . .* She bit off a small section of skin from the arch between thumb and forefinger.

"Hell!" she screamed and spat it out and let the fleece drop over top. She sucked the wound before turning away to search in the ruins for something to wear. Eventually, she found a pair of leather boots and a musty jerkin amongst perished items in a broken chest.

I've not been away that long, have I?

Jade spotted a body behind a collapsed beam. She thought it was Freya and her mind locked up. But this wasn't the younger Freya she had seen in the distance. This was the one they had buried a few days ago. The one she saw escape into the well. Nancy had said Freya's soul would seek out her other self. *This must be what had been left behind, like my body in the cave.*

Jade stared at the corpse for some time before turning away.

Exploring further, she found her backpack where it had been dropped, and she looped it over her shoulder.

A noise drew her attention to a blood-smeared, weary lynx that padded towards her. She stood to approach it as a bang and then an ear-piercing crack sounded. The hall shook, and the left wall exploded. Immense heat radiated as pink-and-rose-red flames roared into the room.

The purge had arrived, tearing the hall apart.

With nowhere to turn, no way to outrun it, Jade stood still as the lynx leapt towards her. She had returned too late.

The Thousand-Year Plan

Two weeks after Jade's disappearance

THE RÓBERT'S KIKÖTŐ Café claimed to make the finest hot chocolate in Budapest. Lena wanted to agree but she'd only tried three cafés during their short stay. They sat in the gallery, overlooking marble tables and dark oak-panelled walls of the ground floor. A great crystal chandelier more than two metres high hung at eye level to her right. But Lena hadn't chosen the place for its decor. She had selected it because of the peeling street number, reversed in the glass above the door. Her sisters liked their games, and most people missed the signs that told of things to come.

Lena unwrapped a chocolate flake and hesitated. Would dunking it into her cup cause a sugar-induced chain reaction that would destroy the city? She dipped it in and bit off the molten end.

Henri sat opposite, sipping an espresso. At intervals, he glanced down towards the entrance. "She's late," he observed.

Lena checked the time on her phone. "Please just remember to get her to leave quickly. You must talk like a New Yorker, not a Provençal."

A moment later, the door opened to the sound of traffic on a rain-washed street. A tall woman tipped an umbrella towards the floor and closed it, showering drops on the concrete tiles.

Lena watched the woman ask a question to the barista on the ground floor and then look up at her. She spoke to the barista again before climbing the circular iron staircase to the gallery.

Nancy removed her coat. "Hell, this place is hard to find. You're Lena?"

Lena nodded, and Henri rose and offered his hand.

"We finally meet," he said.

"Yes," she said.

Henri lowered himself back into his chair as Nancy took a seat.

Nancy twisted her head slowly towards Lena. "So . . . what do you want?"

"You know what," Lena hissed. "You left Jade in Asgard."

"I'm sure she'll find a way back," Nancy said without any sign of being bothered by Lena's outburst.

"You know she can't get out without wings, and you took the pair meant for her."

"Yes. But it worked out. One Norn gone."

"You'll need Jade for the other two. So stop burying your head in the sand."

Nancy looked confused for a moment, as if she was pondering Lena's remark. "You know ostriches don't actually do that? They are smart and run away when there's danger."

"There is nowhere to run," Lena hissed. "Why couldn't you have just killed them centuries ago in Asgard? It would've been a lot easier."

"If I did it then, Frigg would've just imprisoned me again when the deed was done. She was a traditionalist, set in her ways. Here I can make things happen. The possibilities are endless."

"They were endless. But you pushed everything too quickly and now all is being consumed without the knowledge needed to deal with the consequences."

"They would've worked it out eventually. I doubt everything will die at the hands of mankind."

"It's too late now. The Norns won't wait and watch the scornful demise of their blue gem. They will start again, and destroy you in the process. You must kill them all."

"I'm doing it. Okay. But I must wait now. You can't just walk up to a Norn and shoot them in the head."

"Jade did," Lena said.

"How do you know that?" Nancy asked, raising one eyebrow.

"I have my messengers. Some of them travel between the realms."

Nancy nodded slowly. "I see . . .."

"Fetch Jade back," Lena screeched.

The waitress placed a coffee onto the marble top and back-stepped quickly without saying a word.

Nancy picked it up and took a sip. "I may never find her," she said over the rim of her cup.

Lena leant towards Nancy. "Try." She glanced at her phone that sat at the table's centre. "You have three minutes."

"It will take a long time. Asgard is much bigger then Midgard . . . and they will follow us back." Nancy glanced at Henri.

"We know," Lena said. "Go now, Ereshkigal. And good luck."

"A Norn cannot offer luck." Nancy gave a half smile that changed to a frown. "All right, then." She never removed her eyes from Lena's as she stood. She collected her felt pea-green jacket. "You know, after this is all over, I want to be in New York. In the Hamptons. Somewhere with a hot tub," she said to Henri.

"It'll be arranged," he answered.

Lena and Henri watched as Nancy raced down the stairs and out the door.

"Do you think the two remaining Norns can be stopped?" Henri asked.

"*Merde!* We talked about this. It will be messy, very messy. Things were set in motion a thousand years ago, so don't worry about it now."

The waitress slipped the bill onto the table and darted off.

"I think we scared her," Henri muttered.

Lena shrugged. "She shouldn't eavesdrop." She tucked her long black hair around her ears. "Speaking of which, we need to go." She tipped her head towards the glass windows of the café front. A jackdaw had landed on the sill and was shaking the rain out of its wings. "*L'addition.*" She tapped the plastic disc containing the bill for their drinks.

Henri laughed. "I knew I had something useful to do." He pulled a couple of notes from his wallet. "Although, paying for your sugar addiction doesn't seem that prestigious a role."

"Someone has to do it," Lena said before popping the remaining crumb of her chocolate flake into her mouth.

The Gift

"HAPPY BIRTHDAY, PRINCESS."

"Henri!" Freya stood and threw her arms around his shoulders. "I didn't expect you to be here."

"Well, it's not every year you're eighteen."

She released him and laughed. "I've been told this is my second eighteenth birthday."

"True. Everyone is getting younger while I'm getting older. It's not fair."

"Life is not fair. That is what they say . . . I don't know who these 'they' are, but they must be assholes."

Henri laughed. "I must tell Lena to stop teaching you English swear words."

Freya smiled and then craned her neck to look behind him. "Is Lena here? Elise?"

"They are in the kitchen. Lena wanted to wrap up a present for you, and Elise is talking with Max. They've not really met before."

"So Lena has a present for me. That will be interesting. I hope it is not a dead raven's eyeball."

"No guessing," Henri joked.

"It is an eyeball?"

"I hope not." He laughed and reached into his pocket. He took Freya's hand and pressed a large old-fashioned iron key into her palm. "My present. I think it's time you took back your title in France."

Freya blinked, holding it firmly. "What title?"

"Comtessa de Baux. When you next visit I'll show you. You have a house there and land."

She looked at the key. "Why was I not told before?"

Henri shrugged. "Karen didn't want to hurry your recovery. She cares about you a lot. But perhaps she's overly protective, and this is a rather complicated situation. Now that you're eighteen it will be easier to get the legalities sorted again. The French government was pretty keen to acquire your land, so they were a bit annoyed with me when I explained that you're still alive. It's not an inconsiderable portion of France."

"I didn't know about this at all." Freya turned the large key in her hand.

"You've just forgotten. When you're in France again, we'll have to see the officials and have them confirm your identity."

Freya nodded slowly. "So the same as I had to do here?"

"Yes, but the Norwegian royal family is more, let's say, accepting of your nature. They are overjoyed to have you return. It fits in with the traditions of the country. France, well, royals are not so loved, as you know . . . Maybe you don't remember why."

"No. You will tell me?"

"Of course, but first I need to find Karen."

"Thanks for this, and for always being straight with me." She then kissed Henri's cheek.

Henri smiled and scratched his beard while scanning for Karen in the garden. "Where is she?"

"Down on the dock, talking with Linn. Secret fox stuff that I am happy not to be part of."

"I think 'secret squirrel stuff' is what they say."

"I know. But this looks bigger. They have been talking for a while."

Henri laughed and headed down the steps of the deck.

Freya sat down and looked at the lid of the puzzle she had been working on. Bygul was stretched out on the sofa beside her. She pulled her legs up and tucked her feet under the cat's neck to keep them warm.

It was early June and chilly in the mornings. The wind was still, and the waves of the bay, to the west of the modern villa, were just wide furrows in the sea. In front of her, through the rails of the deck, she could see Henri marching towards the boathouse.

It had been more than two years since Nancy had dragged her back from Asgard, and a lot of her past had been just a blur. It had taken some time before the threads of her life started to twine together. Memories of her village, Kari, Ragnvi poisoning the children, and her own death seemed like they'd happened yesterday.

It was considered best that Freya spend time away from Norway, and so Karen sent her to stay with Henri in Provence. There, slowly, very slowly, as Lena told her about herself, she started to remember and reorder events in her mind. Her discordant selves reintegrated, until she felt whole again. As time passed, what surprised her most was how that once she started to learn something, she already knew how to do it. She knew how to speak other languages with only a small amount of practice. She knew how to drive, except Henri told her she never knew how to do that in the first place. And she felt at ease in this world of soft furnishings.

However, a sense of sadness filled her when she stopped and listened to her feelings. Kari was dead, and that was long ago. But there was someone else. Someone she wasn't being told about. There had been too many hushed whispers for her not to notice the secrets hidden from her.

Freya leaned forward and picked up a piece of the puzzle. She wished she'd started a smaller one. The piece didn't quite fit and she whacked it into position with the bottom of her fist. She was making a new picture and not the one on the lid of the box.

"To hell with you, moth-hair-four-king puzzle," she muttered. One thing she had learnt from Lena was how to curse. She didn't really know what the words meant, but they always sounded intriguing. She grabbed three other pieces, using colour to guide where she put them. Squashing them like bugs, she wedged them into submission with her thumb. "Puzzle, you are sofa-king owned—"

"Hey," someone said softly from behind her.

Freya bolted up, knocking Bygul's chin with her heel. "Lena. Henri told me you were here."

Lena shoved a large parcel in her direction. Parts of a garment stuck out of the sides of the messy wrapping. "Happy birthday."

Freya knew better than to try to hug Lena who was not into the bodily contact thing. "Thanks."

She started to put the present down.

"Open it. You need it now," Lena ordered.

"Okay . . ." She wanted to wait for the others, but Lena wasn't someone anyone ignored.

Her long black hair, roman nose, and angular features gave her an air of authority, which usually meant that most eyes were drawn to her when she entered a room. Freya could see she had aged a bit. Now she was looking more like she was in her early twenties than the nineteen she was. She was dressed in black, with a bomber jacket. Other than heavy mascara, she wore little makeup. Her hair was clean, but not styled, and looked as if its length had been maintained with a breadknife rather than a hairdresser's finesse. A black feather on a slender braid of red silk was tied into her hair, such that it dangled close to her chin.

Freya freed a bulky green coat from the brown paper wrapping, and she held it from its hood. "This is exactly the sort of thing I would expect from you." She laughed. "An arctic coat when summer is on the way. But I love it. It helps a lot. I always feels cold."

"I always feel the cold," Lena corrected. "Put it on."

Freya did, and when she struggled with the zip, Lena assisted. Lena then sat, took off her boots, and handed them to Freya.

"Wear these. There's also a hat and gloves in the pockets."

"But why?"

"You'll need them."

Karen stepped onto the deck with Henri and Linn. Karen paused and inspected Freya who was standing in full winter attire. She glanced at Henri and back to Lena.

The sound of a helicopter spinning up echoed behind the house.

"Why are you dressed like that?" Karen asked.

Freya lifted her shoulders and then let them drop before slipping her hands into the pockets of her coat.

"Because she is going with you," Lena snapped.

Karen, wearing a sour expression, raised a finger. Henri leaned in and whispered into her ear.

Karen sighed, taking the crook of Freya's arm. "Come on, honey." She paused in her stride. "Lena, you stay here."

"I'm not going anywhere with you," Lena said.

Freya was forced to meet Karen's pace as they walked through the house, out the back door, and to the waiting helicopter.

"Where are we going?" Freya yelled over the noise.

"Bodø Main, Royal Air Force base."

"Why?"

"I'll explain later. Let's get underway first," Karen shouted while holding her hair from her eyes as the blades of the helicopter's rotor spun faster.

Bygul jumped into the craft just as the door was closing, and refused to be pushed out or dragged away. In the end, Karen acquiesced, allowing the lynx to take a spot on the floor as they took off.

Midnight Sun

THE FLIGHT TO the Bodø Airbase, above the Arctic Circle, took four hours. At a local airport, they swapped to a helicopter with the range required to fly to the northern edge of Norway. Once there, they were escorted to a prepped transport plane. Freya was surprised to see an armed team of five men already in the troop seats. At the centre of the hold, a four-wheel-drive truck was strapped down, and Freya patted the bonnet of the vehicle to encourage Bygul to leap up onto it. The lynx seemed to approve of the vantage point, keeping a lookout along the length of the plane and into the cockpit.

"So you think I might know this person?" Freya asked.

Karen helped Freya with her complicated multi-strapped seat belt. "You might, yes." She then concentrated on her own belt.

"Where are we heading now?" Freya asked.

"Jan Mayen Island."

Freya rubbed her forehead. She remembered the name. "You said I own that island?"

"Yes. But it's been used by the government for years as a meteorological station."

"How, if it is mine?"

"You granted permission for it to be used in the 1940s."

"There is so much I don't remember," she muttered. Her thoughts swam around without purpose, as if as a fish in an aquarium. Lena had explained that her memory would come back. She had been dead for too long and paths to her past had been broken. But they would reconnect with time.

"Why are you not showing me a picture of this person?" Freya asked.

Karen let out a slow breath. "Well, Henri thinks it's better if you meet her in person. It may help to jog your memory."

"Her . . . A woman." Freya squinted while making eye contact with Karen. "Is this the person no one talks about?"

Karen cleared her throat. "Well, yes."

"Then tell me who she is."

Karen put her hand on top of Freya's. "Let's wait until we get there. If you remember, then great. If not, you don't need to get involved."

Freya withdrew her hand. "Just be straight with me."

"Honey, I'm just being careful . . . I lost you once and by some miracle you returned. I want to know if what happened is the truth—"

"Wait . . . You want proof. That's it. You want to see that I know this woman so you believe I am not a *tvífara*!" Freya had to resort to the language she knew best while trying to think of the words in English. "A body double. Henri asked you to take me so you would believe. Believe what had happened. I do not care what you think." She gripped her hands together. "When we get back I will go to France. Henri says I have a house there. At least I have friends in France." She pulled her hood up and closed her eyes; she wasn't going to talk to Karen ever again.

The flight to the island of Jan Mayen took just over one hour, and Freya had been invited to the cockpit to look over the pilot's shoulder and watch their approach. The sky was clear and there was a great view of a small strip of land sitting in the cold sea.

So this was the island she owned. She wasn't sure she wanted it. It looked bleak; something out of a nightmare of isolation. A snow-covered peak of a volcano loomed at the northern end. The rest was a tadpole's tail of ashen rock, outlined by crashing waves of the Arctic Ocean.

"The volcano is called Beerenberg," the pilot told her via her headset. "Dutch explorers named it after polar bears. Others have said it's a gateway to Hell. The volcano last erupted thirty years ago. Due soon I suspect."

"Where do we land?" Freya asked. There were no roads, buildings, or even trees.

"There is a flat of ash at the narrowest part. It's used as a runway."

"This place is so remote," Freya said to herself but it came over the intercom.

"Yes, ma'am. There is nowhere else like it."

Freya watched their approach until the pilot asked her to take her seat before landing.

She returned and pretended to buckle herself in. She wasn't going to fight with the complicated and constraining straps.

A bang sounded as the plane hit the ground with a jolt and she hit her shoulder against the side of the seat. She checked Karen's expression to decide if they had crashed, while rubbing her aching shoulder.

The stowed contents rattled as the plane slowed and turned a semicircle with an increase in engine noise which then quieted. Everyone unbuckled their seat belts, and Freya took this to mean they had arrived.

She waited patiently as the cargo bay was opened, filling the interior with unsaturated sunlight; the world outside was in black and white.

Bygul bound out first, and Freya hurried after her to see where she was heading. The lynx tore, at a great pace, along the shore towards the northern end of the island. Bygul was one of the few things from her past that she remembered; she didn't want to lose her. She called for Bygul as she disappeared amongst the molehills.

"Where is she going?" Freya asked.

Linn came to stand beside her. "I'll keep a look out for her."

"Thank you, Linn."

The vehicle was unloaded, and Karen opened the rear door. "We can ride there with Corporal Fornes. He is the medic who will be evaluating the Jane Doe."

Freya hesitated, glancing to Linn, who was directing the team of armed personnel, dispersing them in different directions. "What is Linn doing?" she asked, breaking her vow of silence.

"Her team will scout the island."

"Why?"

"We need to find out how the Jane Doe got here. Satellite images are not showing any boats or aircraft; it's a bit of a concern. We are not taking any chances against the real or imaginary."

"Imaginary . . . Great," Freya said, climbing into the vehicle.

She felt under pressure with Karen questioning the foundation on which she had rediscovered herself. But also, she was cold and tired. They drove along the wide stretch of unfertile, frozen ash which served as the runway. At the end of the strip, it merged with banks of andosols that were able to sustain plants.

"So her name is Jane?" Freya asked and then cursed herself. The not-speaking-to-Karen thing wasn't really working out so well.

"No. Jane Doe just means without a name."

"No name? Why not just call her 'the person we want to use to see if I'm an imposter?'"

"That's rather long," Karen said with a hint of concern.

"So what. Why does that matter?"

"We need a name for official reports."

Freya sighed. "Okay . . . then how about, 'The Woman of Hell's Gate'?"

"Still wouldn't fit on the forms. Anyway, I know her name. We want to see if you remember her."

"I do not care anymore. Take me home."

"Freya, just bear with us. This is important."

Freya renewed her vow. She stared out the window and glanced back at the volcano that dominated the island. She thought she sensed the vehicle slip sideways. "What just happened?"

"Sorry?" Karen asked.

"The car slid."

"Just a bump."

Maybe she had dozed off. She felt so tired. "What time is it?"

"Near midnight."

"Oh . . . but it is still light outside."

"We are very far north. The sun won't set for a few months now."

"Months . . ." Freya scraped at a decal stuck on the window with her nail. "At least that will keep demons away."

Karen gave her a confused look and pulled Freya's hand away from the window.

"The pilot said the mountain is supposed to be a gateway to Hell. Demons can't come out in daylight."

"I don't think it's a gateway to anywhere."

"You know things can exist without you first seeing them."

"Honey, please, let's not argue. We are here now."

They pulled up in front of a single-storey aluminium-sided hut. Nearby, a tall, metal pole was held up by strands of radiating cables. There were only two other buildings, painted in dark green, and positioned a short distance from the shore in the shelter of a small hill.

The landscape lacked any distinguishing features. It consisted of rock and ice with occasional patches of yellowing grass. Freya couldn't imagine anyone living here.

A door opened and a bearded man in a thick woollen jumper waved to them. "Come in, it is cold today. I am Corporal Emsky."

"Lieutenant Felds." Karen shook the man's hand as they walked inside. She introduced Freya and the medic.

"You can leave your jackets here." Emsky gestured to a row of coat hooks that lined one wall. "Follow me." He started down a narrow corridor that ran along the entrance side of the building.

Freya kept her coat on. She was still cold from the flight in the unheated transport plane. She followed the others, passing rooms that contained supplies and electronic equipment.

A beep repeated at intervals of a few seconds in one of the rooms. Emsky stopped and listened. "Please go ahead. I need to check this."

They went to a large room at the end of the hut with bunk beds and a central kerosene stove that was pumping out heat. On a bunk in the corner, a person was outlined under layers of army-issued grey woollen blankets.

Freya leaned against the wall, giving Karen and the medic space.

Karen woke the patient and asked a few questions while the medic checked the person's blood pressure and pulse.

From where she was, Freya could see the woman's head, and she gave her name as Nancy Coles.

Freya pulled her hood up, turned, and went back the way she came. The woman in the bunk looked familiar, but she had no idea who she was.

Karen raced after her and took hold of her arm, but she yanked it away. "Freya, wait. That's not—"

Emsky butted in between them, waving a piece of paper at Karen, and Freya ran down the corridor. She needed to find Bygul, and she wanted to be alone.

THE SUN HUNG motionless on the horizon, but Jade guessed she'd been outside for a few hours. In the endless daylight, she had gone out to check that they hadn't been followed, and like the day before, Trjegul appeared and joined her.

Waves broke on a flat beach that was cut into a bank, creating a great crescent of charcoal-coloured coastline patched with white snow. She listened to the sound of the wind, waves, and her boots scrunching on the sand.

Walking had become like breathing to her, after spending so many months staying ahead of Hel's consumption of Asgard. It had been Trjegul who saved her, carrying her as the flames flooded Frigg's hall. After that, they just kept going, keeping away from the progressing sweep of destruction.

It was a journey without end, continuing forward to new mountains, rivers, and forests; all filled with life, allowing Jade to shoot and kill game to eat. She used the matches in her backpack to light fires, and when most of the bullets were gone, Trjegul caught their meals.

Behind, nothing remained; the purge obliterated everything. She struggled to keep it at bay. Some days they would just run to build up a lead they could later use for sleep. During their retreat, Trjegul would disappear for days, only to return with new wounds cut into her fur. Jade knew the lynx was protecting her, clearing their path and killing the new types of beasts that had arrived. She'd not seen one up close, only at a distance, as it disappeared into dense forest.

One morning, a winged shadow was cast over her before a woman landed and blocked her path. "You could've made it easier for me to find you," was the queen of the night's greeting. Jade was hugely relieved to see her.

Nancy knew a way back, and in the pitch-dark, they followed an old lava tube for two days until it ended on the north side of Jan Mayen.

Jade was tired, hoping to see Freya again. But she knew there were more hardships to come. She picked up her pace along the shore. She and Nancy had been on the island for three days, and Jade had spoken to Karen via a satellite phone. The conversation was short; she would be collected as soon as possible. So when the plane had circled and landed, Jade cut her walk short and was on her way back to the small outpost.

The sound of sand and snow being churned up by a running animal caused Jade to spin around and pull her backpack off. She had saved one bullet. Another lynx was darting down the bank and onto the beach. Trjegul ran to meet the lynx and she knew it could only be Bygul.

Her heart missed a beat as she realised the implication.

The two cats bounced around each other and sped back over the bank. Jade started slowly after them. She ran her fingers through her hair. *I must look a mess.*

A young woman appeared, walking and then running in Jade's direction. The two lynx zigzagged back and forth, like dogs that had been released off their leads for the first time in ages.

The woman's fur-trimmed hood fell to her shoulders, revealing chestnut-blond hair. Jade knew, without thinking; her heart had told her . . . Freya was here.

"*Kari!*" Freya screamed, and raced to her. They collided, and she wrapped her in her arms.

Tears welled up in Jade's eyes and she struggled to see Freya's face. "I . . . I can't believe—" Uncontrolled sobs overwhelmed her. "I'm sorry . . . Sorry it took so long . . . I—"

Freya buried her head into Jade's neck while holding her. "You're here."

It felt like hours passed while they held each other, until Freya touched Jade's cheek. "Where have you been? Are you okay? What happened? Were you hurt?"

"I'm good now that you're here." Jade took Freya's hands in hers. "You're cold."

"Yes, always. But stop that." Freya laughed and sobbed at the same time. "How did find me? Never mind. There is too much to understand. Kari, I cannot believe you are here."

Jade narrowed her eyes slightly and she frowned.

"Why do you look worried now?" Freya squeezed Jade's fingers.

"It's just that you're calling me Kari. And you're younger. Your accent is different."

"Oh . . . Lena said I was dead too long. I can't remember things. But you are Kari. I know that. Right? I am right?" Freya's voice wavered, but then held fast. "We are friends?"

Jade opened her mouth but didn't speak.

"Please. You know me."

"We are more than friends," Jade said, hugging her. "I love you."

"You . . ." Freya whispered, her lips against Jade's ear. "I love you too."

Jade laughed, her tension washing away. "I think we've both been through a lot. We need to talk and fill in the gaps."

"Yes," Freya said breathlessly. "I will talk off your ear. There are a lot of gaps. Like what's your name?"

"Jade."

"You don't remember being called Kari?"

"Not really. You told me about Kari before, and I remember bits of things, as dreams from past lives, but I think I need to talk to Lena. She—"

A four-wheel drive rose over a nearby dune, and they both turned.

"Even in the middle of the Arctic Ocean we are not alone," Freya said with her arms still around Jade's neck.

The vehicle skidded to a stop on the sand and Karen jumped out. She hesitated before darting over and hugging Jade briefly. "It's good to see you again. You've changed." She stepped back and straightened. "I'm sorry if this sounds abrupt, but we must leave immediately." She opened the rear door.

A vibration shook the land, and the ground shifted under their feet. Freya held on to Jade until it stopped.

"What's going on?" Freya yelled.

"Seismic activity from the volcano. We're not taking any chances, get in," Karen ordered and pushed them into the vehicle. The jeep sped off with its tyres spinning.

Freya locked her arm into Jade's. "I'm not letting you go."

"I won't either," Jade whispered.

"Where are the others?" Freya asked as the jeep soared over the dunes, jolting everyone back and forth.

"The station personnel are already in the plane."

"Where is Nancy?" Jade asked.

"Nancy has decided to stay with Linn and her team."

"You can't leave them here," Freya said.

Karen turned around to look over the passenger seat as they sped along the flat towards the waiting plane. The propellers of its four engines were already turning. "They need to stay. They have their orders."

"I have no say in this?" Freya's strong will showed itself, and Jade smiled. It was so amazing to be with her again.

"This might just be a minor tremor," Karen explained, "and then nothing for a while. If it looks like more than that, I'll get them out. But right now I want you and Jade off the island."

"You're aware of what might have followed us?" Jade asked.

"Yes. Linn briefed me. We'll keep an eye on things, and if anything happens, well, then we'll have the evidence we need to get the military involved."

Jade nodded.

They drove directly into the plane's cargo bay, and the bay door started to close behind them.

"Wait," Freya yelled. "My cats."

"Stay," Karen insisted. "Linn will keep an eye on them."

"No. I don't want to leave them behind." Freya jumped out of the jeep and ran to the closing door.

Jade and Karen leapt out after her.

"Stand back," Karen ordered, taking hold of Freya's arm.

"Open it again," Freya yelled over the sound of the plane's idling engines. The door had only a small gap remaining.

"Freya, we have to leave."

"Open it. Now."

Karen snatched a headset off a rack and quickly jammed it on. "Hold position. Open the cargo bay." After a moment, the bay door folded down. Karen turned to Freya. "If they are not here in one minute, we leave."

Jade stood next to Freya with a hand on her shoulder. She had learnt that Frigg's lynx had their own purpose. "They'll be where they want to be."

When the door was halfway down, two blurs of white and black darted in. The lynx circled the jeep before leaping up onto its bonnet and then climbing onto its roof and settling there.

"Clear to take off. Do it now," Karen ordered into her headset. "Buckle in." She guided Jade and Freya to their seats with her palms on their backs.

The plane picked up speed, with the cargo door still closing. It made a rapid ascent into the air.

Karen handed headsets, and Jade tried to use hers. "So what's—Hell!" She ducked as a sound like hail on a tin roof echoed throughout the fuselage.

Sunlight vanished from the cargo-bay windows. A shudder slammed everyone to one side, and the plane tilted to the left.

The sky appeared as if it was night when she looked through the cockpit. The engines sputtered and Jade's stomach lurched. They were falling. Sunlight returned to the cargo area just as the engines burst back to life. The plane veered right, followed by a steep ascent.

After everything had stabilized, they unbuckled and everyone took turns looking out the left-side window. A large section of the volcano's summit had been blown away, and a great plume of ash rose into the sky.

Karen used her satellite phone to confirm Linn and her team were safe.

After returning to their seats, Jade looped her arm through Freya's. She had spent so long trying to get back to her. She still couldn't believe she was here. She made an oath, then and there, that nothing would come between them, never again, not even death itself. The thought made her smile, because it was something she'd already done.

"Can I talk to Jade privately?" Freya asked in her headset.

"Of course," Karen answered and requested a private connection for them.

Freya scrunched herself against Jade for a few minutes. "Tell me what happened?"

"There's a lot to tell. But really Nancy found me . . . Asgard is being destroyed, and well, I had to keep ahead of it. Trjegul helped a lot. That's one tough cat. I didn't even know Bygul had a sister until Nancy explained."

"Yes, I'm glad they are together again," Freya said, glancing to the cats who were on top of the jeep as if they were at a safari park. "But also, that we are as well."

"Me too." Jade squeezed Freya's hand. "Is Lena at home? I need to talk to her. There are still two left."

"Yes, she should be. Two what?"

"Norns."

Freya went white and her hands shook. "I . . . I met one of those. Where are they?"

"Not here, not here, it's okay." Jade wrapped her arms around her and drew her in. Their headsets clashed. "Don't think of it. It's not your worry."

Freya tucked her head into Jade's neck as best she could. "I will not go back there. I can't seem to escape its memory. It's some kind of darkness pulling me into a place where I am all alone, forever."

"You're with me now. That's not going to happen." Jade tipped her chin up and kissed her. "Okay?"

Freya smiled and blinked away tears. "Sorry, too much has happened, too fast. I am being a *meyla* . . . a child, I mean."

"No, you're just incredible." Jade kissed her again.

"I can't believe you are back," Freya whispered. "You look so tired; rest now."

Jade relaxed against Freya and closed her eyes. "Tell me what happened to you, and I'll listen. I love hearing your voice again." Her stomach that had been a knot of worry for years started to untie.

Freya smiled and a nuzzled against her. Her lips pressed against Jade's forehead. Freya pushed her hand under the folds of Jade's coat and hugged her, before beginning in a small village, over one thousand years ago, when her name was Eir, and her best friend in the world was a dark-haired *thrall* called Kari.

Alex Pyott grew up in Canada and completed a BSc at Acadia University, before leaping across the pond to London, England. Consuming a mixture of historical fiction, fantasy, and romance has led to a desire to write progressive novels that combine these genres with an underpinning moral subtext. In addition to writing, Alex enjoys music creation, photography, painting, and guitar.

www.ingramcontent.com/pod-product-compliance
Lightning Source LLC
Chambersburg PA
CBHW022146010726

47493CB00002B/366